"You will find warriors of every shape, size, and color in these pages, warriors from every epoch of human history, from yesterday and today and tomorrow, and from worlds that never were. Some of the stories will make you sad, some will make you laugh, and many will keep you on the edge of your seat."

—George R. R. Martin, from his introduction to *Warriors*

PRAISE FOR *WARRIORS*

"Pure entertainment."
—*Publishers Weekly*

"Entirely successful . . . There really is something for everybody in it."
—*Booklist*

"Hero-sized . . . Nary a dud to be found."
—*The Miami Herald*

"Well worth the cover price—consistently entertaining throughout."
—*Locus*

WARRIORS 1

EDITED BY

GEORGE R. R. MARTIN

AND

GARDNER DOZOIS

TOR®
fantasy

A TOM DOHERTY ASSOCIATES BOOK
NEW YORK

WARRIORS 1

Copyright © 2010 by George R. R. Martin and Gardner Dozois

All rights reserved.

A Tor Book
Published by Tom Doherty Associates, LLC
175 Fifth Avenue
New York, NY 10010

www.tor-forge.com

Tor® is a registered trademark of Tom Doherty Associates, LLC

ISBN 978-0-7653-6026-7

First Edition: March 2010
First Mass Market Edition: April 2011

Printed in the United States of America

0 9 8 7 6 5 4 3 2 1

Copyright Acknowledgments

To Lauren and Jeff,
to Tyler and Isabella,
to Sean and Dean,

may you be strangers to war

Contents

Introduction

Stories from the Spinner Rack
by George R. R. Martin

There were no bookstores in Bayonne, New Jersey, when I was a kid.

Which is not to say there was no place to buy a book. There were plenty of places to buy books, so long as what you wanted was a paperback. (If you wanted a hardcover, you could take the bus into New York City.) Most of those places were what we called "candy stores" back then, but Hershey bars and Milky Ways and penny candy were the least of what they sold. Every candy store was a little different from every other. Some carried groceries and some didn't, some had soda fountains and some didn't, some offered fresh baked goods in the morning and would make you a deli sandwich all day long, some sold squirt guns and hula hoops and those pink rubber balls we used for our stickball games . . . but all of them sold newspapers, magazines, comic books, and paperbacks.

When I was growing up in Bayonne's projects, my local candy store was a little place on the corner of First Street and Kelly Parkway, across the street from the waters of the Kill Van Kull. The "book section" was a wire spinner rack, taller than I was, that stood right next to the comics ... perfect placement for me, once my reading had expanded beyond funny books. My allowance was a dollar a week, and figuring out how I was going to split that up between ten-cent comic books (when the price went up to twelve cents, it really blew the hell out of my budget), thirty-five-cent paperbacks, a candy bar or two, the infrequent quarter malt or ice cream soda, and an occasional game of Skee-Ball at Uncle Milty's down the block was always one of the more agonizing decisions of the week, and honed my math skills to the utmost.

The comic book racks and the paperback spinner had more in common than mere proximity. Neither one recognized the existence of genre. In those days, the superheroes had not yet reached the same level of dominance in comics that they presently enjoy. Oh, we had Superman and Batman and the JLA, of course, and later on Spider-Man and the Fantastic Four came along to join them, but there were all sorts of other comic books as well—war comics, crime comics, western comics, romance comics for the girls, movie and television tie-ins, strange hybrids like *Turok: Son of Stone* (Indians meet dinosaurs, and call them "honkers"). You had Archie and Betty and Veronica and *Cosmo the Merry Martian* for laughs, you had Casper the Friendly Ghost and Baby Huey for littler kids (I was much too sophisticated for those), you had

Carl Barks drawing Donald Duck and Uncle Scrooge. You had hot rod comics, you had comics about models complete with cut-out clothes, and, of course, you had *Classics Illustrated*, whose literary adaptations served as my first introduction to everyone from Robert Louis Stevenson to Herman Melville. *And all these different comics were mixed together.*

The same was true of the paperbacks in the adjacent spinner rack. There was only the one spinner, and it had only so many pockets, so there were never more than one or two copies of any particular title. I had been a science fiction fan since a friend of my mother's had given me a copy of Robert A. Heinlein's *Have Space Suit—Will Travel* one year for Christmas (for the better part of the decade, it was the only hardcover I owned), so I was always looking for more Heinlein, and more SF, but with the way all the books were mixed together, the only way to be sure of finding them was to flip through every book in every pocket, even if it meant getting down on your knees to check the titles in the back of the bottom level. Paperbacks were thinner then, so each pocket might hold four or five books, and every one was different. You'd find an Ace Double SF title cheek-by-jowl with a mass market reprint of *The Brothers Karamazov*, sandwiched in between a nurse novel and the latest Mike Hammer yarn from Mickey Spillane. Dorothy Parker and Dorothy Sayers shared rack space with Ralph Ellison and J. D. Salinger. Max Brand rubbed up against Barbara Cartland. (Barbara would have been mortified.) A. E. van Vogt, P. G. Wodehouse, and H. P. Lovecraft were crammed in together with F. Scott Fitzgerald. Mysteries, westerns, gothics, ghost stories, classics of English literature, the latest contemporary "literary" novels, and, of course, SF and fantasy and horror—you could find it all on that spinner rack in the little candy store at First Street and Kelly Parkway.

Looking back now, almost half a century later, I can see that that wire spinner rack had a profound impact on my later development as a writer. All writers are readers first, and all of us write the sort of books we want to read. I started out loving science fiction and I still love science fiction . . . but inevitably, digging through those paperbacks, I found myself intrigued by other sorts of books as well. I started reading horror when a book with Boris Karloff on the cover caught my attention. Robert E. Howard and L. Sprague de Camp hooked me on fantasy, just in the time for J. R. R. Tolkien and *The Lord of the Rings*. The historical epics of Dumas and Thomas B. Costain featured sword fights too, so I soon started reading those as well, and that led me to other epochs of history and other authors. When I came upon Charles Dickens and Mark Twain and Rudyard Kipling on the spinner rack, I grabbed them up too, to read the original versions of some of my favorite stories, and to see how they differered from the *Classics Illustrated* versions. Some of the mysteries I found on the rack had cover art so salacious that I had to smuggle them into the apartment and read them when my mother wasn't watching, but I sampled those as well, and have been reading mysteries ever since. Ian Fleming and James Bond led me into the world of thrillers and espionage novels, and Jack Schaefer's *Shane* into westerns. (Okay, I confess, I never did get into romances or nurse novels.) Sure, I knew the differences between a space opera and a hard-boiled detective story and a historical novel . . . but I never *cared* about such differences. It seemed to me, then as now, that there were good stories and bad stories, and that was the only distinction that truly mattered.

My views on that have not changed much in the half century since, but the world of publishing and bookselling certainly has. I don't doubt that there are still some old spinner racks out there, with all the books jumbled up together, but these days most people buy their reading material in chain superstores, where genre is king. SF and fantasy over here, mystery over there, romance back of that, bestsellers up front. No mixing and no mingling, please, keep to your own kind. "Literature" has its own section, now that the so-called "literary novel" has become a genre itself. Children's books and YAs are segregated.

It's good for selling books, I guess. It's convenient. Easy to find the sort of books you like. No one has to get down on their knees in hopes of finding Jack Vance's *Big Planet* behind that copy of *How to Win Friends and Influence People*.

But it's not good for readers, I suspect, and it's definitely not good for writers. Books should broaden us, take us to places we have never been and show us things we've never seen, expand our horizons and our way of looking at the world. Limiting your reading to a single genre defeats that. It limits us, makes us smaller.

Yet genre walls are hardening. During my own career, I have written science fiction, fantasy, and horror, and occasionally a few hybrids that were part this and part that, sometimes with elements of the murder mystery and the literary novel blended in. But younger writers starting out today are actively discouraged from doing the same by their editors and publishers. New fantasists are told that they had best adopt a pseudonym if they want to do a science fiction novel . . . and god help them if they want to try a mystery.

It's all in the name of selling more books, and I suppose it does.

But I say it's spinach, and I say to hell with it.

Bayonne may not have had any bookstores when I was growing up, but it did have a lot of pizza parlors, and a bar pie from Bayonne is among the best pizza anywhere. Small wonder that pizza is my favorite food. That doesn't mean I want to eat it every day, and to the exclusion of every other food in the world.

Which brings me to the book you hold in your hands.

These days I am best known as a fantasy writer, but *Warriors* is not a fantasy anthology . . . though it does have some good fantasy in it. My co-editor, Gardner Dozois, edited a science fiction magazine for a couple of decades, but *Warriors* is not a science fiction anthology either . . . though it does feature some SF stories as good as anything you'll find in *Analog* or *Asimov's*. It also features a western, and some mystery stories, a lot of fine historical fiction, some mainstream, and a couple of pieces that I won't even begin to try to label. *Warriors* is our own spinner rack.

People have been telling stories about warriors for as long as they have been telling stories. Since Homer first sang the wrath of Achilles and the ancient Sumerians set down their tales of Gilgamesh, warriors, soldiers, and fighters have fascinated us; they are a part of every culture, every literary tradition, every genre. *All Quiet on the Western Front, From Here to Eternity,* and *The Red Badge of Courage* have become part of our literary canons, taught in classrooms all around the country and the world. Fantasy has given us such memorable warriors as Conan the Barbarian, Elric of Melniboné, and Aragorn son of Arathorn. Science fiction offers us glimpses of the wars and warriors of the future, in books like Robert A. Heinlein's *Starship Troopers,* Joe W. Haldeman's *Forever War,* and the space operas of David Weber, Lois McMaster Bujold, and Walter Jon Williams. The gunslinger of the classic western is a warrior. The mystery genre has made an archetype of the urban warrior, be he a cop, a hit man, a wiseguy, or one of those private eyes who walks the mean streets of Chandler and Hammett. Women warriors, child soldiers, warriors of the gridiron and the cricket pitch, the Greek hoplite and Roman legionary, Viking, musketeer, crusader, and doughboy, the GI of World War II and the grunt of Vietnam . . . all of them are warriors, and you'll find many in these pages.

Our contributors make up an all-star lineup of award-winning and bestselling writers, representing a dozen different publishers and as many genres. We asked each of them for the same thing—a story about a warrior. Some chose to write in the genre for which they're best known. Some decided to try something different. You will find warriors of every shape, size, and color in these pages, warriors from every epoch of human history, from yesterday and today and tomorrow, and worlds that never were. Some of the stories will make you sad, some will make you laugh, many will keep you on the edge of your seat.

But you won't know which until you've read them, for Gardner and I, in the tradition of that old wire spinner rack, have mixed them all up. There's no science fiction section here, no shelves reserved just for historical novels, no romance rack, no walls or labels of any sort. Just stories. Some are by your favorite writers, we hope; others, by writers you may never have heard of (yet). It's our hope that by the time you finish this book, a few of the latter may have become the former.

So spin the rack and turn the page. We have some stories to tell you.

WARRIORS 1

Joe Haldeman

Here's a fascinating look at the high-tech future of warfare—which, in its essentials, and particularly in its *costs,* turns out to be not all that different from the way that war has always been. . . .

Born in Oklahoma City, Oklahoma, Joe Haldeman took a B.S. degree in physics and astronomy from the University of Maryland, and did postgraduate work in mathematics and computer science. But his plans for a career in science were cut short by the U.S. Army, which sent him to Vietnam in 1968 as a combat engineer. Seriously wounded in action, Haldeman returned home in 1969 and began to write. He sold his first story to *Galaxy* in 1969, and by 1976 had garnered both the Nebula Award and the Hugo Award for his famous novel *The Forever War,* one of the landmark books of the '70s. He took another Hugo Award in 1977 for his story "Tricentennial," won the Rhysling Award in 1983 for the best science fiction poem of the year (although usually thought of primarily as a "hard-science" writer, Haldeman is, in fact, also an accomplished poet and has sold poetry to most of the major professional markets in the genre), and won both the Nebula and the Hugo Award in 1991 for

the novella version of "The Hemingway Hoax."
His story "None So Blind" won the Hugo Award in
1995. His other books include a mainstream novel,
War Year, the SF novels *Mindbridge, All My Sins
Remembered, There Is No Darkness* (written with
his brother, SF writer Jack C. Haldeman II), *Worlds,
Worlds Apart, Worlds Enough and Time, Buying
Time, The Hemingway Hoax, Tool of the Trade,
The Coming,* the mainstream novel *1968, Camou-
flage,* which won the prestigious James Tiptree, Jr.,
Award, and *Old Twentieth.* His short work has
been gathered in the collections *Infinite Dreams,
Dealing in Futures, Vietnam and Other Alien
Worlds, None So Blind, A Separate War and Other
Stories,* and an omnibus of fiction and nonfiction,
War Stories. As editor, he has produced the antholo-
gies *Study War No More, Cosmic Laughter, Nebula
Award Stories 17,* and, with Martin H. Greenberg,
Future Weapons of War. His most recent books are
two new science fiction novels, *The Accidental Time
Machine* and *Marsbound.* Haldeman lives part of
the year in Boston, where he teaches writing at the
Massachusetts Institute of Technology, and the rest
of the year in Florida, where he and his wife, Gay,
make their home.

Forever Bound

I'd thought that being a graduate student in physics would keep me from being drafted. But I was sitting safely boxed in my library carrel, reading a journal article, when the screen went blank and then blinked PAPER DOCUMENT INCOMING, which had never happened before—who would bother to track you down at the library?—and I had a premonition that was instantly confirmed.

One sheet of paper slid out with the sigil of the National Service Commission. I turned it right side up and pressed my thumb onto the the thumbprint circle, and the words appeared: "You have been chosen to represent your country as a member of the Ninth Infantry Division, Twelfth Remote Combat Infantry Brigade," Soldierboys. "You will report to Fort Leonard Wood, Missouri, to begin RCIU training at 1200, 3 September 2054."

Just before class registration, how considerate. I wouldn't be pulled out of school. I even had two weeks to pack and say my good-byes.

Various options came to mind as I sat staring at the page. I could run to Sweden or Finland, where I'd also face national service, but it wouldn't have to be military. I could take the Commission itself to court, pleading pacifism, asking to be reassigned to Road Service or Forestry. But I didn't belong to any pacifist groups and couldn't claim any religion.

I could do like Bruce Cramer last year. Stoke up on painkillers and vodka and shoot off a toe. But his draft notice had been for the regular infantry, pretty dangerous.

People who ran soldierboys never got shot at directly—they sat in an underground bunker hundreds of miles from the battlefield and operated remote robots that were invincible and armed to the teeth. Sort of like a sim, but the people you kill actually are people, and they actually do die.

Most soldierboys didn't do that, I knew. There were about twenty thousand of them dispersed throughout Ngumi territory, and most of them just stood guard, huge and impregnable, unkillable, symbols of Alliance might. Which is to say, American might, though about 12 percent came from elsewhere.

My adviser, Blaze Harding, was in her office a couple of buildings away, and said to bring the document over.

She studied the letter for much longer than it would take to read it. "Let me explain to you . . . in how many dimensions you are fucked.

"You could run. Finland, Sweden, Formosa. Forget Canada. It's a combat assignment, and you'd be extradited. In any case, you'd lose your grant, and it would be the end of your academic career. Likewise with going to jail.

"If you obey the law and go in, you'll be like Sira

Tolliver over in Mac Roman's office. You have to report 'only' ten days a month. But she seems to spend half her time recovering from those ten days."

"Just sitting in a little room?"

"A cage, she calls it. Evidently it's a little more strenuous than sitting.

"The plus side is that the department wouldn't dare drop you. If you just show up for work, your position with the Jupiter Project is as safe as tenure. As long as the grant holds out, which should be approximately forever." The Jupiter Project was building a huge supercollider in orbit around Jupiter, millions of electromagnetic doughnuts circling out by the orbit of Io.

"Once they turn it on," I said, "our worries will be over anyhow. Instantly sucked into a huge black hole."

"No, I favor the 'explode and be scattered to the edge of the universe' theory. I always wanted to travel." We shared a laugh. The Project would simulate conditions 10^{-35} seconds after the Big Bang, and the tabloids loved it.

"Well, at least I'll lose a few pounds in basic training. I've been putting on two or three pounds a year since I graduated and left the soccer team."

"Some of us like them a little plump," she said, pinching the skin on my forearm. It was a funny situation. We'd been attracted to each other since the day we met, three years ago, but it had never gone beyond banter. She was fifteen years older than me, and white. Which was not a problem on campus, but outside, Texas is Texas.

"I goo-wikied something you ought to see. Running a soldierboy isn't really just sitting around." She turned her clipboard around so I could read the screen.

DISABILITY AND DEATH
BY
MILITARY OCCUPATIONAL SPECIALTY
PER 100,00 ANNUALLY

	COMBAT INJURY/DEATH	NONCOMBAT INJURY/DEATH
INFANTRY	949.2/207.4	630.8/123.5
RCI	248.9/201.7	223.9/125.6

"Not really so safe, then."

"And the injuries in the RCI, combat or not, would all be brain injuries. You'd be out of a job here."

"You're just saying that to cheer me up."

"No, but I'm thinking you ought to try switching to the infantry, as crazy as that sounds. With your education and age, they'd put you behind a desk, for sure."

"Well, I've got two weeks to nose around. See how much latitude I'll have. But what about my job here?"

She waved a hand in dismissal. "You can do it in twenty days a month. Actually, I was going to take you off the physics lab babysitting anyhow; just grade papers for 60 and help me with the 299 special projects." She looked at her calendar. "I guess Basic Training will be full-time."

"I don't know. Sounds like it, from what I've heard."

"Find out for me. If I have to kidnap somebody for October and November, I'd better start looking around." She reached across the desk and patted my hand. "It's an inconvenience, Julian, but not a disaster. You'll come out on top."

Blaze hadn't brought up the largest danger and the biggest attraction of being a "mechanic," as the soldiers who operated the soldierboys were called. They all had to be jacked, a hole drilled into the back of the skull and an elecronic interface inserted, so you shared the thoughts and observations, feelings, of the rest of your platoon. There were five men and five women in a platoon, so you become like a mythical beast, with ten brains, twenty arms, and five cocks and five cunts. A lot of people tried to join up for that experience. That was not quite what the army was looking for.

Almost all mechanics were drafted, because the army needed a peculiar mix of attitudes and eptitudes. Empathy is obvious, being able to stay sane with nine other people sharing your deepest feelings and memories. But they also needed people who were comfortable with killing, for the so-called "hunter-killer" platoons. They were the ones who got all the attention, the bonuses, even fan clubs. I could assume I wasn't going to be one of them. I didn't even like to go fishing, because of the blood and guts and hurting the fish.

The installation of the jack was also risky. The rate of failure was classified, but various sources put it between 5 and 15 percent. Most of the failures didn't die, but I wondered how many of them went back to intellectual pursuits.

I found out that Basic Training was indeed full-time, for eight weeks. The first four weeks were intensely physical, old-fashioned boot camp—not obviously useful for people who would spend their military career sitting in a cage, thinking. After four weeks, they installed the jack, and you started training in tandem with your other nine.

I did apply to be reassigned, to infantry or medical or quartermaster. (They crossed that off; you can't join a noncombat arm in time of war.) I was rejected the day I applied.

So I increased my jogging from one mile a day to three, and worked out on the gym machines every other day. Basic training had a bad reputation, and I wanted to be ready for the physical side of it.

I also spent more social time with Blaze than I ever had before. She had no teaching load during the summer. I had legitimate reasons to drop by the Jupiter Project, though I could do most of my work from any computer console anywhere in the world. I tended to show up around lunchtime or when the office nominally closed at five.

You couldn't call it dating, given the difference in our ages, but it wasn't just coworkers having lunch, either. It could have evolved into something if there'd been more than two weeks, perhaps.

But on September 2, she took me to the airport and gave me a tight hug and a kiss that was a little more interesting than a coworker saying "good-bye for now."

When I got off the plane in St. Louis, there was a woman in uniform holding a card with my name and two others on it. She was bigger than me, and white, and looked pretty mean. I stifled the impulse to walk right by her and get a ticket to Finland.

When the other two, a woman and a man, showed up, she walked us to an emergency exit that apparently had been disabled, then down onto the tarmac in the 105-degree heat. We walked a fast quarter mile to where a couple of dozen people stood in ranks, sweating beside a military bus.

"*No* talking. Get your sorry ass in line." A big black man who didn't need a megaphone. "Put your bags on the cart. You'll get them back in eight weeks."

"My medicine—," a woman said.

"*Did I say no talking?*" He glared at her. "If you filled out your medical forms correctly, your pills will be waiting for you. If not, you'll just have to die."

A couple of people chuckled. "Shut up. I'm not kidding." He stepped up to the biggest man and spoke quietly, his face inches away. "I'm not kidding. In the next eight weeks, some of you may die. Usually from not following orders."

When the fiftieth person came, he loaded us all

into the bus, a wheeled oven. My god, I thought, Fort Leonard Wood must be over a hundred miles away. The windows didn't open.

I sat down next to a pretty white woman. She glanced at me and then looked straight ahead. "Are you going to mechanics' school?"

"Go where they send me," she said with a South Texas drawl, not looking at me. Later that day, I would learn that mechanics train with the regular infantry, "shoes," for the first month, and it's not wise to reveal that you were going to spend all your subsequent career sitting down in the air-conditioning.

We drove only a couple of miles, though, to the military airport adjacent to the civil one, and piled into a flying-wing troop transport, where we were stuffed onto benches without seat belts. It was a fast and bumpy twenty-minute flight, the big sergeant standing in front of us, hanging on to a strap, glaring. "Anybody pukes, he has to clean it up while everybody else waits." Nobody did.

We landed on a seriously bumpy runway and were separated by gender and marched off in two different directions. The men, or "dicks," were led into a hot metal building, where we took off all our clothes and put them in plastic bags marked with our names. If they were going to ferment for eight weeks, the army could keep them.

They said we would get clothes when we needed them, and had us shuffle through a line, where we contributed blood and urine and got two shots in each arm and one in the butt, the old-fashioned way, painful. Then we walked through a welcome shower into a room with piles of towels and clothing, fatigues sorted more or less by size. Then we actually got to sit down while three dour men with robot assistants measured our feet and brought us boots.

There was a rotating holo of a handsome guy showing us what we were supposed to look like—the trouser legs "bloused" into boots, shirt seam perfectly aligned with belt buckle and fly, shirtsleeves neatly rolled to midforearm. His fatigues were new and tailored, though; ours were used and approximate. He wasn't sweating.

I thought I'd second-guessed the army by having my hair cut down to a half-inch burr. They shaved me down to the skin, in retribution.

The sun was low, and it had cooled down to about ninety, so they took us for a little run. That didn't bother me except for being overdressed. We went around a quarter-mile cinder track, in formation. After four laps, the women joined us, and together we did eight more.

Then they piled all of us, hot and dripping, into a freezing mess hall. We waited in a long line for cold greasy fried chicken, cold mashed potatoes, and warm wilted salad.

The woman who sat down across from me watched me strip the sodden fried batter from the chicken. "On a diet?"

"Yeah. No disgusting food."

"I think you goin' to lose a lot of weight." We shook hands across the table. Carolyn from Georgia, a pretty black woman a little younger than me. "What, you graduated and got nailed?"

"Yeah. Ph.D. in physics."

She laughed. "I know where *you're* goin'."

"You, too?"

"Yeah, but I don't know why. BFA in Creative Viewing."

"So what's your favorite show?"

"Hate 'em all. Unlike most folks, I *know* why I hate 'em. Now tell me you'd die if you didn't get your *Kill Squad* fix every week."

"Don't have a cube, or time to watch it. When I was a kid, my parents let me watch only ten hours a week."

"Wow . . . would you marry me? Or you got somethin' goin' already."

"I'm gay, except for sheep."

"Ewe." We both laughed a little too hard at that.

Shoe training was about half PT and half learning how to use weapons we'd never see again, as mechanics. Even the shoes would probably never use a bayonet or knife or bare hands—how often would you not have a gun, and face an enemy who didn't have one either?

(I knew the rationale was more subtle, training us to be aggressive. I wasn't sure that was a good idea for mechanics, though—your soldierboy might wipe out a village because you lost your temper.)

Carolyn's last name was Collins, and we were next to each other in the alphabet. We spent a lot of time talking, sometimes sotto voce when we were standing in formation, which got us into trouble a couple of times. ("One of you lovebirds runs around the track while the other finishes painting this wall.")

I was really smitten with her—I mean the kind of brain-chemistry-level addiction that you ought to be able to control by the time you're eighteen. I thought of her all the time, and lived to see her face when we mustered in the mornings. Her expressions and gestures made me think she felt the same way about me, though we carefully wouldn't use the word *love*.

After two weeks of constant training, they unexpectedly gave us half a Sunday off. A bus took us into St. Robert, a small town that existed to separate soldiers from their money. We had to be back by 6:00 sharp, or we'd be AWOL.

On the way to the bus station in St. Robert, we passed several hotels and motels that advertised HOURLY RATES / CLEAN SHEETS. When we got off the bus, I faltered, trying to frame a proposition, and she grabbed me by the arm and pulled me through the closest place's door.

We'd never even kissed before. So we did some of that while trying to get each other's fatigues off without popping any buttons.

Speaking of popping, I was not exactly the long-lasting partner-oriented lover I would've liked to have been. But I had a certain amount of hydrostatic as well as psychological pressure built up; the barracks offered no privacy for masturbation.

She laughed that off, though, and we just played around for a while, until I was ready for a more patient and slow coupling. It was better than my dreams.

We had an hour before we had to be on the bus. There was a bar next door, but Carolyn didn't feel like being stared at by our fellow draftees. So we sat on the damp and rumpled sheets and shared a glass of metallic-tasting water.

"Did you try to get out of it?" she asked.

"Well, yeah. My adviser pointed out that if I joined the infantry, at my age and with my education, I'd just have a desk job for a couple of years."

"Yeah, right. You believe that now?"

I laughed. "They'd put me in a bayonets-only platoon. Get out there and stab for your country."

"God and country. Don't forget God."

"If it weren't for God, we wouldn't get half of Sunday off."

"Praise the Lord." She took my penis between two fingers and wiggled it. "Don't suppose there's any juice left in this little guy."

"Not for a while. We could do it on the bus."

"Okay. Hold you to it." She yawned and stretched so hard, a couple of joints popped. "Maybe we should go get a beer. Show those lonely cunts who got her man."

"Let's." Though I doubted there was much loneliness in town.

She dressed me carefully, smoothing the uniform

down with long slow strokes. Then she stroked my face and my hands, eyes closed, as if she were memorizing.

She held me close then, and took a long deep breath. "Thank you, Julian," she whispered. "It's been some while."

So I tried to dress her, but got the buttons wrong. All very romantic. It's also easier to take panties off of someone than to put them back on.

The nonsmoking part of the bar still had a whiff of tobacco and light weed. Ice-cold beer but no place to sit. So we stayed at the bar, loud with music and laughing, and nodded hello to some of our fellow trainees.

"You didn't grow up in the South," she said. "You talk funny, you don't mind my sayin'."

"Actually, I was born in Georgia, but my parents moved north before I started school, Delaware. Then four years at Harvard will screw up your accent forever."

"You majored in science."

"Physics, then astrophysics for the master's. Moved into particle physics for the doctorate. Post-doc, too, assuming basic doesn't kill me."

"I don't know shit about any of that."

"Never expect anyone to." I put my hand on hers. "Like I know anything about film."

"Joo-lian." She slid her hand away. "Never condescend to someone who can kill you with a single blow. Six different ways."

"Sorry. Takes you four years to get a degree at Harvard, and then forty to get over it."

"Well, I ain't waitin' forty. You best get your shit together." But she smiled and put her hand back.

A short private from the permanent party walked through the door with a megaphone. "Aw-right, you listen up. Trainees Charlie Company, you bus is heah. You not in that bus in five minutes, you AWOL. We come back heah and put you ass in chains."

There was a moment of silence when he went through the door, and then a low murmur.

"How could they put just your ass in chains, and not the rest of you?"

"Think big stapler," she said, and finished off her beer. "Chariot awaits."

The next two weeks didn't have any Sundays. Now that they were pretty sure no one was going to have a heart attack doing laps, they pushed us to the wall. The morning after our afternoon-long furlough, they woke us up at 2:30, striding through the barracks, beating on metal pans. Five minutes to dress, then a ten-mile run with full pack and rifle. When people stopped to puke, we had to run in place, shouting "Pussy, pussy!"

They continued with the early-morning runs about every third day, increasing them by a mile each time. The drill instructors acted like it was malicious torture, but it was obviously well planned. We had to get the running in, but if we did it during those hundred-degree-plus days, people would get heatstroke and die.

The instructors also made sure everybody knew that the intensity of training was our own fault. "Only got four weeks to turn these CGI pussies into soldiers" was the refrain.

Carolyn and I did have one more opportunity, a thirty-minute lunch break in thick woods. I got poison ivy on my butt, and she on her feet. We had the same medic look at us, and he advised us to next time take along something like a shelter half or at least a newspaper. But there never was a next time, not in Basic Training.

The first day of CGI training, they took the fifty of us in a bus with blacked-out windows to someplace that might have been a half hour away, or a mile, going in circles. It was in deep woods, though, and underground.

A camouflaged door slid open to reveal dimly lit stairs going down. The entrance was guarded by two huge soldierboys, whose camouflage perfectly mimicked the woods behind them. If you stood still, you couldn't see them; walking by them, they looked like a heat shimmer roughly the shape of a nine-foot-tall man.

The underground complex was large. We stood in formation in a foyer, and a private read our names off a clipboard and gave us platoon designations and room numbers. Carolyn and I were both Alpha Platoon and went to room A.

There were ten hard chairs in the room and, incongruously, a table with party snacks and a tub full of iced drinks. An older man in a jumpsuit with no insignia watched us file in.

He didn't speak until the last of us sat down. "I'm going to leave you here alone for one hour and thirty minutes. Your job is to get to know one another.

"In a couple of days, you're all going to be jacked, and none of you will have any secrets from the others. That's all I'm going to say.

"When I leave the room, please take off all your clothes. Get a drink and a snack and . . . tell each other your secrets, your problems. It will be easier for you to deal with one another if you have some preparation.

"When the bell rings, you should get dressed, and I'll come back to talk with you. Yes, private?"

"Sir," she said, "I . . . I've never been naked in front of a man. I—"

"You're about to be. You didn't have brothers?"

"No, sir."

"In a couple of days, you'll have five of them. And 'naked' does not begin to describe how exposed you'll be. But you will all be gentlemen?"

"Yes, sir," we all said. She was a pretty little blonde, and I was half looking forward to seeing the rest of her and half sympathetic with her anxiety.

He smiled, face crinkling. "Just look each other in the eyes and you'll be all right." He left the room.

I talked with Lou Mangiani while we undressed, both of us studiously not looking at the women (but *seeing* them with some intensity). Lou's in his late twenties, working as a baker in New York City for his father's Italian restaurant. That's about as much as I knew about anybody except Carolyn. For the past four weeks, we had trained till we dropped and got up hours before our bodies wanted to; not much time for chat.

Carolyn and Candi joined us. We'd wondered in shoe training what Candi was doing here. She was a gentle—you'd have to say "delicate"—woman, whose civilian job was grief counseling. I suppose you have to be pretty tough to do that, actually.

She was also a natural leader for this sort of thing. She clapped once. "Let's get these chairs in a circle," she said to everyone. "Get sorted out boy-girl, boy-girl."

Richard Lasalle was beet-red, with a large prominent erection. I was myself trying to think about anything else, running through prime numbers and tables of integrals.

None of the women were eager to sit next to him. Carolyn gave my hand a little tug and strode over to him, and stuck her hand out. "You're Richard, aren't you?" He nodded—"Dick" would not be a good choice—and she introduced herself and sat down. I took the other seat next to her and the pretty little blonde, Arlie, quickly perched on the other side of me, probably figuring I was "taken" and therefore safe. She crossed her perfect legs and hid her breasts behind folded arms.

Candi was the opposite, totally casual, leaning back, legs akimbo. Samantha and Sara, who had been in modest crouches, looked at Candi and unfolded.

"So let's go around the circle and everybody come up with something important that you normally keep secret. After tomorrow, we won't have any secrets." Slow nods. "I should start it." She paused for some time, rubbing her chin and the side of her face. "My clients, my patients, don't know this. Why I became a grief counselor. I was once so devastated I, I killed myself.

"I jumped off a bridge. In Cape Cod in January. I was dead for ten or twelve minutes, but the water was so cold, they were able to bring me back."

"What was it like?" Akeem said. "Being dead."

"Nothing; I just went unconscious. I think the impact knocked me out." She ran a finger between her breasts. "I woke up when they shocked my heart, in the ambulance."

"You had a reason," I said.

She nodded. "Watched my father die. We were on the interstate and the steering and the fail-safes cut out at the same time. We flipped and crashed into traffic. The air bags inflated, but the accident kept happening; another truck smashed into us and knocked us off an overpass. When we finally came to rest . . . my mother's head was crushed and my father was drowning in his own blood. I wasn't in too bad shape, but was pinned in place. I had to just hang there upside down and watch my father die. About two feet away.

"I couldn't get his image out of my head. So I

jumped off the bridge. And somehow wound up here. Lou?"

He shrugged. "God, I never had anything like that." He shook his head a couple of times, looking down. "I was maybe thirteen. There was a gang my parents forbade me to hang around with, so of course I did. They thought I was out doing church stuff, but they never went, so I could fake it, I thought.

"These were junior goombahs, apprentice Mafia. I was the lookout while they did nickel-and-dime stuff. Robbing machines, shoplifting. Stealing cars for joyrides when people were careless enough to leave them unlocked.

"We got word that this old Jew who ran a news shop and candy store in the Bronx sold guns under the table. The back door looked like it would be easy enough to break in. So at one in the morning, I snuck down the fire escape and ran down a bunch of side streets to meet them.

"They knew for sure the old guy locked up and went home about ten. It was easy to crack the back door with a crowbar.

"This was the first thing we'd done where I wasn't 'the kid.' A younger boy stood lookout, and I went in first, because I was still a juvenile. If something went wrong, I wouldn't get hard time.

"I went in with a flashlight and started opening drawers, looking for guns. Well, I found one, but it was in the fist of the old Jew. He hadn't gone home that night.

"I heard him cock the gun and swung around, and I guess dazzled him with the light. 'Turn that off, boy,' he said. But the guy with the crowbar had come up behind him and bashed his head with a two-handed swing. He went down like a log, but the guy kept hitting him. Then he picked the gun up off the floor and thanked me for thinking fast.

"We ransacked the place, wearing rubber gloves, but there were no other guns, nor anything else of much value. We couldn't open or even move the cash box. We took a bunch of candy and cigarettes.

"The next day the newspaper reported the murder-robbery. I didn't say anything to anybody. I could have called in anonymously and identified the murderer, but I was afraid."

"He ever get caught?" Mel asked.

"Not that I know of. He went down for drug dealing and I went off to college. Now I'm here."

Everybody looked at Arlie. "I got caught having sex. With the wrong person." She looked at the floor. "By my husband. In our bedroom. I promised not to see this person again . . . not to see *her* again." She looked up with a trembling smile. "Details tomorrow."

My turn. "I got caught jerking off?" Some nervous laughter. "I guess the worst thing . . . it might seem even more trivial, to some. But it drove me crazy with guilt at the time, and it still bothers me, more than ten years later.

"I was, what, fifteen, walking down an alley, and I saw a turtle, which was rare. A pretty big box turtle. It pulled in its head and legs. I poked it with a stick and it just sat there, of course.

"On impulse, I picked up a brick and threw it down with all my might. The shell cracked open and the turtle squirmed around, all pale and bloody. I ran away as fast as I could go."

After a pause, Candi said, "Yeah, I can see that. Even though my family used to fish for turtles and cut them up for soup. I grew up thinking of them as food." She looked at Carolyn and raised her eyebrows.

She shook her head. "Guess I've led a sheltered life. Nothing sexy or violent. I did get caught masturbating, but my mother just laughed and told me to do it in my own room.

"There was a test, a chemistry final, when I was a junior in high school. A girl who worked in the office found a copy of it and sold it to me for ten bucks.

"That was bad enough; I mean, I'd never done anything like that before. But what was worse was that I already knew most of the answers— would've gotten a B, anyhow. And now this girl had proof that I was a cheat, and could tell anybody anytime.

"So I killed her." She looked up and grinned. "Only in my dreams, actually."

Richard had enlivened a grown-ups' party by putting a laxative in the punch, but he used a bit too much, and put several people in the hospital. (Including himself, to deflect attention.)

Samantha stole money from her mother's purse for years, whenever she came home drunk.

Mel played vicious tricks on his retarded brother.

Sara helped her father die.

Akeem struggled, and finally confessed that he had never believed in Allah, not even as a child, but had lacked the courage to admit it and leave the faith.

It was an exhausting and awkward two hours, but obviously necessary.

When we got the bell to get dressed, I was a little surprised to find that I wasn't looking at the women sexually anymore. But there were a couple that perhaps I could love.

We never went back to Fort Leonard Wood. The blacked-out bus took us to the St. Louis airport, where they gave us back the personal effects we'd surrendered a month before, laundered, and put us aboard a flight to Portobello.

The plane went over a lot of water, staying carefully away from Nicaraguan and Costa Rican airspace. Ngumi nations don't have air forces; our flyboys would just disintegrate them. But they could still throw missiles at us.

It was nighttime when we landed, the air thick and greasy. The base was an unremarkable collection of low buildings, with the solid gleaming presence of the occasional soldierboy. They stood guard around the perimeter of the base, which they said had never been successfully attacked. I had to wonder how much damage an "unsuccessful" attack could do.

But that's good. We would be spending a third of our lives here, somewhere underground, only dozens of miles from enemy territory. Nice to be safe behind a phalanx of invulnerable telepathic robots. Feel safe, anyhow.

Not really robots, and not completely invulnerable. Each was really an oversized, heavily armed suit of armor that was the telepresent avatar of one man or woman, who operated in instant concert with nine others. Each ten-person platoon was a telepathic family that, with training, would work as one powerful entity.

The enemy could destroy an individual soldierboy, but its operator, the mechanic, could instantly be switched to a reserve machine and be back in the field in minutes—or even seconds, if the backup was stored nearby. And whoever had destroyed the first one, they well knew, would get special attention from its replacement.

I suspected that was just propaganda, part of the mystique that personified the machines, to make them more effective psychological weapons. Any emotion that makes a human being dangerous, they had. But they couldn't die, or even be hurt.

(The "hurt" part was not completely true, which was a closely guarded secret and perennial rumor. If a soldierboy was disabled and captured, the Ngumi would elaborately torture it in front of cameras, before destroying it.)

Americans laughed that off, saying that it might

work with voodoo dolls, but not machines. You turn a machine off, it's just a bag of bolts.

But you have to turn it off in time.

Our quarters in Portobello were neat but perfunctory, and barely large enough to turn around in. But we wouldn't be spending much time in them. Mechanics worked and slept, ate and drank and eliminated, without being unplugged, which took a certain amount of intrusive plumbing. But they didn't open you up for that surgery until they knew whether you could be jacked.

The first day in Portobello, we were wheeled off one at a time for the most dramatic "routine" surgery known to medicine—the installation of cybernetic cranial implants, or jacks, as they were always called. It seems more dangerous than it is. They've done it a hundred thousand times, and it's worked for about ninety thousand.

Of the one in ten for whom it doesn't work, most simply go back to regular life, without the ambiguous gift of being able to share another's mind and body totally. Some few for whom it doesn't work become mentally or emotionally handicapped. Some few die.

The numbers are not published.

Being a physicist, I can figure out some numbers by myself. If something—jacking successfully—has a 90 percent chance of success, and if ten people do it, the probability of one of them *failing* is one minus 0.9 to the tenth power, which equals 0.65. So

65 percent of the time, more than half, at least one of the ten is going to fail.

So logic would say "do eleven." But what if all eleven made it? You'd have to pull one out, and that would be like a casualty, they say. It's easier to add to a family than to subtract.

All ten of us made it, and spent the next two days in bed rest. The third day, we started exploring the gift.

The man who first led us through it, Kerry, was apparently a civilian, a therapist in his seventies.

"Your first time shouldn't be with a beginner," he said. We were back in a place like Room A, government-green walls, the hard chairs and tub of drinks, but with an addition: two couches waiting with a black box between them. Two cables snaked out of the black box.

"You're all going to jack with me for a few minutes first. That will take about an hour for ten people. I don't foresee any trouble, but if there is, best to have someone like me in the circuit."

"Like you, sir?" Candi said.

"You'll see why." He looked at a clipboard. "Azuzi first." Akeem stood and followed him to the couches.

"Close your eyes. Lie down." He took a cable and planted the jack in the base of Akeem's skull with a soft click. Then he sat on the edge of the other couch and did the same to himself.

He closed his eyes and rocked gently for a couple of minutes. Then he unplugged himself and Akeem.

Akeem shook his head and sat up with a shiver. "Oh. That was . . . extreme," he whispered.

Kerry nodded. Neither of them elaborated. "Julian Class?"

I went over and lay down and faced the wall away from him. There was a little click when the jack touched the metal implant, and then I was sort of seeing double with my whole body.

It's hard to describe accurately. I still saw the wall, two feet away, but almost as clearly, I saw what Kerry was looking at, the group of mechanics staring back at him and me.

And all at once, I *knew* him, almost the way I knew myself. I could feel the body in his clothes as well as the clothes on his body; the somatic shifting of soft organs inside, and the complex array of muscle and bone—things that we feel all the time, but which become invisible with familiarity—small twinges and itches and deep pain in the right shoulder I'd have to, he'd have to, stop ignoring. . . .

I remembered everything he routinely remembered about himself, bad and good and neutral. Comfortable childhood cut short by divorce, college a magnificent escape; a rewarding doctorate in developmental psychology. Sex with two women and dozens of men. Somehow that didn't seem even odd. Four years as a mechanic in Africa, driving trucks that got blown up regularly.

Like a memory of a memory, I could feel the union he'd felt with the other mechanics in his transportation platoon, and his longing for the sensation.

It was over with a click. I looked at him. "That's why you're doing this?"

He smiled. "Though it's not the same. Like singing in the shower when you used to be in a choir."

Carolyn was next, and when she sat back down next to me, she softly nudged me with her hip, and you didn't need telepathy to know we were thinking the same thing.

One by one, the others had their sample.

"Okay," Kerry said, "That was the first stage of your warm-up. Now we go to the next level." We followed him into an adjacent room.

Ten of the so-called cages were lined up along the far wall. They were like recliners with lots of plumbing and electronics attached.

We wouldn't have to do the plumbing until the end of Basic, since we wouldn't be plugged in for more than a few hours at a time. When it became ten days, our usual monthly stint, we'd have to be fed and emptied automatically, which they said wasn't bad once you got used to it.

The soldierboys we were going to be plugged into were in a vacant lot somewhere outside. For the first couple of days, we did "raise your right foot, raise your left foot" exercises; then walking and going up stairs. By the third day, we were jogging in formation, having crossed a major threshold: knowing you had to stop thinking about what you were doing, and just do it. Trust the machine. The machine is you.

Meanwhile, we started hooking up to each other

in the evenings, without the soldierboys, one on one and then in larger groups.

Being with Carolyn was thrilling and a little scary—if anything, she felt even more strongly about me than I did about her. And we were so totally different—her intuitive intelligence versus my analytical nature, her streetwise emotionally jarring youth played out against the support and love I'd gotten from my family. Our bodies were different, not just in female/male matters; she was small and fast and I was neither. We enjoyed experimenting with each other's bodies; she said every girl should have a dick of her own for a while. I enjoyed the strangeness of being her, and then the familiarity, though the first time I menstruated, it was like a shocking wound, even though I was ready for it. She was sympathetic but amused—"you big pussy"—and I eventually got over it, though I never got to the point, like her, of looking forward to it, as a kind of affirmation of "my" womanhood.

(None of the other women had that attitude, I came to find out. Sara and Arlie had suppressed ovulation for an indefinite length of time, and the other two didn't especially like it, but didn't like the anti-fertility drugs either.)

Being linked to the others, male and female, was less intense than with Carolyn, though it was pretty sexual with Sara, Candi, and Mel. That was odd enough—Mel wasn't like Kerry; he'd never had or desired sex with a man. When he was linked with me or one of the other guys, though, it was pretty obvious that he'd been suppressing a natural attraction to his own sex, and that's something you couldn't hide from another mechanic even if you wanted to. After some initial embarrassment, he didn't want to hide it.

When we were just doing one-on-one, the other eight people's life stories were pretty far away, like a novel you'd intensely studied in school. When we started doing threesomes and more, it was a lot more complicated. At first, you'd lose track of who—or where—the "I" was. With two, you could be in a state where both lives merged in a kind of selfless integration. I could do that with about half of them.

With three in the circuit, that couldn't happen. At first, there was a kind of existential battle for possession, for "turf," but with experience, it became obvious that each person had to hold on to his or her own sense of "I," or the asymmetries would drive everybody crazy. It was hard for me and Carolyn, and a few other pairs, like Samantha and Arlie, to let go of one another and let a third person in, but if you didn't, the triad would never work together. One person always on the outside, looking in on a love feast.

We spent a lot of time, about four days, switching around among triads. That made the foursomes and larger groups pretty simple, having mastered the basic trick: Each of us was an "I" identified by the life story we had when we weren't jacked, but you had a number of partners, between two and nine of them, each with the same degree of autonomy as you, who intimately shared their pasts and presence.

We could be jacked for a maximum of only two hours running, followed by at least thirty minutes unplugged, which was frustrating. It would be years before we understood why: if you stayed jacked for too long, the feeling of empathy with others became so strong that any human became a part of you; killing anybody would be as impossible as suicide. Which could be a real handicap for a soldier.

We did learn about soldiering at visceral secondhand, by jacking into crystals other people had recorded during battle. It was confusing at first, because you were intimate with ten strangers, and you had no physical control over the soldierboy you inhabited. But the combat was real enough, more real than it could ever be, secondhand, merely human.

Candi was deeply depressed by the experience, and I think only Mel was eager to repeat it. But we all saw how necessary it was. A dress rehearsal for Hell.

I was surprised when they made me platoon leader. I was the oldest, but not by much, and the most educated, but particle physics wasn't exactly relevant to leadership. The unflattering truth became obvious early on. They didn't want a "natural leader," like Lou or Candi, in charge, because he or she would take over the platoon too completely—

instead of ten people working in concert, you'd have one guy making all the decisions, with nine people reviewing them after the fact. That would mirror old-fashioned hierarchic military organization, with the alpha male calling the shots and the lesser doggies falling into line. But if that happened, you'd just wasted a lot of time and money, and risked ten brains in surgery, for no advantage. A soldierboy platoon was like one huge machine that could take over acres of battlefield, making instant decisions with a kind of gestalt intelligence. It was eerie to watch, but became less and less strange to be part of.

We had the minor surgery that took care of nutrition, hydration, and excretion, recovered for a couple of days, and then went out on our first "field exercise"—in the middle of enemy territory.

The ten of us, of course, were safe underground, in a bombproof bunker in Portobello. But our soldierboys walked out ten miles beyond the perimeter, where any pedro could risk his life and attack. But there was an experienced hunter-killer platoon in a protective circle around our machines. Safer than sitting at home, watching it on the cube. You could get struck by lightning there.

We had two more walkabouts like that, never confronting an enemy, and then Basic was over, and we could go home for twenty days. None of us went straight home, though. We had to try the jack joints that ringed the base at Portobello.

At a jack joint, you could pay to plug into other people's experiences. A lot of them were records of soldierboy battle encounters, which we didn't have to pay for, thank you. The flyboy crystals did look appealing, "being" an aircraft capable of banks and dives and accelerations that no human pilot could execute.

But apart from the military ones, there were adventure crystals, of people doing dangerous things in odd places, and "appetite" ones, where you could experience food and drink you could never afford. There were even suicide crystals, for the most extreme experience possible, though you had to sign a waiver before they'd let you enjoy it, in case you empathized enough to die yourself. It was the ultimate in something, like that Japanese sushi with natural neurotoxins, that will kill you if the chef makes a mistake.

And of course, there was sex. Sex with beautiful people who in real life would never even say hello to you, sex in places where you would be arrested if they caught you, daredevil sex, weird sex, sweet and sour and salty sex.

Sex with Carolyn.

During training they only jacked you through cages, to get used to it, so you couldn't physically touch anyone you were jacked with. Most of the jack joints outside the base offered only solitary experiences, but in a few expensive ones, two people could jack together in real time, in private. Sort of like the motels in Rock City, though they advertised *environmentos sanitos* rather than clean sheets, and charged by the minute rather than by the hour.

We asked around and went to Cielito Lindo, a place that did look clean. The women who hovered around the entrance, so-called jills, didn't molest us, but stared deeply at me, and some at Carolyn: if you think it's good with an amateur, come back and try it again with a pro.

The *mamacita* in charge was fat and jolly, and told us the rules: Timer starts the second you close the door, and stops when you come back to the desk and pick up your credit card. Lie there and murmur sweet nothings; they cost the same as sweet somethings.

I asked her whether people ever burst out of the room stark naked and sprint for the credit card. "I have them arrested for indecent exposure," she said, "unless I'm extremely entertained." I decided not to press my luck.

The room was small and clean and smelled heavily of jasmine. There was nothing in it but a large bed with a pile of pillows. The sheet felt like freshly starched cotton, but was dispensed by a practical and unromantic roller.

We'd had sex a couple of hours earlier, so it wouldn't be over immediately, but we were both more than ready when we shucked our clothes and jacked and fell into bed. I kissed and tasted her all over, feeling our mutual tongue on the skin we shared. When we tasted me inside her, I shared her orgasm, but kept just enough "I" not to ejaculate.

She straddled me and slid back and forth once,

and I snapped into her with the springy force of a horny teenager. She held my hips still, telling me wordlessly not to thrust, and for a few moments we merged completely, as I flowed into her and she into me, until neither of us could stand it, and we bucked so hard, we rolled off the bed and lay there gasping.

"Nice carpet," she said while we felt our skin against the rough pile. One of us had bruised a hip in the fall. When we unjacked, I realized it was hers.

"Sorry," I said. "Clumsy." She stroked my retreating dick.

"That musta been at least ten seconds," she said huskily. "Why don't you put on some pants and go get your card."

We went to the Cielito Lindo three more times, and once tried *Falling In Love,* where you made love, or had sex, during an endless fall from an airplane, and floated gently to earth afterwards. But then we did have to literally get back down to earth, Carolyn to her studies and me to my measurements and equations.

Parting was like losing a limb, or part of your mind, but knowing you'd be whole again in three weeks.

I tried to explain it to Blaze, the first day I was back. We were having coffee in a quiet corner of the Student Center.

"You know what it sounds like," she said, "and I'm just being an old mother hen here . . . but it's like you had an intense summer romance, rendered even more intense by the pressure of the military environment, and then the jacking squared it, and then making love while you were jacked cubed it. But you can square x and cube x, and it's still x."

"Still just an infatuation."

She nodded. "You really think it will last forever, though."

"As much of forever as we get."

She sipped her coffee, still nodding. "The Siamese twin aspect. That's a little creepy."

I laughed. "It is. It's really impossible to explain in words."

She stared at me in a funny way. "Wish I could try it. I'm just jealous." Maybe I blushed. "Not of *Carolyn*, silly. Of you both, of the whole experience."

Blaze would lose her grant and her job if she got jacked. Most contracts for intellectual jobs had no-jacking clauses, for obvious reasons; I was protected because my military jack wasn't voluntary. The operation for jacking wasn't even legal in the States for civilians, though hundreds crossed the border every day to have it done.

I had tremendous respect for Blaze, and wanted so much for her to understand. But I suppose it was like a deeply religious person trying to explain her ecstasy to someone like me, before. Samantha was like that, and I understood her instantly, below the level of words, the moment we jacked together. As she understood me, and forgave my unbelief.

Blaze did have legitimate professional concerns,

because I was far from being an ideal coworker. I couldn't concentrate well. At some level, I was never not thinking about Carolyn, and at another level it had to show. I couldn't look at a calendar without counting the days until I gave up my freedom again.

"Why don't you take the weekend off and go to Georgia?" Blaze said on Thursday morning. "Can't you soldierboys fly for free?"

I was a mechanic, and the machine was a soldierboy, but it was a mistake often made. "I was planning to work over the weekend, catch up."

She laughed. "Why don't you catch up with Carolyn instead? The Jupiter Project will lurch along somehow without you."

I wasn't happy about being so transparent, but couldn't pass it up. I called Carolyn, and she was ecstatic. Her roommate agreed to get lost for a few days, and I got booked on a transport headed for Macon Friday afternoon.

It turned out strange. Of course, there was no place to jack in Macon, and we were back to basics. We had the unspoken assumption that that would be enough, but in fact, it wasn't. I wasn't impotent, exactly, and she wasn't unreceptive, exactly. But early Saturday morning we took a bus to Atlanta and got a cheap room a couple of blocks from the jack joints outside Fort McPherson.

The Stars and Stripes Forever was the cheapest place, no frills, which was fine with both of us. Sunday morning, though, we counted our pennies and splurged on Private Space, which gave the illusion of zero gravity, surrounded by whirling galaxies, and that was extraordinary.

We did talk a little bit about it. It was unsettling, but we agreed it was in large measure the fact that jacking was still new to us. We parted very much in love, but a little shaken by the contrast between the normal and enhanced states.

Making love in her apartment, we'd both been fantasizing like mad about the previous week.

In a couple of weeks, we were on our first independent combat mission.

Bravo Platoon was H&I, a Harassment and Interdiction unit. So our main job was to go in there and screw things up for the enemy. Confusion rather than killing.

In this case, our assignment was a little focused chaos. The Ngumi had put together a command center in a remote valley in Costa Rica, laboriously carrying in equipment and munitions by night, by hand. No heat signature visible from above the tree canopy. They didn't know yet that we had seeded the entire countryside with microscopic olfactory devices whose simple job was to ping their location when a sweating human walked by. So we knew exactly where the enemy was and what trails they had taken.

We stayed off those trails. If you're careful and slow, you can move the heavy soldierboy through pretty thick brush without a sound. I guided the ten of us up both sides of the main trail, averaging about one mile per hour. Twice, their patrols tip-toed right through our platoon without noticing us, our suits set on camo in the dark.

Arlie got to their perimeter first. She stood qui-etly a few yards away from a dozing sentry while the rest of us encircled the camp. I was poised to start the attack instantly if one of us was detected, but we all got into place without a hitch.

I was nominally in charge, but all ten of us were essentially wired in parallel. At my thought, we all attacked at once.

No weapons at first but light and sound: ten lights much brighter than the sun; ten deafening speakers shrieking a dissonant chord. Then a bil-low of gas from ten directions.

They were out of their tents firing wildly, but almost all took one breath of KO gas and fell un-conscious. Two had been able to don gas masks. Mel took one and I took the other. Knocked away his rifle and tapped him on the chest, which flung him to the ground. I pulled off his gas mask and tossed it away, and moved with the others to the central objective, a tetrahedral mini-fort of some bulletproof plastic. They'd evidently brought it up piecemeal and glued it together.

Our forces had encountered them in the African desert (invisible to radar and tough on flyboys), but this was the first one we knew of in Costa Rica. They fired 155 mm explosive armor-piercing shells, which could disable a soldierboy, but the barrel was external. It spun around fast, but we could anticipate it and duck. They were firing dumb shells, fortunately.

We could just keep ducking and dodging until he ran out of ammunition, but he was firing all over the place, and liable to kill some of his own people, or civilian mules. So Carolyn and I fried two corners of the thing with lasers, reaiming several times a second as we evaded its fire, which finally heated up the inside and filled it with burning-plastic fumes. A door popped open and two people spilled out, coughing. We KO'ed them, too, and then gathered up all the sleeping bodies and stacked them. Then we lasered a clearing out of the forest to use as a landing zone and called for a chopper to come get them.

From turning on the lights to loading the "captives" aboard the chopper, it was about twelve minutes. No casualties.

Mel was not able to hide his resentment at that. *Thanks . . . we're still virgins.* He apologized, but it hung in the air.

I would have called it a textbook-perfect operation, but while we were waiting for pickup, we got the word from the officers' review board, which had been hooked up with us for evaluation. Three out of the seven thought we should have destroyed the mini-fort and its two occupants immediately, before they could harm a soldierboy or bystanders.

Okay, I thought, *you* come down and kill them. While the soldierboys were on the chopper back, and we were unjacked in the relative privacy of the situation room, we chewed that over. Seven of the platoon agreed with me, predictably; all but Mel and Sara. The disagreement was mild, though; they said they would have done it differently, but it was my call. They didn't think much of the long-distance quarterbacking.

Of course, the officers had really been no further from the action than we were.

They gave us Sunday afternoon off, and I managed to get an advance in pay (borrowing against it, actually; paying the government 10 percent interest) so we could go downtown and jack.

It was called the *Hotel de Dream*. An uninhabited desert island this time, and I paid ahead for thirty minutes, so after we made love in the low morning sun, we swam in the warm water for a few minutes, and then sat and held each other while the gentle surf rolled over us. It was jarring when the time ran out suddenly and we were in that hard plain bed, hardly even touching.

No money for a hotel room. We had hot dogs for dinner and a couple of beers, and then walked back to the base and our separate beds.

Blaze was amused but shook her head. "You're in for four years, ten days at a time?"

"Yeah. I see what you mean." We were alone at the coffee place, midmorning.

"By the time you get out, you'll owe the army a million dollars. At ten percent interest."

I could just shrug, and I guess smile sheepishly.

"You know it's like addictive behavior. If the army had gotten you hooked on DDs, we'd be down there with a brace of lawyers, getting you pulled from service and into detox. But they've got you hooked on *love*!"

"Come on . . ."

"Try to be objective about it. I know Carolyn's a nice girl and so forth—"

"Watch out, Blaze."

"Listen to me for just one minute, okay?" She took out her notebook and clicked a couple of times. "Do you know what your brain chemistry looks like when you go down to that *Motel de Dream*?"

"Hotel. Pretty strange, I suppose."

"Not strange at all. It's a seething stew of oxytocin, serotonin, and endogenous opioids. Your vasopressin receptors are wide open. You would be totally juiced even if Carolyn was a gerbil!"

I could feel myself almost grinning. "Nice job of objectifying it. But if you haven't been there, you just don't know. It really *is* love."

"Okay. So do me a favor. Do it with one of the other women. Watch yourself fall in love with *her*."

"No." Just the thought was disgusting. "Blaze, that's awful. It's like I was a lovesick teenager, and Dad gives me a wad of money to go to a whorehouse and get it out of my system."

"Nothing like that. I just want you to engage your critical side, your objectivity."

"Yeah. That always works with love."

We didn't talk about that any more that month—or much else. I went to the airport alone.

Carolyn and I had one embrace, and then off to the cages.

It was a routine show of force. The governor-general of Panama, our well-loved puppet, was giving a speech in Panama City, and we were there to stand at attention and look ominous. Which we did, I had to admit, nine of the soldierboys set to "camouflage" in the bright sun. That didn't hide them; it made them glittering, shifting statues you couldn't quite focus on. Scary. My own soldier-boy, platoon leader, was shiny black.

Our presence wasn't really needed, except for the press. The crowd was hand-selected, and applauded and cheered on cue, no doubt eager to have it over with and get back into the air-conditioning. It was in the high nineties and steamy still.

Do you feel warm? Carolyn asked without words. I thought back that it was psychosomatic, sympathy for those poor proles outside, and she agreed.

Then the speech was over, and we got together in a line for our dramatic exit. It was a routine extraction, but it was a good demonstration of our inhuman strength: we stood shoulder to shoulder with our left hands raised, and a cargo helicopter with a retrieval bar came swooping in, churning along below treetop-level at more than a hundred miles per hour, and snatched us away. It would have torn off a human's arm, but we hardly felt it.

Carolyn's output suddenly went black, apparently unplugged by the mechanical shock. "Carolyn?" I said over the emergency vocal circuit.

When she didn't respond, I asked permission to disengage. There was no reason for us to stay in the soldierboys, other than the convenience of walking them to storage after we landed. My request wasn't answered by Command. They were probably off fighting a war someplace, I figured.

So we landed by the service bay and walked our machines in. Carolyn's wasn't under her control, obviously; the soldierboy normally mimicked her natural physical grace. This time it staggered like a cartoon robot, some tech moving it with a joystick.

I popped our cages and we were suddenly in the real world, naked and sweaty, joints popping as we stretched.

Carolyn's cage was open, but she wasn't there.

One person in the room was dressed, a medical officer. She walked over. "Private Collins had a massive cerebrovascular failure, just prior to extraction. She's in surgery now."

I felt the blood chase away from my face and arms. "She'll be all right?"

"No, Sergeant. They're trying, but I'm afraid she's . . . well, she's clinically dead."

I sat down on the edge of the cage base, hard concrete, my head spinning. "How is that different from plain dead?"

"She has no higher brain function. We are contacting her next of kin. I'm sorry."

"But . . . I—I was *in* her brain just minutes ago."

She looked at her clipboard. "Time of death was 13:47. Twenty-five minutes."

"That's not enough time. They bring people back."

"They're trying, Sergeant. Mechanics are too valuable to throw away. That's all I can tell you." She turned to go.

"Wait! Can I see her?"

"I don't know where she is, Sergeant. Sorry."

The others had gathered around me. I was surprised I wasn't crying, or even trying not to cry. I felt gut-punched, helpless.

"She's gotta be at the base hospital," Mel said. "Let's go find her."

"And do what?" Candi said. "Get in the way?" She sat down next to me and put an arm around my shoulders. "We should go into the lounge and wait."

We did, me walking like a zombie. Like a soldierboy without a mechanic. Lou got a credit card from his locker and bought us all beers from the machine. We dressed and drank in awkward silence.

Akeem didn't drink. "Sometimes one wishes one could pray." Samantha looked up from her meditation and nodded. The rest of us just drank and watched the door.

I got up to buy a round, and the medical officer came back. I took one look at her eyes and collapsed.

I woke up suddenly in a hospital bed, like a noiseless splash of ice water. A nurse stepped away with a hypodermic, and behind her was Blaze.

"What time is it?"

"Five in the morning," she said. "Wednesday. I came as soon as I heard, and they said they were about to wake you up anyway." She picked up a plastic cup and held the straw toward me. "Water?"

I shook my head. "What, I just passed out? Twelve hours ago?"

"And they gave you something, to help you sleep. It's what they do, when someone has a loss like yours."

It all came back and hit me like a car. "Carolyn." She took my hand in both of hers, and I jerked it away. Then I sat partway up and took her hand back.

I closed my eyes and I was floating, falling. Maybe the drug. I swallowed, and couldn't find my voice.

"They said you're on compassionate leave for the rest of the month. Come home with me."

"What about my people? My platoon?"

"Most of them are waiting in the hall. They let me come in first."

I sat up and held her, she held me, until I was ready to see my mates. They came in as a group, and Blaze waited outside in the hall while we made a wheel, each right arm a spoke. Mel and Candi and Samantha whispered a few words, but it was more the silent communion than any specific sentiment, that gave me a place to be. A place where I could breathe for a while.

Blaze took me home with her, and after some long time, I was her lover rather than the friend who needed a strong arm, a soft breast. Later on, we laughed because neither of us could remember the exact night, or afternoon or morning, when it became sex. But I think I know when it became love.

The army counselor I'd been going to said I should see my loss as a wound, which had to be protected by stitches, which is to say a set of responses that could protect me while it healed. Stitches that would fall away when they were no longer needed.

But Blaze, a doctor of physics rather than of medicine, said he didn't understand. There are wounds too large to close with stitches. You have to leave them open, and protect them, while keloid tissue grows over them. Keloid tissue doesn't have normal nerve endings. It keeps you alive, but numb.

That's where I am, years later. For ten days each month, I lock myself into the cage that gives me superhuman power. The rest of the time, I have her calm and sweet acceptance of the loss that will always be my center.

The soft cage of arms and legs that protects me, and gives me a measure of amnesia.

Steven Saylor

New York Times bestselling author Steven Saylor is one of the brightest stars in the "historical mystery" subgenre, along with authors such as Lindsey Davis, John Maddox Roberts, and the late Ellis Peters. He is the author of the long-running Roma Sub Rosa series, which details the adventures of Gordianus the Finder, a detective in a vividly realized Ancient Rome, in such novels as *Roman Blood, Arms of Nemesis, Catilina's Riddle, The Venus Throw, A Murder on the Appian Way, Rubicon, Last Seen in Massilia, A Mist of Prophecies*, and *The Judgment of Caesar*. Gordianus's exploits at shorter lengths have been collected in *The House of the Vestals: The Investigations of Gordianus the Finder* and *A Gladiator Dies Only Once: The Further Investigations of Gordianus the Finder*. Saylor's other books include *A Twist at the End, Have You Seen Dawn?* and a huge non-Gordianus historical novel, *Roma*. His most recent book is a new Gordianus novel, *The Triumph of Caesar*. He lives in Berkeley, California.

Here he takes us back to the last days of ancient Carthage, to the aftermath of a devastating victory and an even more complete and more devastating conquest, for the grim tale of just how far a man can be forced to go if you push him hard enough—and *cleverly* enough.

The Eagle and the Rabbit

I

The Romans made us stand in a row, naked, our wrists tied behind our backs. Man to man we were linked together by chains attached to the iron collars around our necks.

The tall one appeared, the one the others called Fabius, their leader. I had seen his face close up in the battle; it had been the last thing I had seen, followed by a merciful rain of stars as his cudgel struck my head. Merciful, because in the instant I glimpsed his face, I knew true terror for the first time. The jagged red scar that began at his forehead, disfigured his nose and mouth, and ended at his chin was terrible enough, but it was the look in his eyes that chilled my blood. I had never seen such a look. He had the face of a warrior who laughs at his own pain and delights in the pain of others, who knows nothing of pity or remorse. The cold, hard face of a Roman slave raider.

You may wonder why Fabius struck me with a cudgel, not a sword. The blow was meant to stun, not to kill. Carthage was destroyed. We few survivors, fugitive groups of men, women, and children, were poorly fed and poorly armed. Months of fearful hiding in the desert had weakened us. We were no match for battle-hardened Roman soldiers. Their goal was not to kill, but to capture. We were the final scattered trophies of an annihilated city, to be rounded up and sold into slavery.

Carthago delenda est! Those words are Latin, the harsh, ugly language of our conquerors; the words of one of their leaders, the bloodthirsty Cato. The wars between Carthage and Rome began generations ago, with great battles fought on the sea and bloody campaigns all across Sicily, Spain, Italy, and Africa, but for a time there was peace. During that truce, Cato made it his habit to end every speech before the Roman Senate and every conversation with his colleagues, no matter what the subject, with those words: *Carthago delenda est!* "Carthage must be destroyed!"

Cato died without seeing his dream come true, a bitter old man. When news of his death reached Carthage, we rejoiced. The madman who relentlessly craved our destruction, who haunted out nightmares, was gone.

But Cato's words lived on. *Carthago delenda est!* The war resumed. The Romans invaded our shores. They laid siege to Carthage. They cut off the city by land and by sea. They seized the great harbor. Finally they breached the walls. The city was taken street by street, house by house. For six days the battle raged. The streets became rivers of blood. When it was over, the Carthaginians who survived were rounded up, to be sold into slavery and dispersed to the far corners of the earth. The profit from their bodies would pay for the cost of Rome's war. Their tongues were cut out or burned with hot irons, so that the Punic language would die with them.

The houses were looted. Small items of value—precious stones, jewelry, coins—were taken by the Roman soldiers as their reward. Larger items—fine furniture, magnificent lamps, splendid chariots—were assessed by agents of the Roman treasury and loaded onto trading vessels. Heirlooms of no commercial value—spindles and looms, children's toys, images of our ancestors—were thrown onto bonfires.

The libraries were burned, so that no books in the Punic language should survive. The works of our great playwrights and poets and philosophers, the speeches and memoirs of Hannibal and his father, Hamilcar, and all our other leaders, the tales of Queen Dido and the Phoenician seafarers who founded Carthage long ago—all were burned to ashes.

The gods and goddesses of Carthage were pulled from their pedestals. Their temples were reduced to rubble. The statues made of stone were smashed; the inlaid eyes of ivory and onyx and lapis were plucked from the shards. The statues made of gold and silver were melted down and made into bullion—more booty to fill the treasury of Rome. Tanit the great mother, Baal the great father, Melkart the fearless hero, Eshmun who heals the sick—all of them vanished from the earth in a single day.

The walls were pulled down and the city was razed to the ground. The ruins were set afire. The fertile fields near the city were scattered with salt, so that not even weeds should grow for a generation.

Some of us were outside the city when the siege began and escaped the destruction. We fled from the villas and fishing villages along the coast into the stony, dry interior. The Romans decreed that not a single Carthaginian should escape. To round up the fugitives they sent not regular legionaries but decommissioned soldiers especially trained to hunt down and capture fugitive slaves. That was why Fabius and the rest carried cudgels along with swords. They were hunters. We were their prey.

We stood naked in chains with our backs against the sheer cliff of a sandstone crag.

It was from the top of that crag that I had seen the approach of the Romans that morning and called the alarm. Keeping watch was a duty of the young, of those with the strength and agility to climb the jagged peaks and with sharp eyes. I had resented the duty, the long, lonely hours of boredom spent staring northward at the wide valley that led to the sea. But the elders insisted that the watch should never go untended.

"They will come," old Matho had wheezed in his singsong voice. "Never mind that we've managed to escape them for more than a year. The Romans are relentless. They know the nomads of the desert refuse to help us. They know how weak we've become, how little we have to eat, how pathetic our weapons are. They will come for us, and when they do, we must be ready to flee, or to fight. Never think that we're safe. Never hope that they've forgotten us. They will come."

And so they had. I had been given night duty. I did not sleep. I was not negligent. I fixed my eyes to the north and watched for the signs that Matho had warned of—a band of torches moving up the valley like a fiery snake, or the distant glint of metal under moonlight. But the night was moonless and the Romans came in utter darkness.

I heard them first. The hour was not quite dawn when I thought I heard the sound of hooves somewhere in the distance, carried on the dry wind that sweeps up the valley on summer nights. I should have sounded the alarm then, at the first suspicion of danger, as Matho had always instructed; but peering down into the darkness that blanketed the valley I could see nothing. I kept silent, and I watched.

Dawn came swiftly. The edge of the sun glinted across the jagged peaks to the east, lighting the broken land to the west with an amber haze. Still I did not see them. Then I heard a sudden thunder of hoofbeats. I looked down and saw a troop of armed men at the foot of the cliff.

I gave a cry of alarm. Down below, old Matho and the others rushed out of the shallow crevices that offered shelter for the night. A little ridge still hid them from Romans, but in moments the Romans would be across the ridge and upon them. Matho and the others turned their eyes up to me. So did the horseman who rode at the head of the Romans. He wore only light armor and no helmet. Even at such a distance, and in the uncertain early light, I could see the scar on his face.

The Romans swarmed over the ridge. In miniature, as if on the palm of my hand, I saw the people scatter and I heard their distant cries of panic.

I descended as quickly as I could, scurrying down the rugged pathway, scraping my hands and knees when I slipped. Near the bottom, I met Matho. He pressed something into my right hand—a precious silver dagger with an image of Melkart on the handle. It was one of the few metal weapons we possessed.

"Flee, Hanso! Escape if you can!" he wheezed. Behind him I heard the wild whooping and war cries of the Romans.

"But the women, the children . . . ," I whispered.

"Done," Matho said. His eyes darted toward a narrow crevice amid the rocks opposite the sandstone cliff. From most angles, the crevice was impossible to see; it opened into a cave of substantial size, where the elders and the unmarried women slept. At the first warning, the mothers and children had been sent to join them in hiding. This was a plan Matho had made in anticipation of an attack, that if all could not flee together, then only the strongest among us should face the Romans while the others hid themselves in the cave.

The battle was brief. The Romans overwhelmed us in minutes. They held back, fighting to capture rather than kill, while we fought with everything we had, in utter desperation. Even so, we were no match for them. All was a tumult of shouting, confusion, and terror. Some of us were struck by cudgels and knocked to the ground. Others were trapped like beasts in nets. I saw the tall rider in the midst of the Romans, the one with the scar, barking orders at the others, and I ran for him. I raised my dagger and leaped, and for an instant I felt that I could fly. I meant to stab him, but his mount wheeled about, and instead I stabbed the horse in the neck. The beast whinnied and reared, and my hand was covered by hot red blood. The horseman glared down at me, his mouth contorted in a strange, horrible laugh. A gust of wind blew the unkempt blond hair from his face, revealing the whole length of the scar from his forehead to his chin. I saw his wild, terrifying eyes.

He raised his mallet. Then the stars, and darkness.

My head still rang from that blow as we were made to stand, chained together, against the sandstone cliff. The stone was warm against my back, heated by the midday sun. My nostrils were choked by dust and smoke. They had found our sleeping places and our small stores of food and clothing. Anything that could be burned, they had set to the torch.

The Romans were mounted on their horses. They were relaxed now, laughing and joking among themselves but keeping their eyes on us. They held long spears cradled against their bent elbows and pointed at our throats. Occasionally one of the Romans would poke the tip of his spear against the man he guarded, prodding his chest or pricking his neck, smirking at the shudder that ran through the unguarded flesh. They outnumbered us, three Romans to every captive. Matho had always warned that they would come in overwhelming numbers. If only there had been more of us, I thought, then remembered how pitiful our resistance had been. If all the Carthaginian fugitives scattered across the desert had been gathered in one place to fight the slave raiders, we still would have lost.

Then the Romans drew back, and down the aisle left in their wake their leader came riding, leading Matho behind him by a tether fitted around the old man's neck. Like the rest, Matho was naked and bound. To see him that way made me lower my eyes in shame. Thus I avoided seeing the face of the Roman leader again as he rode slowly by, the hooves of his mount ringing on the stone.

He reached the end of the row and wheeled his horse about, and then I heard his voice, piercing and harsh. He spoke Punic well, but with an ugly Latin accent.

"Twenty-five!" he announced. "Twenty-five

male Carthaginians taken today for the glory of Rome!"

The Romans responded by beating their spears against the stony ground and shouting his name: "Fabius! Fabius! Fabius!"

I looked up, and was startled to see that his eyes were on me. I quickly lowered my face.

"You!" he shouted. I gave a start and almost looked up. But from the corner of my eye I saw him pull sharply on the tether. It was Matho he addressed. "You seem to be the leader, old man."

Fabius slowly rotated his wrist, coiling the tether around his fist to shorten the lead, drawing Matho closer to him until the old man was forced to his toes. "Twenty-five men," he said, "and not a woman or child among you, and you the only graybeard. Where are the others?"

Matho remained silent, then choked as the tether was drawn even tighter around his throat. He stared up defiantly. He drew back his lips. He spat. A gasp issued from the line of captives. Fabius smiled as he wiped the spittle from his cheek and flicked it onto Matho's face, making him flinch.

"Very well, old man. Your little troop of fugitives won't be needing a leader any longer, and we have no use for an old weakling." There was a slithering sound as he drew a sword from his scabbard, then a flash of sunlight on metal as he raised it above his head. I shut my eyes. I instinctively moved to cover my ears, but my hands were bound. I heard the ragged slicing sound, then the heavy thud as Matho's severed head struck the ground.

In the midst of the cries and moans of the captives, I heard a whisper to my right: "Now it begins." It was Lino who spoke—Lino, who knew the ways of the slave raiders, because he had been captured once himself, and alone of all his family had escaped. He was even younger than I, but at that moment he looked like an old man. His shackled body slumped. His face was drawn and pale. Our eyes met briefly. I looked away first. The misery in his eyes was unbearable.

Lino had joined us a few months ago, ragged and thin, as naked as now and blistered by the sun. He spoke a crude Punic dialect, different from the cosmopolitan tongue of us city-dwellers. His family had been shepherds, tending flocks in the foothills outside Carthage. They had thought themselves safe when the Romans laid siege to the city, beneath the notice of the invaders. When the Romans turned their wrath against even shepherds and farmers in the distant countryside, Lino's tribe fled into the desert, but the Romans hunted them down. Many were killed. The rest, including Lino, had been captured. But on the journey toward the coast he had somehow escaped, and found his way to us.

Some of the men had argued that Lino should be turned away, for if there were Romans pursuing him, he would lead them straight to us. "He's not one of us," they said. "Let him hide somewhere else." But Matho had insisted that we take him in, saying that any youth who had escaped the Romans might know something of value. Time passed, and when it became clear that Lino had not led the

Romans to us, even those who had argued for his expulsion accepted him. But to any question about his time in captivity, he gave no reply. He seldom talked. He lived among us, but as an outsider, keeping himself guarded and apart.

I felt Lino's eyes on me as he whispered again: "The same as last time. The same leader, Fabius. He kills the chief elder first. And then—"

His words were drowned by the clatter of hoof-beats as Fabius galloped down the line of captives. At the far end of the row he wheeled about and began a slow parade up the line, looking at each of the captives in turn.

"This one's leg is too badly wounded. He'll never survive the journey."

Two of the Romans dismounted, unshackled the wounded man, and led him away.

"A shame," Fabius said, sauntering on. "That one had a strong body, the makings of a good slave." Again he paused. "And this one's too old. No market for his kind, not worth the care and feeding. And this one—see the blank stare and the drool on his lips? An idiot, common among these inbreeding Carthaginians. Useless!"

The Romans removed the men from the line and closed the links, so that I was forced to shuffle sideways, pulling Lino along with me.

The men removed from the line were taken behind a large boulder. They died with hardly a sound—a grunt, a sigh, a gasp.

Fabius continued down the line, until the shadow of man and beast loomed above me, blocking the sun. I bit my lip, praying for the shadow to move on. Finally I looked up.

I couldn't make out his face, which was obscured by the blinding halo that burned at the edges of his shaggy blond mane of hair. "And this one," he said, with grim amusement in his voice, "this one slew my mount in the battle. The best fighter among you lot of cowards, even if he is hardly more than a boy." He lifted his spear and jabbed my ribs, grazing the skin but not quite drawing blood. "Show some spirit, boy! Or have we already broken you? Can't you even spit, like the old man?"

I stared back at him and didn't move. It wasn't bravery, though perhaps it looked like it. I was frozen with terror.

He produced the silver dagger I had buried to the hilt in his mount's neck. The blood had been cleaned away. The blade glinted in the sunlight.

"A fine piece of workmanship, this. A fine image of Hercules on the handle."

"Not Hercules," I managed to whisper. "Melkart!"

He laughed. "There is no Melkart, boy! Melkart no longer exists. Don't you understand? Your gods are all gone, and they're never coming back. This is an image of the god we Romans call Hercules, and that's the name by which the world shall know him from now until eternity. Our gods were stronger than your gods. That's why I'm sitting on this horse, and you're standing there naked in chains."

My body trembled and my face turned hot. I shut my eyes, trying not to weep. Fabius chuckled, then moved on, reining his mount sharply after only a few paces. He stared down at Lino. Lino didn't look up. After a very long pause, longer than he had spent staring at me, Fabius moved on without saying a word.

"He remembers me," Lino whispered, in a voice so low, he could only have been speaking to himself. He began to shake, so violently that I felt the vibration through the heavy chain that linked our necks. "He remembers me! It will happen all over again. . . ."

Fabius removed two more captives from the line, then finished his inspection and cantered to the center. "Well, then—where are the women?" he said quietly. No one answered. He raised his spear and cast it so hard against the cliff wall above our heads that it splintered with a thunderous crack. Every face in the line jerked upright.

"Where are they?" he shouted. "A single woman is more valuable than the whole lot of you worthless cowards! Where have you hidden them?"

No one spoke.

I glanced past him, at the place where the crevice opened into the hidden cave, then quickly looked away, fearing he would see and read my thoughts. Fabius leaned forward on his mount, crossing his arms. "Before we set out in the morning, one of you will tell me."

II

That night we slept, still chained together, under the open sky. The night was cold, but the Romans gave us nothing to cover ourselves. They huddled under blankets and built a bonfire to keep themselves warm. While some slept, others kept watch on us.

During the night, one by one, each of us was removed from the circle, taken away, and then brought back. When the first man returned and the second was taken in his stead, someone whispered, "What did they do to you? Did you tell?" Then a guard jabbed the man who spoke with a spear, and we all fell silent.

Late that night, they came for Lino. I would be next. I braced myself for whatever ordeal was to come, but Lino was kept for so long that my courage began to fade, drained away by imagined terrors and then by utter exhaustion. I was only barely conscious when they came for me. I didn't notice that Lino was still missing from the circle.

They led me over the ridge and through a maze of boulders to the open place where Fabius had pitched his tent. A soft light shone through its green panels.

Within the tent was another world, the world the Romans carried with them in their travels. A thick carpet was underfoot. Glowing griffon-headed lamps were mounted on elegantly crafted tripods. Fabius himself reclined on a low couch, his weapons and battle gear discarded for a finely embroidered tunic. In his hand he held a silver cup brimming with wine. He smiled.

"Ah, the defiant one." He waved his hand. The guards pushed me forward, forcing me to kneel and pressing my throat into the bottom panel of stocks mounted at the foot of Fabius's couch. They closed the yoke over the back of my neck, locking my head in place.

"I suppose you'll say the same as all the rest: 'Women? Children? But there are no women and children, only us men! You've killed our beloved old leader and culled out the weaklings, so what more do you want?'" He lifted the cup to his lips, then leaned forward and spat in my face. The wine burned my eyes.

His voice was hard and cold, and slightly slurred from the wine. "I'm not stupid, boy. I was born a Roman patrician. I used to be a proud centurion in the legions, until . . . until there was a slight problem. Now I hunt for runaway slaves. Not much honor in that, but I'm damned good at it."

"I'm not a slave," I whispered.

He laughed. "Granted, you weren't born a slave. But you were born a Carthaginian, and I know the ways of you Carthaginians. Your men are weak. You can't bear to be without your women and children. You refugees out here in the desert always travel in a group, dragging the old bones and infants after you. What sort of worthless life are you leading out here in the wilderness? You should be grateful that we've come for you at last. Even life as a slave should seem like Elysium after this pathetic existence. What's your name, boy?"

I swallowed. It wasn't easy, with the stocks pressed so tightly against my throat. "Hanso. And I'm not a boy."

"Hanso." His curled his upper lip. "A common enough Carthaginian name. But I'm remembering the spirit you showed in the battle this morning, and I'm wondering if there's not some Roman blood in your veins. My grandfather used to boast about all the Carthaginian girls he raped when he fought your colonists in Spain. He was proud to spill some Fabius seed to bolster your cowardly stock!"

I wanted to spit at him, but my neck was bent and the stocks were too tight around my throat.

"You're not a boy, you say? Then you shall be tested as a man. Now tell me: Where are the women hidden?"

I didn't answer. He raised his hand, making a signal to someone behind me. I heard a whoosh, then felt an explosion of fire across my back. The whip seared my flesh, then slid from my shoulders like a heavy snake.

I had never felt any pain like it. I had never been beaten as a child, as the Romans are said to beat their children. The pain stunned me.

Fabius seemed to revel in the punishment, laughing softly and repeating the same question as the whip struck me again and again. My flesh burned as if glowing coals had been poured on my back.

I promised myself I wouldn't weep or cry out, but soon my mouth lost its shape and I began to sob.

Fabius leaned forward, peering at me with one eyebrow raised. His scar was enormous, the only thing I could see. "You *are* a strong one," he said, nodding. "As I thought. So you won't tell me where the women are hidden?"

I thought of Matho, of all his fretful plans, of my own fault in sounding the alarm too late. I took a deep shuddering breath and managed a single word: "Never."

Fabius sipped his wine. A few drops trickled from the corner of his mouth as he spoke. "As you wish. It doesn't matter anyway. We already know where they are. My men are busy flushing them out even now."

I looked up at him in disbelief, but the grim amusement in his eyes showed that he wasn't lying. I spoke through gritted teeth. "But how? Who told you?"

Fabius clapped his hands. "Come out, little eagle."

Lino emerged from behind a screen. His hands were no longer bound, and the collar had been removed from his neck. Like Fabius he was dressed in a finely embroidered tunic, but his expression was fearful and he trembled. He wouldn't look me in the eye.

The guard who had wielded the whip removed me from the stocks and pulled me to my feet. If my hands hadn't been bound behind my back, I would have strangled Lino then and there. Instead,

I followed Matho's example. I spat. The spittle clung to Lino's cheek. He began to raise his hand to brush it away, then dropped his arm, and I thought: He knows he deserves it.

"Restrain yourself," Fabius said. "After all, you two will have all night together in close quarters to settle your differences."

Lino looked up, panic in his eyes. "No! You promised me!"

He squealed and struggled, but against the Romans he was helpless. They stripped the tunic off him, twisted his arms behind his back, and returned the collar to his neck. They attached us by a link of chain and pushed us from the tent.

Behind us, I heard Fabius laugh. "Sleep well," he called out. "Tomorrow the *temptatio* begins!"

Even as we stumbled from the tent, the Romans were herding their new captives from the hidden cave. The scene was chaotic—wavering torchlight and shadow, the shrieking of children, the wailing of mothers, the clatter of spears and the shouts of the Romans barking orders as the last of my people were taken into captivity.

The bonfire burned low. Most of the Romans were occupied in flushing out the new captives. The few Romans who guarded us grew careless and dozed, trusting in the strength of our chains.

I lay on my side, my back turned to Lino, staring into the flames, longing for sleep to help me escape from the pain of the whipping. Behind me

I heard Lino whisper: "You don't understand, Hanso. You can't understand."

I glared at him over my shoulder. "I understand, Lino. You betrayed us. What does it matter to you? We're not your tribe. You're an outsider. You always were. But we took you in when you came to us starving and naked, and for that you owed us something. If my hands are ever free again, I swear I'll kill you. For Matho." My voice caught in my throat. I choked back a sob.

After a long moment, Lino spoke again. "Your back is bleeding, Hanso."

I turned to face him, wincing at the pain. "And yours?" I hissed. "Show me *your* wounds, Lino!"

He paused, then showed his back to me. It was covered with bloody welts. He had been whipped even more severely than I. He turned back. His face, lit by the dying firelight, was so haggard and pale that for a moment my anger abated. Then I thought of Matho and the women. "So what? So the monster beat you. He beat us all. Every man here has wounds to show."

"And do you think I was the only one to betray the hiding place?" His voice became shrill. One of the guards muttered in his sleep.

"What do you mean?" I whispered.

"You kept silent, Hanso. I know, because I was there. Every time the lash fell on you, I cringed, and when you resisted him I felt . . . I felt almost alive again. But what about the others? Why do you think they're so silent? A few may be sleeping, but the rest are awake and speechless, afraid to talk.

Because they're ashamed. You may be the only man among us who kept Matho's secret."

I was quiet for a long time, wishing I hadn't heard him. When he began to whisper again, I longed to cover my ears.

"It's their way, Hanso. The Roman way. To divide us. To isolate each man in his misery, to shame us with our weakness, to sow mistrust among us. Fabius plays many games with his captives. Every game has a purpose. The journey to the coast is long, and he must control us at every moment. Each day he'll find some new way to break us, so that by the time we arrive, we'll be good slaves, ready for the auction block."

I thought about this. Matho had been right. Of all of us, only Lino knew the ways of the Roman slave raiders. If I was to survive, Lino might help me. Perhaps I could learn from him—and still hate him for what he had done.

"Fabius spoke of something called the *temptatio*," I whispered.

Lino sighed. "A Latin word. It means a trial, a test, an ordeal. In this case, the *temptatio* is the journey across the wasteland. The *temptatio* turns free men into slaves. It begins tomorrow. They'll make the men march like this, naked and in chains. They'll simply bind the hands of the women and children and herd them like sheep. By nightfall we'll reach the place where the path splits. They'll separate us from the women and children then, and some of the Romans will take them to a different destination by way of a shorter, easier route to the sea. But the men will be driven up the long valley until we finally reach the coast and the slave galleys that are waiting there."

"Why do they separate the men and women?"

"I think it's because Fabius wants the women to be kept soft and unharmed; that's why they take an easier route. But the men he wants tested and hardened. That's why Fabius will drive us on foot across the desert. Those who falter will be left to die. Those with the strength to survive the journey will be stronger than when they set out, hardy slaves worth a fortune to Fabius and his men when we reach the coast. That's how the *temptatio* works."

He spoke as dispassionately as if he were explaining the workings of a flint or a pulley, but when the firelight caught his eyes, I could see the pain that came from remembering. It took an effort of will to hold fast to my hatred for him, and to keep my voice as cold and flat as his. "Fabius called you his little eagle. What did he mean?"

Lino drew in a sharp breath and hid his face in the shadows. "He lied when he called me that. He said it only to be cruel." His voice faltered and he shuddered. "All right, I'll tell you—tell you what I would never speak of before, because like a fool I hoped that it was all past and I would never have to face it again. Once the *temptatio* begins, Fabius will choose two of us from among the captives. One for punishment, the other for reward. The rabbit and the eagle. Both will serve as examples to the other captives, clouding their minds, shaming them with fear, tempting them with hope. The eagle he'll elevate above the other captives, making sure he's well fed and clothed, treating him almost like one of his own men, testing him to see if he can turn him against the others, seducing him with promises of freedom." He fell silent.

"And the rabbit?"

Lino was silent.

"The rabbit, Lino. Tell me!"

"The fate of the rabbit will be very different." His voice grew dull and lifeless. A chill passed though me as I understood.

"And last time," I whispered, "when Fabius captured your tribe—you were his rabbit."

He made no answer.

I sighed. "And tonight, in his tent, Fabius promised that you would be the eagle. That's why you told him where the women were hidden."

Lino nodded. He began to sob.

"But you escaped him, Lino. You escaped last time. It *can* be done."

He shook his head. His voice was so choked, I could hardly understand him. "It could never happen again. I beat him, Hanso, don't you understand? By escaping, I beat him at the game. Do you think he would let me do it again? Never! When he rode down the line of captives, when he saw us standing side by side and recognized me, that was when he chose his rabbit."

"I see. But if you're to be his rabbit, then who is the eagle?"

Lino lifted his face into the firelight. Tears ran

down his cheeks. He stared straight at me with a strange, sad fury, amazed that I had not yet understood.

III

In the morning, the Romans fed each of us a ladle full of gruel, then led us to the place where the women and children were gathered. The elders were missing. Fabius did not explain what he had done with them, but vultures were already circling over the open space beyond the ridge.

They marched us through the boulder-strewn foothills, over rugged, winding paths. The pace was slow to allow the children to keep up, but the mounted Romans used their whips freely, barking at us to stay in formation, punishing those who stumbled, shouting at the children when they wept.

At sundown, still in the foothills, we came to a place where the path diverged. The women and children were taken in a different direction. No words of parting were allowed. Even furtive glances were punished by the whip. We slept that night in the open, laid out in a straight line with our chains bolted to iron stakes driven into the ground. The Romans pitched tents for themselves. At some point they came and took Lino. All through the night, I could hear them singing and laughing. Fabius laughed louder than all the rest.

Just before dawn, Lino was returned. The clatter of his chains woke me. He couldn't stop trembling.

I asked him what had happened. He hid his face and wouldn't answer.

On the second day we descended from the foothills into the long valley. The mountains gradually became more distant on either side until there was only harsh blue sky from horizon to horizon. The vegetation grew scarcer as the parched earth beneath our feet turned into a vast sheet of white stone dusted with sand, as flat and featureless as if it had been pounded by a great hammer.

In the midst of this expanse, amazingly, we came to a small river, too wide for a man to jump across and quite deep. It snaked northward up the middle of the valley flanked by steep banks of stone.

The sun blazed down on my naked shoulders. Though the river was only paces away—we could hear it lapping against its banks—the Romans gave us water only at dawn and sunset. We thirsted, and the sight and sound of so much water, so near, was enough to drive a man mad.

That afternoon, Fabius rode up alongside me and offered me water to drink, leaning down from his mount and holding the spout of his waterskin to my lips. I looked up and saw him smile. I felt Lino's eyes on my back. But as the spout passed between my lips, I didn't refuse it. I let the cool water fill my mouth. I could not swallow fast enough, and it spilled over my chin.

That night I was given an extra portion of gruel. The others noticed, but when they began to whisper among themselves, the Romans silenced them with a crack of the whip.

After all the others slept, Lino was taken to Fabius's tent again. He did not return for hours.

On the third day, the *temptatio* claimed its first victim: Gebal, my mother's brother. It was Uncle Gebal who had given me my first bow and arrow when I was no taller than a man's knee, and taught me to hunt the deer in the hills outside Carthage; Gebal who told me tales of Queen Dido and her brother, King Pumayyaton of Tyre; Gebal who taught me to honor the great Hannibal in our prayers, even though Hannibal had failed to conquer Rome and died a broken man in exile. At midday he began to shout, and then he bolted toward the river, dragging along the rest of us chained to him. The Romans were on him in an instant, forcing him back with their spears, but he struggled and screamed, cutting himself on the sharp points.

Fabius himself dismounted, removed Gebal from the line, lifted him off his feet, and threw him from the steep bank into the water. Weighted by his iron collar, Gebal must have sunk like a stone. There was the sound of a splash, then a silence so complete, I could hear the low moan of the arid north wind across the sand. The captives didn't make a sound. We were too stunned to speak. Our eyes were too dry for tears.

"So much for those who thirst," said Fabius.

It was also on that day that Fabius truly set me above and apart from the others. Until then his favors had extended only to the extra portions of water and gruel. But that day, as the sun reached its zenith and even the strongest among us began to stagger from the relentless heat, Fabius removed me from the line.

"Have you ever ridden a horse?" he asked.

"No," I said.

"Then I'll teach you," he said.

The chains were removed from the collar around my neck. My hands were released and retied in front of me, and a thin robe was thrown over my shoulders. The Romans lifted me onto the back of a black stallion. Two sets of reins were fixed to the beast's bridle, one tied to Fabius's saddle and the other placed in my hands. A waterskin was hung around my neck, so that I could drink at will. I knew the others were watching in envy and confusion, but my legs were weak, my throat dry, and my shoulders blistered from the sun. I didn't refuse his favors.

As we rode side by side, Fabius tersely pointed out the parts of the harness and saddle and explained the art of riding. I had been apprehensive when they first placed me on the beast, thinking it would throw me to the ground. But our pace was slow, and I soon felt at home on its back. I also felt a strange kind of pride, to be elevated so high above the ground and moving so effortlessly forward, the master of so much power tamed between my legs.

That night I was chained apart from the others, given a pallet to sleep on and as much as I wanted to eat and drink. As I fell asleep, I heard the others muttering. Did they think I had betrayed the women, and this was my reward? I was too sleepy from the heat of the day and the food that filled my belly to care. I slept so soundly, I didn't even notice when Lino was taken away that night.

The days blurred into one another. For me they were long and grueling but not beyond endurance. My worst complaints were the sores that chafed my thighs and buttocks, which were unaccustomed to the friction of the saddle.

For the others it was very different. Day by day, I saw them grow more desperate. The ordeal was worst for Lino. He was moved to the head of the line, where he was forced to set the pace. The Romans swarmed about him like hornets, stinging him with theirs whips, driving him on. Whenever anyone faltered behind him, the chain pulled at his iron collar, so that his neck became ringed with blisters and bruises. I did my best not to see his suffering.

"You're not like the others, Hanso," said Fabius one day, riding along beside me. "Look at them. The *temptatio* doesn't change a man, it only exposes his true nature. See how weak they are, how they stumble and walk blindly on, their minds as empty as the desert. And for all their sentimental vows of loyalty to one another, there's no true brotherhood among them, no honor. See how they shove and snarl, blaming each other for every misstep."

It was true. Chained together, the captives constantly jostled each other, tripping and pulling at each other's throats. Any interruption in the march brought the whips on their shoulders. The men were in a constant state of anger, fear, and desperation; unable to strike back at the Romans, they turned against each other. The Romans now spent

as much time breaking up fights among the captives as driving them on. I looked down on the
captives from the high vantage of my mount, and
I could hardly see them as men any longer. They
looked like wild animals, their hair tangled and
knotted, their skin darkened by the sun, their faces
beastlike and snarling one moment, slavish and
cowering the next.

"You're not like them, Hanso," Fabius whispered, leaning close. "They're rabbits, cowering in
holes, nervously sniffing the air for danger, living
only to breed and be captured. But you, Hanso,
you're an eagle, strong and proud and born to fly
above the rest. I knew it from the first moment
I saw you, flying at me with that dagger. You're the
only brave man among them. You have nothing in
common with this lot, do you?"

I looked down at the haggard line of captives,
and did not answer.

As the *temptatio* wore on, I felt more and more
removed from the suffering of the others. I still
slept in chains at night, but I began to take my evening meal in Fabius's tent along with the Romans. I
drank their wine and listened to their stories of
battles fought in faraway places. They had spilled
much blood, and they were proud of that fact,
proud because the city they fought for was the
greatest on earth.

Rome! How the soldiers' eyes lit up when they
spoke of the city. In the great temples they wor-
shipped gods with outlandish names—Jupiter, Mi-

nerva, Venus, and, especially, Mars, the war god, who loved the Romans and guided them always to victory. In the vast marketplaces, they spent their earnings on luxuries from every corner of the world. In the Circus Maximus, they gathered by the tens of thousands to cheer the world's fastest charioteers. In the arena, they watched slaves and captives from all over the world fight combats to the death. In the sumptuous public baths, they took their leisure, soothed their battle-weary muscles, and watched naked athletes compete. In the wild taverns and brothels of the Subura (a district so notorious, even I had heard of it), they took their pleasure with pliant slaves trained to satisfy every lust.

I began to see how cramped and pitiful had been our lives as fugitives in the desert, fraught with fear and hopelessness and haunted by memories of a city that was gone forever. Carthage was only a memory now. Rome was the greatest of all cities, and stood poised to become greater still as her legions looked to the East for fresh conquests. Rome was a hard place to be a slave, but for her free citizens, she offered endless opportunities for wealth and pleasure.

As I was led out of the tent each night, not wanting to leave its cool and cushioned comfort, the Romans would be leading Lino in. I saw the terror in his eyes only in glimpses, for I always averted my face. What they did to him in the tent after I left, I didn't want to know.

IV

It was on the fourteenth day of the *temptatio* that Lino escaped.

The featureless desert had gradually given way to a region of low hills carpeted with scrubby grass and dotted with small trees. The mountains had drawn close on either side. In the northern distance, they almost converged at a narrow pass that led to the coast beyond. The river flowed through the pass into a hazy green distance where, framed by the steep walls of the gorge, I could barely discern a glimpse of the sea, a tiny glint of silver under the morning sun.

I first learned of Lino's escape from the whisperings of the captives. When dawn came and he still hadn't been brought back from the tent, an excited exchange ran up and down the line. Their hoarse voices became more animated than at any time since the *temptatio* began, hushed and hopeful, as if the prospect of Lino's escape restored a part of their broken humanity to them.

"He said he would escape," one of them whispered. "He's done it!"

"But how?"

"He did it once before—"

"Unless he's still in the tent. Unless they've finally killed him with their cruel games . . ."

The Romans came for me. As I was led past the

line of captives, I heard them mutter the word "traitor" and spit into the grass.

In the tent, I glanced about and saw only the familiar faces of the Romans, busy with their morning preparations. What the captives had said was true, then. Somehow, during the long night of wine and laughter, Lino had escaped.

One of the Romans pulled the thin robe from my shoulders and freed my hands. Suddenly I had a sudden terrible premonition that I was to take Lino's place.

Instead, they placed a pair of riding boots before me, along with a soldier's tunic and a bronze cuirass—the same uniform that they wore. They handed me a saddlebag and showed me what it contained: a length of rope, a whip, a waterskin, a generous supply of food, and a silver dagger—the very knife that Matho had given me, with its engraving of Melkart on the handle. Atop the pile they laid a spear.

I turned to Fabius, who reclined on his couch, taking his morning meal. He watched me with a smile, amused at my consternation. He gestured to the items laid out before me.

"These are the supplies for your mission."

I looked at him dumbly.

"The rabbit has escaped, boy. Haven't you heard? Now it's time for you to repay my generosity to you."

"I don't understand."

Fabius grunted. "The *temptatio* is almost over.

The sea is only a day's march away. A ship will already be waiting there, to load the captives and take them to whatever market is currently offering the best price. Antioch, Alexandria, Massilia—who knows? But one of my captives has escaped. He can't have gone far, not weighted down by his chains. There's the river to the east, and the desert to the south, so I figure he must have gone west, where he thinks he can hide among the low hills. My men could probably flush him out in a matter of hours, but I have another idea. *You* will find him for me."

"Me?"

"You know how to ride well enough, and he should be easy to take with his arms bound behind his back. If he gives you too much trouble, kill him—I know you can do it, I've seen you fight—but bring back his head for proof."

I thought of Lino's suffering, of the others calling me traitor. Then I realized that I might escape myself; but Fabius, seeing the hope that lit my face, shook his head.

"Don't even think of it, boy. Yes, you might take the horse and the food and make your way back south. If you can survive the desert. If you don't meet another troop of Romans on the way. Don't think the clothing will disguise you; your Latin is terrible. And even if you did manage to escape me this time, I'll find you in the end. It might take me a year, perhaps two; but I'll find you again. There are still a few stray Carthaginians to be rounded up. My men and I won't rest until we've scoured every

crevice and looked under every stone. They're easier to take every time—weaker, more starved, more
demoralized. Less and less like men willing to fight,
and more and more like slaves ready to accept their
fate. The reach of Rome is long, Hanso, and her
appetite for vengeance is endless. You'll never escape her. You'll never escape *me*.

"Besides, you haven't yet heard my offer. Return here within three days with the rabbit trailing behind you—or the rabbit's head on your
spear, I don't care which—and when we reach the
coast, I'll make you a free man, a citizen of Rome.
You're young, Hanso. You have spirit. Your accent will be held against you, but even so, freedom
and a strong young body, and a bit of ruthless-
ness, will take you far in Rome. Consider the al-
ternative, and make your choice."

I looked at the gleaming boots at my feet, the
spear, the whip, the coil of rope, the dagger with
Melkart—or Hercules, as Fabius would have it. I
thought of Lino—Lino who had come to us as a
stranger and an outsider, who had betrayed the
women, who would only be captured again and
forced to endure the *temptatio* a third time if I
didn't bring him back myself. What did I owe Lino,
after all?

"What if you're lying?" I said. "Why should I
trust you? You lied to Lino—you told him he would
be your eagle, didn't you? Instead you made him
your rabbit."

Fabius drew his sword from its scabbard, the
same blade he had used to decapitate Matho. He

pressed the point to his forearm and drew a red line across the flesh. He held out his arm. "When a Roman shows his blood, he doesn't lie. By Father Jupiter and great Mars, I swear that my promise to you is good." I looked at the shallow wound and the blood that oozed from the flesh. I looked into Fabius's eyes. There was no amusement there, no deceit, only a twisted sense of honor, and I knew he spoke the truth.

V

I remember the faces of the captives as I left the tent, their astonishment when they saw the outfit I wore. I remember their jeering as I rode out of the camp, followed by the snapping of whips as the Romans quieted them. I remember turning my back to them and gazing north, through the pass in the mountains, where the faraway sea glimmered like a shard of lapis beneath the sun.

It didn't take me three days to find Lino, or even two. The trail he had left was easy to follow. I could see from the spacing of his steps and the way the grass had been flattened by the ball of each foot that he had run very fast at first, seldom pausing to rest. Then his stride grew shorter and his tread heavier, and I saw how quickly he had wearied.

I followed his trail at a slow pace, unsure of my skill at driving the horse at a gallop. The sun began to sink behind the western range. In the twilight, his trail became more difficult to follow. I pushed on, sensing that I was close.

I crested the ridge of a low hill and surveyed the dim valley below. He must have seen me first; from the corner of my eye I caught his hobbling gait and I heard the rattling of his chains as he sought to hide behind a scrubby tree.

I approached him warily, thinking that he might somehow have freed his hands, that he might still have strength to fight. But when I saw him shivering against the tree, naked, his hands still tied behind him, his face pressed against the bark as if he could somehow conceal himself, I knew there would be no contest.

The only sound was the dry rustling of the grass beneath my horse's hooves. As I drew closer, Lino's shivering increased, and in that moment, it seemed to me that he was exactly what Fabius had named him—a rabbit, twitching and paralyzed by panic.

He's not like me, I thought. I owe him nothing. On a sudden impulse, I lifted the spear, cradling the shaft in the crook of my arm as I had seen the Romans do. I prodded his shoulder with the sharp point. As he quivered in response, a strange excitement ran through me, a thrilling sensation of power.

"Look at me," I said. The sound of my own voice, so harsh and demanding, surprised me. It was a voice I had learned from Fabius. That voice wielded its own kind of power, and Lino's response—the way he cowered and wheeled about—showed that I had mastered it on my first attempt. Fabius must have seen the seeds of power inside me at first glance, I thought. It was no mistake that he had made me his eagle, that he had separated me from the rest, as a miner separates gold from sand.

This was the moment, in any other hunt, when I would have killed the prey. A flood of memories poured through me. I remembered the first time I hunted and killed a deer. It was Uncle Gebal who taught me the secrets of pursuit—and I remembered how Gebal had died, sinking like a stone in the river. I thought of Matho, of the head that had held so much wisdom severed from his shoulders, sent tumbling like a cabbage onto the stony ground. I clenched my jaw and crushed these thoughts inside me. I prodded Lino again with the spear.

Lino stopped trembling. He turned from the tree and stood beneath me with his face bowed. "Do it, then," he whispered. His voice was dry and hoarse. "Let Fabius win his game this time."

I reached into the saddlebag and began to uncoil the rope.

"No!" Lino shouted and started back. "You won't take me to him alive. You'll have to kill me, Hanso. It's what you wanted anyway, isn't it? On the night that I betrayed the women, you said you would kill me if you had the chance. Do it now! Didn't Fabius say you could bring back my head?"

His eyes flashed in the growing darkness. They were not the eyes of a hunted animal, but of a man. The rush of power inside me suddenly dwindled, and I knew I couldn't kill him. I began to knot the rope, fashioning a noose. Then I paused.

"How did you know what Fabius told me—that I could bring back your head for proof?"

Lino's scarred shoulders, squared and defiant before, slumped against the tree. "Because those are the rules of his game."

"But how would you know the instructions he gave me? You were his rabbit the last time—"

"No."

"But you told me, that night when you first explained the *temptatio*—"

"You assumed I had been his rabbit. *You* spoke those words, Hanso, not me." Lino shook his head and sighed. "When Fabius captured me a year ago, I was his eagle. Do you understand now? *I* was granted all the privileges; *I* was mounted on a horse; *I* was given my meals in his tent and told stories of glorious Rome. And when the time came, Fabius promised me my freedom and sent me out to hunt the rabbit—just as he now sends you."

His voice dropped to a whisper. "It took me many days to make my way to your people, skulking southward through the mountain gorges, hiding from Romans, living on roots and weeds. The horse died, and for a while Carabal and I lived on its flesh—Carabal the rabbit, the man I was sent to recapture. And then Carabal died—he was too weak and broken to live—and what was the use of it all? I should have done what Fabius wanted. I should have done what you're about to do. It all comes to this in the end."

My head was burning. I couldn't think. "But this time you really did escape. . . ."

Lino laughed, then choked, his throat too dry for laughter. "I've never met a man as stupid as you, Hanso. Do you think I escaped on my own, with my arms tied behind my back and Romans all around me? Fabius drove me from his tent at spear-point in the middle of the night. The rabbit doesn't escape; the rabbit is forced to flee for his life! And why? So that you could hunt me. The rabbit flees, and the eagle is sent after him. And when you return to the camp, with my head mounted on your spear, he'll reward you with your freedom. Or so he says. Why not? He will have had his way. He will have made you one of his own. You will have proven that everything Fabius believes is true."

The heady sense of power I had felt only moments before now seemed very far away. "I can't kill you, Lino."

Lino stamped his foot and twisted his arms to one side, so that I could see the ropes that bound his wrists. "Then cut me free and I'll do it myself. I'll slice my wrists with your knife, and when I'm dead you can behead me. He'll never know the difference."

I shook my head. "No. I could let you escape. I'll tell him that I couldn't find you—"

"Then you'll end up a slave like all the rest, or else he'll devise some even more terrible punishment for you. Fabius has a boundless imagination for cruelty. Believe me, I know."

I twisted the rope in my hands, staring at the

noose I had made, at the emptiness it contained. "We could escape together—"

"Don't be a fool, Hanso. He'll only find you again, just as he found me. Do you want to be his rabbit on your next *temptatio*? Imagine that, Hanso. No, take what Fabius has offered you. Kill me now! Or let me do it myself, if you don't have the stomach for it—if the precious eagle finds his claws too delicate to do Fabius's dirty work."

The twilight had given way to darkness. A half moon overhead illuminated the little valley with a soft silver sheen. The reddish glow of the Romans' campfires loomed beyond the ridge. I stared at that smoky red glare, and for a moment it seemed that time stopped and the world all around receded, leaving me utterly alone in that dim valley. Even Lino seemed far away, and the horse beneath me might have been made of mist.

I saw the future as a many-faceted crystal, each facet reflecting a choice. To kill Lino; to cut his bonds and watch while he killed himself; to turn my back and allow him to flee, and then to face Fabius with my failure; to take flight myself. But the crystal was cloudy and gave no glimpse of where these choices would lead.

The temptatio *turns free men into slaves*: that was what Lino had told me on our first night of captivity. What had the *temptatio* done to me? I thought of the scorn I had felt for the other captives, riding high above them, proud and vain upon my mount, and my face grew hot. I thought of the sense of power that had surged through me when I came upon Lino cringing naked in the valley, and saw what Fabius had done to me. I was no more a free man than Lino in his bonds. I stood on the brink of becoming just as much a slave as all the others, seduced by Fabius's promises, bent to his will, joining in the cruel game he forced us to play for his amusement.

Lino had once played the same game. Lino had defied the cruelty of Fabius and taken flight, like a true eagle, not like the caged scavenger that Fabius would have made him, and now was determined to make me. But Lino had lost in the end, I told myself—and immediately saw the lie, for this was not the end of Lino, unless I chose it to be. Lino had faced the same choice himself, when Fabius had groomed him as his eagle and set him upon the rabbit Carabal. Lino had chosen freedom, whatever its cost. I saw that I faced only two choices: to take the course that Lino had taken, or to submit to Fabius and be remade in his image.

I turned my eyes from the dull red glow of the campfires and looked down at Lino's face by moonlight, close enough to touch and yet far away, framed by my clouded thoughts like a face in a picture. I remembered the tears he had wept on the night of our capture, and the lines of suffering that had creased his brow on all the nights since then. But now his cheeks and forehead shone smooth and silver in the moonlight. His eyes were bright and dry. There was no anger or pain or guilt there. I saw the face of a free man, unconquered and defiant, composed and ready for death.

The crystal turned in my mind, and I strained to catch a glint of hope; that glint was the brightness in Lino's eyes. Fabius had told me that escape was impossible, that freedom was only a fugitive's dream, that no other game existed except the *temptatio* that ground men into the same coarse matter as himself, or else crushed them altogether. But how could Fabius know the future, any more than I—especially if there were those like Lino who could still summon the will to defy him?

The power of Rome could not last forever. Once, Carthage had been invincible and men had thought her reign would never end—and now Carthage was nothing but ashes and a fading memory. So it would someday be with Rome. Who could say what realms might rise to take Rome's place?

I closed my eyes. It was such a thin hope! I would not delude myself. I would not let wishful fantasies soften the harshness of the choice I was making. Call me fool. Call me rabbit or eagle, there is finally no difference. But let no man say that I became Fabius's creature.

I slid from the saddle and pulled the dagger from its sheath. Lino turned and offered his wrists. I sliced through the heavy bindings. He turned back and reached for the knife.

For an instant, we clutched the hilt together, his finger laced with mine over the image of Melkart. I looked into his eyes and saw that he was still ready to die, that he didn't know the choice I had made. I pulled the hilt from his grasp, returned the dagger to its sheath, and mounted the horse.

A sudden tremor of doubt ran through me; the reins slipped from my grasp. To steady myself, I took inventory of the supplies that Fabius had given me. How long could three days' rations last if I split them between us? I looked down at the clothing I wore, the uniform of a Roman soldier, and wanted to tear it from my body in disgust; but I would need its protection for the journey.

Lino hadn't moved. A band of clouds obscured the moon, casting a shadow across his face. He stood so still that he might have been carved from stone. "What are you waiting for?" I said. I moved forward in the saddle and gestured to the space behind me. "There's room enough for two. It will only slow us down if one walks while the other rides."

Lino shook his head. "You're an even bigger fool than I thought, Hanso." But his whisper held no malice, and he turned his face away as he spoke. He couldn't resist a final jab—or was he offering me one last chance to betray him?

"And perhaps I'm a better man than I thought," I answered. Lino stood still for a long moment, then his shoulders began to shake and he drew a shuddering breath. I averted my face so I wouldn't see him weeping. "Hurry," I said. "We have a long, hard journey ahead of us."

I felt him climb into the saddle behind me and settle himself, felt the trembling of his body, then spurred the horse across the valley and up to the crest of the hill. There I paused for a moment, looking to the east. The Romans' campfires flashed tiny but distinct in the darkness. The river glimmered beyond, like a thin ribbon of black marble beneath the moon. Far to the north, through the mountain pass, I could glimpse the black marble sea.

I stared at that glistening sliver of the sea for a long time. Then I snapped the reins and kicked my heels against the horse's flanks, turning the beast southward, and we began the uncertain journey.

Tad Williams

Tad Williams became an international bestselling writer with his very first novel, *Tailchaser's Song*, and the high quality of his output and the devotion of his readers have kept him on the top of the charts ever since as a *New York Times* and *London Sunday Times* bestseller. His other novels include *The Dragonbone Chair*, *Stone of Farewell*, *To Green Angel Tower*, *City of Golden Shadow*, *River of Blue Fire*, *Mountain of Black Glass*, *Sea of Silver Light*, *Caliban's Hour*, *Child of an Ancient City* (with Nina Kiriki Hoffman), *Tad Williams' Mirrorworld: An Illustrated Novel*, *The War of the Flowers*, *Shadowmarch*, and a collection of two novellas, one by Williams and one by Raymond E. Feist, *The Wood Boy/The Burning Man*. As editor, he has produced the big retrospective anthology *A Treasury of Fantasy*. His most recent book is a collection, *Rite: Short Work*. In addition to his novels, Williams writes comic books and film and television scripts, and is cofounder of an interactive television company. He lives with his family in Woodsie, California.

And Ministers of Grace

The seed whispers, sings, offers, instructs.

A wise man of the homeworld once said, "Human beings can alter their lives by altering their attitudes of mind." Everything is possible for a committed man or woman. The universe is in our reach.

Visit the Orgasmium—now open 24 hours. We take Senior Credits. The Orgasmium—where you come first!

Your body temperature is normal. Your stress levels are normal, tending toward higher than normal. If this trend continues, you are recommended to see a physician.

I'm almost alive! And I'm your perfect companion—I'm entirely portable. I want to love you. Come try me. Trade my personality with friends. Join the fun!

Comb properties now available. Consult your local environment node. Brand new multifamily and single-family dwellings, low down payment with government entry loans! ...

Commodity prices are up slightly on the Sackler Index at this hour, despite a morning of sluggish trading. The Prime Minister will detail her plans to reinvigorate the economy in her speech to Parliament. . . .

A wise woman of the homeworld once said, "Keep your face to the sunshine and you cannot see the shadow."

His name is Lamentation Kane and he is a Guardian of Covenant—a holy assassin. His masters have placed a seed of blasphemy in his head. It itches like unredeemed sin and fills his skull with foul pagan noise.

The faces of his fellow travelers on the landing shuttle are bored and vacuous. How can these infidels live with this constant murmur in their heads? How can they survive and stay sane with the constant pinpoint flashing of attention signals at the edge of vision, the raw, sharp pulse of a world bristling and burbling with information?

It is like being stuck in a hive of insects, Kane thinks—insects doing their best to imitate human existence without understanding it. He longs for the sweet, singular voice of Spirit, soothing as cool water on inflamed skin. Always before, no matter the terrors of his mission, that voice has been with him, soothing him, reminding him of his holy purpose. All his life, Spirit has been with him. All his life until now.

Humble yourselves therefore under the strong

hand of God, so that He may raise you up in due time.

Sweet and gentle like spring rain. Unlike this unending drizzle of filth, each word Spirit has ever spoken has been precious, bright like silver.

Cast all your burdens on Him, for He cares for you. Be in control of yourself and alert. Your enemy, the devil, prowls around like a roaring lion, looking for someone to devour.

Those were the last words Spirit spoke to him before the military scientists silenced the Word of God and replaced it with the endless, godless prattle of the infidel world, Archimedes.

For the good of all mankind, they assured him: Lamentation Kane must sin again so that one day all men would be free to worship God. Besides, the elders pointed out, what was there for him to fear? If he succeeds and escapes Archimedes, the pagan seed will be removed and Spirit will speak in his thoughts again. If he does not escape—well, Kane will hear the true voice of God at the foot of His mighty throne. *Well done, my good and faithful servant. . . .*

Beginning descent. Please return to pods, the pagan voices chirp in his head, prickling like nettles. *Thank you for traveling with us. Put all food and packaging in the receptacle and close it. This is your last chance to purchase duty-free drugs and alcohol. Cabin temperature is twenty degrees centigrade. Pull the harness snug. Beginning descent. Cabin pressure stable. Lander will detach in twenty seconds. Ten seconds. Nine seconds. Eight seconds . . .*

It never ends, and each godless word burns, prickles, itches.

Who needs to know so much about nothing?

A child of one of the Christian cooperative farms on Covenant's flat and empty plains, he was brought to New Jerusalem as a candidate for the elite Guardian unit. When he saw for the first time the white towers and golden domes of his planet's greatest city, Kane had been certain that Heaven would look just that way. Now, as Hellas City rises up to meet him, capital of great Archimedes and stronghold of his people's enemies, it is bigger than even his grandest, most exaggerated memories of New Jerusalem—an immense sprawl with no visible ending, a lumpy white and gray and green patchwork of complex structures and orderly parks and lacy polyceramic web skyscrapers that bend gently in the cloudy upper skies like an oceanic kelp forest. The scale is astounding. For the first time ever in his life, Lamentation Kane has a moment of doubt—not in the rightness of his cause, but in the certainty of its victory.

But he reminds himself of what the Lord told Joshua: *Behold I have given into thy hands Jericho, and the king thereof, and all the valiant men. . . .*

Have you had a Creemy Crunch today? It blares through his thoughts like a Klaxon. *You want it! You need it! Available at any food outlet. Creemy*

Crunch makes cream crunchy! Don't be a bitch, Mom! Snag me a CC—or three!

The devil owns the Kingdom of Earth. A favorite saying of one of his favorite teachers. *But even from his high throne, he cannot see the City of Heaven.*

Now with a subdermal glow-tattoo in every package! Just squeeze it in under the skin—and start shining!

Lord Jesus, protect me in this dark place and give me strength to do your work once more, Kane prays. *I serve You. I serve Covenant.*

It never stops, and only gets more strident after the lander touches down and they are ushered through the locks into the port complex. *Remember the wise words, air quality is in the low thirties on the Teng Fuo scale today, first-time visitors to Archimedes go here, returning go there,* where to stand, what to say, what to have ready. Restaurants, news feeds, information for transportation services, overnight accommodations, immigration law, emergency services, yammer yammer yammer until Kane wants to scream. He stares at the smug citizens of Archimedes around him and loathes every one of them. How can they walk and smile and talk to each other with this Babel in their heads, without God in their hearts?

Left. Follow the green tiles. Left. Follow the green tiles. They aren't even people, they can't be— just crude imitations. And the variety of voices with which the seed bedevils him! High-pitched, low-pitched, fast and persuasive, moderately slow and persuasive, adult voices, children's voices, accents of a dozen sorts, most of which he can't even identify and can barely understand. His blessed Spirit is one voice and one voice only, and he longs for her desperately. He always thinks of Spirit as "her," although it could just as easily be the calm, sweet voice of a male child. It doesn't matter. Nothing so crass as earthly sexual distinctions matter, any more than with God's holy angels. Spirit has been his constant companion since childhood, his advisor, his inseparable friend. But now he has a pagan seed in his brain and he may never hear her blessed voice again.

I will never leave thee, or forsake thee. That's what Spirit told him the night he was baptized, the night she first spoke to him. Six years old. *I will never leave thee, or forsake thee.*

He cannot think of that. He will not think of anything that might undermine his courage for the mission, of course, but there is a greater danger: some types of thoughts, if strong enough, can trigger the port's security E-Grams, which can perceive certain telltale patterns, especially if they are repeated.

A wise man of the homeworld once said, "Man is the measure of all things. . . ." The foreign seed doesn't want him thinking of anything else, anyway.

Have you considered living in Holyoake Harbor? another voice asks, cutting through the first.

Only a twenty-minute commute to the business district, but a different world of ease and comfort.

. . . And of things which are not, that they are not, the first voice finishes, swimming back to the top. *Another wise fellow made the case more directly: "The world holds two classes of men— intelligent men without religion, and religious men without intelligence."*

Kane almost shivers despite the climate controls. *Blur your thoughts,* he reminds himself. He does his best to let the chatter of voices and the swirl of passing faces numb and stupefy him, making himself a beast instead of a man, the better to hide from God's enemies.

He passes the various mechanical sentries and the first two human guard posts as easily as he hoped he would—his military brethren have prepared his disguise well. He is in line at the final human checkpoint when he catches a glimpse of her, or at least he thinks it must be her—a small brown-skinned woman sagging between two heavily armored port security guards who clutch her elbows in a parody of assistance. For a moment their eyes meet and her dark stare is frank before she hangs her head again in a convincing imitation of shame. The words from the briefing wash up in his head through the fog of Archimedean voices—*Martyrdom Sister*—but he does his best to blur them again just as quickly. He can't imagine any word that will set off the E-Grams so quickly as *martyrdom.*

The final guard post is more difficult, as it is meant to be. The sentry, almost faceless behind an array of enhanced light scanners and lenses, does not like to see Arjuna on Kane's itinerary, his last port of call before Archimedes. Arjuna is not a treaty world for either Archimedes or Covenant, although both hope to make it so, and is not officially policed by either side.

The official runs one of his scanners over Kane's itinerary again. "Can you tell me why you stopped on Arjuna, Citizen McNally?"

Kane repeats the story of staying there with his cousin who works in the mining industry. Arjuna is rich with platinum and other minerals, another reason both sides want it. At the moment, though, neither the Rationalists of Archimedes nor the Abramites of Covenant can get any traction there: the majority of Arjuna's settlers, colonists originally from the homeworld's Indian subcontinent, are comfortable with both sides—a fact that makes both Archimedes and Covenant quite uncomfortable indeed.

The guard post official doesn't seem entirely happy with Lamentation Kane's explanation and is beginning to investigate the false personality a little more closely. Kane wonders how much longer until the window of distraction is opened. He turns casually, looking up and down the transparent U-glass cells along the far wall until he locates the one in which the brown-skinned woman is being questioned. Is she a Muslim? A Copt? Or perhaps something entirely different—there are

Australian Aboriginal Jews on Covenant, remnants of the Lost Tribes movement back on the homeworld. But whoever or whatever she is doesn't matter, he reminds himself: she is a sister in God and she has volunteered to sacrifice herself for the sake of the mission—*his* mission.

She turns for a moment, and their eyes meet again through the warping glass. She has acne scars on her cheeks but she's pretty, surprisingly young to be given such a task. He wonders what her name is. When he returns—if he returns—he will go to the Great Tabernacle in New Jerusalem and light a candle for her.

Brown eyes. She seems sad as she looks at him before turning back to the guards. Could that be true? The Martyrs are the most privileged of all during their time in the training center. And she must know she will be looking on the face of God Himself very soon. How can she not be joyful? Does she fear the pain of giving up her earthly body?

As the sentry in front of him seems to stare out at nothing, reading the information that marches across his vision, Lamentation Kane opens his mouth to say something—to make small talk the way a real returning citizen of Archimedes would after a long time abroad, a citizen guilty of nothing worse than maybe having watched a few religious broadcasts on Arjuna—when he sees movement out of the corner of his eye. Inside the U-glass holding cell, the young brown-skinned woman lifts her arms. One of the armored guards lurches back from the table, half-falling; the other reaches out his gloved hand as though to restrain her, but his face has the hopeless slack expression of a man who sees his own death. A moment later, bluish flames run up her arms, blackening the sleeves of her loose dress, and then she vanishes in a flare of magnesium white light.

People are shrieking and diving away from the glass wall, which is now spiderwebbed with cracks. The light burns and flickers, and the insides of the walls blacken with a crust of what Kane guesses must be human fat turning to ash.

A human explosion—nanobiotic thermal flare—that partially failed. That will be their conclusion. But of course, the architects of Kane's mission didn't want an actual explosion. They want a distraction.

The sentry in the guardpost polarizes the windows and locks up his booth. Before hurrying off to help the emergency personnel fight the blaze that is already leaking clouds of black smoke into the concourse, he thrusts Kane's itinerary into his hand and waves him through, then locks off the transit point.

Lamentation Kane would be happy to move on, even if he were the innocent traveler he pretends to be. The smoke is terrible, with the disturbing, sweet smell of cooked meat.

What had her last expression been like? It is hard to remember anything except those endlessly deep, dark eyes. Had that been a little smile or is he trying to convince himself? And if it had been fear, why should that be surprising? Even the saints must have feared to burn to death.

Yea, though I walk through the valley of the shadow of death, I will fear no evil. . . .

Welcome back to Hellas, Citizen McNally! a voice in his head proclaims, and then the other voices swim up beneath it, a crowd, a buzz, an itch.

He does his best not to stare as the cab hurtles across the metroscape, but he cannot help being impressed by the sheer size of Archimedes' first city. It is one thing to be told how many millions live there and to try to understand that it is several times the size of New Jerusalem, but another entirely to see the hordes of people crowding the sidewalks and skyways. Covenant's population is mostly dispersed on pastoral settlements like the one on which Kane was raised, agrarian cooperatives that, as his teachers explained to him, keep God's children close to the earth that nurtures them. Sometimes it is hard to realize that the deep, reddish soil he had spent his childhood digging and turning and nurturing was not the same soil as the Bible described. Once he even asked a teacher why if God made Earth, the People of the Book had left it behind.

"God made all the worlds to be earth for His children," the woman explained. "Just as he made all the lands of the old Earth, then gave them to different folk to have for their homes. But he always kept the sweetest lands, the lands of milk and honey, for the children of Abraham, and that's why when we left earth, he gave us Covenant."

As he thinks about it now, Kane feels a surge of warmth and loneliness commingled. It's true that the hardest thing to do for love is to give up the beloved. At this moment he misses Covenant so badly, it is all he can do not to cry out. It is astounding in one as experienced as himself. *God's warriors don't sigh*, he tells himself sternly. *They make others sigh instead. They bring lamentation to God's enemies. Lamentation.*

He exits the cab some distance from the safe house and walks the rest of the way, floating in smells both familiar and exotic. He rounds the neighborhood twice to make sure he is not followed, then enters the flatblock, takes the slow but quiet elevator up to the eighteenth floor, and lets himself in with the key code. It looks like any other Covenant safe house on any of the other colony worlds, cupboards well stocked with nourishment and medical supplies, little in the way of furniture but a bed and a single chair and a small table. These are not places of rest and relaxation; these are way stations on the road to Jericho.

It is time for him to change.

Kane fills the bathtub with water. He finds the chemical ice, activates a dozen packs and tosses them in. Then he goes to the kitchen and locates the necessary mineral and chemical supplements. He pours enough water into the mixture to make himself a thick, bitter milk shake and drinks it down while he waits for the water in the tub to cool. When the temperature has dropped far enough, he strips naked and climbs in.

"You see, Kane," one of the military scientists had explained, "we've reached a point where we can't smuggle even a small hand-weapon onto Archimedes, let alone something useful, and they regulate their own citizens' possession of weapons so thoroughly that we cannot chance trying to obtain one there. So we have gone another direction. We have created Guardians—human weapons. That is what you are, praise the Lord. It started in your childhood. That's why you've always been different from your peers—faster, stronger, smarter. But we've come to the limit of what we can do with genetics and training. We need to give you what you need to make yourself into the true instrument of God's justice. May He bless this and all our endeavors in His name. Amen."

"Amen," the Spirit in his head told him. "You are now going to fall asleep."

"Amen," said Lamentation Kane.

And then they gave him the first injection.

When he woke up that first time he was sore, but nowhere near so sore as he was the first time he activated the nanobiotes or "notes" as the scientists liked to call them. When the notes went to work, it was like a terrible sunburn on the outside and the inside both, and like being pounded with a round-ball bat for at least an hour, and like lying in the road while a good-sized squadron of full-dress Holy Warriors marched over him.

In other words, it hurt.

Now, in the safe house, he closes his eyes, turns down the babble of the Archimedes seed as far as it will let him, and begins to work.

It is easier now than it used to be, certainly easier than that terrible first time when he was so clumsy that he almost tore his own muscles loose from tendon and bone.

He doesn't just *flex*, he thinks about where the muscles are that would flex if he wanted to flex them, then how he would just begin to move them if he were going to move them extremely slowly, and with that first thought comes the little tug of the cells unraveling their connections and reknitting in different, more useful configurations, slow as a plant reaching toward the sun. Even with all this delicacy his temperature rises and his muscles spasm and cramp, but not like the first time. That was like being born—no, like being judged and found wanting, as though the very meat of his earthly body were trying to tear itself free, as though devils pierced his joints with hot iron pitchforks. Agony.

Had the sister felt something like this at the end? Was there any way to open the door to God's house without terrible, holy pain? She had brown eyes. He thinks they were sad. Had she been frightened? Why would Jesus let her be frightened, when even He had cried out on the cross?

I praise You, Lord, Lamentation Kane tells the pain. *This is Your way of reminding me to pay at-*

tention. I am Your servant, and I am proud to put on Your holy armor.

It takes him at least two hours to finish changing at the best of times. Tonight, with the fatigue of his journey and long entry process and the curiously troubling effect of the woman's martyrdom tugging at his thoughts, it takes him over three.

Kane gets out of the tub shivering, most of the heat dispersed and his skin almost blue-white with cold. Before wrapping the towel around himself he looks at the results of all his work. It's hard to see any differences except for a certain broadness to his chest that was not there before, but he runs his fingers along the hard shell of his stomach and the sheath of gristle that now protects his windpipe and is satisfied. The thickening beneath the skin will not stop high-speed projectiles from close up, but they should help shed the energy of any more distant shot and will allow him to take a bullet or two from nearer and still manage to do his job. Trellises of springy cartilage strengthen his ankles and wrists. His muscles are augmented, his lungs and circulation improved mightily. He is a Guardian, and with every movement he can feel the holy modifications that have been given to him. Beneath the appearance of normality he is strong as Goliath, scaly and supple as a serpent.

He is starving, of course. The cupboards are full of powdered nutritional supplement drinks. He adds water and ice from the kitchen unit, mixes the first one up and downs it in a long swallow. He drinks five before he begins to feel full.

Kane props himself up on the bed—things are still sliding and grinding a little inside him, the last work of change just finishing—and turns the wall on. The images jump into life and the seed in his head speaks for them. He wills his way past sports and fashion and drama, all the unimportant gibberish with which these creatures fill their empty hours, until he finds a stream of current events. Because it is Archimedes, hive of Rationalist pagans, even the news is corrupted with filth, gossip and whoremongering, but he manages to squint his way through the offending material to find a report on what the Hellas City, authorities are calling a failed terrorist explosion at the port. A picture of the Martyrdom Sister flashes onto the screen—taken from her travel documents, obviously, anything personal in her face well hidden by her training—but seeing her again gives him a strange jolt, as though the notes that tune his body have suddenly begun one last forgotten operation.

Nefise Erim, they call her. Not her real name, that's almost certain, any more than Keenan McNally is his. *Outcast*, that's her true name. *Scorned*—that could be her name too, as it could be his. Scorned by the unbelievers, scorned by the smug, faithless creatures who like Christ's ancient tormentors fear the Word of God so much, they try to ban Him from their lives, from their entire planet! But God can't be banned, not so long as one human heart remains alive to His voice. As long as the Covenant system survives, Kane knows, God will wield his mighty sword and the unbelievers will learn real fear.

Oh, please, Lord, grant that I may serve you well. Give us victory over our enemies. Help us to punish those who would deny You.

And just as he lifts this silent prayer, he sees *her* face on the screen. Not his sister in martyrdom, with her wide, deep eyes and dark skin. No, it is her—the devil's mistress, Keeta Januari, Prime Minister of Archimedes.

His target.

Januari is herself rather dark skinned, he cannot help noticing. It is disconcerting. He has seen her before, of course, her image replayed before him dozens upon dozens of times, but this is the first time he has noticed a shade to her skin that is darker than any mere suntan, a hint of something else in her background beside the pale Scandinavian forebears so obvious in her bone structure. It is as if the martyred sister Nefise has somehow suffused everything, even his target. Or is it that the dead woman has somehow crept into his thoughts so deeply that he is witnessing her everywhere?

If you can see it, you can eat it! He has mostly learned to ignore the horrifying chatter in his head, but sometimes it still reaches up and slaps his thoughts away. *Barnstorm Buffet! We don't care if they have to roll you out the door afterwards— you'll get your money's worth!*

It doesn't matter what he sees in the Prime

Minister, or thinks he sees. A shade lighter or darker means nothing. If the devil's work out here among the stars has a face, it is the handsome, narrow-chinned visage of Keeta Januari, leader of the Rationalists. And if God ever wanted someone dead, she is that person.

She won't be his first: Kane has sent eighteen souls to judgment already. Eleven of them were pagan spies or dangerous rabble-rousers on Covenant. One of those was the leader of a cryptorationalist cult in the Crescent—the death was a favor to the Islamic partners in Covenant's ruling coalition, Kane found out later. Politics. He doesn't know how he feels about that, although he knows the late Dr. Hamoud was a doubter and a liar and had been corrupting good Muslims. Still . . . politics.

Five were infiltrators among the Holy Warriors of Covenant, his people's army. Most of these had half-expected to be discovered, and several of them had resisted desperately.

The last two were a politician and his wife on the unaffiliated world of Arjuna, important Rationalist sympathizers. At his masters' bidding, Kane made it look like a robbery gone wrong instead of an assassination: this was not the time to make the Lord's hand obvious in Arjuna's affairs. Still, there were rumors and accusations across Arjuna's public networks. The gossipers and speculators had even given the unknown murderer a nickname— the Angel of Death.

Dr. Prishrahan and his wife had fought him. Neither of them had wanted to die. Kane had let them resist even though he could have killed them both in a moment. It gave credence to the robbery scenario. But he hadn't enjoyed it. Neither had the Prishrahans, of course.

He will avenge the blood of His servants, and will render vengeance to His adversaries, Spirit reminded him when he had finished with the doctor and his wife, and he understood. Kane's duty is not to judge. He is not one of the flock, but closer to the wolves he destroys. Lamentation Kane is God's executioner.

He is now cold enough from his long submersion that he puts on clothes. He is still tender in his joints as well. He goes out onto the balcony, high in the canyons of flatblocks pinpricked with illuminated windows, thousands upon thousands of squares of light. The immensity of the place still unnerves him a little. It's strange to think that what is happening behind one little lighted window in this expanse of sparkling urban night is going to rock this massive world to its foundations.

It is hard to remember the prayers as he should. Ordinarily Spirit is there with the words before he has a moment to feel lonely. *"I will not leave you comfortless: I will come to you."*

But he does not feel comforted at this moment. He is alone.

"Looking for love?" The voice in his head

whispers this time, throaty and exciting. A bright twinkle of coordinates flicker at the edge of his vision. *"I'm looking for you . . . and you can have me for almost nothing. . . ."*

He closes his eyes tight against the immensity of the pagan city.

Fear thou not; for I am with thee: be not dismayed; for I am thy God.

He walks to the auditorium just to see the place where the Prime Minister will speak. He does not approach very closely. It looms against the grid of light, a vast rectangle like an axe head smashed into the central plaza of Hellas City. He does not linger.

As he slides through the crowds, it is hard not to look at the people around him as though he has already accomplished his task. What would they think if they knew who he was? Would they shrink back from the terror of the Lord God's wrath? Or would a deed of such power and piety speak to them even through their fears?

I am ablaze with the light of the Lord, he wants to tell them. *I have let God make me His instrument—I am full of glory!* But he says nothing, of course, only walks amid the multitudes with his heart grown silent and turned inward.

Kane eats in a restaurant. The food is so over-spiced as to be tasteless, and he yearns for the simple meals of the farm on which he was raised. Even military manna is better than this! The customers twitter and laugh just like the Archimedes seed in their heads, as if it is that babbling obscenity that has programmed them instead of the other way around. How these people surrounded themselves with distraction and glare and noise to obscure the emptiness of their souls!

He goes to a place where women dance. It is strange to watch them, because they smile and smile and they are all as beautiful and naked as a dark dream, but they seem to him like damned souls, doomed to act out this empty farce of love and attraction throughout eternity. He cannot get the thought of martyred Nefise Erim out of his head. At last he chooses one of the women—she does not look much like the martyred one, but she is darker than the others—and lets her lead him to her room behind the place where they dance. She feels the hardened tissues beneath his skin and tells him he is very muscular. He empties himself inside her and then, afterwards, she asks him why he is crying. He tells her she is mistaken. When she asks again, he slaps her. Although he holds back his strength, he still knocks her off the bed. The room adds a small surcharge to his bill.

He lets her go back to her work. She is an innocent, of sorts: she has been listening to the godless voices in her head all her life and knows nothing else. No wonder she dances like a damned thing.

Kane is soiled now as he walks the streets again, but his great deed will wipe the taint from him as it always does. He is a Guardian of Covenant, and soon he will be annealed by holy fire.

His masters want the deed done while the crowd is gathered to see the Prime Minister, and so the question seems simple: Before or after? He thinks at first that he will do it when she arrives, as she steps from the car and is hurried into the corridor leading to the great hall. That seems safest. After she has spoken it will be much more difficult, with her security fully deployed and the hall's own security acting with them. Still, the more he thinks about it, the more he feels sure that it must be inside the hall. Only a few thousand would be gathered there to see her speak, but millions more will be watching on the screens surrounding the massive building. If he strikes quickly his deed will be witnessed by this whole world—and other worlds, too.

Surely God wants it that way. Surely He wants the unbeliever destroyed in full view of the public waiting to be instructed.

Kane does not have time or resources to counterfeit permission to be in the building—the politicians and hall security will be checked and rechecked, and will be in place long before Prime Minister Januari arrives. Which means that the only people allowed to enter without going through careful screening will be the Prime Minister's own party. That is a possibility, but he will need help with it.

Making contact with local assets is usually a bad sign—it means something has gone wrong with the original plan—but Kane knows that with a task this important he cannot afford to be superstitious.

He leaves a signal in the established place. The local assets come to the safe house after sunset. When he opens the door, he finds two men, one young and one old, both disconcertingly ordinary-looking, the kind of men who might come to tow your car or fumigate your flat. The middle-aged one introduces himself as Heinrich Sartorius, his companion just as Carl. Sartorius motions Kane not to speak while Carl sweeps the room with a small object about the size of a toothbrush.

"Clear," the youth announces. He is bony and homely, but he moves with a certain grace, especially while using his hands.

"Praise the Lord," Sartorius says. "And blessings on you, brother. What can we do to help you with Christ's work?"

"Are you really the one from Arjuna?" young Carl askes suddenly.

"Quiet, boy. This is serious." Sartorius turns back to Kane with an expectant look on his face. "He's a good lad. It's just—that meant a lot to the community, what happened there on Arjuna."

Kane ignores this. He is wary of the Death Angel nonsense. "I need to know what the Prime Minister's security detail wears. Details. And I want the layout of the auditorium, with a focus on air and water ducts."

The older man frowns. "They'll have that all checked out, won't they?"

"I'm sure. Can you get it for me without attracting attention?"

"Course." Sartorius nods. "Carl'll find it for

you right now. He's a whiz. Ain't that right, boy?"
The man turns back to Kane. "We're not backward, you know. The unbelievers always say it's
because we're backward, but Carl here was up
near the top of his class in mathematics. We just
kept Jesus in our hearts when the rest of these
people gave Him up, that's the difference."

"Praise Him," says Carl, already working the
safe house wall, images flooding past so quickly
that even with his augmented vision Kane can
barely make out a tenth of them.

"Yes, *praise* Him," Sartorius agrees, nodding his
head as though there has been a long and occasionally heated discussion about how best to deal with
Jesus.

Kane is beginning to feel the ache in his joints
again, which usually means he needs more pro-
tein. He heads for the small kitchen to fix himself
another nutrition drink. "Can I get you two anything?" he asks.

"We're good," says the older man. "Just happy
doing the Lord's work."

They make too much noise, he decides. Not that
most people would have heard them, but Kane
isn't most people.

I am the sword of the Lord, he tells himself silently. He can scarcely hear himself think it over
the murmur of the Archimedes seed, which although turned down low is still spouting meteo-
rological information, news, tags of philosophy

and other trivia like a madman on a street corner. Below the spot where Kane hangs, the three men of the go-suited security detail communicate among themselves with hand signs as they investigate the place he has entered the building. He has altered the evidence of his incursion to look like someone has tried and failed to get into the auditorium through the intake duct.

The guards seem to draw the desired conclusion: after another flurry of hand signals, and presumably after relaying the all clear to the other half of the security squad, who are doubtless inspecting the outside of the same intake duct, the three turn and begin to walk back up the steep conduit, the flow of air making their movements unstable, headlamps splashing unpredictably over the walls. But Kane is waiting above them like a spider, in the shadows of a high place where the massive conduit bends around one of the building's pillars, his hardened fingertips dug into the concrete, his augmented muscles tensed and locked. He waits until all three pass below him then drops down silently behind them and crushes the throat of the last man so he can't alert the others. He then snaps the guard's neck and tosses the body over his shoulder, then scrambles back up the walls into the place he has prepared, a hammock of canvas much the same color as the inside of the duct. In a matter of seconds he strips the body, praying fervently that the other two will not have noticed that their comrade is missing. He pulls on the man's go-suit, which is still warm, then leaves the guard's body in the hammock and springs down to the ground just as the second guard realizes there is no one behind him.

As the man turns toward him, Kane sees his lips moving behind the face shield and knows the guard must be talking to him by seed. The imposture is broken, or will be in a moment. Can he pretend his own communications machinery is malfunctioning? Not if these guards are any good. If they work for the Prime Minister of Archimedes, they probably are. He has a moment before the news is broadcast to all the other security people in the building.

Kane strides forward, making nonsensical hand signs. The other guard's eyes widen: he does not recognize either the signs or the face behind the polymer shield. Kane shatters the man's neck with a two-handed strike even as the guard struggles to pull his sidearm. Then Kane leaps at the last guard just as he turns.

Except it isn't a he. It's a woman and she's fast. She actually has her gun out of the holster before he kills her.

He has only moments, he knows: the guards will have a regular check-in to their squad leader. He sprints for the side shaft that should take him to the area above the ceiling of the main hall.

Women as leaders. Women as soldiers. Women dancing naked in public before strangers. Is there anything these Archimedeans will not do to debase the daughters of Eve? Force them all into whoredom, as the Babylonians did?

The massive space above the ceiling is full of riggers and technicians and heavily armed guards. A dozen of those, at least. Most of them are sharp-shooters keeping an eye on the crowd through the scopes on their high-powered guns, which is lucky. Some of them might not even see him until he's on his way down.

Two of the heavily armored troopers turn as he steps out into the open. He is being queried for identification, but even if they think he is one of their own, they will not let him get more than a few yards across the floor. He throws his hands in the air and takes a few casual steps toward them, shaking his head and pointing at his helmet. Then he leaps forward, praying they do not understand how quickly he can move.

He covers the twenty yards or so in just a little more than a second. To confound their surprise, he does not attack but dives past the two who have already seen him and the third just turning to find out what the conversation is about. He reaches the edge and launches himself out into space, tucked and spinning to make himself a more difficult target. Still, he feels a high-speed projectile hit his leg and penetrate a little way, slowed by the guard's go-suit and stopped by his own hardened flesh.

He lands so hard that the stolen guard helmet pops off his head and bounces away. The first screams and shouts of surprise are beginning to rise from the crowd of parliamentarians but Kane can hardly hear them. The shock of his fifty-foot fall swirls through the enhanced cartilage of his knees and ankles and wrists, painful but manageable. His heart is beating so fast it almost buzzes, and he is so accelerated that the noise of the audience seemed like the sound of something completely inhuman, the deep scrape of a glacier, the tectonic rumbling of a mountain's roots. Two more bullets snap into the floor beside him, chips of concrete and fragments of carpet spinning slowly in the air, hovering like ashes in a fiery updraft. The woman at the lectern turns toward him in molasses-time, and it is indeed her, Keeta Januari, the Whore of Babylon. As he reaches toward her he can see the individual muscles of her face react—eyebrows pulled up, forehead wrinkling, surprised . . . but not frightened.

How can that be?

He is already leaping toward her, curving the fingers of each hand into hardened claws for the killing strike. A fraction of a second to cross the space between them as bullets snap by from above and either side, the noise scything past a long instant later, *wow, wow, wow.* Time hanging, disconnected from history. God's hand. He *is* God's hand, and this is what it must feel like to be in the presence of God Himself, this shimmering, endless, bright NOW. . . .

And then pain explodes through him and sets his nerves on fire and everything goes suddenly and irrevocably

black.

———

Lamentation Kane wakes in a white room, the light from everywhere and nowhere. He is being watched, of course. Soon the torture will begin.

"*Beloved, think it not strange concerning the fiery trial which is to try you, as though some strange thing happened unto you.* . . ." Those were the holy words Spirit whispered to him when he lay badly wounded in the hospital after capturing the last of the Holy Warrior infiltrators, another augmented soldier like himself, a bigger, stronger man who almost killed him before Kane managed to put a stiffened finger through his eyeball into his brain. Spirit recited the words to him again and again during his recuperation: "*But rejoice, inasmuch as ye are partakers of Christ's sufferings; that, when his glory* . . . *when his glory* . . ."

To his horror, he cannot remember the rest of the passage from Peter.

He cannot help thinking of the martyred young woman who gave her life so that he could fail so utterly. He will see her soon. Will he be able to meet her eye? Is there shame in Heaven?

I will be strong, Kane promises her shade, *no matter what they do to me.*

One of the cell's walls turns from white to transparent. The room beyond is full of people, most of them in military uniforms or white medical smocks. Only two wear civilian clothing, a pale man and . . . her. Keeta Januari.

"You may throw yourself against the glass if you want." Her voice seems to come out of the air on all sides. "It is very, very thick and very, very strong."

He only stares. He will not make himself a beast, struggling to escape while they laugh. These people are the ones who think themselves related to animals. Animals! Kane knows that the Lord God has given his people dominion.

"Over all the beasts and fowls of the earth," he says out loud.

"So," says Prime Minister Januari. "So, this is the Angel of Death."

"That is not my name."

"We know your name, Kane. We have been watching you since you reached Archimedes."

A lie, surely. They would never have let him get so close.

She narrows her eyes. "I would have expected an angel to look more . . . angelic."

"I'm no angel, as you almost found out."

"Ah, if you're not, then you must be one of the ministers of grace." She sees the look on his face. "How sad. I forgot that Shakespeare was banned by your mullahs. 'Angels and ministers of grace defend us!' From *Macbeth*. It precedes a murder."

"We Christians do not have mullahs," he says as evenly as he can. He does not care about the rest of the nonsense she speaks. "Those are the people of the Crescent, our brothers of the Book."

She laughed. "I thought you would be smarter than the rest of your sort, Kane, but you parrot the same nonsense. Do you know that only a few generations back your 'brothers' as you call them set off a thermonuclear device, trying to kill your grandparents and the rest of the Christian and Zionist 'brothers'?"

"In the early days, before the Covenant, there was confusion." Everyone knew the story. Did she think to shame him with old history, ancient quotations, banned playwrights from the wicked old days of Earth? If so, then both of them had underestimated each other as adversaries.

Of course, at the moment she did hold a somewhat better position.

"So, then, not an angel but a minister. But you don't pray to be protected from death, but to be able to cause it."

"I do the Lord's will."

"Bullshit, to use a venerable old term. You are a murderer many times over, Kane. You tried to murder me." But Januari does not look at him as though at an enemy. Nor is there kindness in her gaze, either. She looks at him as though he is a poisonous insect in a jar—an object to be careful with, yes, but mostly a thing to be studied. "What shall we do with you?"

"Kill me. If you have any of the humanity you claim, you will release me and send me to Heaven. But I know you will torture me."

She raises an eyebrow. "Why would we do that?"

"For information. Our nations are at war, even though the politicians have not yet admitted it to their peoples. You know it, woman. I know it. Everyone in this room knows it."

Keeta Januari smiles. "You will get no argument from me or anyone here about the state of affairs between Archimedes and the Covenant system. But why would we torture you for information we already have? We are not barbarians. We are not primitives—like some others. We do not force our citizens to worship savage old myths—"

"You force them to be silent! You punish those who would worship the God of their fathers. You have persecuted the People of the Book wherever you have found them!"

"We have kept our planet free from the mania of religious warfare and extremism. We have never interfered in the choices of Covenant."

"You have tried to keep us from gaining converts."

The Prime Minister shakes her head. "Gaining converts? Trying to hijack entire cultures, you mean. Stealing the right of colonies to be free of Earth's old tribal ghosts. We are the same people that let your predecessors worship the way they wished to—we fought to protect their freedom, and were repaid when they tried to force their beliefs on us at gunpoint." Her laugh is harsh. "'Christian tolerance'—two words that do not belong together no matter how often they've been coupled. And we all know what your Islamist and Zionist brothers are like. Even if you destroy all of the Archimedean alliance and every single one of us unbelievers, you'll only find yourself fighting your allies instead. The madness won't stop until the last living psychopath winds up all alone on a hill of ashes, shouting praise to his god."

Kane feels his anger rising and closes his mouth. He suffuses his blood with calming chemicals. It confuses him, arguing with her. She is a woman and she should give comfort, but she is speaking only lies—cruel, dangerous lies. This is what happens when the natural order of things is upset. "You are a devil. I will speak to you no more. Do whatever it is you're going to do."

"Here's another bit of Shakespeare," she says. "If your masters hadn't banned him, you could have quoted it at me. '*But man, proud man,/ dressed in a little brief authority,/most ignorant of what he's most assured*'—that's nicely put, isn't it?—'*His glassy essence, like an angry ape,/plays such fantastic tricks before high heaven/as make the angels weep.*'" She puts her hands together in a gesture disturbingly reminiscent of prayer. He cannot turn away from her gaze. "So—what *are* we going to do with you? We could execute you quietly, of course. A polite fiction—died from injuries sustained in the arrest—and no one would make too much fuss."

The man behind her clears his throat. "Madame Prime Minster, I respectfully suggest we take this conversation elsewhere. The doctors are waiting to see the prisoner—"

"Shut up, Healy." She turns to look at Kane again, really look, her blue eyes sharp as scalpels. She is older than the Martyrdom Sister by a good twenty years, and despite the dark tint, her skin is much paler, but somehow, for a dizzying second, they are the same.

Why do you allow me to become confused, Lord, between the murderer and the martyr?

"Kane comma Lamentation," she says. "Quite a name. Is that your enemies lamenting, or is it you, crying out helplessly before the power of your God?" She holds up her hand. "Don't bother to answer. In parts of the Covenant system you're a hero, you know—a sort of superhero. Were you aware of that? Or have you been traveling too much?"

He does his best to ignore her. He knows he will be lied to, manipulated, that the psychological torments will be more subtle and more important than the physical torture. The only thing he does not understand is this: Why her—why the prime minister herself? Surely he isn't so important. The fact that she stands in front of him at this moment instead of in front of God is, after all, a demonstration that he is a failure.

As if in answer to this thought, a voice murmurs in the back of his skull, *"Arjuna's Angel of Death captured in attempt on PM Januari."* Another inquires, *"Have you smelled yourself lately? Even members of Parliament can lose freshness—just ask one!"* Even here, in the heart of the beast, the voices in his head will not be silenced.

"We need to study you," the Prime Minister says at last. "We haven't caught a Guardian-class agent before—not one of the new ones, like you. We didn't know if we could do it—the scrambler field was only recently developed." She smiles again, a quick icy flash like a first glimpse of snow in high mountains. "It wouldn't have meant anything if you'd succeeded, you know. There are at least a dozen more in my party who can take my place and keep this system safe against you and your masters. But I made good bait—and you leaped into the trap. Now we're going to find out what makes you such a nasty instrument, little Death Angel."

He hopes now that the charade is over they will at least shut off the seed in his head. Instead, they leave it in place but disable his controls so that he can't affect it at all. Children's voices sing to him about the value of starting each day with a healthy breakfast, and he grinds his teeth. The mad chorus yammers and sings to him nonstop. The pagan seed shows him pictures he does not want to see, gives him information about which he does not care, and always, always, it denies that Kane's God exists.

The Archimedeans claim they have no death penalty. Is this what they do instead? Drive their prisoners to suicide?

If so, he will not do their work for them. He has internal resources they cannot disable without killing him, and he was prepared to survive torture of a more obvious sort—why not this? He dilutes the waves of despair that wash through him at night when the lights go out and he is alone with the idiot babble of their idiot planet.

No, Kane will not do their job for him. He will not murder himself. But it gives him an idea.

If he had done it in his cell, they might have been more suspicious, but when his heart stops in the course of a rather invasive procedure to learn how the note biotech has grown into his nervous system, they are caught by surprise.

"It must be a fail-safe!" one of the doctors cries. Kane hears him as though from a great distance—already his higher systems are shutting down. "Some kind of autodestruct!"

"Maybe it's just cardiac arrest . . . ," says another, but it's only a whisper, and he is falling down a long tunnel. He almost thinks he can hear Spirit calling after him. . . .

And God shall wipe away all tears from their eyes; and there shall be no more death, neither sorrow, nor crying, neither shall there be any more pain: for the former things are passed away.

His heart starts pumping again twenty minutes later. The doctors, unaware of the sophistication of his autonomic control, are trying to shock his system back to life. Kane hoped he would be down longer and that they would give him up for dead, but that was overly optimistic: instead he has to roll off the table, naked but for trailing wires and tubes, and kill the startled guards before they can draw their weapons. He must also break the neck of one of the doctors who has been trying to save him but now makes the mistake of attacking him. Even after he leaves the rest of the terrified medical staff cowering on the emergency room floor and escapes the surgical wing, he is still in a prison.

"Tired of the same old atmosphere? Holyoake Harbor, the little village under the bubble—we make our own air and it's guaranteed fresh!"

His internal modifications are healing the surgical damage as quickly as possible, but he is staggering, starved of nutrients and burning energy at brushfire speed. God has given him this chance and he must not fail, but if he does not replenish his reserves, he *will* fail.

Kane drops down from an overhead air duct into a hallway and kills a two-man patrol team. He tears the uniform off one of them and then, with stiffened, clawlike fingers, pulls gobbets of meat off the man's bones and swallows them. The blood is salty and hot. His stomach convulses at what he is doing—the old, terrible sin—but he forces himself to chew and swallow. He has no choice.

Addiction a problem? Not with a NeoBlood transfusion! We also feature the finest life-tested and artificial organs. . . .

He can tell by the sputtering messages on the guards' communicators that the security personnel are spreading out from the main guardroom. They seem to have an idea of where he has been and where he now is. When he has finished his terrible meal he leaves the residue on the floor of the closet and then makes his way toward the central security office, leaving red footprints behind him. He looks, he feels sure, like a demon from the deepest floors of Hell.

The guards make the mistake of coming out of their hardened room, thinking numbers and weaponry are on their side. Kane takes several bullet wounds, but they have nothing as terrible as the scrambling device that captured him in the first place; he moves through his enemies like a whirlwind, snapping out blows of such strength that one guard's head is knocked from his shoulders and tumbles down the hall.

Once he has waded through the bodies into the main communication room, he throws open as many of the prison cells as he can and turns on the escape and fire alarms, which howl like the damned. He waits until the chaos is ripe, then pulls on a guard's uniform and heads for the exercise yard. He hurries through the shrieking, bloody confusion of the yard, then climbs over the three sets of razor-wire fencing. Several bullets smack into his hardened flesh, burning like hot rivets. A beam weapon scythes across the last fence with a hiss and pop of snapping wire, but Kane has already dropped to the ground outside.

He can run about fifty miles an hour under most circumstances, but fueled with adrenaline he can go almost half again that fast for short bursts. The only problem is that he is traveling over open, wild ground and has to watch for obstacles—even he can badly injure an ankle at this speed because he cannot armor his joints too much without losing flexibility. Also, he is so exhausted and empty even after consuming the guard's flesh that black spots caper in front of his eyes: he will not be able to keep up this pace very long.

Here are some wise words from an ancient statesman to consider: "You can do what you have to do, and sometimes you can do it even better than you think you can."

Kids, all parents can make mistakes. How about yours? Report religious paraphernalia or overly superstitious behavior on your local Freedom Council tip node. . . .

Your body temperature is far above normal. Your stress levels are far above normal. We recommend you see a physician immediately.

Yes, Kane thinks. *I believe I'll do just that.*

He finds an empty house within five miles of the prison and breaks in. He eats everything he can find, including several pounds of frozen meat, which helps him compensate for a little of the heat he is generating. He then rummages through the upstairs bedrooms until he finds some new clothes to wear, scrubs offs the blood that marks him out, and leaves.

He finds another place some miles away to hide for the night. The residents are home—he even hears them listening to news of his escape, although it is a grossly inaccurate version that concentrates breathlessly on his cannibalism and his terrifying nickname. He lays curled in a box in their attic like a mummy, nearly comatose. When they leave in the morning, so does Kane, reshaping the bones of his face and withdrawing color from his hair. The pagan seed still chirps in his head. Every few minutes, it reminds him to keep an eye open for himself, but not to approach himself, because he is undoubtedly very, very dangerous.

"Didn't know anything about it." Sartorius looks worriedly up and down the road to make sure they are alone, as if Kane hadn't already done that better, faster, and more carefully long before the two locals had arrived at the rendezvous. "What can I say? We didn't have any idea they had that scrambler thing. Of course, we would have let you know if we'd heard."

"I need a doctor—somebody you'd trust with your life, because I'll be trusting him with mine."

"Cannibal Christian," says young Carl in an awed voice. "That's what they're calling you now."

"That's crap." He is not ashamed, because he was doing God's will, but he does not want to be reminded, either.

"Or the Angel of Death, they still like that one, too. Either way, they're sure talking about you."

The doctor is a woman too, a decade or so past her child-bearing years. They wake her up in her small cottage on the edge of a blighted park that looks like it was manufacturing space before a halfway attempt to redeem it. She has alcohol on her breath and her hands shake, but her eyes, although a little bloodshot, are intelligent and alert.

"Don't bore me with your story and I won't bore you with mine," she says when Carl begins to introduce them. A moment later, her pupils dilate. "Hang on—I already know yours. You're the Angel everyone's talking about."

"Some people call him the Cannibal Christian," says young Carl helpfully.

"Are you a believer?" Kane asks her.

"I'm too flawed to be anything else. Who else but Jesus would keep forgiving me?"

She lays him out on a bedsheet on her kitchen table. He waves away both the anesthetic inhaler and the bottle of liquor.

"They won't work on me unless I let them, and I can't afford to let them work. I have to stay alert. Now please, cut that godless thing out of my head. Do you have a Spirit you can put in?"

"Beg pardon?" She straightens up, the scalpel already bloody from the incision he is doing his best to ignore.

"What do you call it here? My kind of seed, a seed of Covenant. So I can hear the voice of Spirit again—"

As if to protest its own pending removal, the Archimedes seed abruptly fills his skull with a crackle of interference.

A bad sign, Kane thinks. He must be overworking his internal systems. When he finishes here he'll need several days' rest before he decides what to do next.

"Sorry," he tells the doctor. "I didn't hear you. What did you say?"

She shrugs. "I said I'd have to see what I have. One of your people died on this very table a few years ago, I'm sad to say, despite everything I did to save him. I think I kept his communication seed." She waves her hand a little, as though such things happen or fail to happen every day. "Who knows? I'll have a look."

He cannot let himself hope too much. Even if she has it, what are the odds that it will work, and even more unlikely, that it will work here on Archimedes? There are booster stations on all the other colony worlds, like Arjuna, where the Word is allowed to compete freely with the lies of the Godless.

The latest crackle in his head resolves into a calm, sweetly reasonable voice. . . . *No less a philosopher than Aristotle himself said, "Men create gods after their own image, not only with regard to their form, but with regard to their mode of life."*

Kane forces himself to open his eyes. The room is blurry, the doctor a faint shadowy shape bending over him. Something sharp probes in his neck.

"There it is," she says. "It's going to hurt a bit coming out. What's your name? Your real name?"

"Lamentation."

"Ah." She doesn't smile, at least he doesn't think she does—it's hard for him to make out her features—but she sounds amused. "'She weepeth sore in the night, and her tears are on her cheeks: among all her lovers she hath none to comfort her: all her friends have dealt treacherously with her, they are become her enemies.' That's Jerusalem they're talking about," the doctor adds. "The original one."

"Book of Lamentations," he says quietly. The pain is so fierce that it's all he can do not to reach up and grab the hand that holds the probing, insupportable instrument. At times like this, when he most needs to restrain himself, he can most clearly feel his strength. If he were to lose control and loose that unfettered power, he feels that he could blaze like one of the stellar torches in heaven's great vault, that he could destroy an entire world.

"Hey," says a voice in the darkness beyond the pool of light on the kitchen table—young Carl "Hey. Something's going on."

"What are you talking about?" demands Sartorius. A moment later, the window explodes in a shower of sparkling glass and the room fills with smoke.

Not smoke, gas. Kane springs off the table, accidentally knocking the doctor back against the wall. He gulps in enough breath to last him a quarter of an hour and flares the tissues of his pharynx to seal his air passages. If it's a nerve gas, there is nothing much he can do, though—too much skin exposed.

In the corner, the doctor struggles to her feet, emerging from the billows of gas on the floor with her mouth wide and working but nothing coming out. It isn't just her. Carl and Sartorius are holding their breath as they shove furniture against the door as a makeshift barricade. The bigger, older man already has a gun in his hand. Why is it so quiet outside? What are they doing out there?

The answer comes with a stuttering roar. Small arms fire suddenly fills the kitchen wall with holes. The doctor throws up her hands and begins a terrible jig, as though she is being stitched by an invisible sewing machine. When she falls to the ground, it is in pieces.

Young Carl stretches motionless on the floor in a pool of his own spreading blood and brains. Sartorius is still standing unsteadily, but red bubbles seep through his clothing in several places.

Kane is on the ground—he has dropped without realizing it. He does not stop to consider the near-certainty of failure, but instead springs to the ceiling and digs his fingers in long enough to smash his way through with the other hand, then hunkers in the crawlspace until the first team of troopers comes in to check the damage, flashlights darting through the fog of gas fumes. How did they find him so quickly? More important, what have they brought to use against him?

Speed is his best weapon. He climbs out through the vent. He has to widen it, and the splintering brings a fusillade from below. When he reaches the roof dozens of shots crack past him and two actually hit him, one in the arm and one in the back, these from the parked security vehicles where the rest of the invasion team are waiting for the first wave to signal them inside. The shock waves travel through him so that he shakes like a wet dog. A moment later, as he suspected, they deploy the scrambler. This time, though, he is ready: he saturates his neurons with calcium to deaden the electromagnetic surge, and although his own brain activity ceases for a moment and he drops bonelessly across the roof crest, there is no damage. A few seconds later, he is up again. Their best weapon spent, the soldiers have three seconds to shoot at a dark figure scrambling with incredible speed along the roofline; then Lamentation Kane jumps down into the hot tracery of their fire, sprints forward and leaps off the hood of their own vehicle and over them before they can change firing positions.

He can't make it to full speed this time—not enough rest and not enough refueling—but he can go fast enough that he has vanished into the Hellas City sewers by time the strike team can remobilize.

The Archimedes seed, which has been telling his enemies exactly where he is, lies behind him now, wrapped in bloody gauze somewhere in the ruins of the doctor's kitchen. Keeta Januari and her Rationalists will learn much about the ability of the Covenant scientists to manufacture imitations of Archimedes technology, but they will not learn anything more about Kane. Not from the seed. He is free of it now.

———

He emerges almost a full day later from a pumping station on the outskirts of one of Hellas City's suburbs, but now he is a different Kane entirely, a Kane never before seen. Although the doctor removed the Archimedes seed, she had no time to locate, let alone implant, a Spirit device in its place: for the first time in as long as he can remember his thoughts are entirely his own, his head empty of any other voices.

The solitude is terrifying.

He makes his way up into the hills west of the great city, hiding in the daytime, moving cautiously by night because so many of the rural residents have elaborate security systems or animals who can smell Kane even before he can smell them. At last he finds an untended property. He could break in easily, but instead extrudes one of his fingernails and hardens it to pick the lock. He wants to minimize his presence whenever possible—he needs time to think, to plan. The ceiling has been lifted off his world and he is confused.

For safety's sake, he spends the first two days exploring his new hiding place only at night, with the lights out and his pupils dilated so far that even the sudden appearance of a white piece of paper in front of him is painful. From what he can tell, the small modern house belongs to a man traveling for a month on the eastern side of the continent. The owner has been gone only a week, which gives Kane ample time to rest and think about what he is going to do next.

The first thing he has to get used to is the silence in his head. All his life since he was a tiny unknowing child, Spirit has spoken to him. Now he cannot hear her calm, inspiring voice. The godless prattle of Archimedes is silenced too. There is nothing and no one to share Kane's thoughts.

He cries that first night as he cried in the whore's room, like a lost child. He is a ghost. He is no longer human. He has lost his inner guide, he has botched his mission, he has failed his God and his people. He has eaten the flesh of his own kind, and for nothing.

Lamentation Kane is alone with his great sin.

He moves on before the owner of the house returns. He knows he could kill the man and stay for many more months, but it seems time to do things differently, although Kane can't say precisely why. He can't even say for certain what things he is going to do. He still owes God the death of Prime Minister Januari, but something seems to have changed inside him, and he is in no hurry to fulfill that promise. The silence in his head, at first so frightening, has begun to seem something more. Holy, perhaps, but certainly different from anything he has experienced before, as though every moment is a waking dream.

No, it is more like waking up from a dream. But what kind of dream has he escaped, a good one or a bad one? And what will replace it?

Even without Spirit's prompting, he remembers Christ's words: *You shall know the truth, and the truth shall set you free.* In his new inner silence, the ancient promise seems to have many meanings. Does Kane really want the truth? Could he stand to be truly free?

Before he leaves the house, he takes the owner's second-best camping equipment, the things the man left behind. Kane will live in the wild areas in the highest parts of the hills for as long as seems right. He will think. It is possible that he will leave Lamentation Kane there behind him when he comes out again. He may leave the Angel of Death behind as well.

What will remain? And whom will such a new sort of creature serve? The angels, the devils . . . or just itself?

Kane will be interested to find out.

Cecelia Holland

Cecelia Holland is one of the world's most highly acclaimed and respected historical novelists, ranked by many alongside other giants in that field, such as Mary Renault and Larry McMurtry. Over the span of her thirty-year career, she's written almost thirty historical novels, including *The Firedrake, Rakóssy, Two Ravens, Ghost on the Steppe, The Death of Attila, The King's Road, Pillar of the Sky, The Lords of Vaumartin, Pacific Street, The Sea Beggars, The Earl, The Kings in Winter, The Belt of Gold,* and more than a dozen others. She also wrote the well-known science fiction novel *Floating Worlds,* which was nominated for a Locus Award in 1975, and of late has been working on a series of fantasy novels, including *The Soul Thief, The Witches' Kitchen, The Serpent Dreamer,* and *Varanger,* the most recent volume in the Soul Thief series. *The High City,* a historical novel set in the Byzantine Empire, was published in 2009.

In the violent and bloody story that follows, she takes us back to the days of the Vikings and sweeps us along with a swift-moving raiding party (hope you know how to row!) who find the stakes for that particular raid set a little higher than they had bargained for. . . .

The King of Norway

I

Conn Corbansson had fought for Sweyn Tjugas when Sweyn was just an outlaw rebelling against his father, King Harald Bluetooth, and the prince had promised him a war with England when he became King of Denmark. Now that Sweyn actually wore the crown, he had let the English king buy his peace with a ship full of silver. Conn took this very ill.

"England is the greatest prize. You swore this to me."

Sweyn pulled furiously at his long forked mustaches. His eyes glittered. "I have not forgotten. And the time will come. Meanwhile, there is Hakon the Jarl, up in Norway. I cannot turn my back on him."

"So you called in the Jomsvikings instead of fighting him yourself," Conn said. "I see being King has made you womanish as well as pursefond."

He turned on his heel, before Sweyn could speak, and walked off down the boardwalk toward the King's great hall. His cousin Raef, who went everywhere with him, followed at his side. Sweyn bellowed after them, but neither of them paid heed.

Conn said, "How can I believe anything he says ever again?"

Raef said, "Who would you rather fight for?"

"I don't know," Conn said. "But I will find out."

That night in his great hall at Helsingor, Sweyn had a feasting, and there came many of his own hird-men, including Conn and Raef, but also the chiefs of the Jomsvikings, Sigvaldi Haraldsson and Bui the Stout. Raef sat down at the low table, since with Conn he was now on the King's sour side.

Conn sat beside him, his black curly hair and beard a wild mane around his head. His gaze went continually to the Jomsvikings at the table across the way. Raef knew his curiosity; they had heard much of the great company of the Jomsvikings, of their fortress in the east, and their skill at war, which they gave to whoever would pay them enough. They weren't actually supposed to have chiefs, but to hold all in common as free men, and Raef wondered if Sigvaldi here and the barrel-shaped Bui were messengers more than chiefs. They wore no fancy clothes, such as Sweyn's red coats of silk and fur, and their beards and hair hung shaggy and long. Sigvaldi was a big man, square shouldered, with curling yellow hair that flowed into his beard.

Beside him, Conn said, "I like their looks. They are hard men, and proud."

Raef said nothing, being slower to judgment. Across the way, Sigvaldi had seen Conn watching, indeed, and lifted a cup to him, and Conn drank with him. It was the strong beer, thick as bear piss, and the slaves were carrying around ewers of it to refill any cup that went even half-empty. Raef reached out and turned his empty cup upside down.

When they were finished with the meat and settling in to drink, Sweyn stood up and lifted his cup, and called on Thor and Odin and gave honor to them. The men all shouted and drank, but Sweyn was not finished.

"In their honor also, it's our Danish custom to offer vows, which are most sacred now—" He held out his cup to be filled again. "And here in the names of those most high, I swear one day to make myself King of England!"

The men all through the hall gave up a roar of excitement; across the field of waving arms and cheering faces, Raef saw Sweyn turn and glare at Conn. "Who else offers such a vow as this?"

The uproar faded a moment, and Sigvaldi lurched to his feet. "When the war for England comes, let it be, but we are here for the sake of Hakon the Jarl, in Norway, who is an oathbreaker and a turncoat."

Voices rose, calling Hakon the Jarl every sort of evil thing, traitor and thief and liar. And the slaves went around and filled the cups. Steeped in drink, red-faced Sigvaldi held his cup high so that all would look. When the hall was hushed, he shouted, "Therefore I vow here before the high gods to lead the Jomsvikings against Hakon, wherever he hides! And I will not give up until he is beaten."

There was a great yell from all there, and they drank. The hall was crowded with men now, those sitting at the tables, many of them Jomsvikings, and many others standing behind them who were Sweyn's housecarls and crews.

"A mighty vow," Sweyn called. "An honor to the gods Hakon has betrayed. The rest of you— will you follow your chief in this?" His eyes shot an oblique glance at Conn, down at the lower table. "Which of you will join the Jomsvikings?"

At this, Dane and Jomsviking alike began shouting out oaths and vows against Hakon, while the slaves with the jugs plied their work.

Then Conn rose.

Raef held his breath, alarmed at this, and around the hall, the other men hushed.

Conn held out his cup.

"I swear I will sail with you, Sigvaldi, and call out Hakon face-to-face, and not come back until I am the King of Norway." He raised his cup toward Sweyn and tilted it to his mouth.

There was a brief hush at this, as everybody saw it was an insult, or a challenge, but then they erupted again in another great roaring and stamping all through the hall, and more outpourings of vows. Raef, who had touched nothing since the first cup, marked that up there at the high seat, Sweyn's glinting eyes were fixed on Conn and his mouth wound tight with rage. Raef thought they had all probably gotten more than they wished for in this oath-taking at Helsingor.

The next morning Conn woke, sprawled on his bench in the hall, and went out into the yard to piss. His head pounded and his mouth tasted evil. He could not remember much of the night before. When he turned away from the fence, Sigvaldi the Jomsviking chief was walking up to him, beaming all across his face.

"Well," he boomed out, "maybe we promised some mighty doings, last night, with those vows, hah? But I'm glad you're with us, boy. We'll see if you'll make a Jomsviking." He put out his hand to Conn, who shook it, having nothing else to do. Sigvaldi went on, "Meet at the Limsfjord at the full moon, and we'll go raiding in Norway, and draw Hakon to us. Then we'll find out how well you fight."

He tramped away across the yard, where more of the Jomsvikings were coming out into the sun. Raef stood by the door into the hall.

Conn went over by him.

"What did I swear to?"

His cousin's long homely face was expressionless. "You said you would sail with them and challenge Hakon the Jarl face-to-face, and not return to Denmark until you were King of Norway."

Conn gave a yelp, amazed, and said, "What a

fool I am in beer! That's something great to do, though, isn't it."

Raef said, "I'd say that."

"Well, then," Conn said, "let's get started."

II

So they sailed north to raid in Norway, around the Vik, where the riches were. Sometimes the whole fleet raided a village together, and sometimes they went out in parties and attacked farmsteads along the fjord, driving the people out and then ransacking their holdings. Whatever anybody found of gold went into a great chest, which Bui the Stout guarded like a dragon. All else they ate or drank, or packed off to the Jomsberg. Several ships went heavy-laden to the Jomsberg, but there was no sign of Hakon the Jarl.

They turned north, following the passageways between the islands and the coast, raiding as they went. Every day the sun stayed longer in the sky, and the nights barely darkened enough to let a man sleep an hour. Around them, above thin green seaside meadows, the land rose in curtains of rock, snow-cloaked. They stood far out to sea to weather the cloud-shrouded wind-blasted cape at Stad, and then rowed on, still north but now easterly, attacking whatever they found in the fjords. They were within a few good days' rowing now of the long waterway that led to the Trondelag, and still Hakon offered them no opposition.

III

Conn's muscles hurt; all day he had been rowing against the fierce north wind, and he stood on the beach and stretched the ache out of his arms. The sun was a great fat orange blob floating just above the western horizon. The sky burned with its fiery glow, the few low streaks of cloud gilt-edged. The dark sea rolled up against the pebble shore, broke, and withdrew in a long seething growl. Out past the ships, sixty of them, drawn up onto the beach like resting monsters, he caught a glimpse of a shark.

The coppery light of the long sundown made the campfires that covered the beach almost invisible. Over every pit a haunch turned, strips of meat and fish hung dripping on tripods and spits, their fats exploding in the coals below, and a man stood by in the hot glow with a cup, putting out burns with a douse of beer. Conn saw Sigvaldi Haraldsson up on the beach and went to him.

The chief of the Jomsvikings sat on a big log, his feet out in front of him, watching some lesser men turn his spit. Bui the Stout sat next to him, the Jomsvikings' treasure chest at his feet. As Conn came up, they raised their faces toward him. They were passing a cup between them, and Sigvaldi with a bellowed greeting held it out to him.

Conn drank. The beer tasted muddy. "Hakon has to come after us soon."

Sigvaldi gave a harsh crackle of a laugh, clapping his hands on his knees. "I told you, lad, he won't willingly fight us. We will have to go all the way up to the Trondelag to drag him out of his hole."

Bui laughed. "By then we will have beggared him anyway." He kicked the chest at his feet.

"Yes," Sigvaldi said, and reached out and slapped Conn's arm companionably. "We've taken great boot, and we'll feast again tonight as we do every night. This is the life of a Jomsviking, boy."

Conn blurted, "I came to throw down Hakon the Jarl, not to stick a few burghers for their gold chains."

Bui threw his head back at that. "There's a bit of Hakon in every link."

Sigvaldi gave another laugh at that. "Conn, heed me. You need to match this green eagerness with a cold wit. Before we can get to any real fighting, we have to run Hakon to ground like the rabbit he is. Meanwhile, we can feast on these villages."

Bui was still staring at Conn, unfriendly. "You know, your ship isn't bringing me much gold." He pushed at the treasure chest. "Maybe you ought to think about that more."

Conn said, "I'm not a Jomsviking," and turned and walked away. He did not say, I am not Sweyn Tujgas's hirdman anymore either.

He went back down the shore, past the ships, going toward his own fire. His crew had camped at the end of the beach, where the sandy bank cut the wind. The sundown cast a pink veil over the sea, which the waves broke in lines of light and dark.

The wind sang among the ships, as if the dragons spoke to one another in their secret voices. Beyond, to the east, against the red-and-purple sky, the gaunt mountains of the coast seemed like sheer walls of rock, capped with the rosy glisten of a glacier.

He went in among his crew, clustered around the fire, cooking cow parts and drinking beer; they greeted him in a chorus. His cousin Raef was off by the foot of the sandy slope, sitting beside the wounded man, who lay stretched out flat on the ground.

Conn squatted down on his heels by the fire. He took the beer horn out of the hand of the man next to him, who was Finn, the youngest of them. "Go ask Aslak to come drink with me."

Finn got up and trotted off, a short, thin boy who had been pushing a plow two summers before. Conn drank what was left in the horn, which was better beer than Sigvaldi's. Since he had found out that after every raid any gold or silver they took went into Bui's chest, he shifted his interest to looting the best food and drink.

Opposite him, pop-eyed Gorm grinned at him over a half-burnt chunk of meat.

"Any word?"

Conn said, "Nothing." He looked around again at Raef, off in the gloom with the dying man, but then Aslak came up.

Conn got to his feet; Aslak was a captain, like him, and although he was a Jomsviking, he and Conn got on well. Also, he was from the Trondelag. They shook hands and sat, and Conn waited until Aslak had taken a long pull of the drinking horn.

Aslak smacked his lips. "That's the best of the sacred stuff I've tasted since the oath-taking at Helsingor."

Conn growled. He did not like being reminded of that. He said, "You're from here, aren't you? What's this coast?"

"Same as we've been sailing," Aslak said. "All inlets and bays and islands. Lots of wind. Lots of rock. And poor, these people, poor as an old field. Bui won't be happy here."

Conn laughed. "Bui isn't happy with me anyway."

Aslak saluted him with the horn. "You steal the wrong kind of gold, Conn."

Conn gave him back the salute and drank. "Sigvaldi thinks Hakon is too afraid to come after us, no matter how we harry his people."

Aslak grunted. The other men by the fire were watching them both intently. "That's wrong. Sigvaldi's making a bad mistake if he really believes that. Hakon's a devil of a fighter." Aslak wiped foam off his beard with one hand. "Hakon's kindred goes back to the Frost Giants, to gods older than Odin. That's why he didn't come south when we sacked Tonsberg, or come out to meet us below Stad. His power is in the North. And so now we are going North, and I doubt we'll be too much longer waiting."

"Let it happen," Conn said, and spat between his fingers. He nodded toward the fire. "Drink another horn, Aslak. Gorm, save me some of that meat." He got up and went in toward the bank, to where Raef sat beside the dying man.

This was Ketil, one of their rowers, no older than Conn himself. Their whole crew were boys who had joined off their farms when they first took their ship *Seabird*. After two years' sailing with Conn and Raef, none of them was green anymore, whatever Sigvaldi thought.

That day they had stormed a village on an inlet; some of the people had fought back, for a few moments, and one had bashed in the side of Ketil's head with a stick. He was still alive, and they had brought him here to keep him safe while he died. Raef was sitting there beside him, his back to the sandbank and his long legs drawn up to his chest. Conn sank down on his heels.

"Is he—?"

Raef shook his head. His pale hair hung lank to his shoulders. "Less and less."

Conn sat there thinking about the fight in the village, and he said, "These are Hakon's people. Why does he not defend them?" He put out one hand toward Ketil, but he did not touch him.

Raef shrugged. "Because we want him to."

"Then what will he do?"

"What we don't want," Raef said. "Here comes Bui."

The keg-shaped Jomsviking had sauntered up the beach toward the *Seabird*'s fire, and now seeing them apart from it, veered toward them.

"Hail, King of Norway!" he called, and snickered.

Conn stood up. "Let the Fates hear you. What is it?"

"Sigvaldi commands you. Just you. Right now. For a council."

Conn turned and glanced at Raef. "Are you coming?"

"Sigvaldi says you only," Bui said with a sniff.

"I'm staying here with Ketil," Raef said, and Conn went off without him.

IV

When he first sailed with the Jomsvikings, Conn had expected their council to be a great shouting and arguing and talking of everybody, but now he knew better; there was plenty of food and beer, but in the end, Sigvaldi stood in front of them and said what would happen, and they nodded. They were supposed to be free men, but they did as they were told. There was much about the Jomsvikings he liked better in the idea than in the actual practice.

Sigvaldi said, "We have word now that Hakon is just inside the bay, over there. Where that big island is."

A roar went up from the gathered captains. Bui stood.

"How many ships?"

"Not many," Sigvaldi said. "Six. Eight. He's waiting for his fleet to gather, that's clear. But we're going to catch him before they come." He swept his gaze around them all. "We'll leave before dawn. I'll take the left, with Bui. Aslak, you take the right, with Sigurd Cape, and Havard." His teeth shone. Conn felt a sudden shiver of excitement. Sigvaldi turned and fixed his gaze on him.

"And since you're so wild to get him, Conn Corbansson, you go first, in the middle."

In the short, bright night, they buried Ketil. The rest of *Seabird*'s crew laid him on his back at the foot of the sand bank, with his sword beside him and a little meat and beer for the last journey. Then each brought a stone from the beach.

Finn said, "Better to die like this than behind a plow, like an ox." He put his stone by Ketil's feet.

"Better still, in the battle tomorrow," Gorm said, at Ketil's head. He turned his wide eyes on Conn; he always looked a little pop-eyed. "How many ships does Hakon have?"

Conn said, "Sigvaldi says only a few. But I don't trust Sigvaldi anymore."

"Tomorrow," said Grim, "when we catch Hakon—"

Somebody else laughed; Rugr said, "If we catch him—"

"That will be a deed that will ring around the world."

Conn stooped and laid his stone down by Ketil's shoulder, moving other stones to fit. "Whatever we do tomorrow, we do it together."

"We take Ketil with us." Raef bent and put his stone by Ketil's hip.

"If we beat Hakon—" Odd laid his stone by Ketil's knee. Now the shape of stones was closed around the dead man, a ship to carry him on. "They will tell the story until the end of the world."

"The end of the world."

They stood then a moment silent, their eyes on Ketil, and then they brought the sand bank down to cover him. They all turned and looked at one another. They clasped each other's hands and laughed, sharp and uneasy and wild, their eyes shining. "Together," they said. "All together."

Then they went off to get ready, to see to their weapons, to sleep, if they could, so they could sail before dawn. Conn and Raef fetched extra water and food and stowed it on the ship, where she lay on the beach.

The others were lying down by the fire. Conn sat down beside his cousin on the sand beside the round breast of their ship. He thought he would never sleep. In his mind he thought about every fight and battle he had ever been in, but everything seemed like a blur suddenly.

It would all be different, anyway; it always was.

After a while, he said to Raef, "Are you ready?"

"I guess so," Raef said. His voice was tight as a plucked wire. "No. This feels bad to me. He put us first, out in front of everybody?"

"Yes," Conn said. "We have the chance to take Hakon ourselves, alone."

"Or be taken ourselves. He's trying to kill us," Raef said.

Conn nudged him with his elbow. "You think too much. When it starts, you won't have time to think." He yawned, leaning against the ship's side, suddenly exhausted. "Just follow me," he said, and shut his eyes finally, and slept.

Conn dreamt.

He was in a great battle, around him the clash of axes and shields, the horns blaring, a boat rocking under him, arms and hair and twisted faces packed around him. He could not tell his enemies from his friends. The heaving and screaming and struggle around him were like something trying to devour him, and in a frenzy he hacked around him with his sword to make himself room to stand. The blood sprayed over him, so he tasted it on his lips.

Then the clash of blades on shields became thunder rolling, and lightning flashed so bright, he was blinded. When he could see again, he was alone, fighting alone, a tiny man against a towering storm, not even on a ship anymore. The clouds rose hundreds of feet above him, billowing black and gray, and the lightning shot forth its arrows at him, the rain itself felt like showers of stones, and the fists of the thunder battered him.

The wind streamed out the cloud's long hair; in the billows he saw eyes, a mouth with teeth like boulders, a monstrous woman's shape of fog and mist. High above him, she stretched out her arm toward him, and from each fingertip the lightning blazed. He could not move, bound where he was, and the lightning bolts came straight at him and blasted him into pieces, so that where he had been, there was nothing.

He woke up on the ground beside the ship. The dream gripped him; he was surprised to find himself whole. He got to his feet and walked down the shore, toward the sunrise.

On the far edge of the purple sky, a hot red glow was spreading, and the air glimmered. He stood on the pebble beach, and the dream went on in his head, stronger than the day around him.

In a moment, Raef came up beside him. Conn told him the dream and, even in the dim light, saw his cousin turn pale.

"Is it true, do you think?" Conn asked.

"All dreams are true, somehow."

The crew was gathering by *Seabird*, and the sun was about to rise. "Fate takes us," Conn said, "and all there is for us to do is meet it well. Simple enough. Come on, let's get going."

V

They rowed out into the swelling sunlight, rounding the top end of the island and turning southeast toward the opening of the bay. The sea was high and rolling. *Seabird* flew over the water like a hunting hawk; without Ketil, Conn was rowing his oar, the first bench on the steerboard side. As he leaned into each stroke, he saw the rest of the fleet swinging out to row after them, ship after ship, stalking along on their oars, their bare masts and tall curled prows dark against the pale sky, the sea breaking white along their bows.

Something swelled in him, some irresistible joy. He glanced forward over his shoulder. They were passing the tip of the island, set to weather the low cape on the mainland, with the bay opening before them between the gaunt gouged hillsides. Behind hung the white curtain of the mountains. The sun was rising, spilling a sheet of light out over the water. The sky was white. He was glad they were turning south now, so he would fight with the glare of the sun on his side instead of in his eyes. He felt the sea smooth out as they came into the shelter of the hills; he called an order, and the crew gave a single shout in answer, flattened their oars so the blades bit the top of the sea and the ship seemed to lift into the air, skimming over the low chop. He felt a giddy pride in this, his crew, the best rowers in the fleet.

The bay opened its arms. In the middle of the channel, a ragged island humped up dark under a cloak of trees. Raef, at the helm, set them to pass to the west of it. The ship flew by a cluster of low rocks that barely broke up through the trough of the waves. Looking past the seven rowers in front of him, Conn saw Raef with his white hair streaming, staring up ahead and all around the bay, Raef with his long sight.

A pale spit ran like a tongue down into the

water from the southern tip of the island. Beyond, the bay widened out, glistening with fresh light. Near the shore on either side, the waves broke white on barren skerries. Then Raef shouted, "Ship! Ship!" and pointed straight ahead of them.

Conn crossed his oar and leapt up, climbing onto the gunwale, one hand on the stempost. At first, all he saw was the broad glittering expanse of the water, another tree-covered island, farther south. Then, halfway to that island, the fresh new sun glinted on something gold.

Conn remembered that golden-headed dragon, which he had seen once before, in Denmark. He gave a yell. "That's him! That's Hakon's ship!"

Behind him, Raef shouted an answer. On one of the ships coming after them, a warhorn sounded its deep hollow note. *Seabird* shot out past the island onto the open bay, the rowers pulling strong and long. Conn twisted to look quickly back.

Behind them, the narrow waters between the island and the west shore were packed with the ships of the Jomsvikings, the masts like a moving forest. More horns sounded, and a roar of voices went up. They had seen the golden ship too.

He wheeled around. Up there, half a mile into the bay, the golden gleam turned and ran off into the south. His crew bellowed, and *Seabird* surged forward. The long warhorns were braying behind him. Conn slid down quickly to his oar again. On his left, Sigvaldi in his big dragon was striding after him, and on the right, Aslak's ship with its fanged and horned head was only a few lengths behind.

Conn screamed, "Go! Go!" and leaned into his stroke, and the rest of the crew smoothly picked up the rhythm with him. The fleet behind him was spreading out, as they rowed into the open water past the first island, and all were racing to be first. A screech of urgent voices rose. Conn saw Sigvaldi in the bow of his big dragon, bellowing orders. On the other side, Aslak was waving his men on with milling arms.

Smallest of them, still *Seabird* flew ahead of them all. Behind her was the great pack of the Jomsvikings, but ahead of her was only the dragon with the golden head, running away.

Then Raef shouted, "Ships! Ships—"

Conn crossed his oar again and leapt up onto the gunwale by the bow. His eyes swept the end of the bay, through the confusion of the ragged shore and the islands and the low skerries. Down there, the golden dragon was turning, was facing them, not running anymore. He climbed higher on the prow, teetering on the gunwale, and now he saw, first, the low hulls sliding through the water after Hakon, and then, on either side, other ships stroking hard into the bay from inlets, from behind capes.

"How many?" Raef bellowed.

"I don't know! Half row!" Conn sprang down from the bow, and as the ship slowed a little, he went back through his ship, from man to man. "Get ready," he said. "Get your swords, get your helmets on." Their eyes were already wild, and Finn's face was white as an egg, Gorm was swearing under his breath, Skeggi was swallowing over and over as if he were about to be sick. Conn reached the stern, where Raef had climbed up on the gunwale to see.

"A lot of ships," Raef said. "More than us. Hakon laid a trap for us, and we walked right into it."

"Sigvaldi did," Conn said. He reached into the stern counter and got his helmet out and pulled it on over his hair. "Just get us to Hakon." He shouted, "Full row! One! Two!" and ran back up to his oar in the forecastle.

Seabird surged forward. While they had slowed, the rest of the fleet had all but caught up to them, on every ship shouting and horns. Conn could see Aslak on his right, the big bald Jomsviking standing by his third oarsmen. He wore no helmet; he was bawling to the crew. Conn swung forward again, his heart hammering, and rowed. His ship hurtled across the flat water. Ahead, now, faint, he heard other horns and more shouting.

Raef shouted, "They're throwing something! Duck!"

Conn doubled over, hunching his shoulders; the bow would shield him well enough. A rattle of spears clattered down around *Seabird*, mostly just sharpened sticks, which hit nothing. Raef shouted, "Get ready!"

Conn crossed his oar again. "Gorm! Arn— Sigurd—" He leapt up; he had almost called Ketil's name. He drew his sword and, with his free hand, grabbed up a sharpened stick that had fallen into the ship. When he whirled around, the round head of a dragon was looming toward him, closing rapidly.

Not golden. A big black beast, a round weather-beaten curve of a prow. Behind him, Raef shouted: "Up oars!"

With the hand holding the sharp stick, Conn grabbed the gunwale, and *Seabird* plowed in past the black dragon, snapping off a few of her oars before the other crew managed to get them out of the way. Conn stepped up onto the gunwale and jumped across the narrowing water between the two ships.

Three men met him with their axes swinging. For a moment, balancing on the gunwale with his back to the sea, all he could do was weave and parry, jabbing with the stick with his left hand and his sword in his right. Then somebody else from *Seabird* landed next to him and one of the axemen staggered and Conn stuck him through and then lunging sideways and all the way onto the ship hacked down another Tronder axeman.

It was pop-eyed Gorm beside him. His whole forecastle crew was piling onto the enemy ship after him. The ship was pitching hard, as if it tried to throw them off. He ducked down under an axe blade swinging by him and thrust toward the body behind it. He fought for space on the tilting floor, his feet planted wide, stabbing and jabbing with his sword at the man before him. The Tronder reeled, cut across the chest. Lunging to hack him down,

Conn smacked his knee on a bench and almost collapsed.

Suddenly the Tronders were turning, were leaping off the ship, and beyond them, he saw Aslak's bald head climbing over the black ship's stern.

He wheeled toward *Seabird*; the little dragon was drifting away. From the far side, more Tronders swarmed over her, battling the rest of his crew. Raef. He bellowed and charged back to his ship.

When they first closed with the black ship, half the crew had jumped off, and now the rest were leaning out to watch, their oars idle. *Seabird* was tipped hard to that direction. Raef held the steerboard out, to keep the ship close on the black dragon. Then another Tronder ship was veering straight at him.

He bellowed to the sterncastle crew, who were all backwards to this, and swung the steerboard up out of the way.

The crew wheeled around to meet the Tronders' charge. The bigger ship ground into *Seabird*'s bow and spilled men in a tide, roaring and waving their one-bladed axes. Tronders charged down the middle of the ship; Raef reached down at his feet for his sword, and before he stood up, a shaggy-bearded man was leaping toward him, his red mouth round and howling.

His axe swung, and, still sitting, Raef shrank away. The brow of the axe missed him by a finger's breadth and struck the gunwale just beyond him.

A chunk of wood flew into the air. Awkward, stooping, Raef flailed his sword at the shaggy man, and the flat of the blade hit the Tronder's wrist with a crack like a stone splitting. The Tronder staggered. Raef lunged up and caught him in the gut with his shoulder and heaved him over the side of the ship.

The Tronder ship had backed off, was fighting somebody else. All around him, Raef saw ships jammed against ships, and men fighting up and down them; ahead of him, a big dragon wallowed awash to the tops of its benches, and men swam and bodies floated in the choppy water.

On *Seabird*, the remaining Tronders had taken over the forecastle, but the stern half of the crew had pushed them back and was holding them at the mast. Raef charged up to help them. As he got there, Finn went down hard right in front of him. A big man in a leather tunic reared over him, his single-bladed axe high; he never saw Raef coming and Raef never stopped. Still running, he drove his sword straight through the leather chest.

The Tronder fell backwards. Finn was trying to crawl out of the way, blocked by a sea chest and a misshipped oar, and Raef stepped over him to the mast. There Skeggi and Odd were clubbing away at two axemen in front of them; more beyond in the narrow waist of the ship were struggling to close enough to strike. Then suddenly the ship yawed. Up by the bow, Conn was climbing out of the bay, pulling himself over the gunwale behind the Tronders, his hair streaming in his face, and they wheeled, saw him and the men climbing in after him, and leapt off.

Raef turned around to Finn, who was clinging to the gunwale and trying to stand. His leg looked broken, maybe both legs. Raef hauled him back into the stern and sat him on the bench by the tiller. "Can you steer?"

"I—" The boy threw back his long brown hair. "Yes, I can." He reached out one hand to hold the side of the ship, but the other reached for the tiller. Raef swung the steerboard down and gave him the tiller bar.

"Stay off the rocks. And get us to that golden dragon." He ran back toward Conn, in the forecastle.

The sun was only halfway up the sky and the day already crackled with heat. Raef peeled off his shirt; his hair dripped. Hakon's golden ship seemed always just out of reach. They went side to side with a big snake-headed dragon, fighting across the gunwales. Twice Conn led the whole crew to charge the other ship, and twice the Tronders held them off. Then abruptly the Tronder was veering away, all her oars coming out, fleeing.

For a moment, *Seabird* was in a lull, ships all around them, but nobody fighting them. Raef leaned against the mast, breathing hard, looking around. There were fewer of them than before. Gorm lay flat on his back on the floor, his pop eyes open. But his arm was gone, and he was dead. Beyond him, Egil leaned on the gunwale and then slowly slumped down on his knees between two benches. Skeggi and Grim had simply disappeared. The others looked battered, but whole. They were sitting down, reaching for water or food, talking. He even heard Arn's girly laugh. Raef lifted his gaze toward the fighting.

The battle line stretched across the whole end of the bay in a long crescent moon curve, with Sigvaldi on the left arm of the curve. Raef could see them fighting hard there, every ship engaged. *Seabird* was near the center; on the other arm, the Jomsvikings shoved Hakon's men toward the beach, and here in the middle there were several idle ships— Hakon seemed to be falling back—he could not see the golden dragon. Then, at the end of the line where Sigvaldi fought, another stream of ships was rowing up into sight, past the big island.

"Hiyahh! What's that?"

Conn reared up beside him. Raef pointed to the leader of the line of ships now attacking Sigvaldi. The ship was bigger than most, with a broader bow, and her whole stem below the slender curve of her dragon neck was covered in bands of iron set with iron claws.

Conn said, "I don't know, but if he turns the end of Sigvaldi's line, we're surrounded. Come on."

He shouted, and the men jumped to their oars. Gorm still lay on the floor, and Egil was dead on his own bench, but Finn sat by the steerboard and nodded at Raef when he looked. Raef went up forward and took the oar opposite Conn.

Seabird flew across the choppy water, past clumps of ships fighting. Overhead, ravens and seagulls glided in circles. They passed a dragon sinking, bodies floating around her, loose oars. Raef pointed beyond. "Bui is there."

Conn lifted his head; to his right, he saw Bui the Stout in the bow of his long dragon charging toward the iron ship, and he spun around toward his crew and shouted, "Go—go—go—!"

Smoothly, they quickened their pace, their shoulders sunburnt, slick with sweat. On the backswing, he turned again to look ahead of them.

The great iron dragon was at the center of a wedge-line of ships, pushing slightly ahead of the rest. The armor on her sea swan's breast was set with massive hooks. Conn guessed the barbs stuck out below the waterline too. He thought also she would be slow to steer. He crossed his oar and stood.

Seabird swooped in on the iron ship from one side and Bui from the other. The big ship stayed steady on her course, and Conn yelled, "Half row!" trying to judge the distance so that *Seabird* and Bui's ship got to the Tronder at the same time. He drew his sword. A hail of spears and stones met them, but the iron ship did not veer. Then *Seabird* was sheering in along one bow, and Bui on the other.

The Tronders, caught in the middle, stood up and fought in place. Conn traded blows with the man opposite him, parrying and hitting; Conn flinched back and, when the man lunged after him, chopped his sword through the Tronder's shoulder and then hacked him in the back as he went down. He bounded into the open space this left on the iron ship and stood toe to toe with another man with an axe. Raef was coming behind him. Conn pushed in—so close, he felt the Tronder's hot breath on his face. The axe haft struck him a glancing blow on the elbow and his arm went dead and the sword clattered to the floor. He stooped and with his left hand gripped it and struck upward, and the odd angle caught the Tronder off balance and Conn's sword bit his side and he slumped.

Bui was climbing on over the iron ship's other gunwale. He saw Conn and shouted, "Ho, the King of Norway! Come help me!"

Raef stood at Conn's left shoulder; they fought their way along one line of benches, and Bui fought his way down the other. The Tronders gave way only by dying. Conn's right arm started to tingle alive again, and he switched his sword into that hand. Now he got to use his sword well again, and he and Raef reached the mast a step ahead of Bui. The burly Jomsviking was red in the face, his bare chest slick with blood streaming from a cut on his neck.

"Eirik," he shouted, his voice hoarse. "We've got you!"

In the stern stood a man who, in spite of the heat, wore a dark shirt and a long cloak. His helmet had a gold rim and he was yelling orders. He bellowed, "Somebody has somebody, Bui. Reverse! Reverse!"

Conn wheeled. "They'll take us in with them!" The iron ship was already sliding backwards on her sterncastle oars, rowing back in among the other Tronder ships. By the bow, *Seabird*, with six men at the oars, was staying near as she could, but she dared not go into the midst of the Tronders. Conn shouted and pushed Raef ahead of him, and Raef shoved the other men on up to the bow of the iron ship.

The first four men leapt easily enough into *Seabird*, and then Raef clambered up the gunwale and jumped across the widening water, but Conn threw off his helmet, and dived into the bay.

The iron ship was stroking steadily backwards, into the thick of Hakon's ships. A stretch of clear water opened between the Tronder fleet and the Jomsvikings. Conn swam hard through it toward his ship, her oars coming out, hanging in the air, ready to row. A spear sliced through the water just past his head. He reached the ship and Raef leaned down to haul him up. He went facefirst into the space between the front two benches, into several inches of water.

He rolled over and straightened, on his knees, looking back toward the iron ship. Raef pushed up beside him.

"We're full of water."

"Bail!" Conn yelled, and got his feet under him, to his ankles in water. *Seabird* was rowing rearward, sluggish; she was always stiff going stern first, but this was more sluggish than usual. All around the ship, the crew bent to slinging the water out.

The fighting everywhere had stopped. Between them and the Tronders now was a broad stretch of the bay. Hakon was pulling his whole fleet back toward shore. The water between was scummed with blood, filthy with broken gear, bits of ships and oars, bodies like unsteady islands bobbing in the little waves. Down past his own stempost, he could see an arm floating a few feet below the surface.

The water in his ship did not seem to be going down. He reached into the forecastle and found a bucket and began to throw water over the side. Raef vaulted over the gunwale into the bay, and went hand over hand around the outside of the ship.

"King of Norway!"

Conn straightened, looking around. Aslak's big dragon was gliding up just off his bow. The big bald Jomsviking stood by the mast.

"You don't look so good!" Aslak shouted. "Eirik's claws ripped you."

Conn pointed toward Hakon's fleet. "Is he giving up?" He bent to bail; the water was coming in as fast as he and his crew threw it out again.

"No—he's just gone for help," Aslak bellowed.

Raef's head appeared above the gunwale, near Conn's knee; he boosted himself smoothly up onto the ship. His left side was all bruised, Conn saw, and he was bleeding from a cut on his arm, but he looked hale enough.

Raef said, "The ship is sinking. I think that damned toothed thing tore one of the strakes loose."

Aslak bawled, "Come over here! Come on—half my crew's gone anyway." He turned and gave orders, and his ship began to scull sideways toward Conn's.

Conn shouted, "*Seabird*—everybody—go over!" He waved his arm. They were already scrambling over so fast, the ship rocked, even wallowing half-full of water. Conn went back into the stern and got Finn.

The boy was only half-conscious. His leg had swollen fat enough to split his legging, the flesh black underneath. Conn lifted him up and he whined. Raef came and helped him carry Finn onto Aslak's ship. They set him down in the hollow of the sterncastle, behind the steering bench. Raef went off immediately. Conn found some beer, but Finn choked on it. His eyes opened, wide and dark with pain. Conn left the beer by him and stood up.

Amidships he saw Raef standing also, his arms at his sides, watching *Seabird* go down. Conn went up beside him. For a while, their dragonship seemed to float, still, even awash, but then suddenly it went down out of sight into the dark green deep. The last thing he saw was her little fierce-eyed dragon head. Raef said nothing, only stood there. Conn felt the heart in him crack like a rock in the fire.

He looked around, and found Aslak up by the bow. He went there, looking toward Hakon's fleet against the far shore. Where they were, in the center of the bay, the Jomsvikings were drinking and eating and bailing their ships out. Conn could see three other ships sinking in a single glance.

He said, "What kind of help is Hakon looking for?"

Aslak had a little skin of beer, and he took a pull on it. He nodded with his head toward the island in the middle of the bay.

"You see that island? It's called the Blessed Place. There are altars there half as old as the Ash Tree. Hakon may have a problem. He switched sides once too often. I've heard his patron goddesses are still angry for when he turned Christian."

He slung an arm around Conn's shoulders. "I'm glad to have you on board, boy—you're a damned good fighter."

Conn flushed; to hide this pleasure he turned and glanced around at his crew. That took the glow away. He had not realized how many were gone. He was losing everything—his ship, the crew that made her fly. He had to win now.

He turned back to Aslak. "This Christian thing seems common enough. Even Sweyn's been prime-signed." He took the skin and drank, and leaned out to pass the skin to Raef.

Aslak was sitting on the front bench, his knees wide and his arms bent across them. "Hakon didn't stay a Christer very long—just until he got away from Bluetooth."

"So he's betrayed everybody," Conn said.

"Oh, yes. At least once. And beaten everybody. German, Swede, Dane, and Norse. At least once."

With a grimace, Aslak stretched one leg out and rubbed his calf. Blood squished from the top of his shoe.

Conn said, "But we are winning this one."

Aslak said, "Yes, I think so. So far."

VI

In the blazing sun past noon, Hakon's ships gathered again, and the golden dragon was in the center. They came forward again across the bay, and the Jomsvikings swung into lines to meet them.

Even as they rowed up, a cold wind began to blast. Conn, pulling an oar in the front of Aslak's ship, felt the harsh slash of the air on his cheek and looked west and saw a cloud boiling up over the horizon, black and swelling like a bruise on the sky. His skin went all to gooseflesh, and his dream came back to him. The line of the Jomsviking ships swept toward Hakon, and the stormcloud climbed up over half the sky, heavy and dark, the wind ripping streamers away like hair. Under it, the air flickered, thick and green.

Conn bent to his oar. Up the center of Aslak's ship came four men with spears, which they cast, but the wind flung them off like splinters. A roll of thunder boomed across the sky. Inside the towering cloud, lightning glowed. The first drops fell, and then all at once, sheets of rain hammered down.

Aslak was screaming the oar-chant, because of the mixed crew. Conn threw all his strength into each stroke. The rain battered on his head, his bare shoulders, streamed cold down his chest. Hakon's ships in their line loomed over them; he shipped the oar and, drawing his sword, wheeled toward the bow.

As he rose, the wind met him so hard, he had to stiffen himself against it, and then suddenly, as if the sky broke into tiny pieces and fell on him, it began to hail.

He stooped, half-blinded in the white deluge, feeling the ship under him rub another ship, and saw through the haze of flying ice the shape before him of a man with an axe. He struck. Raef was beside him, hip to hip. The axe came at him and he slashed again, blind, into the white whirling storm. Somebody screamed, somewhere. There was hail all in his beard, his hair, his eyebrows. Abruptly the booming fall stopped. The rain pattered away, and the sun broke through, glaring.

He staggered back a step. The ship was full of hailstones and water; Raef, beside him, slumped down on the bench, gasping for breath. Blood streamed down his face, his shoulders. Conn wheeled to look past the bow, toward Hakon's men.

The Tronder fleet had backed off again, but they were not fleeing; they were letting Sigvaldi flee.

Conn let out a howl of rage. Off toward the west, at the end of the Jomsviking line, Sigvaldi's big dragon suddenly had broken out of line, was stroking fast away up the bay, and behind it, the other Jomsviking ships were peeling out of their formation and following.

Conn leapt up onto the gunwale of Aslak's ship, his hand on the dragon's neck, and shouted, "Run! Run, Sigvaldi, you coward! Remember your vow? The Jomsviking way, is it—I'll not run—not if I'm the last man here and he sends all the gods against me, I'll not run!"

From behind him came a howl from Aslak's ship and the ships beyond. Conn pivoted his head to see them—back there all the other men shouted and shook their fists toward Sigvaldi and waved their swords at Hakon. Bui in their midst bellowed like a bull, red-faced. There were ten ships, he thought. Ten left, from sixty.

Aslak stood before him and put his hand on Conn's shoulder and met his eyes.

"If it's my doom here, I'll meet it like a man. Let's show them how true Jomsvikings fight!"

Conn gripped his hand. "To the last man!"

"It will be that," Raef said, behind him.

Bui shouted from the next dragon, "Aslak! Aslak! King of Norway! Lash the ships together!"

Aslak's head pivoted, looking toward Hakon. "He's coming."

"Hurry," Conn said.

They drew all the ships together, gunwale to gunwale, and lashed them with the rigging through the oar holes; so all the men were free to fight, and the ships formed a sort of fighting floor. The Tronder fleet was spreading out to encircle them. Conn went back into the stern of Aslak's dragon, where Finn lay, his eyes closed, still breathing, and pulled a shield across him. Then he went back up beside Raef.

VII

Horns blew in the Tronder fleet, the sound rolling around the bay, and then the ships all at once closed on the Jomsvikings on their floating ship-island. The air darkened; the cold wind blasted. The rain began to fall, and like icy rocks the hail descended on them again. Conn could barely stand against the wind and the pelting hailstones. Through the driving white, he saw a man with an axe heave up over the gunwale, another just be-hind, and he slashed out, and on the hailstrewn floor, he slipped and fell on his back. Raef strode across him. Raef slashed wildly side to side with his sword, battling two men at once, until Conn staggered up again and cut the first axeman across the knees and dropped him.

The hail stopped. In the rain, they battered at a wall of axeblades trying to hack their way over the gunwale. Horns blew. The Tronders were falling back again. Conn stepped back, breathing hard, his hair in his eyes; his knee was swelling and hurt as if somebody were driving a knife into it. The sun came out again, blazing bright.

On the next ship, Bui swayed back and forth, covered with blood. Both hands were gone. His face was hacked to the bone. He stooped, and looped his stumped arms through the handles of his chest of gold.

"All Bui's men overboard!" he shouted, and leapt into the bay, the gold in his arms. He sank at once into the deep.

The sunlight slanted in under a roof of cloud. The long sundown had begun. Beneath the clouds, the air was already turning dark. Hakon's horns blew their long booming notes, pulling his fleet off.

Aslak sank down on a bench. The side of his face was mashed so that one eye was almost invisible. Raef sat next to him, slack with fatigue. Conn went down the ship, whose whole side had taken the Tronder attack. He was afraid if he sat down, his knee would stiffen entirely. What he saw clenched his belly to a knot.

Arn lay dead on the floor, his head split to the red mush of his brain. The two men next to him, bleeding but alive, were Jomsvikings, not his. Beyond them, Rugr slumped, and Conn stooped beside him and tried to rouse him, but he fell over, lifeless. Two other dead men lay on the floor of the ship, and he had to climb across a bench to get around them. He went up to the stern, where Finn lay, still breathing, in the dark.

Conn laid one hand on him, as if he could hold the life in him. He looked back along the ship, at the living and wounded, and saw no other face that had rowed on *Seabird* with him save Raef's. Along the length of Aslak's ship, he met Raef's eyes and knew his cousin was thinking this too.

The ship-fortress was sinking. All over the cluster

of lashed hulls, men were dipping and rising, bailing out the water and ice. Several other men came walking across the wooden island, stepping from gunwale to gunwale. They were gathering down by Aslak, and Conn went back that way, wading through a soup of hail and rainwater that got deeper toward the bow. He sat down next to Raef, with the other men, slumped wearily around Aslak.

All save him and Raef were Jomsvikings. Havard had a skin of beer and held it out to Conn as he sat. Beside him, another captain was looking around them. "How many of us are left?"

Aslak shrugged. "Maybe fifty. Half wounded. Some really bad wounded." His voice was a little thick from the mess of his face.

Conn took a deep pull on the skin of beer. The drink hit his stomach like a fist. But a moment later, warmth spread through him. He handed the skin on to Raef, just behind him.

The Jomsviking across from Conn said, "Hakon will sit out the night on the shore, in comfort. Then they'll finish us off tomorrow, unless we all just drown tonight."

Conn said, "We have to swim for it." He had a vague idea of reaching shore and walking around and surprising Hakon from behind.

Havard leaned forward, his bloody hands in front of him. "That's a good idea. We could probably make that side, there." He pointed the other way from Hakon.

"That's far," Raef said. "Some of these men can't swim two strokes."

Aslak said, "We could lash some spars together. Make a raft."

Havard leaned closer to Conn, his voice sinking. "Look. The ones who can make it, should. Leave the rest behind—they're dying anyway."

Conn thought of Finn, and red rage drove him to his feet. He hit Havard in the face as hard as he could. The Jomsviking pitched backwards head over heels into the half foot of water on the floor. Conn wheeled toward the others.

"We take everybody. All or none."

Aslak was grinning at him. The other men shifted a little, glaring down at Havard, who sat up.

"Look. I was just—"

"Shut up," Aslak said. "Let's get moving. This ship is sinking."

In the slow-gathering dark, they tied spars together into a square and bound sails over it. The rain held off. On the raft, they laid the ten wounded men who could not move by themselves, and the other men swam behind the raft to push it.

The icy water gripped them. They left the sinking ships behind them. At first, they moved steadily along, but after a while, men started to lag behind, to drag on the raft. Havard cried, "Keep up!" Across the way, someone tried to climb onto the spars, and the men beside him pulled him back.

Next to Conn, Aslak said, "We'll never make it." He was gasping; he laid his head down on the spar a moment. Conn knew it was true. He was exhausted; he could barely kick his legs. Aslak lost his grip, and Conn reached out and grabbed hold of him until the Jomsviking could get his hands back to the spar.

Raef said, breathless, "There's a skerry—"

"Go," Conn said.

The skerry was only a bare rock rising just above the surface of the bay. They hauled and kicked and dragged the raft into the low waves lapping it. The rock was slippery, and it took all Conn's strength to haul Finn up off the raft. Raef dragged Aslak after them, and above the waterline they lay down on the rock, and instantly Conn was asleep.

Hail fell again in the night. Conn woke and crawled over to Finn to protect him from the worst of it. After the brief crash abruptly stopped, he realized that the body under him was as cold as the rock.

He thought of the other dead—of pop-eyed Gorm; and Odd, whose sister he had loved once; and Skeggi and Orm; Sigurd and Rugr—he remembered how only the night before, they were all alive, speaking of the battle to come, how its fame and theirs would ring around the world until the end of time—now who would even remember their names, when all those who knew them were dead with them? The battle might be a long-told story, but the men were already forgotten.

He would remember. But he would be dead soon himself. Hakon had beaten him. He put his face against the cold stone and shut his eyes.

In the morning, Raef woke up, battered and stiff, starving and thirsty. All around him on the rock, the other men lay slumped asleep, or dead. Between him and Conn, Finn was dead. Raef crawled up higher on the skerry and found a hollow where some hail had fallen and mostly melted. He plunged his face into the ice-studded water and drank. When he lifted his head, he saw, on the bay, the dragons coming for them.

He slid back to Conn, yelling, the men stirring awake, all but the dead, but then the dragons reached them, and Hakon's men swarmed over them.

VIII

Raef had never heard exactly how the Jomsvikings had offended Thorkel Leira, but clearly the wergild was going to be very high. The big Tronder had killed three men already, all nearly dead anyway, and he was lining up the rest of the prisoners for the same. Now another wounded man stumbled exhausted between two slaves, who made him kneel down, and twisted a stick in his hair.

Raef had already counted; there were nine men in the line between him and Conn. The Tronders had tied their hands behind their backs and strung them along the beach, here, and bound their feet together, like trussed lambs. Down the shore, on

the pebbles between them and the beached dragons, stood several men, passing a drinking horn
and watching Thorkel Leira at his work. One was
the man in the gold-rimmed helmet, captain of the
iron ship, who was Eirik the Jarl; another was his
father, Hakon the Jarl himself.

Thorkel Leira took a long pull on a drinking
horn and gave it to one of the slaves. As he took
hold of his sword again, Hakon said, "You, there,
what do you think about dying?"

The Jomsviking, kneeling there, his hands
bound, his head stretched out for the killing stroke,
said, "I don't care. My father did it. Tonight I'll
drink Odin's ale, Thorkel, but you will be despised
for this forever. Slash away."

Thorkel raised the sword and struck off his
head. The slave took the head by the hair and carried it off to the heap by the shore.

Conn said, "You know, I don't like how this is
going."

Raef thought the Jomsvikings were too ready
for dying. He was not; he rubbed his bound wrists
frantically back and forth, and up and down, trying to get some play in the rope. The sun was hot
on his shoulders. Another man went up before
Thorkel Leira.

"I don't mind dying, but I will do it the way I
have lived, facing everything. So I ask you to kill
me straight ahead, and not bent over, and not from
behind."

"So be it," said Thorkel, and stepping forward
raised his sword over his shoulder and struck the

man straight down the face, cleaving through the top of his skull. The Jomsviking never flinched, his eyes open until his body slumped.

Thorkel was getting tired, Raef thought; the big Tronder had trouble getting his sword out of the body. He called for the drinking horn again and drained it. Now another was kneeling down in front of Hakon and Eirik and the others, and Thorkel again asked him if he was afraid to die.

"I'm a Jomsviking," the kneeling man said. "I don't care one way or the other. But we have often spoken among us about whether a man remains conscious at all after his head is cut off, and here is a chance to prove it. Cut off my head, and if I am still conscious, I will raise my hand."

Beside Raef, Conn gave a choked incredulous laugh. Thorkel stepped forward and slashed off the head; it took him two strokes to get it entirely off. The two jarls and their men crowded around the body and looked. Then they stepped back, and solemnly Eirik the Jarl turned to the Jomsvikings and announced, "His hand did not move."

Conn said, "That was pretty stupid. In a few minutes, we'll all know for ourselves." Along the rope line, the Jomsvikings laughed as if they were at table hearing jokes.

Thorkel turned and glared at him, and then the next man knelt before him, and when he turned to this one, he missed the first stroke. He hit the back of the man's head, knocking him down, and then his shoulders, and didn't cut off his head until the third try.

"I hope you have better aim with your prick, Thorkel!" Conn shouted.

The Jomsvikings let up a yell of derision, and even Eirik the Jarl smiled, his hands on his hips. Someone called, "That's why his wife's always so glad to see me coming, I guess!"

Half a dozen men shouted, "You mean Ingebjorg? Is that why, do you think?"

Thorkel's face twisted. He wheeled around and pointed at Conn.

"Bring him. Bring him next!"

The guard came and untied Conn's feet. Raef suddenly saw some chance here; he licked his lips, afraid of croaking, a weakling voice, and called out, "Wait."

The Jomsvikings were yelling taunts at Thorkel, who stood there with his mouth snarling, his long sword tilted down, but Eirik heard Raef and looked toward him. "What do you want?"

"Kill me first," Raef said. "I love my brother too much, I don't want to see him die. If you kill me first, I won't have to."

Eirik scowled at him, and Hakon made a snort. "Why should we do what you want?" But Thorkel strode forward, the sword in both hands, shouting.

"Bring him! Bring him! I'll kill them both at once!"

The slave untied Raef's feet and pulled him up. Conn was already standing, and his feet were already untied. Raef gave him a swift look, walking past, and went down before the jarls on the shore. His ribs hurt where he had taken blows in the battle, he was walking a little crooked, and he was tired and hungry, but he summoned himself together. Thorkel's slaves came up beside him and pushed him on the shoulder to make him kneel down; one had the stick to twist in his hair.

He stepped back from the hands on him. "I am a free man. No slave shall put his dirty hands in my hair."

The Norse all laughed, except Eirik the Jarl, who snapped, "He's just stalling. He's afraid to die. Somebody hold his hair for him, and we'll see how he does it."

One of his hirdmen stepped forward. "My privilege." He came up before Raef. "Kneel by yourself, then, if you're free."

Raef knelt down, and the Tronder took hold of his long pale hair and stepped back again, and so stretched Raef's head forward like a chicken on the block. Raef's heart was hammering in his chest, and he was sick to his stomach. His neck felt ten feet long and thin as a whisker; he watched Thorkel approaching in the corner of his eye.

He said, "Try to do this right, will you?" Up on the beach there was a chorus of jeers.

Thorkel snarled. He swung up his sword, the long sun glinting off the blade, and brought it down hard.

With all his strength, Raef lunged back and out from under that falling blade, yanking after him the man holding his hair, so that the Tronder's hands passed under the falling sword and Thorkel slashed them both off at the wrist. The Tronder howled, his arms spurting blood. Still on his knees, Raef staggered his chest up straight. The Tronder's hands had clenched in his hair, and he had to toss his head to get them out.

Thorkel wheeled around, hauling the sword back for a fresh blow. His hands still tied behind his back, Raef rolled sideways against the big man's ankles and brought him crashing down, so that the sword flew out of his hands.

Raef struggled to get to his feet. Thorkel sprawled on the ground. Even the jarls were laughing at him. But Conn had leapt forward even as the sword fell. He knelt astride it, ran his bound hands down the edge, and leapt up again, freed, the sword in his fists.

Thorkel staggered up. Conn took a long stride toward him, the sword swinging around level, and sliced Thorkel's head off while the big man was still rising.

A roar went up from the Jomsvikings. Conn wheeled toward Hakon.

"Hakon, I challenge you, face-to-face!"

Eirik the Jarl had drawn his sword, was shouting, waving his arms, calling his hirdmen to him. Raef lurched to his feet, close to Conn. Conn's hands were dripping blood; in his fury to get free, he had cut himself all over. Quickly he turned and sliced through Raef's bonds. Eirik and his men were closing in on them.

Then Hakon called out again. "Hold. Hold your hands. Who are you, there, Jomsviking? I've seen you two before."

The Tronders stood where they were. Conn lowered the sword. "I'm not a Jomsviking. I'm Conn Corbansson."

"I thought so," Hakon said. "These are the sons of that Irish wizard who helped Sweyn Tjugas overcome Bluetooth. I told you Sweyn was behind this."

Eirik said, "So." He lowered the long sword in his hand. "Still, we've won. Good enough. That just now was cleverly done, and to go on is a waste of men. Thorkel's dead, he needs no more revenge. Let me have these two."

Hakon said, "Well, I remember the wizard, who once gave me good advice. I will not say his name. Do what you like with them all."

Eirik said, "You, Corbanssons, if I let you live, will you come into my service?"

Conn said, "You are a generous man, Jarl Eirik. But you should know I swore at Helsingor never to go back to Denmark until I was King of Norway, which I don't think will sit well with either Sweyn or you Tronders. But those men—" He swung his arm at the hillside, at the twenty men still roped together on the grass. "Those men will serve you, better than any other. Those are the true Jomsvikings!"

At that, there was a yell that went on for a while. Raef saw that Eirik started to smile, his hands on his hips, and Hakon shrugged and walked away toward the ships. Eirik gave a word, and the Jomsvikings were set free.

Then Hakon the Jarl came up to Conn. He was

as Raef remembered him—not tall, with a crisp black beard, and the coldest eyes he had ever seen.

He said, "King of Norway, was it? I think anyone you do choose to serve will find you more trouble than help. But tell me what you will do now that you are free again."

Conn glanced at Raef beside him. "We won't go back to Sweyn, that's certain. We promise to go somewhere else and not bother you."

Aslak came up to them and shook their hands and clapped them both on the back. Even Havard grinned at them, over Hakon's shoulder.

Hakon said, "Then go. But if I catch you again in Norway you're done."

"Agreed," Conn said, and went on down the beach, Raef beside him. After a while, he said, "I think we hammered that vow."

"We, it is now," Raef said. "Don't get so drunk next time. We should both be dead. Like everybody else."

"But we're not," Conn said. He had lost his sword, his ship, his crew, but he felt light, fresh, as if he had just come new alive again. "I don't know what to make of that, but I will make something. I swear it. Let's go."

Robert Silverberg

Soldiers in every age have learned that the military's unofficial motto is "Hurry up and wait." But suppose all you ever did was wait? And wait. And *wait* . . .

Robert Silverberg is one of the most famous SF writers of modern times, with dozens of novels, anthologies, and collections to his credit. As both writer and editor (he was editor of the original anthology series *New Dimensions,* perhaps the most acclaimed anthology series of its era), Silverberg was one of the most influential figures of the Post–New Wave era of the '70s, and continues to be at the forefront of the field to this very day, having won a total of five Nebula Awards and four Hugo Awards, plus SFWA's prestigious Grandmaster Award.

His novels include the acclaimed *Dying Inside, Lord Valentine's Castle, The Book of Skulls, Downward to the Earth, Tower of Glass, Son of Man, Nightwings, The World Inside, Born with the Dead, Shadrach in the Furnace, Thorns, Up the Line, The Man in the Maze, Tom O'Bedlam, Star of Gypsies, At Winter's End, The Face of the Waters, Kingdoms of the Wall, Hot Sky at Midnight,*

The Alien Years, Lord Prestimion, The Mountains of Majipoor, two novel-length expansions of famous Isaac Asimov stories, *Nightfall* and *The Ugly Little Boy, The Longest Way Home,* and the mosaic novel *Roma Eterna.* His collections include *Unfamiliar Territory, Capricorn Games, Majipoor Chronicles, The Best of Robert Silverberg, The Conglomeroid Cocktail Party, Beyond the Safe Zone,* and four massive retrospective collections, *Secret Sharers* (in two volumes), *To the Dark Star* (in two volumes), *Something Wild Is Loose: The Collected Stories, Phases of the Moon,* and a collection of early work, *In the Beginning.* His reprint anthologies are far too numerous to list here but include *The Science Fiction Hall of Fame, Volume One,* and the distinguished Alpha series, among dozens of others. Coming up, as editor, is *The Science Fiction Hall of Fame, Volume Two B.* He lives with his wife, writer Karen Haber, in Oakland, California.

Defenders of the Frontier

Seeker has returned to the fort looking flushed and exhilarated. "I was right," he announces. "There is one of them hiding quite close by. I was certain of it, and now I know where he is. I can definitely feel directionality this time."

Stablemaster, skeptical as always, lifts one eyebrow. "You were wrong the last time. You're always too eager these days to find them out there."

Seeker merely shrugs. "There can be no doubt," he says.

For three weeks now, Seeker has been searching for an enemy spy—or straggler, or renegade, or whatever he may be—that he believes is camped in the vicinity of the fort. He has gone up to this hilltop and that one, to this watchtower and that, making his solitary vigil, casting forth his mind's net in that mysterious way of his that none of us can begin to fathom. And each time he has come back convinced that he feels enemy emanations, but he has never achieved a strong enough sense of directionality to warrant our sending out a search party. This time he has the look of conviction about him. Seeker is a small, flimsy sort of man, as his kind often tends to be, and much of the time in recent months he has worn the slump-shouldered look of dejection and disappointment. His trade is in finding enemies for us to kill. Enemies have been few and far between of late. But now he is plainly elated. There is an aura of triumph about him, of vindication.

Captain comes into the room. Instantly he sizes up the situation. "What have we here?" he says brusquely. "Have you sniffed out something at last, Seeker?"

"Come. I'll show you."

He leads us all out onto the flat roof adjacent to our barracks. To the right and left, the huge turreted masses of the eastern and western redoubts, now unoccupied, rise above us like vast pillars, and before us lies the great central courtyard, with the massive wall of tawny brick that guards us on the north beyond it. The fort is immense, an enormous sprawling edifice designed to hold ten thousand men. I remember very clearly the gigantic effort we expended in the building of it, twenty years before. Today just eleven occupants remain, and we rattle about it like tiny pebbles in a colossal jug.

Seeker gestures outward, into the gritty yellow wasteland that stretches before us like an endless ocean on the far side of the wall. That flat plain of twisted useless shrubs marks the one gap in the line of precipitous cliffs that forms the border here between Imperial territory and the enemy lands. It has been our task these twenty years past—we were born to it; it is an obligation of our caste—to guard that gap against the eventual incursion of the enemy army. For two full decades we have inhabited these lonely lands. We have fortified that gap, we have patrolled it, we have dedicated our lives to guarding it. In the old days, entire brigades of enemy troops would attempt to breach our line, appearing suddenly like clouds of angry insects out of the dusty plain, and with great loss of life on both sides we would drive them back. Now things are quieter on this frontier, very much quieter indeed, but we are still here, watching for and intercepting the occasional spies that periodically attempt to slip past our defenses.

"There," says Seeker. "Do you see those three little humps over to the northeast? He's dug in not very far behind them. I know he is. I can feel him the way you'd feel a boil on the back of your neck."

"Just one man?" Captain asks.

"One. Only one."

Weaponsmaster says, "What would one man hope to accomplish? Do you think he expects to come tiptoeing into the fort and kill us one by one?"

"There's no need for us to try to understand them," Sergeant says. "Our job is to find them and kill them. We can leave understanding them to the wiser heads back home."

"Ah," says Armorer sardonically. "Back home, yes. Wiser heads."

Captain has walked to the rim of the roof and stands there with his back to us, clutching the rail and leaning forward into the dry, crisp wind that eternally blows across our courtyard. A sphere of impenetrable chilly silence seems to surround him. Captain has always been an enigmatic man, solitary and brooding, but he has become stranger than ever since the death of Colonel, three years past, left him the ranking officer of the fort. No one knows his mind now, and no one dares to attempt any sort of intimacy with it.

"Very well," he says, after an interval that has become intolerably long. "A four-man search party: Sergeant to lead, accompanied by Seeker, Provisioner, and Surveyor. Set out in the morning. Take three days' food. Search, find, and kill."

It has been eleven weeks since the last successful search mission. That one ended in the killing of three enemies, but since then, despite Seeker's constant efforts, there have been no signs of any hostile presence in our territory. Once, six or seven weeks back, Seeker managed to convince himself that he felt emanations coming from a site along the river, a strange place for an enemy to have settled because it was well within our defense perimeter, and a five-man party led by Stablemaster hastened out to look. But they found no one there except a little band of the Fisherfolk, who swore that they had seen nothing unusual thereabouts, and the Fisherfolk do not lie. Upon their return, Seeker himself had to admit that he no longer felt the emanations and that he was now none too certain he had felt any in the first place.

There is substantial feeling among us that we have outlived our mission here, that few if any enemies still occupy the territory north of the gap, that quite possibly the war has long since been over. Sergeant, Quartermaster, Weaponsmaster, and Armorer are the chief proponents of this belief. They note that we have heard nothing whatsoever from the capital in years—no messengers have come, let alone reinforcements or fresh supplies— and that we have had no sign from the enemy, either, that any significant force of them is gathered anywhere nearby. Once, long ago, war seemed imminent, and indeed real battles often took place. But it has been terribly quiet here for a long time. There has been nothing like a real battle for six years, only a few infrequent skirmishes with small enemy platoons, and during the past two years we have detected just a few isolated outliers, usually no more than two or three men at a time, whom we catch relatively easily as they try to infiltrate our territory. Armorer insists that they are not spies but stragglers, the last remnants of whatever enemy force once occupied the region to our north, who have been driven by hunger or loneliness or who knows what other compulsion to take up positions close to our fort. He argues that in the twenty years we have been here, our own numbers have dwindled from ten thousand men to a mere eleven, at first by losses in battle but later by the attrition of age and ill-health, and he thinks it is reasonable that the same dwindling has occurred on the other side of the border, so that we few defenders now confront an enemy that may be even fewer in number than ourselves.

I myself see much to concur with in Armorer's position. I think it might very well be the case that we are a lost platoon, that the war is over and the Empire has forgotten us, and that there is no purpose at all in our continued vigilance. But if the Empire has forgotten us, who can give the order that withdraws us from our post? That is a decision that only Captain can make, and Captain has not given us the slightest impression of where he stands on the issue. And so we remain, and may remain to the end of our days. What folly that would be, says Armorer, to languish out here forever defending this forlorn frontier country against invaders that no longer choose to invade! And I half agree with him, but only half. I would not want to spend such time as remains to me working at a fool's task; but equally I do not wish to be guilty of dereliction of duty, after having served so long and so honorably on this frontier. Thus I am of two minds on the issue.

There is, of course, the opposite theory that holds that the enemy is simply biding its time, waiting for us to abandon the fort, after which a great army will come pouring through the gap at long last and strike at the Empire from one of its most vulnerable sides. Engineer and Signalman are the most vocal proponents of this viewpoint. They think it would be an act of profound treason to withdraw, the negation of all that we have dedicated our lives to, and they become irate when the idea is merely suggested. When they propound this position, I find it hard to disagree.

Seeker is the one who works hardest to keep our mission alive, constantly striving to pick up threatening emanations. That has been his life's work, after all. He knows no other vocation, that sad little man. So day by day Seeker climbs his hilltops and haunts his watchtowers and uses his one gift to detect the presence of hostile minds, and now and then he returns and sounds the alarm, and off we go on yet another search foray. More often than not, they prove to be futile, nowadays: either Seeker's powers are failing or he is excessively anxious to interpret his inputs as the mental output from nearby enemies.

I confess I feel a certain excitement at being part of this latest search party. Our days are spent in such terrible empty routine, normally. We tend our little vegetable patch, we look after our animals, we fish and hunt, we do our regular maintenance jobs, we read the same few books over and again, we have the same conversations, chiefly reminiscing about the time when there were more than eleven of us here, recalling as well as we can the robust and earthy characters who once dwelled among us but are long since gone to dust. Tonight, therefore, I feel a quickening of the pulse. I pack my gear for the morning, I eat my dinner with unusual gusto, I couple passionately with my little Fisherfolk companion. Each of us, all but Seeker, who seems to know no needs of that sort, has taken a female companion from among the band of simple people who live along our one feeble river. Even Captain takes one sometimes into his bed, I understand, although unlike the rest of us, he has no regular woman. Mine is called Wendrit. She is a pale and slender creature, surprisingly skillful in the arts of love. The Fisherfolk are not quite human—we and they are unable to conceive children together, for example—but they are close enough to human to serve most purposes, and they are pleasant, unassuming, uncomplaining companions. So I embrace Wendrit vigorously this night, and in the dawn the four of us gather, Sergeant, Provisioner, Seeker, and I, by the northern portcullis.

It is a bright, clear morning, the sun a hard, sharp-edged disk in the eastern sky. The sun is the only thing that comes to us from the Empire, visiting us each day after it has done its work back there, uncountable thousands of miles to the east. Probably the capital is already in darkness by now, just as we are beginning our day. The world is so large, after all, and we are so very far from home.

Once there would have been trumpeters to celebrate our departure as we rode through the portcullis, hurling a brassy fanfare for us into the quiet air. But the last of our trumpeters died years ago, and though we still have the instruments, none of us knows how to play them. I tried once, and made a harsh squeaking sound like the grinding of metal against metal, nothing more. So the only sound we hear as we ride out into the desert is the soft steady thudding of our mounts' hooves against the brittle sandy soil.

In truth, this is the bleakest of places, but we are used to it. I still have memories from my childhood of the floral splendor of the capital, great trees thick with juicy leaves, and shrubs clad in clusters of flowers, red and yellow and orange and purple, and the dense green lawns of the grand boulevards. But I have grown accustomed to the desert, which has become the norm for me, and such lush abundance as I remember out of my earlier life strikes me now as discomfortingly vulgar and excessive, a wasteful riot of energy and resources. All that we have here in the plain that runs out to the north between the wall of hills is dry yellow soil sparkling with the doleful sparkle of overabundant quartz, small gnarled shrubs and equally gnarled miniature trees, and occasional tussocks of tough, sharp-edged grass. On the south side of the fort the land is not quite so harsh, for our little river runs past us there, a weak strand of some much mightier one that must pour out of one of the big lakes in the center of the continent. Our river must be looking for the sea, as rivers do, but of course we are nowhere near the sea, and doubtless it exhausts itself in some distant reach of the desert. But as it passes our outpost, it brings greenery to its flanks, and some actual trees, and enough fish to support the tribe of primitive folk who are our only companions here.

Our route lies to the northeast, toward those three rounded hillocks behind which, so Seeker staunchly asserts, we will find the campsite of our solitary enemy. The little hills had seemed close enough when we viewed them from the barracks roof, but that was only an illusion, and we ride all day without visibly diminishing the span between them and us. It is a difficult trek. The ground, which is merely pebbly close by the fort, becomes rocky and hard to traverse farther out, and our steeds pick their way with care, heedful of their fragile legs. But this is familiar territory for us. Everywhere we see traces of hoofprints or tire tracks, five years old, ten, even twenty, the scars of ancient forays, the debris of half-forgotten battles of a decade and more ago. Rain comes perhaps twice a year here at best. Make a mark on the desert floor and it remains forever.

We camp as the first lengthening of the shadows begins, gather some scrubby wood for our fire, pitch our tent. There is not much in the way of conversation. Sergeant is a crude, inarticulate man at best; Seeker is too tense and fretful to be pleasant company; Provisioner, who has grown burly and red-faced with the years, can be jovial enough after a drink or two, but he seems uncharacteristically moody and aloof tonight. So I am left to my own resources, and once we have finished our meal, I walk out a short way into the night and stare, as I often do, at the glittering array of stars in this western sky of ours, wondering, as ever, whether each has its own collection of worlds, and whether those worlds are peopled, and what sort of lives the peoples of those worlds might lead. It is a perverse sort of amusement, I suppose: I who have spent half my life guarding a grim brick fort in this parched isolated outpost stare at the night sky and imagine the gleaming palaces and fragrant gardens of faraway worlds.

We rise early, make a simple breakfast, ride on through a cutting wind toward those three far-off hills. This morning, though, the perspective changes quickly: suddenly the hills are much closer, and then they are upon us, and Seeker, excited now, guides us toward the pass between the southernmost hill and its neighbor. "I feel him just beyond!" he cries. For Seeker, the sense that he calls directionality is like a compass, pointing the way toward our foes. "Come! This is the way! Hurry! Hurry!"

Nor has he led us wrongly this time. On the far side of the southernmost hill someone has built a little lean-to of twisted branches covered with a heaping of grass, no simple project in these stony ungenerous wastes. We draw our weapons and take up positions surrounding it, and Sergeant goes up to it and says, "You! Come out of there, and keep your hands in the air!"

There is a sound of stirring from within. In a moment or two a man emerges.

He has the classic enemy physiognomy: a short, stumpy body, sallow waxen skin, and heavy features

with jutting cheekbones and icy blue eyes. At the
sight of those eyes I feel an involuntary surge of
anger, even hatred, for we of the Empire are a
brown-eyed people and I have trained myself
through many years to feel nothing but hostility
for those whose eyes are blue.

But these are not threatening eyes. Obviously
the man had been asleep, and he is still making the
journey back into wakefulness as he comes forth
from his shelter, blinking, shaking his head. He is
trembling, too. He is one man and we are four, and
we have weapons drawn and he is unarmed, and he
has been taken by surprise. It is an unfortunate way
to start one's day. I am amazed to find my anger
giving way to something like pity.

He is given little time to comprehend the gravity of his situation. "Bastard!" Sergeant says, and
takes three strides forward. Swiftly he thrusts his
knife into the man's belly, withdraws it, strikes
again, again.

The blue eyes go wide with shock. I am shocked
myself, in a different way, and the sudden cruel
attack leaves me gasping with amazement. The
stricken enemy staggers, clutches at his abdomen
as though trying to hold back the torrent of blood,
takes three or four tottering steps, and falls in a
series of folding ripples. There is a convulsion or
two, and then he is still, lying face downward.

Sergeant kicks the entrance of the shelter open
and peers within. "See if there's anything useful in
there," he tells us.

Still astounded, I say, "Why did you kill him so quickly?"

"We came here to kill him."

"Perhaps. But he was unarmed. He probably would have given himself up peacefully."

"We came here to kill him," Sergeant says again.

"We might have interrogated him first, at least. That's the usual procedure, isn't it? Perhaps there are others of his kind somewhere close at hand."

"If there were any more of them around here," Sergeant says scornfully, "Seeker would have told us, wouldn't he have? Wouldn't he have, Surveyor?"

There is more that I would like to say, about how it might have been useful or at any rate interesting to discover why this man had chosen to make this risky pilgrimage to the edge of our territory. But there is no point in continuing the discussion, because Sergeant is too stupid to care what I have to say, and the man is already dead, besides.

We knock the shelter apart and search it. Nothing much there: a few tools and weapons, a copper-plated religious emblem of the kind that our enemies worship, a portrait of a flat-faced blue-eyed woman who is, I suppose, the enemy's wife or mother. It does not seem like the equipment of a spy. Even to an old soldier like me, it is all very sad. He was a man like us, enemy though he was, and he died far from home. Yes, it has long been our task to kill these people before they can kill us. Certainly I have killed more than a few of them myself.

But dying in battle is one thing; being slaughtered like a pig while still half-asleep is something else again. Especially if your only purpose had been to surrender. Why else had this solitary man, this lonely and probably desperate man, crossed this unrelenting desert, if not to give himself up to us at the fort?

I am softening with age, I suppose. Sergeant is right that it was our assignment to kill him: Captain had given us that order in the most explicit way. Bringing him back with us had never been part of the plan. We have no way of keeping prisoners at the fort. We have little enough food for ourselves, and guarding him would have posed a problem. He had had to die; his life was forfeit from the moment he ventured within the zone bordering on the fort. That he might have been lonely or desperate, that he had suffered in crossing this terrible desert and perhaps had hoped to win shelter at our fort, that he had had a wife or perhaps a mother whom he loved, all of that was irrelevant. It did not come as news to me that our enemies are human beings not all that different from us except in the color of their eyes and the texture of their skins. They are, nevertheless, our enemies. Long ago they set their hands against us in warfare, and until the day arrives when they put aside their dream of destroying what we of the Empire have built for ourselves, it is the duty of people like us to slay men like him. Sergeant had not been kind or gentle about it. But there is no kind or gentle way, really, to kill.

The days that followed were extremely quiet ones. Without so much as a discussion of what had taken place in the desert, we fell back into our routines: clean and polish this and that, repair whatever needs repair and still can be repaired, take our turns working in the fields alongside the river, wade in that shallow stream in quest of water-pigs for our table, tend the vats where we store the mash that becomes our beer, and so on, so forth, day in, day out. Of course I read a good deal, also. I have ever been a man for reading.

We have nineteen books; all the others have been read to pieces, or their bindings have fallen apart in the dry air, or the volumes have simply been misplaced somewhere about the fort and never recovered. I have read all nineteen again and again, even though five of them are technical manuals covering areas that never were part of my skills and which are irrelevant now anyway. (There is no point in knowing how to repair our vehicles when the last of our fuel supply was exhausted five years ago.) One of my favorite books is *The Saga of the Kings*, which I have known since childhood, the familiar account, probably wholly mythical, of the Empire's early history, the great charismatic leaders who built it, their heroic deeds, their inordinately long lifespans. There is a religious text, too, that I value, though I have grave doubts about the existence of the gods. But for me the choice volume of our library is the one called *The Register of Strange Things Beyond the Ranges*, a thousand-year-old account of the natural wonders to be found in the outer reaches of the Empire's great expanse. Only half the book remains to us now—perhaps one of my comrades ripped pages out to use as kindling, once upon a time—but I cherish that half, and read it constantly, even though I know it virtually by heart by this time.

Wendrit likes me to read to her. How much of what she hears she is capable of understanding, I have no idea: she is a simple soul, as all her people are. But I love the way she turns her big violet-hued eyes toward me as I read, and sits in total attention.

I read to her of the Gate of Ghosts, telling her of the customs shed there that spectral phantoms guard: "Ten men go out; nine men return." I read to her of the Stones of Shao, two flat-sided slabs flanking a main highway that on a certain day every ten years would come crashing together, crushing any wayfarers who happened to be passing through just then, and of the bronze Pillars of King Mai, which hold the two stones by an incantation that forbids them ever to move again. I read to her of the Mountain of a Thousand Eyes, the granite face of which is pockmarked with glossy onyx boulders that gleam down upon passersby like stern black eyes. I tell her of the Forest of Cinnamon, and of the Grotto of Dreams, and of the Place of Galloping Clouds. Were such places real, or simply the fantasies of some ancient spinner of tall tales? How would I know, I who spent my childhood and youth at the capital, and have passed the rest of my years here at this remote desert fort, where there is nothing to be seen but sandy yellow soil, and twisted shrubs, and little scuttering scorpions that run before our feet? But the strange places described in *The Register of Strange Things Beyond the Ranges* have grown more real to me in these latter days than the capital itself, which has become in my mind a mere handful of vague and fragmentary impressions. So I read with conviction, and Wendrit listens in awe, and when I weary of the wonders of the *Register*, I put it aside and take her hand and lead her to my bed, and caress her soft pale-green skin and kiss the tips of her small round breasts, and so we pass another night.

In those quiet days that followed our foray, I thought often of the man Sergeant had killed. In the days when we fought battles here, I killed without compunction, five, ten, twenty men at a time, not exactly taking pleasure in it, but certainly feeling no guilt. But the killing in those days was done at a decent distance, with rifles or heavy guns, for we still had ammunition then and our rifles and guns were still in good repair. It was necessary now in our forays against the occasional spies who approached the fort to kill with spears or knives, and to kill at close range feels less like a deed of warfare to me and more like murder.

My mind went back easily to those battles of

yesteryear: the sound of the sentry's alarm, the first view of the dark line of enemy troops on the horizon, the rush to gather our weapons and start our vehicles. And out we would race through the portcullis to repel the invaders, rushing to take up our primary defensive formation, then advancing in even ranks that filled the entire gap in the hills, so that when the enemy entered that deadly funnel we could fall upon them and slaughter them. It was the same thing every time. They came; we responded; they perished. How far they must have traveled to meet their dismal deaths in our dreary desert! None of us had any real idea how far away the country of the enemy actually was, but we knew it had to be a great distance to the north and west, just as our own country is a great distance to the south and east. The frontier that our own outpost defends lies on the midpoint between one desert and another. Behind us is the almost infinite terrain of sparse settlements that eventually culminates in the glorious cities of the Empire. Before us are equally interminable wastes that give way, eventually, to the enemy homeland itself. For one nation to attack the other, it must send its armies far across an uncharted and unfriendly nothingness. Which our enemy was willing to do, the gods only knew why, and again and again their armies came, and again and again we destroyed them in the fine frenzy of battle. That was a long time ago. We were not much more than boys then. But finally the marching armies came no more, and the only enemies we had to deal with were those few infrequent spies or perhaps stragglers whom Seeker pinpointed for us, and whom we went out and slew at close range with our knives and spears, looking into their frosty blue eyes as we robbed them of their lives.

Seeker is in a bad way. He can go from one day to the next without saying a word. He still heads up to his watchtowers almost every morning, but he returns from his vigils in a black cloak of gloom and moves through our midst in complete silence. We know better than to approach him at such times, because, though he is a man of no great size and strength, he can break out in savage fury sometimes when his depressions are intruded upon. So we let him be; but as the days pass and his mood grows ever darker, we fear some sort of explosion.

One afternoon I saw him speaking with Captain out on the rooftop terrace. It appeared that Captain had initiated the conversation, and that Seeker was answering Captain's questions with the greatest reluctance, staring down at his boots as he spoke. But then Captain said something that caused Seeker to react with surprising animation, looking up, gesticulating. Captain shook his head. Seeker pounded his fists together. Captain made a gesture of dismissal and walked away.

What they were saying to each other was beyond all guessing. And beyond all asking, too, for if anyone is more opaque than Seeker, it is Captain, and while it is at least possible at certain times to ask Seeker what is on his mind, making such an inquiry of Captain is inconceivable.

In recent days, Seeker has taken to drinking with us after dinner. That is a new thing for him. He has always disliked drinking. He says he despises the stuff we make that we call beer and wine and brandy. That is reasonable enough, because we make our beer from the niggardly sour grain of a weed that grows by the river, and we wrest our thin wine and our rough brandy from the bitter gray fruits of a different weed, and they are pitiful products indeed to anyone who remembers the foaming beers of the capital and the sweet vintages of our finest wine-producing districts. But we have long since exhausted the supplies of such things that we brought with us, and, of course, no replenishments from home ever come, and, since in this somber landscape there is comfort to be had from drinking, we drink what we can make. Not Seeker, no. Not until this week.

Now he drinks, though, showing no sign of pleasure, but often extending his glass for another round. And at last one night when he has come back with his glass more than once, he breaks his long silence.

"They are all gone," he says, in a voice like the tolling of a cracked bell.

"Who are?" Provisioner asks. "The scorpions? I saw three scorpions only yesterday." Provisioner is well along in his cups, as usual. His reddened, jowly face creases in a broad toothy smile, as if he has uttered the cleverest of witticisms.

"The enemy," says Seeker. "The one we killed—he was the last one. There's nobody left. Do you know how empty I feel, going up to the towers to listen, and hearing nothing? As if I've been hollowed out inside. Can you understand what sort of feeling that is? Can you? No, of course you can't. What would any of you know?" He stares at us in agony. "The silence . . . the silence . . ."

Nobody seems to know how quite to respond to that, so we say nothing. And Seeker helps himself to yet another jigger of brandy, and full measure at that. This is alarming. The sight of Seeker drinking like this is as strange as the sight of a torrential downpour of rain would be.

Engineer, who is probably the calmest and most reasonable of us, says, "Ah, man, can you not be a bit patient? I know you want to do your task. But more of them will come. Sooner or later, there'll be another, and another after that. Two weeks, three, six, who knows? But they'll come. You've been through spells like this before."

"No. This is different," says Seeker sullenly. "But what would you know?"

"Easy," Engineer says, laying his strong hand across the back of Seeker's frail wrist. "Go easy, man. What do you mean, 'this is different'?"

Carefully, making a visible effort at self-control, Seeker says, "All the other times when we've gone several weeks between incursions, I've always felt a low inner hum, a kind of subliminal static, a barely perceptible mental pressure, that tells me there are at least a few enemies out there somewhere, a hundred miles away, five hundred, a thousand. It's just a kind of quiet buzz. It doesn't give me any directionality. But it's there, and sooner or later the signal becomes stronger, and then I know that a couple of them are getting close to us, and then I get directionality and I can lead us to them, and we go out and kill them. It's been that way for years, ever since the real battles stopped. But now I don't get anything. Not a thing. It's absolutely silent in my head. Which means that either I've lost my power entirely, or else there aren't any enemies left within a thousand miles or more."

"And which is it that you think is so?"

Seeker scans us all with a haggard look. "That there are no enemies out there anymore. Which means that it is pointless to remain here. We should pack up, go home, make some sort of new lives for ourselves within the Empire itself. And yet we have to stay, in case they come. I must stay, because this is the only task that I know how to perform. What sort of new life could I make for myself back there? I never had a life. This is my life. So my choice is to stay here to no purpose, performing a task that does not need to be performed any longer, or to return home to no existence. Do you see my predicament?" He is shivering. He reaches for the brandy, pours yet another drink with a trembling hand, hastily downs it, coughs, shudders, lets his head drop to the tabletop. We can hear him sobbing.

That night marks the beginning of the debate among us. Seeker's breakdown has brought into the open something that has been on my own mind for some weeks now, and which Armorer, Weaponsmaster, Quartermaster, and even dull-witted Sergeant have been pondering also, each in his own very different way.

The fact is unanswerable that the frequency of enemy incursions has lessened greatly in the past two years, and when they do come, every five or six or ten weeks apart, they no longer come in bands of a dozen or so, but in twos or threes. This last man whom Sergeant slew by the three little hills had come alone. Armorer has voiced quite openly his notion that just as our own numbers have dwindled to next to nothing over the years, the enemy confronting us in this desert must have suffered great attrition, too, and like us, has had no reinforcement from the home country, so that only a handful of our foes remain—or, perhaps, as Seeker now believes, none at all. If that is true, says Armorer, who is a wry and practical man, why do we not close up shop and seek some new occupation for ourselves in some happier region of the Empire?

Sergeant, who loves the excitement of warfare, for whom combat is not an ugly necessity but an act of passionate devotion, shares Armorer's view that we ought to move along. It is not so much that inactivity makes him restless—*restlessness* is not a word that really applies to a wooden block of a man like Sergeant—but that, like Seeker, he lives only to perform his military function. Seeker's function is to seek and Sergeant's function is to kill, and Seeker now feels that he will seek forever here and nevermore find, and Sergeant, in his dim way, believes that for him to stay here any longer would be a waste of his capability. He, too, wants to leave.

As does Weaponsmaster, who has had no weapons other than knives and spears to care for since our ammunition ran out and thus passes his days in a stupefying round of makework, and Quartermaster, who once presided over the material needs of ten thousand men and now, in his grizzled old age, lives the daily mockery of looking after the needs of just eleven. Thus we have four men—Armorer, Sergeant, Weaponsmaster, Quartermaster—fairly well committed to bringing the life of this outpost to an end, and one more, Seeker, who wants both to go and to stay. I am more or less of Seeker's persuasion here myself, aware that we are living idle and futile lives at the fort but burdened at the same time with a sense of obligation to my profession that leads me to regard an abandonment of the fort as a shameful act. So I sway back and forth. When Armorer speaks, I am inclined to join his faction. But when one of the others advocates remaining here, I drift back in that direction.

Gradually it emerges in our circular nightly discussion that the other four of us are strongly committed to staying. Engineer enjoys his life here: there are always technical challenges for him, a new canal to design, a parapet in need of repair, a harness to mend. He also is driven by a strong sense of duty and believes it is necessary to the welfare of the Empire that we remain here. Stablemaster, less concerned about duty, is fond of his beasts and similarly has no wish to leave. Provisioner, who is rarely given to doubts of any sort, would be content to remain so long as our supply of food and drink remains ample, and that appears to be the case. And Signalman still believes, Seeker's anguish to the contrary, that the desert beyond the wall is full of patient foes who will swarm through the gap and march against the capital like ravening beasts the moment we relinquish the fort.

Engineer, who is surely the most rational of us, has raised another strong point in favor of staying. We have scarcely any idea of how to get home. Twenty years ago we were brought here in a great convoy, and who among us bothered to take note of the route we traversed? Even those who might have paid attention to it then have forgotten almost every detail of the journey. But we do have a vague general idea of the challenge that confronts us. Between us and the capital lies, first of all, a great span of trackless dry wasteland and then forested districts occupied by autonomous savage tribes. Uncharted and, probably, well-nigh impenetrable tropical jungles are beyond those, and no doubt we would encounter a myriad other hazards. We have no maps of the route. We have no working communications devices. "If we leave here, we might spend the rest of our lives wandering around hopelessly lost in the wilderness," Engineer says. "At least here we have a home, women, something to eat, and a place to sleep."

I raise another objection. "You all speak as though this is something we could just put to a vote. 'Raise hands, all in favor of abandoning the fort.'"

"If we did take a vote," Armorer says, "We'd have a majority in favor of getting out of here. You, me, Sergeant, Quartermaster, Weaponsmaster, Seeker—that's six out of eleven, even if Captain votes the other way."

"No. I'm not so sure I'm with you. I don't think Seeker is, either. Neither of us has really made up his mind." We all looked toward Seeker, but Seeker was asleep at the table, lost in winy stupor. "So at best we're equally divided right now, four for leaving, four for staying, and two undecided. But in any case this place isn't a democracy and how we vote doesn't matter. Whether we leave the fort is something for Captain to decide, and Captain alone. And we don't have any idea what his feelings are."

"We could ask him," Armorer suggests.

"Ask my elbow," Provisioner says, guffawing.

"Who wants to ask Captain anything? The man who does will get a riding crop across the face."

There is general nodding around the table. We all have tasted Captain's unpredictable ferocity.

Quartermaster says, "If we had a majority in favor of going home, we could all go to him and tell him how we feel. He won't try to whip us all. For all we know, he might even tell us that he agrees with us."

"But you don't have a majority," Engineer points out.

Quartermaster looks toward me. "Come over to our side, Surveyor. Surely you see there's more merit in our position than in theirs. That would make it five to four for leaving."

"And Seeker?" Engineer asks. "When he sobers up, what if he votes the other way? That would make it a tie vote again."

"We could ask Captain to break the tie, and that would settle the whole thing," Armorer says.

That brings laughter from us all. Captain is very sensitive to anything that smacks of insubordination. Even the dullest of us can see that he will not react well to hearing that we are trying to determine a serious matter of policy by majority vote.

I lie awake for hours that night, replaying our discussion in my mind. There are strong points on both sides. The idea of giving up the fort and going home has great appeal. We are all getting along in years; at best each of us has ten or fifteen years left to him, and do I want to spend those years doing nothing but hunting water-pigs in the river and toiling over our scrawny crops and rereading the same handful of books? I believe Seeker when he says that the man we killed a few weeks ago was the last of the enemy in our territory.

On the other hand, there is the question of duty. What are we to say when we show up in the capital? Simply announce that by our own authority we have abandoned the outpost to which we have devoted our lives, merely because in our opinion there is no further need for us to stay on at it? Soldiers are not entitled to opinions. Soldiers who are sent to defend a frontier outpost have no option but to defend that outpost until orders to the contrary are received.

To this argument I oppose another one, which is that duty travels both ways. We might be abandoning our fort, an improper thing for soldiers to be doing, but is it not true that the Empire has long ago abandoned us? There has been no word from home for ages. Not only have we had no reinforcements or fresh supplies from the Empire, but there has not been so much as an inquiry. They have forgotten we exist. What if the war ended years ago and nobody at the capital has bothered to tell us that? How much do we owe an Empire that does not remember our existence?

And, finally, there is Engineer's point that going home might be impossible anyway, for we have no maps, no vehicles, no clear idea of the route we must follow, and we know that we are an almost unimaginable distance from any civilized district of the Empire. The journey will be a terrible struggle, and we may very well perish in the course of it. For me, in the middle of the night, that is perhaps the most telling point of all.

I realize, as I lie there contemplating these things, that Wendrit is awake beside me, and that she is weeping.

"What is it?" I asked. "Why are you crying?"

She is slow to answer. I can sense the troubled gropings of her mind. But at length she says, between sobs, "You are going to leave me. I heard things. I know. You will leave and I will be alone."

"No," I tell her, before I have even considered what I am saying. "No, that isn't true. I won't leave. And if I do, I'll take you with me. I promise you that, Wendrit." And I pull her into my arms and hold her until she is no longer sobbing.

I awaken knowing that I have made my decision, and it is the decision to go home. Along with Armorer, Sergeant, Weaponsmaster, and Stablemaster, I believe now that we should assemble whatever provisions we can, choose the strongest of our beasts to draw our carts, and, taking our women with us, set out into the unknown. If the gods favor our cause, we will reach the Empire eventually, request retirement from active duty, and try to form some sort of new lives for ourselves in what no doubt is a nation very much altered from the one we left behind more than twenty years ago.

That night, when we gather over our brandy, I announce my conversion to Armorer's faction. But Seeker reveals that he, too, has had an epiphany in the night, which has swung him to the other side: weak and old as he is, he fears the journey home more than he does living out the rest of his life in futility at the fort. So we still are stalemated, now five to five, and there is no point in approaching Captain, even assuming that Captain would pay the slightest attention to our wishes.

Then there is an event that changes everything. It is the day of our weekly pig-hunt, when four or five of us don our high boots and go down to the river with spears to refresh our stock of fresh meat. The water-pigs that dwell in the river are beasts about the size of cattle, big sleek purple things with great yellow tusks, very dangerous when angered but also very stupid. They tend to congregate just upriver from us, where a bend in the flow creates a broad pool thick with water-plants, on which they like to forage. Our hunting technique involves cutting one beast out of the herd with proddings of our spears and moving him downriver, well apart from the others, so that we can kill him in isolation, without fear of finding ourselves involved in a chaotic melee with seven or eight furious pigs snapping at us from all sides at once. The meat from a single pig will last the eleven of us a full week, sometimes more.

Today the hunting party is made up of Provisioner, Signalman, Weaponsmaster, Armorer, and me. We are all skilled hunters and work well together. As soon as the night's chill has left the air, we go down to the river and march along its banks to the water-pig pool, choose the pig that is to be our prey, and arrange ourselves along the bank so that we will be in a semicircular formation when we enter the water. We will slip between the lone pig and the rest of his fellows and urge him away from them, and when we think it is safe to attack, we will move in for the kill.

At first everything goes smoothly. The river is hip-deep here. We form our arc, we surround our pig, we nudge him lightly with the tips of our spears. His little red-rimmed eyes glower at us in fury, and we can hear the low rumblings of his annoyance, but the half-submerged animal pulls back from the pricking without attempting to fight, and we prod him twenty, thirty, forty feet downstream, toward the killing-place. As usual, a few Fisherfolk have gathered on the bank to watch us, though there is, as ever, a paradoxical incuriosity about their bland stares.

And then, catastrophe. "Look out!" cries Armorer, and in the same moment I become aware of the water churning wildly behind me, and I see two broad purple backs breaching the surface of the river, and I realize that this time other pigs—at least a couple, maybe more, who knows?—have followed on downstream with our chosen one and intend to defend their grazing grounds against our intrusion. It is the thing we have always dreaded but never experienced, the one serious danger in these hunts. The surface of the water thrashes and boils. We see pigs leaping frenetically on all sides of us. The river is murky at best, but now, with maddened water-pigs snorting and snuffling all about us, we have no clear idea of what is happening, except that we have lost control of the situation and are in great jeopardy.

"Out of the water, everybody!" Weaponsmaster yells, but we are already scrambling for the riverbank. I clamber up, lean on my spear, catch my breath. Weaponsmaster and Armorer stand beside me. Provisioner has gone to the opposite bank. But there is no sign of Signalman, and the river suddenly is red with blood, and great yellow-tusked pig-snouts are jutting up everywhere, and then Signalman comes floating to the surface, belly upward, his body torn open from throat to abdomen.

We carry him back borne on our shoulders, like a fallen hero. It is our first death in some years. Somehow we had come to feel, in the time that has elapsed since that one, that we eleven who still remain would go on and on together forever, but now we know that that is not so. Weaponsmaster takes the news to Captain and reports back to us that that stony implacable man had actually seemed to show signs of real grief upon hearing of Signalman's death. Engineer and Provisioner and I dig the grave, and Captain presides over the service, and for several days there is a funereal silence around the fort.

Then, once the shock of the death has begun to ebb a little, Armorer raises the point that none of us had cared to mention openly since the event at the river. Which is, that with Signalman gone, the stalemate has been broken. The factions stand now at five for setting out for home, four for remaining indefinitely at the fort. And Armorer is willing to force the issue on behalf of the majority by going to Captain and asking whether he will authorize an immediate retreat from the frontier.

For hours, there is an agitated discussion, verging sometimes into bitterness and rage. We all recognize that it must be one way or another, that we cannot divide: a little group of four or five would never be able to sustain itself at the fort, nor would the other group of about the same size have any hope of success in traversing the unknown lands ahead. We must all stay together or assuredly we will all succumb; but that means that the four who would remain must yield to the five who wish to leave, regardless of their own powerful desires in the matter. And the four who would be compelled to join the trek against their wishes are fiercely resentful of the five who insist on departure.

In the end, things grow calmer and we agree to leave the decision to Captain, in whose hands it belongs anyway. A delegation of four is selected to go to him: Engineer and Stablemaster representing those who would stay, and Armorer and me to speak for the other side.

Captain spends most of his days in a wing of the fort that the rest of us rarely enter. There, at a huge ornate desk in an office big enough for ten men, he studies piles of documents left by his predecessors as commanding officer, as though hoping to learn from the writings of those vanished colonels how best to carry out the responsibilities that the vagaries of time have placed upon his shoulders. He is a brawny, dour-faced man, thin-lipped and somber-eyed, with dense black eyebrows that form a single forbidding line across his forehead, and even after all these years he is a stranger to us all.

He listens to us in his usual cold silence as we set forth the various arguments: Seeker's belief that there are no more enemies for us to deal with here, Armorer's that we are absolved of our duty to the Empire by its long neglect of us, Engineer's that the journey home would be perilous to the point of foolhardiness, and Signalman's, offered on his behalf by Stablemaster, that the enemy is simply waiting for us to go and then will launch its long-awaited campaign of conquest in Imperial territory. Eventually we begin to repeat ourselves and realize that there is nothing more to say, though Captain has not broken his silence by so much as a single syllable. The last word is spoken by Armorer, who tells Captain that five of us favor leaving, four remaining, though he does not specify who holds which position.

Telling him that strikes me as a mistake. It

implies—rightly—that a democratic process has gone on among us, and I expect Captain to respond angrily to the suggestion that any operational issue here can be decided, or even influenced, by a vote of the platoon. But there is no thunderstorm of wrath. He sits quietly, still saying nothing, for an almost unendurable span of time. Then he says, in a surprisingly moderate tone, "Seeker is unable to pick up any sign of enemy presence?" He addresses the question to Engineer, whom, apparently, he has correctly identified as one of the leaders of the faction favoring continued residence at the fort.

"This is so," Engineer replies.

Captain is silent once again. But finally he says, to our universal amazement, "The thinking of those who argue for withdrawal from the frontier is in line with my own. I have considered for some time now that our services in this place are no longer required by the Empire, and that if we are to be of use to the country at all, we must obtain reassignment elsewhere."

It is, I think, the last thing any of us had expected. Armorer glows with satisfaction. Engineer and Stablemaster look crestfallen. I, ambivalent even now, simply look at Captain in surprise.

Captain goes on, "Engineer, Stablemaster, make plans for our departure at the soonest possible date. I stipulate one thing, though: We go as a group, with no one to remain behind, and we must stay together as one group throughout what I know will be a long and arduous journey. Anyone who attempts to leave the group will be considered a deserter and treated accordingly. I will request that you all take an oath to that effect."

That is what we had agreed among ourselves to do anyway, so there is no difficulty about it. Nor do our four recalcitrants indicate any opposition to the departure order, though Seeker is plainly terrified of the dangers and stress of the journey. We begin at once to make our plans for leaving.

It turns out that we do have some maps of the intervening territory after all. Captain produces them from among his collection of documents, along with two volumes of a chronicle of our journey from the capital to the frontier that the first Colonel had kept. He summons me and gives me this material, ordering me to consult it and devise a plan of route for our journey.

But I discover quickly that it is all useless. The maps are frayed and cracked along their folds, and such information as they once might have held concerning the entire center of the continent has faded into invisibility. I can make out a bold star-shaped marker indicating the capital down in the lower right-hand corner, and a vague ragged line indicating the frontier far off to the left, and just about everything between is blank. Nor is the old Colonel's chronicle in any way helpful. The first volume deals with the organization of the expeditionary force and the logistical problems involved in transporting it from the capital to the interior.

The second volume that we have, which is actually the third of the original three, describes the building of the fort and the initial skirmishes with the enemy. The middle volume is missing, and that is the one, I assume, that speaks of the actual journey between the capital and the frontier.

I hesitate to tell Captain this, for he is not one who receives bad news with much equanimity. Instead I resolve that I will do my best to improvise a route for us, taking my cues from what we find as we make our way to the southeast. And so we get ourselves ready, choosing our best wagons and our sturdiest steeds and loading them with tools and weapons and with all we can carry by way of provisions: dried fruit and beans, flour, casks of water, cartons of preserved fish, parcels of the air-dried meat that Provisioner prepares each winter by laying out strips of pig-flesh in the sun. We will do as we can for fresh meat and produce on the march.

The women placidly accept the order to accompany us into the wilderness. They have already crossed over from their Fisherfolk lives to ours, anyway. There are only nine of them, for Seeker has never chosen to have one, and Captain has rarely shown more than fitful interest in them. Even so we have one extra: Sarkariet, Signalman's companion. She has remained at the fort since Signalman's death and says she has no desire to return to her village, so we take her along.

The day of our departure is fair and mild, the sun warm but not hot, the wind gentle. Perhaps that is a good omen. We leave the fort without a backward glance, going out by way of the eastern gate and descending to the river. A dozen or so of the Fisher-folk watch us in their blank-faced way as we cross the little wooden bridge upstream of their village. Once we are across, Captain halts our procession and orders us to destroy the bridge. From Engineer comes a quick grunt of shock: the bridge was one of his first projects, long ago. But Captain sees no reason to leave the enemy any easy path eastward, should the enemy still be lurking somewhere in the hinterlands. And so we ply our axes for half a morning until the bridge goes tumbling down into the riverbed.

We have never had any reason in the past twenty years to venture very far into the districts east or south of the fort, but we are not surprised to find them pretty much the same as the region north and west of the fort that we have patrolled so long. That is, we are in a dry place of pebbly yellowish soil, with low hills here and there, gnarled shrubs, tussocks of saw-bladed grass. Now and again some scrawny beast scampers quickly across our path, or we hear the hissing of a serpent from the underbrush, and solitary melancholy birds sometimes go drifting high overhead, cawing raucously, but by and large the territory is deserted. There is no sign of water all the first day, nor midway through the second, but that afternoon Seeker reports that he detects the presence of Fisherfolk somewhere nearby, and before long we reach a straggling little stream that is probably another fork of the river whose other tributary runs close below our fort. On its farther bank we see a Fisherfolk camp, much smaller than the village on the banks of our river.

Wendrit and the other women become agitated at the sight of it. I ask her what the matter is, and she tells me that these people are ancient enemies of her people, that whenever the two tribes encounter each other, there is a battle. So even the passive, placid Fisherfolk wage warfare among themselves! Who would have thought it? I bring word of this to Captain, who looks untroubled. "They will not come near us," he says, and this proves to be so. The river is shallow enough to ford; and the strange Fisherfolk gather by their tents and stand in silence as we pass by. On the far side we replenish our water-casks.

Then the weather grows unfriendly. We are entering a rocky, broken land, a domain of sandstone cliffs, bright red in color and eroded into jagged, fanciful spires and ridges, and here a hard, steady wind blows out of the south through a gap in the hills into our faces, carrying a nasty freight of tiny particles of pinkish grit. The sun now is as red as new copper in that pinkish sky, as though we have a sunset all day long. To avoid the sandstorm that I assume will be coming upon us, I swing the caravan around to due east, where we will be traveling along the base of the cliffs and perhaps will be sheltered from the worst of the wind. In this I am incorrect, because a cold, inexorable crosswind arises abruptly, bringing with it out of the north the very sandstorm that I had hoped to avoid, and we find ourselves pinned down for a day and a half just below the red cliffs, huddling together miserably with our faces masked by scarves. The wind howls all night; I sleep very badly. At last it dies down and we hurry through the gap in the cliffs and resume our plodding southeastward march.

Beyond, we find what is surely a dry lakebed, a broad flat expanse covered with a sparse incrustation of salt that glitters in the brutal sunlight like newly fallen snow. Nothing but the indomitable saw grass grows here, and doubtless the lake has been dry for millennia, for there is not even a skeletal trace of whatever vegetation, shrubs, and even trees might have bordered its periphery in the days when there was water here. We are three days crossing this dead lake. Our supply of fresh water is running troublesomely low already, and we have exhausted all of our fresh meat, leaving only the dried stuff that increases our thirst. Nor is there any game to hunt here, of course.

Is this what we are going to have to face, week after week, until eventually we reach some kinder terrain? The oldest men, Seeker and Quartermaster, are showing definite signs of fatigue, and the women, who have never been far from their river for even a day, seem fretful and withdrawn. Clearly dismayed and even frightened, they whisper constantly among themselves in the Fisherfolk language that none of us has ever bothered to learn, but draw away whenever we approach. Even our pack animals are beginning to struggle. They have had little to eat or drink since we set out, and the effects are only too apparent. They snap listlessly at the tufts of sharp gray grass and look up at us with doleful eyes, as though we have betrayed them.

The journey has only just begun, and already I am beginning to regret it.

One evening, when we are camped at some forlorn place near the farther end of the lake, I confess my doubts to Captain. Since he is our superior officer and I am the officer who is leading us on our route, I have come to assume some sort of equality of rank between us that will allow for confidential conversations. But I am wrong. When I tell him that I have started to believe that this enterprise may be beyond our powers of endurance, he replies that he has no patience with cowards, and turns his back on me. We do not speak again in the days that follow.

There are indications of the sites of ancient villages in the region beyond, where the river that fed that dry lake must once have flowed. There is no river here now, though my practiced eye detects the faint curves of its prehistoric route, and the fragmentary ruins of small stone settlements can be seen on the ledges above what once were its banks. But nowadays all is desert here. Why did the Empire need us to defend the frontier, when there is this gigantic buffer zone of desert between its rich, fertile territories and the homeland of the enemy?

Later we come to what must have been the capital city of this long-abandoned province, a sprawling maze of crumbled stone walls and barely comprehensible multi-roomed structures. We find some sort of temple sanctuary where devilish statues still stand, dark stone idols with a dozen heads and thirty arms, each one grasping the stump of what must have been a sword. Carved big-eyed snakes twine about the waists of these formidable forgotten gods. The scholars of our nation surely would wish to collect these things for the museums of the capital, and I make a record of our position, so that I can file a proper report for them once we have reached civilization. But by now I have arrived at serious doubt that we ever shall.

I draw Seeker aside and ask him to cast his mind forth in the old way and see if he can detect any intimation of inhabited villages somewhere ahead.

"I don't know if I can," he says. He is terribly emaciated, trembling, pale. "It takes a strength that I don't think I have anymore."

"Try. Please. I need to know."

He agrees to make the effort, and goes into his trance, and I stand by, watching, as his eyeballs roll up into his head and his breath comes in thick, hoarse bursts. He stands statue-still, utterly motionless for a very long while. Then, gradually, he returns to normal consciousness, and as he does so, he begins to topple, but I catch him in time and ease him to the ground. He sits blinking for a time, drawing deep breaths, collecting his strength. I wait until he seems to have regained himself.

"Well?"

"Nothing. Silence. As empty ahead as it is behind."

"For how far?" I ask. "How do I know?" he said. "There's no one there. That's all I can say."

We are rationing water very parsimoniously and we are starting to run short of provisions, too. There is nothing for us to hunt, and none of the vegetation, such as it is, seems edible. Even Sergeant, who is surely the strongest of us, now looks hollow-eyed and gaunt, and Seeker and Quartermaster seem at the verge of being unable to continue. From time to time we find a source of fresh water, brackish but at any rate drinkable, or slay some unwary wandering animal, and our spirits rise a bit, but the environment through which we pass is unremittingly hostile and I have no idea when things will grow easier for us. I make a show of studying my maps, hoping it will encourage the others to think that I know what I am doing, but the maps I have for this part of the continent are blank and I might just as well consult my wagon or the beasts that pull it as try to learn anything from those faded sheets of paper.

"This is a suicidal trek," Engineer says to me one morning as we prepare to break camp. "We should never have come. We should turn back while we still can. At least at the fort we would be able to survive."

"You got us into this," Provisioner says, scowling at me. "You and your switched vote." Burly Provisioner is burly no longer. He has become a mere shadow of his former self. "Admit it, Surveyor: We'll never make it. It was a mistake to try."

Am I supposed to defend myself against these charges? What defense can I possibly make?

A day later, with conditions no better, Captain calls the nine of us together and makes an astonishing announcement. He is sending the women back. They are too much of a burden on us. They will be given one of the wagons and some of our remaining provisions. If they travel steadily in the direction of the sunset, he says, they will sooner or later find their way back to their village below the walls of our fort.

He walks away from us before any of us can reply. We are too stunned to say anything, anyway. And how could we reply? What could we say? That we oppose this act of unthinkable cruelty and will not let him send the women to their deaths? Or that we have taken a new vote, and we are unanimous in our desire that all of us, not just the women, return to the fort? He will remind us that a military platoon is not a democracy. Or perhaps he will simply turn his back on us, as he usually does. We are bound on our path toward the inner domain of the Empire; we have sworn an oath to continue as a group; he will not release us.

"But he can't mean it!" Stablemaster says. "It's a death sentence for them!"

"Why should he care about that?" Armorer asks. "The women are just domestic animals to him. I'm surprised he doesn't just ask us to kill them right here and now, instead of going to the trouble of letting them have some food for their trip back."

It says much about how our journey has weakened us that none of us feels capable of voicing open opposition to Captain's outrageous order. He confers with Provisioner and Stablemaster to determine how much of our food we can spare for them and which wagon to give them, and the conference proceeds precisely as though it is a normal order of business.

The women are unaware of the decision Captain has made. Nor can I say anything to Wendrit when I return to our tent. I pull her close against me and hold her in a long embrace, thinking that this is probably the last time.

When I step back and look into her eyes, my own fill with tears, and she stares at me in bewilderment. But how can I explain? I am her protector. There is no way to tell her that Captain has ordered her death and that I am prepared to be acquiescent in his monstrous decision.

Can it be said that it is possible to feel love for a Fisherfolk woman? Well, yes, perhaps. Perhaps I love Wendrit. Certainly it would cause me great pain to part from her.

The women will quickly lose their way as they try to retraverse the inhospitable desert lands that we have just passed through. Beyond doubt they will die within a few days. And we ourselves, in all likelihood, will be dead ourselves in a week or two as we wander ever onward in this hopeless quest for the settled districts of the Empire. I was a madman to think that we could ever succeed in that journey simply by pointing our noses toward the capital and telling ourselves that by taking one step after another we would eventually get there.

But there is a third way that will spare Wendrit and the other women, and my friends as well, from dying lonely deaths in these lonely lands. Sergeant had shown me, that day behind the three little hillocks north of the fort, how the thing is managed.

I leave my tent. Captain has finished his conference with Provisioner and Stablemaster and is standing off by himself to one side of our camp, as though he is alone on some other planet.

"Captain?" I say.

My blade is ready as he turns toward me.

Afterwards, to the shaken, astounded men, I say quietly, "I am Captain now. Is anyone opposed? Good." And I point to the northwest, back toward the place of the serpent-wrapped stone idols, and the dry lakebed beyond, and the red cliffs beyond those. "We all know we won't ever find the Empire. But the fort is still there. So come, then. Let's break camp and get started. We're going back. We're going home."

George R. R. Martin

Hugo, Nebula, and World Fantasy Award winner George R. R. Martin, *New York Times* bestselling author of the landmark A Song of Ice and Fire fantasy series, has been called "the American Tolkien."

Born in Bayonne, New Jersey, George R. R. Martin made his first sale in 1971 and soon established himself as one of the most popular SF writers of the '70s. He quickly became a mainstay of the Ben Bova *Analog* with stories such as "With Morning Comes Mistfall," "And Seven Times Never Kill Man," "The Second Kind of Loneliness," "The Storms of Windhaven" (in collaboration with Lisa Tuttle, and later expanded by them into the novel *Windhaven*), "Override," and others, although he also sold to *Amazing, Fantastic, Galaxy, Orbit,* and other markets. One of his *Analog* stories, the striking novella "A Song for Lya," won him his first Hugo Award in 1974.

By the end of the '70s, he had reached the height of his influence as a science fiction writer and was producing his best work in that category with stories such as the famous "Sandkings," his best-known story, which won both the Nebula and the

Hugo in 1980 (he'd later win another Nebula in 1985 for his story "Portraits of His Children"), "The Way of Cross and Dragon," which won a Hugo Award in the same year (making Martin the first author ever to receive two Hugo Awards for fiction in the same year), "Bitterblooms," "The Stone City," "Starlady," and others. These stories would be collected in *Sandkings*, one of the strongest collections of the period. By now, he had mostly moved away from *Analog*, although he would have a long sequence of stories about the droll interstellar adventures of Haviland Tuf (later collected in *Tuf Voyaging*) running throughout the '80s in the Stanley Schmidt *Analog*, as well as a few strong individual pieces such as the novella "Nightflyers"; most of his major work of the late '70s and early '80s, though, would appear in *Omni*. The late '70s and '80s also saw the publication of his memorable novel *Dying of the Light*, his only solo SF novel, while his stories were collected in *A Song for Lya, Sandkings, Songs of Stars and Shadows, Songs the Dead Men Sing, Nightflyers*, and *Portraits of His Children*. By the beginning of the '80s, he'd moved away from SF and into the horror genre, publishing the big horror novel *Fevre Dream* and winning the Bram Stoker Award for his horror story "The Pear-Shaped Man" and the World Fantasy Award for his werewolf novella "The Skin Trade." By the end of that decade, though, the crash of the horror market and the commercial failure of his ambitious horror novel *The Armageddon Rag* had driven him out of the print world and to a successful career in television instead, where for more than a decade he worked as story editor or producer on such shows as the new *Twilight Zone* and *Beauty and the Beast*.

After years away, Martin made a triumphant return to the print world in 1996 with the publication of the immensely successful fantasy novel *A Game of Thrones*, the start of his Song of Ice and Fire sequence. A free-standing novella taken from that work, "Blood of the Dragon," won Martin another Hugo Award in 1997. Further books in the Song of Ice and Fire series, *A Clash of Kings, A Storm of Swords, A Feast for Crows*, and forthcoming *A Dance with Dragons*, have made it one of the most popular, acclaimed, and bestselling series in all of modern fantasy. His most recent books are a massive retrospective collection spanning the entire spectrum of his career, *GRRM: A RRetrospective*; a novella collection, *Starlady and Fast-Friend*; a novel written in collaboration with Gardner Dozois and Daniel Abraham, *Hunter's Run*; and, as editor, three new volumes in his long-running Wild Cards anthology series, *Busted Flush, Inside Straight*, and *Suicide Kings*.

Martin first introduced the baseborn "Hedge Knight," Ser Duncan the Tall, and his squire, Egg, in his novella "The Hedge Knight," a finalist for the World Fantasy Award. The two characters became wildly popular and returned for further adventures in "The Sworn Sword." In the vivid and hugely entertaining novella that follows, Martin takes Dunk and Egg on a further adventure, as they participate in a sinister tourney where absolutely nothing is as it seems—including Dunk and Egg!

The "Dunk and Egg" stories have recently been published in graphic novel form as *The Hedge Knight* and *The Hedge Knight II: Sworn Sword*.

The Mystery Knight

A Tale of the Seven Kingdoms

A light summer rain was falling as Dunk and Egg took their leave of Stoney Sept.

Dunk rode his old warhorse Thunder, with Egg beside him on the spirited young palfrey he'd named Rain, leading their mule Maester. On Maester's back were bundled Dunk's armor and Egg's books, their bedrolls, tent, and clothing, several slabs of hard salt beef, half a flagon of mead, and two skins of water. Egg's old straw hat, wide-brimmed and floppy, kept the rain off the mule's head. The boy had cut holes for Maester's ears. Egg's new straw hat was on his own head. Except for the ear holes, the two hats looked much the same to Dunk.

As they neared the town gates, Egg reined up sharply. Up above the gateway, a traitor's head had been impaled upon an iron spike. It was fresh from the look of it, the flesh more pink than green, but the carrion crows had already gone to work on it. The dead man's lips and cheeks were torn and ragged; his eyes were two brown holes weeping slow red tears as raindrops mingled with the crusted blood. The dead man's mouth sagged open, as if to harangue travelers passing through the gate below.

Dunk had seen such sights before. "Back in King's Landing when I was a boy, I stole a head right off its spike once," he told Egg. Actually it had been Ferret who scampered up the wall to snatch the head, after Rafe and Pudding said he'd never dare, but when the guards came running he'd tossed it down, and Dunk was the one who'd caught it. "Some rebel lord or robber knight, it was. Or maybe just a common murderer. A head's a head. They all look the same after a few days on a spike." Him and his three friends had used the head to terrorize the girls of Flea Bottom. They'd chase them through the alleys and make them give the head a kiss before they'd let them go. That head got kissed a lot, as he recalled. There wasn't a girl in King's Landing who could run as fast as Rafe. Egg was better off not hearing that part, though. *Ferret, Rafe, and Pudding. Little monsters, those three, and me the worst of all.* His friends and he had kept the head until the flesh turned black and began to slough away. That took the fun out of chasing girls, so one night they burst into a pot shop and tossed what was left into the kettle. "The crows always go for the eyes," he told Egg. "Then the cheeks cave in, the flesh turns green. . . ." He squinted. "Wait. I know that face."

"You do, ser," said Egg. "Three days ago. The hunchbacked septon we heard preaching against Lord Bloodraven."

He remembered then. *He was a holy man sworn to the Seven, even if he did preach treason.* "His hands are scarlet with a brother's blood, and the blood of his young nephews too," the hunchback had declared to the crowd that had gathered in the market square. "A shadow came at his command to strangle brave Prince Valarr's sons in their mother's womb. Where is our Young Prince now? Where is his brother, sweet Matarys? Where has Good King Daeron gone, and fearless Baelor Breakspear? The grave has claimed them, every one, yet he endures, this pale bird with bloody beak who perches on King Aerys's shoulder and caws into his ear. The mark of hell is on his face and in his empty eye, and he has brought us drought and pestilence and murder. Rise up, I say, and remember our true king across the water. Seven gods there are, and seven kingdoms, and the Black Dragon sired seven sons! Rise up, my lords and ladies. Rise up, you brave knights and sturdy yeomen, and cast down Bloodraven, that foul sorcerer, lest your children and your children's children be cursed forevermore."

Every word was treason. Even so, it was a shock to see him here, with holes where his eyes had been. "That's him, aye," Dunk said, "and another good reason to put this town behind us." He gave Thunder a touch of the spur, and he and Egg rode through the gates of Stoney Sept, listening to the soft sound of the rain. *How many eyes does Lord Bloodraven have?* the riddle ran. *A thousand eyes, and one.* Some claimed the King's Hand was a student of the dark arts who could change his face, put on the likeness of a one-eyed dog, even turn into a mist. Packs of gaunt gray wolves hunted down his foes, men said, and carrion crows spied for him and whispered secrets in his ear. Most of the tales were only tales, Dunk did not doubt, but no one could doubt that Bloodraven had informers everywhere.

He had seen the man once with his own two eyes, back in King's Landing. White as bone were the skin and hair of Brynden Rivers, and his eye—he had only the one, the other having been lost to his half brother Bittersteel on the Redgrass Field—was red as blood. On cheek and neck he bore the wine-stain birthmark that had given him his name.

When the town was well behind them, Dunk cleared his throat and said, "Bad business, cutting off the heads of septons. All he did was talk. Words are wind."

"Some words are wind, ser. Some are treason." Egg was skinny as a stick, all ribs and elbows, but he did have a mouth.

"Now you sound a proper princeling."

Egg took that for an insult, which it was. "He might have been a septon, but he was preaching lies, ser. The drought wasn't Lord Bloodraven's fault, nor the Great Spring Sickness either."

"Might be that's so, but if we start cutting off the heads of all the fools and liars, half the towns in the Seven Kingdoms will be empty."

Six days later, the rain was just a memory.

Dunk had stripped off his tunic to enjoy the warmth of sunlight on his skin. When a little breeze came up, cool and fresh and fragrant as a maiden's breath, he sighed. "Water," he announced. "Smell it? The lake can't be far now."

"All I can smell is Maester, ser. He stinks." Egg gave the mule's lead a savage tug. Maester had stopped to crop at the grass beside the road, as he did from time to time.

"There's an old inn by the lakeshore." Dunk had stopped there once when he was squiring for the old man. "Ser Arlan said they brewed a fine brown ale. Might be we could have a taste while we waited for the ferry."

Egg gave him a hopeful look. "To wash the food down, ser?"

"What food would that be?"

"A slice off the roast?" the boy said. "A bit of duck, a bowl of stew? Whatever they have, ser."

Their last hot meal had been three days ago. Since then, they had been living on windfalls and strips of old salt beef as hard as wood. *It would be good to put some real food in our bellies before we started north. That Wall's a long way off.*

"We could spend the night as well," suggested Egg.

"Does m'lord want a feather bed?"

"Straw will serve me well enough, ser," said Egg, offended.

"We have no coin for beds."

"We have twenty-two pennies, three stars, one stag, and that old chipped garnet, ser."

Dunk scratched at his ear. "I thought we had two silvers."

"We did, until you bought the tent. Now we have the one."

"We won't have any if we start sleeping at inns. You want to share a bed with some peddler and wake up with his fleas?" Dunk snorted. "Not me. I have my own fleas, and they are not fond of strangers. We'll sleep beneath the stars."

"The stars are good," Egg allowed, "but the ground is hard, ser, and sometimes it's nice to have a pillow for your head."

"Pillows are for princes." Egg was as good a squire as a knight could want, but every so often he would get to feeling princely. *The lad has dragon blood, never forget.* Dunk had beggar's blood himself . . . or so they used to tell him back in Flea Bottom, when they weren't telling him that he was sure to hang. "Might be we can afford some ale and a hot supper, but I'm not wasting good coin on a bed. We need to save our pennies for the ferryman." The last time he had crossed the lake, the ferry cost only a few coppers, but that had been six years ago, or maybe seven. Everything had grown more costly since then.

"Well," said Egg, "we could use my boot to get across."

"We could," said Dunk, "but we won't." Using the boot was dangerous. *Word would spread. Word always spreads.* His squire was not bald by chance. Egg had the purple eyes of old Valyria, and hair that shone like beaten gold and strands of silver woven together. He might as well wear a three-headed dragon as a brooch as let that hair grow out. These were perilous times in Westeros, and . . . well, it was best to take no chances. "Another word about your bloody boot, and I'll clout you in the ear so hard you'll *fly* across the lake."

"I'd sooner swim, ser." Egg swam well, and Dunk did not. The boy turned in the saddle. "Ser? Someone's coming up the road behind us. Hear the horses?"

"I'm not deaf." Dunk could see their dust as well. "A large party. And in haste."

"Do you think they might be outlaws, ser?" Egg raised up in the stirrups, more eager than afraid. The boy was like that.

"Outlaws would be quieter. Only lords make so much noise." Dunk rattled his sword hilt to loosen the blade in its scabbard. "Still, we'll get off the road and let them pass. There are lords and lords." It never hurt to be a little wary. The roads were not so safe as when Good King Daeron sat the Iron Throne.

He and Egg concealed themselves behind a thornbush. Dunk unslung his shield and slipped it onto his arm. It was an old thing, tall and heavy, kite-shaped, made of pine and rimmed with iron. He had bought it in Stoney Sept to replace the shield the Longinch had hacked to splinters when they fought. Dunk had not had time to have it painted with his elm and shooting star, so it still bore the arms of its last owner: a hanged man swinging grim and gray beneath a gallows tree. It was not a sigil that he would have chosen for himself, but the shield had come cheap.

The first riders galloped past within moments; two young lordlings mounted on a pair of coursers. The one on the bay wore an open-faced helm of gilded steel with three tall feathered plumes: one white, one red, one gold. Matching plumes adorned his horse's crinet. The black stallion beside him was barded in blue and gold. His trappings rippled with the wind of his passage as he thundered past. Side by side the riders streaked on by, whooping and laughing, their long cloaks streaming behind.

A third lord followed more sedately, at the head of a long column. There were two dozen in the party, grooms and cooks and serving men, all to attend three knights, plus men-at-arms and mounted crossbowmen, and a dozen drays heavy-laden with their armor, tents, and provisions. Slung from the lord's saddle was his shield, dark orange and charged with three black castles.

Dunk knew those arms, but from where? The lord who bore them was an older man, sour-mouthed and saturnine, with a close-cropped salt-and-pepper beard. *He might have been at Ashford Meadow,* Dunk thought. *Or maybe we served at his castle when I was squiring for Ser Arlan.* The old hedge knight had done service at so many different keeps and castles through the years that Dunk could not recall the half of them.

The lord reined up abruptly, scowling at the thornbush. "You. In the bush. Show yourself." Behind him, two crossbowmen slipped quarrels into the notch. The rest continued on their way.

Dunk stepped through the tall grass, his shield upon his arm, his right hand resting on the pommel of his longsword. His face was a red-brown mask from the dust the horses had kicked up, and he was naked from the waist up. He looked a scruffy sight, he knew, though it was like to be the size of him that gave the other pause. "We want no quarrel, m'lord. There's only the two of us, me and my squire." He beckoned Egg forward.

"Squire? Do you claim to be a knight?"

Dunk did not like the way the man was looking at him. *Those eyes could flay a man.* It seemed prudent to remove his hand from his sword. "I am a hedge knight, seeking service."

"Every robber knight I've ever hanged has said the same. Your device may be prophetic, ser . . . if *ser* you are. A gallows and a hanged man. These are your arms?"

"No, m'lord. I need to have the shield repainted."

"Why? Did you rob it off a corpse?"

"I bought it, for good coin." *Three castles, black on orange . . . where have I seen those before?* "I am no robber."

The lord's eyes were chips of flint. "How did you come by that scar upon your cheek? A cut from a whip?"

"A dagger. Though my face is none of your concern, m'lord."

"I'll be the judge of what is my concern."

By then, the two younger knights had come trotting back to see what had delayed their party. "There you are, Gormy," called the rider on the black, a young man lean and lithe, with a comely, clean-shaven face and fine features. Black hair fell shining to his collar. His doublet was made of dark blue silk edged in gold satin. Across his chest an engrailed cross had been embroidered in gold thread, with a golden fiddle in the first and third quarters, a golden sword in the second and the fourth. His eyes caught the deep blue of his doublet and sparkled with amusement. "Alyn feared you'd fallen from your horse. A palpable excuse, it seems to me; I was about to leave him in my dust."

"Who are these two brigands?" asked the rider on the bay.

Egg bristled at the insult: "You have no call to name us brigands, my lord. When we saw your dust, we thought *you* might be outlaws—that's the only reason that we hid. This is Ser Duncan the Tall, and I'm his squire."

The lordlings paid no more heed to that than they would have paid the croaking of a frog. "I believe that is the largest lout that I have ever seen," declared the knight of three feathers. He had a pudgy face beneath a head of curly hair the color of dark honey. "Seven feet if he's an inch, I'd wager. What a mighty crash he'll make when he comes tumbling down."

Dunk felt color rising to his face. *You'd lose your wager,* he thought. The last time he had been measured, Egg's brother Aemon pronounced him an inch shy of seven feet.

"Is that your warhorse, Ser Giant?" said the

feathered lordling. "I suppose we could butcher it for the meat."

"Lord Alyn oft forgets his courtesies," the black-haired knight said. "Please forgive his churlish words, ser. Alyn, you will ask Ser Duncan for his pardon."

"If I must. Will you forgive me, ser?" He did not wait for reply, but turned his bay about and trotted down the road.

The other lingered. "Are you bound for the wedding, ser?"

Something in his tone made Dunk want to tug his forelock. He resisted the impulse and said, "We're for the ferry, m'lord."

"As are we . . . but the only lords hereabouts are Gormy and that wastrel who just left us, Alyn Cockshaw. I am a vagabond hedge knight like yourself. Ser John the Fiddler, I am called."

That was the sort of name a hedge knight might choose, but Dunk had never seen any hedge knight garbed or armed or mounted in such splendor. *The knight of the golden hedge*, he thought. "You know my name. My squire is called Egg."

"Well met, ser. Come, ride with us to Whitewalls and break a few lances to help Lord Butterwell celebrate his new marriage. I'll wager you could give a good account of yourself."

Dunk had not done any jousting since Ashford Meadow. *If I could win a few ransoms, we'd eat well on the ride north*, he thought, but the lord with the three castles on his shield said, "Ser Duncan needs to be about his journey, as do we."

John the Fiddler paid the older man no mind. "I would love to cross swords with you, ser. I've tried men of many lands and races, but never one your size. Was your father large as well?"

"I never knew my father, ser."

"I am sad to hear it. Mine own sire was taken from me too soon." The Fiddler turned to the lord of the three castles. "We should ask Ser Duncan to join our jolly company."

"We do not need his sort."

Dunk was at a loss for words. Penniless hedge knights were not oft asked to ride with highborn lords. *I would have more in common with their servants.* Judging from the length of their column, Lord Cockshaw and the Fiddler had brought grooms to tend their horses, cooks to feed them, squires to clean their armor, guards to defend them. Dunk had Egg.

"His sort?" The Fiddler laughed. "What sort is that? The big sort? Look at the *size* of him. We want strong men. Young swords are worth more than old names, I've oft heard it said."

"By fools. You know little and less about this man. He might be a brigand, or one of Lord Bloodraven's spies."

"I'm no man's spy," said Dunk. "And m'lord has no call to speak of me as if I were deaf or dead or down in Dorne."

Those flinty eyes considered him. "Down in Dorne would be a good place for you, ser. You have my leave to go there."

"Pay him no mind," the Fiddler said. "He's a

sour old soul—he suspects everyone. Gormy, I have a good feeling about this fellow. Ser Duncan, will you come with us to Whitewalls?"

"M'lord, I . . ." How could he share a camp with such as these? Their serving men would raise their pavilions, their grooms would curry their horses, their cooks would serve them each a capon or a joint of beef, whilst Dunk and Egg gnawed on strips of hard salt beef. "I couldn't."

"You see," said the lord of the three castles. "He knows his place, and it is not with us." He turned his horse back toward the road. "By now Lord Cockshaw is half a league ahead."

"I suppose I must chase him down again." The Fiddler gave Dunk an apologetic smile. "Perchance we'll meet again someday. I hope so. I should love to try my lance on you."

Dunk did not know what to say to that. "Good fortune in the lists, ser," he finally managed, but by then Ser John had wheeled about to chase the column. The older lord rode after him. Dunk was glad to see his back. He had not liked his flinty eyes, nor Lord Alyn's arrogance. The Fiddler had been pleasant enough, but there was something odd about him as well. "Two fiddles and two swords, a cross engrailed," he said to Egg as they watched the dust of their departure. "What house is that?"

"None, ser. I never saw that shield in any roll of arms."

Perhaps he is a hedge knight after all. Dunk had devised his own arms at Ashford Meadow, when a puppeteer called Tanselle Too-Tall asked him what he wanted painted on his shield. "Was the older lord some kin to House Frey?" The Freys bore castles on their shields, and their holdings were not far from here.

Egg rolled his eyes. "The Frey arms are two blue *towers* connected by a bridge, on a gray field. Those were three *castles*, black on orange, ser. Did you see a bridge?"

"No." *He just does that to annoy me.* "And next time you roll your eyes at me, I'll clout you on the ear so hard they'll roll back into your head for good."

Egg looked chastened. "I never meant—"

"Never mind what you meant. Just tell me who he was."

"Gormon Peake, the Lord of Starpike."

"That's down in the Reach, isn't it? Does he really have three castles?"

"Only on his shield, ser. House Peake did hold three castles once, but two of them were lost."

"How do you lose two castles?"

"You fight for the Black Dragon, ser."

"Oh." Dunk felt stupid. *That again.*

For two hundred years, the realm had been ruled by the descendants of Aegon the Conquerer and his sisters, who had made the Seven Kingdoms one and forged the Iron Throne. Their royal banners bore the three-headed dragon of House Targaryen, red on black. Sixteen years ago, a bastard son of King Aegon IV named Daemon Blackfyre had risen in revolt against his trueborn brother. Daemon had used the three-headed dragon on his banners too, but he reversed the colors, as many bastards did. His revolt had ended on the Redgrass Field, where Daemon and his twin sons died beneath a rain of Lord Bloodraven's arrows. Those rebels who survived and bent the knee were pardoned, but some lost land, some titles, some gold. All gave hostages to ensure their future loyalty.

Three castles, black on orange. "I remember now. Ser Arlan never liked to talk about the Redgrass Field, but once in his cups he told me how his sister's son had died." He could almost hear the old man's voice again, smell the wine upon his breath. "Roger of Pennytree, that was his name. His head was smashed in by a mace wielded by a lord with three castles on his shield." *Lord Gormon Peake. The old man never knew his name. Or never wanted to.* By that time Lord Peake and John the Fiddler and their party were no more than a plume of red dust in the distance. *It was sixteen years ago. The Pretender died, and those who followed him were exiled or forgiven. Anyway, it has nought to do with me.*

For a while they rode along without talking, listening to the plaintive cries of birds. Half a league on, Dunk cleared his throat and said, "Butterwell, he said. His lands are near?"

"On the far side of the lake, ser. Lord Butterwell was the master of coin when King Aegon sat the Iron Throne. King Daeron made him Hand, but not for long. His arms are undy green and white and yellow, ser." Egg loved showing off his heraldry.

"Is he a friend of your father?"

Egg made a face. "My father never liked him. In the Rebellion, Lord Butterwell's second son fought for the pretender and his eldest for the king. That way he was certain to be on the winning side. Lord Butterwell didn't fight for anyone."

"Some might call that prudent."

"My father calls it craven."

Aye, he would. Prince Maekar was a hard man, proud and full of scorn. "We have to go by Whitewalls to reach the kingsroad. Why not fill our bellies?" Just the thought was enough to cause his guts to rumble. "Might be that one of the wedding guests will need an escort back to his own seat."

"You said that we were going north."

"The Wall has stood eight thousand years, it will last awhile longer. It's a thousand leagues from here to there, and we could do with some more silver in our purse." Dunk was picturing himself atop Thunder, riding down that sour-faced old lord with the three castles on his shield. That would be sweet. *"It was old Ser Arlan's squire who defeated you," I could tell him when he came to ransom back his arms and armor. "The boy who replaced the boy you killed." The old man would like that.*

"You're not thinking of entering the lists, are you, ser?

"Might be it's time."

"It's not, ser."

"Maybe it's time I gave you a good clout in the ear." *I'd only need to win two tilts. If I could collect two ransoms and pay out only one, we'd eat like kings for a year.* "If there was a melee, I might enter that." Dunk's size and strength would serve him better in a melee than in the lists.

"It's not customary to have a melee at a marriage, ser."

"It's customary to have a feast, though. We have a long way to go. Why not set out with our bellies full for once?"

The sun was low in the west by the time they saw the lake, its waters glimmering red and gold, bright as a sheet of beaten copper. When they glimpsed the turrets of the inn above some willows, Dunk donned his sweaty tunic once again and stopped to splash some water on his face. He washed off the dust of the road as best he could, and ran wet fingers through his thick mop of sun-streaked hair. There was nothing to be done for his size, or the scar that marked his cheek, but he wanted to make himself appear somewhat less the wild robber knight.

The inn was bigger than he'd expected, a great gray sprawl of a place, timbered and turreted, half of it built on pilings out over the water. A road of rough-cut planks had been laid down over the muddy lakeshore to the ferry landing, but neither the ferry nor the ferrymen were in evidence. Across the road stood a stable with a thatched roof. A dry stone wall enclosed the yard, but the gate was open. Within, they found a well and a watering trough. "See to the animals," Dunk told Egg, "but see that they don't drink too much. I'll ask about some food."

He found the innkeep sweeping off the steps. "Are you come for the ferry?" the woman asked him. "You're too late. The sun's going down, and Ned don't like to cross by night unless the moon is full. He'll be back first thing in the morning."

"Do you know how much he asks?"

"Three pennies for each of you, and ten for your horses."

"We have two horses and a mule."

"It's ten for mules as well."

Dunk did the sums in his head, and came up with six-and-thirty, more than he had hoped to spend. "Last time I came this way, it was only two pennies, and six for horses."

"Take that up with Ned, it's nought to me. If you're looking for a bed, I've none to offer. Lord Shawney and Lord Costayne brought their retinues. I'm full to bursting."

"Is Lord Peake here as well?" *He killed Ser Arlan's squire.* "He was with Lord Cockshaw and John the Fiddler."

"Ned took them across on his last run." She looked Dunk up and down. "Were you part of their company?"

"We met them on the road, is all." A good smell was drifting out the windows of the inn, one that made Dunk's mouth water. "We might like some of what you're roasting, if it's not too costly."

"It's wild boar," the woman said, "well peppered, and served with onions, mushrooms, and mashed neeps."

"We could do without the neeps. Some slices off the boar and a tankard of your good brown ale would do for us. How much would you ask for that? And maybe we could have a place on your stable floor to bed down for the night?"

That was a mistake. "The stables are for horses. That's why we call them stables. You're big as a horse, I'll grant you, but I see only two legs." She swept her broom at him, to shoo him off. "I can't be expected to feed all the Seven Kingdoms. The boar is for my guests. So is my ale. I won't have lords saying that I run short of food or drink before they were surfeit. The lake is full of fish, and you'll find some other rogues camped down by the stumps. Hedge knights, if you believe them." Her tone made it quite clear that she did not. "Might be they'd have food to share. It's nought to me. Away with you now, I've work to do." The door closed with a solid thump behind her, before Dunk could even think to ask where he might find these stumps.

He found Egg sitting on the horse trough, soaking his feet in the water and fanning his face with his big floppy hat. "Are they roasting pig, ser? I smell pork."

"Wild boar," said Dunk in a glum tone, "but who wants boar when we have good salt beef?"

Egg made a face. "Can I please eat my boots instead, ser? I'll make a new pair out of the salt beef. It's tougher."

"No," said Dunk, trying not to smile. "You can't eat your boots. One more word and you'll eat my fist, though. Get your feet out of that trough." He found his greathelm on the mule and slung it underhand at Egg. "Draw some water from the well and soak the beef." Unless you soaked it for a good long time, the salt beef was like to break your teeth. It tasted best when soaked in ale, but water would serve. "Don't use the trough either, I don't care to taste your feet."

"My feet could only improve the taste, ser," Egg said, wriggling his toes. But he did as he was bid.

The hedge knights did not prove hard to find. Egg spied their fire flickering in the woods along the lakeshore, so they made for it, leading the animals behind them. The boy carried Dunk's helm beneath one arm, sloshing with each step he took. By then the sun was a red memory in the west. Before long the trees opened up, and they found themselves in what must once have been a weirwood grove. Only a ring of white stumps and a tangle of bone-pale roots remained to show where the trees had stood, when the children of the forest ruled in Westeros.

Amongst the weirwood stumps, they found two men squatting near a cook fire, passing a skin of wine from hand to hand. Their horses were cropping at the grass beyond the grove, and they had stacked their arms and armor in neat piles. A much younger man sat apart from the other two, his back against a chestnut tree. "Well met, sers," Dunk called out in a cheerful voice. It was never wise to take armed men unawares. "I am called Ser Duncan the Tall. The lad is Egg. May we share your fire?"

A stout man of middling years rose to greet them, garbed in tattered finery. Flamboyant ginger whiskers framed his face. "Well met, Ser Duncan. You are a large one . . . and most welcome, certainly, as is your lad. *Egg*, was it? What sort of name is that, pray?"

"A short one, ser." Egg knew better than to admit that Egg was short for Aegon. Not to men he did not know.

"Indeed. What happened to your hair?"

Rootworms, Dunk thought. *Tell him it was rootworms, boy.* That was the safest story, the tale they told most often . . . though sometimes Egg took it in his head to play some childish game.

"I shaved it off, ser. I mean to stay shaven until I earn my spurs."

"A noble vow. I am Ser Kyle, the Cat of Misty Moor. Under yonder chestnut sits Ser Glendon, ah, Ball. And here you have the good Ser Maynard Plumm."

Egg's ears pricked up at that name. "Plumm . . . are you kin to Lord Viserys Plumm, ser?"

"Distantly," confessed Ser Maynard, a tall, thin, stoop-shouldered man with long straight flaxen hair, "though I doubt that His Lordship would admit to it. One might say that he is of the sweet Plumms, whilst I am of the sour." Plumm's cloak was as purple as his name, though frayed about the edges and badly dyed. A moonstone brooch big as a hen's egg fastened it at the shoulder. Elsewise he wore dun-colored roughspun and stained brown leather.

"We have salt beef," said Dunk.

"Ser Maynard has a bag of apples," said Kyle the Cat. "And I have pickled eggs and onions. Why, together we have the makings of a feast! Be seated, ser. We have a fine choice of stumps for your comfort. We will be here until midmorning, unless I miss my guess. There is only the one ferry, and it is not big enough to take us all. The lords and their tails must cross first."

"Help me with the horses," Dunk told Egg. Together the two of them unsaddled Thunder, Rain, and Maester.

Only when the animals had been fed and watered and hobbled for the night did Dunk accept the wineskin that Ser Maynard offered him. "Even sour wine is better than none," said Kyle the Cat. "We'll drink finer vintages at Whitewalls. Lord Butterwell is said to have the best wines north of the Arbor. He was once the King's Hand, as his father's father was before him, and he is said to be a pious man besides, and very rich."

"His wealth is all from cows," said Maynard Plumm. "He ought to take a swollen udder for his arms. These Butterwells have milk running in their veins, and the Freys are no better. This will be a marriage of cattle thieves and toll collectors, one lot of coin clinkers joining with another. When the

Black Dragon rose, this lord of cows sent one son to Daemon and one to Daeron, to make certain there was a Butterwell on the winning side. Both perished on the Redgrass Field, and his youngest died in the spring. That's why he's making this new marriage. Unless this new wife gives him a son, Butterwell's name will die with him."

"As it should." Ser Glendon Ball gave his sword another stroke with the whetstone. "The Warrior hates cravens."

The scorn in his voice made Dunk give the youth a closer look. Ser Glendon's clothes were of good cloth, but well-worn and ill-matched, with the look of hand-me-downs. Tufts of dark brown hair stuck out from beneath his iron halfhelm. The lad himself was short and chunky, with small close-set eyes, thick shoulders, and muscular arms. His eyebrows were shaggy as two caterpillars after a wet spring, his nose bulbous, his chin pugnacious. And he was young. *Sixteen, might be. No more than eighteen.* Dunk might have taken him for a squire if Ser Kyle had not named him with a *ser.* The lad had pimples on his cheeks in place of whiskers.

"How long have you been a knight?" Dunk asked him.

"Long enough. Half a year when the moon turns. I was knighted by Ser Morgan Dunstable of Tumbler's Falls, two dozen people saw it, but I have been training for knighthood since I was born. I rode before I walked, and knocked a grown man's tooth out of his head before I lost any of my own. I mean to make my name at Whitewalls, and claim the dragon's egg."

"The dragon's egg? Is that the champion's prize? Truly?" The last dragon had perished half a century ago. Ser Arlan had once seen a clutch of her eggs, though. *They were hard as stone, he said, but beautiful to look upon,* the old man had told Dunk. "How could Lord Butterwell come by a dragon's egg?"

"King Aegon presented the egg to his father's father after guesting for a night at his old castle," said Ser Maynard Plumm.

"Was it a reward for some act of valor?" asked Dunk.

Ser Kyle chuckled. "Some might call it that. Supposedly old Lord Butterwell had three young maiden daughters when His Grace came calling. By morning, all three had royal bastards in their little bellies. A hot night's work, that was."

Dunk had heard such talk before. Aegon the Unworthy had bedded half the maidens in the realm and fathered bastards on the lot of them, supposedly. Worse, the old king had legitimized them all upon his deathbed; the baseborn ones born of tavern wenches, whores, and shepherd girls, and the Great Bastards whose mothers had been highborn. "We'd all be bastard sons of old King Aegon if half these tales were true."

"And who's to say we're not?" Ser Maynard quipped.

"You ought to come with us to Whitewalls, Ser

Duncan," urged Ser Kyle. "Your size is sure to catch some lordling's eye. You might find good service there. I know I shall. Joffrey Caswell will be at this wedding, the Lord of Bitterbridge. When he was three, I made him his first sword. I carved it out of pine, to fit his hand. In my greener days my sword was sworn to his father."

"Was that one carved from pine as well?" Ser Maynard asked.

Kyle the Cat had the grace to laugh. "That sword was good steel, I assure you. I should be glad to ply it once again in the service of the centaur. Ser Duncan, even if you do not choose to tilt, do join us for the wedding feast. There will be singers and musicians, jugglers and tumblers, and a troupe of comic dwarfs."

Dunk frowned. "Egg and I have a long journey before us. We're headed north to Winterfell. Lord Beron Stark is gathering swords to drive the krakens from his shores for good."

"Too cold up there for me," said Ser Maynard. "If you want to kill krakens, go west. The Lannisters are building ships to strike back at the ironmen on their home islands. That's how you put an end to Dagon Greyjoy. Fighting him on land is fruitless, he just slips back to sea. You have to beat him on the water."

That had the ring of truth, but the prospect of fighting ironmen at sea was not one that Dunk relished. He'd had a taste of that on the *White Lady*, sailing from Dorne to Oldtown, when he'd donned his armor to help the crew repel some raiders. The battle had been desperate and bloody, and once he'd almost fallen in the water. That would have been the end of him.

"The throne should take a lesson from Stark and Lannister," declared Ser Kyle the Cat. "At least they fight. What do the Targaryens do? King Aerys hides amongst his books, Prince Rhaegel prances naked through the Red Keep's halls, and Prince Maekar broods at Summerhall."

Egg was prodding at the fire with a stick, to send sparks floating up into the night. Dunk was pleased to see him ignoring the mention of his father's name. *Perhaps he's finally learned to hold that tongue of his.*

"Myself, I blame Bloodraven," Ser Kyle went on. "He is the King's Hand, yet he does nothing, whilst the krakens spread flame and terror up and down the sunset sea."

Ser Maynard gave a shrug. "His eye is fixed on Tyrosh, where Bittersteel sits in exile, plotting with the sons of Daemon Blackfyre. So he keeps the king's ships close at hand, lest they attempt to cross."

"Aye, that may well be," Ser Kyle said, "but many would welcome the return of Bittersteel. Bloodraven is the root of all our woes, the white worm gnawing at the heart of the realm."

Dunk frowned, remembering the hunchbacked septon at Stoney Sept. "Words like that can cost a man his head. Some might say you're talking treason."

"How can the truth be treason?" asked Kyle the Cat. "In King Daeron's day, a man did not have to fear to speak his mind, but now?" He made a rude noise. "Bloodraven put King Aerys on the Iron Throne, but for how long? Aerys is weak, and when he dies, it will be bloody war between Lord Rivers and Prince Maekar for the crown, the Hand against the heir."

"You have forgotten Prince Rhaegel, my friend," Ser Maynard objected, in a mild tone. "He comes next in line to Aerys, not Maekar, and his children after him."

"Rhaegel is feeble-minded. Why, I bear him no ill will, but the man is good as dead, and those twins of his as well, though whether they will die of Maekar's mace or Bloodraven's spells . . ."

Seven save us, Dunk thought as Egg spoke up shrill and loud. "Prince Maekar is Prince Rhaegel's *brother*. He loves him well. He'd never do harm to him or his."

"Be quiet, boy," Dunk growled at him. "These knights want none of your opinions."

"I can talk if I want."

"No," said Dunk. "You can't." *That mouth of yours will get you killed someday. And me as well, most like.* "That salt beef's soaked long enough, I think. A strip for all our friends, and be quick about it."

Egg flushed, and for half a heartbeat, Dunk feared the boy might talk back. Instead he settled for a sullen look, seething as only a boy of eleven years can seethe. "Aye, ser," he said, fishing in the bottom of Dunk's helm. His shaven head shone redly in the firelight as he passed out the salt beef.

Dunk took his piece and worried at it. The soak had turned the meat from wood to leather, but that was all. He sucked on one corner, tasting the salt and trying not to think about the roast boar at the inn, crackling on its spit and dripping fat.

As dusk deepened, flies and stinging midges came swarming off the lake. The flies preferred to plague their horses, but the midges had a taste for man flesh. The only way to keep from being bitten was to sit close to the fire, breathing smoke. *Cook or be devoured*, Dunk thought glumly, *now there's a beggar's choice*. He scratched at his arms and edged closer to the fire.

The wineskin soon came round again. The wine was sour and strong. Dunk drank deep, and passed along the skin, whilst the Cat of Misty Moor began to talk of how he had saved the life of the Lord of Bitterbridge during the Blackfyre Rebellion. "When Lord Armond's banner-bearer fell, I leapt down from my horse with traitors all around us—"

"Ser," said Glendon Ball. "Who were these *traitors*?"

"The Blackfyre men, I meant."

Firelight glimmered off the steel in Ser Glendon's hand. The pockmarks on his face flamed as red as open sores, and his every sinew was wound as tight as a crossbow. "My father fought for the Black Dragon."

This again. Dunk snorted. *Red or Black?* was not a thing you asked a man. It always made for trouble. "I am sure Ser Kyle meant no insult to your father."

"None," Ser Kyle agreed. "It's an old tale, the Red Dragon and the Black. No sense for us to fight about it now, lad. We are all brothers of the hedges here."

Ser Glendon seemed to weigh the Cat's words, to see if he was being mocked. "Daemon Blackfyre was no traitor. The old king gave *him* the sword. He saw the worthiness in Daemon, even though he was born bastard. Why else would he put Blackfyre into his hand in place of Daeron's? He meant for him to have the kingdom too. Daemon was the better man."

A hush fell. Dunk could hear the soft crackle of the fire. He could feel midges crawling on the back of his neck. He slapped at them, watching Egg, willing him to be still. "I was just a boy when they fought the Redgrass Field," he said, when it seemed that no one else would speak, "but I squired for a knight who fought with the Red Dragon, and later served another who fought for the Black. There were brave men on both sides."

"Brave men," echoed Kyle the Cat, a bit feebly.

"Heroes." Glendon Ball turned his shield about, so all of them could see the sigil painted there, a fireball blazing red and yellow across a night-black field. "I come from hero's blood."

"You're *Fireball*'s son," Egg said.

That was the first time they saw Ser Glendon smile.

Ser Kyle the Cat studied the boy closely. "How can that be? How old are you? Quentyn Ball died—"

"—before I was born," Ser Glendon finished, "but in me, he lives again." He slammed his sword back into its scabbard. "I'll show you all at White-walls, when I claim the dragon's egg."

The next day proved the truth of Ser Kyle's prophecy. Ned's ferry was nowise large enough to accomodate all those who wished to cross, so Lords Costayne and Shawney must go first, with their tails. That required several trips, each taking more than an hour. There were the mudflats to contend with, horses and wagons to be gotten down the planks, loaded on the boat, and unloaded again across the lake. The two lords slowed matters even further when they got into a shouting match over precedence. Shawney was the elder, but Costayne held himself to be better born.

There was nought that Dunk could do but wait and swelter. "We could go first if you let me use my boot," Egg said.

"We could," Dunk answered, "but we won't. Lord Costayne and Lord Shawney were here before us. Besides, they're lords."

Egg made a face. "Rebel lords."

Dunk frowned down at him. "What do you mean?"

"They were for the Black Dragon. Well, Lord Shawney was, and Lord Costayne's father. Aemon and I used to fight the battle on Maester Mela-quin's green table with painted soldiers and little banners. Costayne's arms quarter a silver chalice on black with a black rose on gold. That banner was on the left of Daemon's host. Shawney was with Bittersteel on the right, and almost died of his wounds."

"Old dead history. They're here now, aren't they? So they bent the knee, and King Daeron gave them pardon."

"Yes, but—"

Dunk pinched the boy's lips shut. "Hold your tongue."

Egg held his tongue.

No sooner had the last boatload of Shawney men pushed off than Lord and Lady Smallwood turned up at the landing with their own tail, so they must needs wait again.

The fellowship of the hedge had not survived the night, it was plain to see. Ser Glendon kept his own company, prickly and sullen. Kyle the Cat judged that it would be midday before they were allowed to board the ferry, so he detached himself from the others to try to ingratiate himself with Lord Smallwood, with whom he had some slight acquaintance. Ser Maynard spent his time gossiping with the innkeep.

"Stay well away from that one," Dunk warned Egg. There was something about Plumm that troubled him. "He could be a robber knight, for all we know."

The warning only seemed to make Ser Maynard more interesting to Egg. "I never knew a robber knight. Do you think he means to rob the dragon's egg?"

"Lord Butterwell will have the egg well guarded, I'm sure." Dunk scratched the midge bites on his neck. "Do you think he might display it at the feast? I'd like to get a look at one."

"I'd show you mine, ser, but it's at Summerhall."

"Yours? Your *dragon's egg*?" Dunk frowned down at the boy, wondering if this was some jape. "Where did it come from?"

"From a dragon, ser. They put it in my cradle."

"Do you want a clout in the ear? There are no dragons."

"No, but there are eggs. The last dragon left a clutch of five, and they have more on Dragonstone, old ones from before the Dance. My brothers all have them too. Aerion's looks as though it's made of gold and silver, with veins of fire running through it. Mine is white and green, all swirly."

"Your dragon's egg." *They put it in his cradle.* Dunk was so used to Egg that sometimes he forgot Aegon was a prince. *Of course they'd put a dragon egg inside his cradle.* "Well, see that you don't go mentioning this egg where anyone is like to hear."

"I'm not *stupid*, ser." Egg lowered his voice. "Someday the dragons will return. My brother Daeron's dreamed of it, and King Aerys read it in a prophecy. Maybe it will be my egg that hatches. That would be *splendid*."

"Would it?" Dunk had his doubts.

Not Egg. "Aemon and I used to pretend that our eggs would be the ones to hatch. If they did, we could fly through the sky on dragonback, like the first Aegon and his sisters."

"Aye, and if all the other knights in the realm should die, I'd be the Lord Commander of the Kingsguard. If these eggs are so bloody precious, why is Lord Butterwell giving his away?"

"To show the realm how rich he is?"

"I suppose." Dunk scratched his neck again and glanced over at Ser Glendon Ball, who was tightening the cinches on his saddle as he waited for the ferry. *That horse will never serve.* Ser Glendon's mount was a swaybacked stot, undersized and old. "What do you know about his sire? Why did they call him Fireball?"

"For his hot head and red hair. Ser Quentyn Ball was the master-at-arms at the Red Keep. He taught my father and my uncles how to fight. The Great Bastards too. King Aegon promised to raise him to the Kingsguard, so Fireball made his wife join the silent sisters, only by the time a place came open, King Aegon was dead and King Daeron named Ser Willam Wylde instead. My father says that it was Fireball as much as Bittersteel who convinced Daemon Blackfyre to claim the crown, and rescued him when Daeron sent the Kingsguard to arrest him. Later on, Fireball killed Lord Lefford at the gates of Lannisport and sent the Grey Lion running back to hide inside the Rock. At the crossing of the Mander, he cut down the sons of Lady Penrose one by one. They say he spared the life of the youngest one as a kindness to his mother."

"That was chivalrous of him," Dunk had to admit. "Did Ser Quentyn die upon the Redgrass Field?"

"Before, ser," Egg replied. "An archer put an arrow through his throat as he dismounted by a stream to have a drink. Just some common man, no one knows who."

"Those common men can be dangerous when they get it in their heads to start slaying lords and heroes." Dunk saw the ferry creeping slowly across the lake. "Here it comes."

"It's slow. Are we going to go to Whitewalls, ser?"

"Why not? I want to see this dragon's egg." Dunk smiled. "If I win the tourney, we'd *both* have dragon's eggs."

Egg gave him a doubtful look.

"What? Why are you looking at me that way?"

"I could tell you, ser," the boy said solemnly, "but I need to learn to hold my tongue."

They seated the hedge knights well below the salt, closer to the doors than to the dais.

Whitewalls was almost new as castles went, having been raised a mere forty years ago by the grandsire of its present lord. The smallfolk hereabouts called it the Milkhouse, for its walls and keeps and towers were made of finely dressed white stone, quarried in the Vale and brought over the mountains at great expense. Inside were floors and pillars of milky white marble veined with gold;

the rafters overhead were carved from the bone-pale trunks of weirwoods. Dunk could not begin to imagine what all of that had cost.

The hall was not so large as some others he had known, though. *At least we were allowed beneath the roof,* Dunk thought as he took his place on the bench between Ser Maynard Plumm and Kyle the Cat. Though uninvited, the three of them had been welcomed to the feast quick enough; it was ill luck to refuse a knight hospitality on your wedding day.

Young Ser Glendon had a harder time, however. "Fireball never had a son," Dunk heard Lord Butterwell's steward tell him, loudly. The stripling answered heatedly, and the name of Ser Morgan Dunstable was mentioned several times, but the steward had remained adamant. When Ser Glendon touched his sword hilt, a dozen men-at-arms appeared with spears in hand, but for a moment it looked as though there might be bloodshed. It was only the intervention of a big blond knight named Kirby Pimm that saved the situation. Dunk was too far away to hear, but he saw Pimm clasp an arm around the steward's shoulders and murmur in his ear, laughing. The steward frowned, and said something to Ser Glendon that turned the boy's face dark red. *He looks as if he's about to cry,* Dunk thought, watching. *That, or kill someone.* After all of that, the young knight was finally admitted to the castle hall.

Poor Egg was not so fortunate. "The great hall is for the lords and knights," an understeward had informed them haughtily when Dunk tried to bring the boy inside. "We have set up tables in the inner yard for squires, grooms, and men-at-arms."

If you had an inkling who he was, you would seat him on the dais on a cushioned throne. Dunk had not much liked the look of the other squires. A few were lads of Egg's own age, but most were older, seasoned fighters who long ago had made the choice to serve a knight rather than become one. *Or did they have a choice?* Knighthood required more than chivalry and skill at arms; it required horse and sword and armor too, and all of that was costly. "Watch your tongue," he told Egg before he left him in that company. "These are grown men; they won't take kindly to your insolence. Sit and eat and listen, might be you'll learn some things."

For his own part, Dunk was just glad to be out of the hot sun, with a wine cup before him and a chance to fill his belly. Even a hedge knight grows weary of chewing every bite of food for half an hour. Down here below the salt, the fare would be more plain than fancy, but there would be no lack of it. Below the salt was good enough for Dunk.

But *peasant's pride is lordling's shame,* the old man used to say. "This cannot be my proper place," Ser Glendon Ball told the understeward hotly. He had donned a clean doublet for the feast, a handsome old garment with gold lace at the cuffs and collar and the red chevron and white plates of House Ball sewn across the chest. "Do you know who my father was?"

"A noble knight and mighty lord, I have no doubt," said the understeward, "but the same is true of many here. Please take your seat or take your leave, ser. It is all the same to me."

In the end, the boy took his place below the salt with the rest of them, his mouth sullen. The long white hall was filling up as more knights crowded onto the benches. The crowd was larger than Dunk had anticipated, and from the looks of it, some of the guests had come a very long way. He and Egg had not been around so many lords and knights since Ashford Meadow, and there was no way to guess who else might turn up next. *We should have stayed out in the hedges, sleeping under trees. If I am recognized . . .*

When a serving man placed a loaf of black bread on the cloth in front of each of them, Dunk was grateful for the distraction. He sawed the loaf open lengthwise, hollowed out the bottom half for a trencher, and ate the top. It was stale, but compared with his salt beef, it was custard. At least it did not have to be soaked in ale or milk or water to make it soft enough to chew.

"Ser Duncan, you appear to be attracting a deal of attention," Ser Maynard Plumm observed as Lord Vyrwel and his party went parading past them toward places of high honor at the top of the hall. "Those girls up on the dais cannot seem to take their eyes off you. I'll wager they have never seen a man so big. Even seated, you are half a head taller than any man in the hall."

Dunk hunched his shoulders. He was used to

being stared at, but that did not mean he liked it. "Let them look."

"That's the Old Ox down there beneath the dais," Ser Maynard said. "They call him a huge man, but seems to me his belly is the biggest thing about him. You're a bloody giant next to him."

"Indeed, ser," said one of their companions on the bench, a sallow man, saturnine, clad in grey and green. His eyes were small and shrewd, set close together beneath thin arching brows. A neat black beard framed his mouth, to make up for his receding hair. "In such a field as this, your size alone should make you one of the most formidable competitors."

"I had heard the Brute of Bracken might be coming," said another man, farther down the bench.

"I think not," said the man in green and grey. "This is only a bit of jousting to celebrate His Lordship's nuptials. A tilt in the yard to mark the tilt between the sheets. Hardly worth the bother for the likes of Otho Bracken."

Ser Kyle the Cat took a drink of wine. "I'll wager my lord of Butterwell does not take the field either. He will cheer on his champions from his lord's box in the shade."

"Then he'll see his champions fall," boasted Ser Glendon Ball, "and in the end, he'll hand his egg to me."

"Ser Glendon is the son of Fireball," Ser Kyle explained to the new man. "Might we have the honor of your name, ser?"

"Ser Uthor Underleaf. The son of no one of importance." Underleaf's garments were of good cloth, clean and well cared for, but simply cut. A silver clasp in the shape of a snail fastened his cloak. "If your lance is the equal of your tongue, Ser Glendon, you may even give this big fellow here a contest."

Ser Glendon glanced at Dunk as the wine was being poured. "If we meet, he'll fall. I don't care how big he is."

Dunk watched a server fill his wine cup. "I am better with a sword than with a lance," he admitted, "and even better with a battleaxe. Will there be a melee here?" His size and strength would stand him in good stead in a melee, and he knew he could give as good as he got. Jousting was another matter.

"A melee? At a marriage?" Ser Kyle sounded shocked. "That would be unseemly."

Ser Maynard gave a chuckle. "A marriage *is* a melee, as any married man could tell you."

Ser Uthor chuckled. "There's just the joust, I fear, but besides the dragon's egg, Lord Butterwell has promised thirty golden dragons for the loser of the final tilt, and ten each for the knights defeated in the round before."

Ten dragons is not so bad. Ten dragons would buy a palfrey, so Dunk would not need to ride Thunder save in battle. Ten dragons would buy a suit of plate for Egg, and a proper knight's pavilion sewn with Dunk's tree and falling star. *Ten dragons would mean roast goose and ham and pigeon pie.*

"There are ransoms to be had as well, for those who win their matches," Ser Uthor said as he hollowed out his trencher, "and I have heard it rumored that some men place wagers on the tilts. Lord Butterwell himself is not fond of taking risks, but amongst his guests are some who wager heavily."

No sooner had he spoken than Ambrose Butterwell made his entrance, to a fanfare of trumpets from the minstrel's gallery. Dunk shoved to his feet with the rest as Butterwell escorted his new bride down a patterned Myrish carpet to the dais, arm in arm. The girl was fifteen and freshly flowered, her lord husband fifty and freshly widowed. She was pink and he was grey. Her bride's cloak trailed behind her, done in undy green and white and yellow. It looked so hot and heavy that Dunk wondered how she could bear to wear it. Lord Butterwell looked hot and heavy too, with his heavy jowls and thinning flaxen hair.

The bride's father followed close behind her, hand in hand with his young son. Lord Frey of the Crossing was a lean man elegant in blue and grey, his heir a chinless boy of four whose nose was dripping snot. Lords Costayne and Risley came next, with their lady wives, daughters of Lord Butterwell by his first wife. Frey's daughters followed with their own husbands. Then came Lord Gormon Peake; Lords Smallwood, and Shawney; various lesser lords and landed knights. Amongst them Dunk glimpsed John the Fiddler and Alyn

Cockshaw. Lord Alyn looked to be in his cups, though the feast had not yet properly begun.

By the time all of them had sauntered to the dais, the high table was as crowded as the benches. Lord Butterwell and his bride sat on plump downy cushions in a double throne of gilded oak. The rest planted themselves in tall chairs with fancifully carved arms. On the wall behind them, two huge banners hung from the rafters: the twin towers of Frey, blue on grey, and the green and white and yellow undy of the Butterwells.

It fell to Lord Frey to lead the toasts. *"The king!"* he began simply. Ser Glendon held his wine cup out above the water basin. Dunk clanked his cup against it, and against Ser Uthor's and the rest as well. They drank.

"Lord Butterwell, our gracious host," Frey proclaimed next. "May the Father grant him long life and many sons."

They drank again.

"Lady Butterwell, the maiden bride, my darling daughter. May the Mother make her fertile." Frey gave the girl a smile. "I shall want a grandson before the year is out. Twins would suit me even better, so churn the butter well tonight, my sweet."

Laughter rang against the rafters, and the guests drank still once more. The wine was rich and red and sweet.

Then Lord Frey said, "I give you the King's Hand, Brynden Rivers. May the Crone's lamp light his path to wisdom." He lifted his goblet high and drank, together with Lord Butterwell and his bride and the others on the dais. Below the salt, Ser Glendon turned his cup over to spill its contents to the floor.

"A sad waste of good wine," said Maynard Plumm.

"I do not drink to kinslayers," said Ser Glendon. "Lord Bloodraven is a sorcerer and a bastard."

"Born bastard," Ser Uthor agreed mildly, "but his royal father made him legitimate as he lay dying." He drank deep, as did Ser Maynard and many others in the hall. Near as many lowered their cups, or turned them upside down as Ball had done. Dunk's own cup was heavy in his hand. *How many eyes does Lord Bloodraven have?* the riddle went. *A thousand eyes, and one.*

Toast followed toast, some proposed by Lord Frey and some by others. They drank to young Lord Tully, Lord Butterwell's liege lord, who had begged off from the wedding. They drank to the health of Leo Longthorn, Lord of Highgarden, who was rumored to be ailing. They drank to the memory of their gallant dead. *Aye*, thought Dunk, remembering. *I'll gladly drink to them.*

Ser John the Fiddler proposed the final toast. "*To my brave brothers!* I know that they are smiling tonight!"

Dunk had not intended to drink so much, with the jousting on the morrow, but the cups were filled anew after every toast, and he found he had a thirst. "Never refuse a cup of wine or a horn of ale," Ser Arlan had once told him, "it may be a year before you see another." *It would have been discourteous not to toast the bride and groom*, he told himself, *and dangerous not to drink to the king and his Hand, with strangers all about.*

Mercifully, the Fiddler's toast was the last. Lord Butterwell rose ponderously to thank them for coming and promise good jousting on the morrow. "Let the feast begin!"

Suckling pig was served at the high table, a peacock roasted in its plumage, a great pike crusted with crushed almonds. Not a bite of that made it down below the salt. Instead of suckling pig, they got salt pork, soaked in almond milk and peppered pleasantly. In place of peacock, they had capons, crisped up nice and brown and stuffed with onions, herbs, mushrooms, and roasted chestnuts. In place of pike, they ate chunks of flaky white cod in a pastry coffyn, with some sort of tasty brown sauce that Dunk could not quite place. There was pease porridge besides, buttered turnips, carrots drizzled with honey, and a ripe white cheese that smelled as strong as Bennis of the Brown Shield. Dunk ate well, but all the while wondered what Egg was getting in the yard. Just in case, he slipped half a capon into the pocket of his cloak, with some hunks of bread and a little of the smelly cheese.

As they ate, pipes and fiddles filled the air with spritely tunes, and the talk turned to the morrow's jousting. "Ser Franklyn Frey is well regarded along the Green Fork," said Uthor Underleaf, who seemed to know these local heroes well. "That's him upon the dais, the uncle of the bride. Lucas Nayland is down from Hag's Mire, he should not be discounted. Nor should Ser Mortimer Boggs, of Crackclaw Point. Elsewise, this should be a tourney of household knights and village heroes. Kirby Pimm and Galtry the Green are the best of those, though neither is a match for Lord Butterwell's good-son, Black Tom Heddle. A nasty bit of business, that one. He won the hand of His Lordship's eldest daughter by killing three of her other suitors, it's said, and once unhorsed the Lord of Casterly Rock."

"What, young Lord Tybolt?" asked Ser Maynard.

"No, the old Grey Lion, the one who died in the spring." That was how men spoke of those who had perished during the Great Spring Sickness. *He died in the spring.* Tens of thousands had died in the spring, among them a king and two young princes.

"Do not slight Ser Buford Bulwer," said Kyle the Cat. "The Old Ox slew forty men upon the Redgrass Field."

"And every year his count grows higher," said Ser Maynard. "Bulwer's day is done. Look at him. Past sixty, soft and fat, and his right eye is good as blind."

"Do not trouble to search the hall for the champion," a voice behind Dunk said. "Here I stand, sers. Feast your eyes."

Dunk turned to find Ser John the Fiddler looming over him, a half smile on his lips. His white silk doublet had dagged sleeves lined with red satin, so long their points drooped down past his knees. A heavy silver chain looped across his chest, studded with huge dark amethysts whose color matched his eyes. *That chain is worth as much as everything I own*, Dunk thought.

The wine had colored Ser Glendon's cheeks and inflamed his pimples. "Who are you, to make such boasts?"

"They call me John the Fiddler."

"Are you a musician or a warrior?"

"I can make sweet song with either lance or resined bow, as it happens. Every wedding needs a singer, and every tourney needs a mystery knight. May I join you? Butterwell was good enough to place me on the dais, but I prefer the company of my fellow hedge knights to fat pink ladies and old men." The Fiddler clapped Dunk upon the shoulder. "Be a good fellow and shove over, Ser Duncan."

Dunk shoved over. "You are too late for food, ser."

"No matter. I know where Butterwell's kitchens are. There is still some wine, I trust?" The Fiddler smelled of oranges and limes, with a hint of some strange eastern spice beneath. Nutmeg, perhaps. Dunk could not have said. What did he know of nutmeg?

"Your boasting is unseemly," Ser Glendon told the Fiddler.

"Truly? Then I must beg for your forgiveness, ser. I would never wish to give offense to any son of Fireball."

That took the youth aback. "You know who I am?"

"Your father's son, I hope."

"Look," said Ser Kyle the Cat. "The wedding pie."

Six kitchen boys were pushing it through the doors, upon a wide wheeled cart. The pie was brown and crusty and immense, and there were noises coming from inside it, squeaks and squawks and thumps. Lord and Lady Butterwell descended from the dais to meet it, sword in hand. When they cut it open, half a hundred birds burst forth to fly around the hall. In other wedding feasts Dunk had attended, the pies had been filled with doves or songbirds, but inside this one were blue-jays and skylarks, pigeons and doves, mocking-birds and nightingales, small brown sparrows and a great red parrot. "One-and-twenty sorts of birds," said Ser Kyle.

"One-and-twenty sorts of bird droppings," said Ser Maynard.

"You have no poetry in your heart, ser."

"You have shit upon your shoulder."

"This is the proper way to fill a pie," Ser Kyle sniffed, cleaning off his tunic. "The pie is meant to be the marriage, and a true marriage has in it many sorts of things—joy and grief, pain and pleasure, love and lust and loyalty. So it is fitting that there be birds of many sorts. No man ever truly knows what a new wife will bring him."

"Her cunt," said Plumm, "or what would be the point?"

Dunk shoved back from the table. "I need a breath of air." It was a piss he needed, truth be told, but in fine company like this, it was more courteous to talk of air. "Pray excuse me."

"Hurry back, ser," said the Fiddler. "There are jugglers yet to come, and you do not want to miss the bedding."

Outside, the night wind lapped at Dunk like the tongue of some great beast. The hard-packed earth of the yard seemed to move beneath his feet . . . or it might be that he was swaying.

The lists had been erected in the center of the outer yard. A three-tiered wooden viewing stand had been raised beneath the walls, so Lord Butterwell and his highborn guests would be well shaded on their cushioned seats. There were tents at both ends of the lists where the knights could don their armor, with racks of tourney lances standing ready. When the wind lifted the banners for an instant, Dunk could smell the whitewash on the tilting barrier. He set off in search of the inner ward. He had to hunt up Egg and send the boy to the master of the games to enter him in the lists. That was a squire's duty.

Whitewalls was strange to him, however, and somehow Dunk got turned around. He found himself outside the kennels, where the hounds caught scent of him and began to bark and howl. *They want to tear my throat out,* he thought, *or else they want the capon in my cloak.* He doubled back the way he'd come, past the sept. A woman went running past, breathless with laughter, a bald knight in hard pursuit. The man kept falling, until finally the woman had to come back and help him up. *I should slip into the sept and ask the Seven to make that knight my first opponent,* Dunk thought, but that would have been impious. *What I really need is a privy, not a prayer.* There were some bushes near at hand, beneath a flight of pale stone steps. *Those will serve.* He groped his way behind them and unlaced his breeches. His bladder had been full to bursting. The piss went on and on.

Somewhere above, a door came open. Dunk heard footfalls on the steps, the scrape of boots on stone. ". . . beggar's feast you've laid before us. Without Bittersteel . . ."

"Bittersteel be buggered," insisted a familiar voice. "No bastard can be trusted, not even him. A few victories will bring him over the water fast enough."

Lord Peake. Dunk held his breath . . . and his piss.

"Easier to speak of victories than to win them." This speaker had a deeper voice than Peake, a bass rumble with an angry edge to it. "Old Milk-blood expected the boy to have it, and so will all the rest. Glib words and charm cannot make up for that."

"A dragon would. The prince insists the egg will hatch. He dreamed it, just as he once dreamed his brothers dead. A living dragon will win us all the swords that we would want."

"A dragon is one thing, a dream's another. I

promise you, Bloodraven is not off dreaming. We need a warrior, not a dreamer. Is the boy his father's son?"

"Just do your part as promised, and let me concern myself with that. Once we have Butterwell's gold and the swords of House Frey, Harrenhal will follow, then the Brackens. Otho knows he cannot hope to stand . . ."

The voices were fading as the speakers moved away. Dunk's piss began to flow again. He gave his cock a shake, and laced himself back up. "His father's son," he muttered. *Who were they speaking of? Fireball's son?*

By the time he emerged from under the steps, the two lords were well across the yard. He almost shouted after them, to make them show their faces, but thought better of it. He was alone and unarmed, and half-drunk besides. *Maybe more than half.* He stood there frowning for a moment, then marched back to the hall.

Inside, the last course had been served and the frolics had begun. One of Lord Frey's daughters played "Two Hearts That Beat As One" on the high harp, very badly. Some jugglers flung flaming torches at each other for a while, and some tumblers did cartwheels in the air. Lord Frey's nephew began to sing "The Bear and the Maiden Fair" while Ser Kirby Pimm beat out time upon the table with a wooden spoon. Others joined in, until the whole hall was bellowing, *"A bear! A bear! All black and brown, and covered with hair!"* Lord Caswell passed out at the table with his face in a puddle of wine, and Lady Vyrwel began to weep, though no one was quite certain as to the cause of her distress.

All the while the wine kept flowing. The rich Arbor reds gave way to local vintages, or so the Fiddler said; if truth be told, Dunk could not tell the difference. There was hippocras as well, he had to try a cup of that. *It might be a year before I have another.* The other hedge knights, fine fellows all, had begun to talk of women they had known. Dunk found himself wondering where Tanselle was tonight. He *knew* where Lady Rohanne was—abed at Coldmoat Castle, with old Ser Eustace beside her, snoring through his mustache—so he tried not to think of her. *Do they ever think of me?* he wondered.

His melancholy ponderings were rudely interrupted when a troupe of painted dwarfs came bursting from the belly of a wheeled wooden pig to chase Lord Butterwell's fool about the tables, walloping him with inflated pig's bladders that made rude noises every time a blow was struck. It was the funniest thing Dunk had seen in years, and he laughed with all the rest. Lord Frey's son was so taken by their antics that he joined in, pummeling the wedding guests with a bladder borrowed from a dwarf. The child had the most irritating laugh Dunk had ever heard, a high shrill hiccup of a laugh that made him want to take the boy over a knee or throw him down a well. *If he hits me with that bladder, I may do it.*

"There's the lad who made this marriage," Ser

Maynard said as the chinless urchin went screaming past.

"How so?" The Fiddler held up an empty wine
cup, and a passing server filled it.

Ser Maynard glanced toward the dais, where the
bride was feeding cherries to her husband. "His
Lordship will not be the first to butter that biscuit.
His bride was deflowered by a scullion at the Twins,
they say. She would creep down to the kitchens to
meet him. Alas, one night that little brother of hers
crept down after her. When he saw them making
the two-backed beast, he let out a shriek, and cooks
and guardsmen came running and found milady
and her pot boy coupling on the slab of marble
where the cook rolls out the dough, both naked as
their name day and floured up from head to heel."

That cannot be true, Dunk thought. Lord Butterwell had broad lands, and pots of yellow gold.
Why would he wed a girl who'd been soiled by a
kitchen scullion, and give away his dragon's egg to
mark the match? The Freys of the Crossing were
no nobler than the Butterwells. They owned a
bridge instead of cows, that was the only difference. *Lords. Who can ever understand them?* Dunk
ate some nuts and pondered what he'd overheard
whilst pissing. *Dunk the drunk, what is it that you
think you heard?* He had another cup of hippocras,
since the first had tasted good. Then he lay his head
down atop his folded arms and closed his eyes just
for a moment, to rest them from the smoke.

———

When he opened them again, half the wedding guests were on their feet and shouting, "Bed them! Bed them!" They were making such an uproar than they woke Dunk from a pleasant dream involving Tanselle Too-Tall and the Red Widow. "Bed them! Bed them!" the calls rang out. Dunk sat up and rubbed his eyes.

Ser Franklyn Frey had the bride in his arms and was carrying her down the aisle, with men and boys swarming all around him. The ladies at the high table had surrounded Lord Butterwell. Lady Vyrwel had recovered from her grief and was trying to pull His Lordship from his chair, while one of his daughters unlaced his boots and some Frey woman pulled up his tunic. Butterwell was flailing at them ineffectually, and laughing. He was drunk, Dunk saw, and Ser Franklyn was a deal drunker . . . so drunk, he almost dropped the bride. Before Dunk quite realized what was happening, John the Fiddler had dragged him to his feet. "Here!" he cried out. "Let the giant carry her!"

The next thing he knew, he was climbing a tower stair with the bride squirming in his arms. How he kept his feet was beyond him. The girl would not be still, and the men were all around them, making ribald japes about flouring her up and kneading her well whilst they pulled off her clothes. The dwarfs joined in as well. They swarmed around Dunk's legs, shouting and laughing and smacking at his calves with their bladders. It was all he could do not to trip over them.

Dunk had no notion where Lord Butterwell's

bedchamber was to be found, but the other men pushed and prodded him until he got there, by which time the bride was red-faced, giggling, and nearly naked, save for the stocking on her left leg, which had somehow survived the climb. Dunk was crimson too, and not from exertion. His arousal would have been obvious if anyone had been looking, but fortunately all eyes were the bride. Lady Butterwell looked nothing like Tanselle, but having the one squirming half-naked in his arms had started Dunk thinking about the other. *Tanselle Too-Tall, that was her name, but she was not too tall for me.* He wondered if he would ever find her again. There had been some nights when he thought he must have dreamed her. *No, lunk, you only dreamed she liked you.*

Lord Butterwell's bedchamber was large and lavish, once he found it. Myrish carpets covered the floors, a hundred scented candles burned in nooks and crannies, and a suit of plate inlaid with gold and gems stood beside the door. It even had its own privy set into a small stone alcove in the outer wall.

When Dunk finally plopped the bride onto her marriage bed, a dwarf leapt in beside her and seized one of her breasts for a bit of a fondle. The girl let out a squeal, the men roared with laughter, and Dunk seized the dwarf by his collar and hauled him kicking off m'lady. He was carrying the little man across the room to chuck him out the door when he saw the dragon's egg.

Lord Butterwell had placed it on a black velvet cushion atop a marble plinth. It was much bigger than a hen's egg, though not so big as he'd imagined. Fine red scales covered its surface, shining bright as jewels by the light of lamps and candles. Dunk dropped the dwarf and picked up the egg, just to feel it for a moment. It was heavier than he'd expected. *You could smash a man's head with this, and never crack the shell.* The scales were smooth beneath his fingers, and the deep, rich red seemed to shimmer as he turned the egg in his hands. *Blood and flame*, he thought, but there were gold flecks in it as well, and whorls of midnight black.

"Here, you! What do you think you're doing, ser?" A knight he did not know was glaring at him, a big man with a coal-black beard and boils, but it was the voice that made him blink; a deep voice, thick with anger. *It was him, the man with Peake*, Dunk realized, as the man said, "Put that down. I'll thank you to keep your greasy fingers off His Lordship's treasures, or by the Seven, you shall wish you had."

The other knight was not near so drunk as Dunk, so it seemed wise to do as he said. He put the egg back on its pillow, very carefully, and wiped his fingers on his sleeve. "I meant no harm, ser." *Dunk the lunk, thick as a castle wall.* Then he shoved past the man with the black beard and out the door.

There were noises in the stairwell, glad shouts and girlish laughter. The women were bringing Lord Butterwell to his bride. Dunk had no wish to encounter them, so he went up instead of down, and found himself on the tower roof beneath the stars, with the pale castle glimmering in the moonlight all around him.

He was feeling dizzy from the wine, so he leaned against a parapet. *Am I going to be sick?* Why did he go and touch the dragon's egg? He remembered Tanselle's puppet show, and the wooden dragon that had started all the trouble there at Ashford. The memory made Dunk feel guilty, as it always did. *Three good men dead, to save a hedge knight's foot.* It made no sense, and never had. *Take a lesson from that, lunk. It is not for the likes of you to mess about with dragons or their eggs.*

"It almost looks as if it's made of snow."

Dunk turned. John the Fiddler stood behind him, smiling in his silk and cloth-of-gold. "What's made of snow?"

"The castle. All that white stone in the moonlight. Have you ever been north of the Neck, Ser Duncan? I'm told it snows there even in the summer. Have you ever seen the Wall?"

"No, m'lord." *Why is he going on about the Wall?* "That's where we were going, Egg and me. Up north, to Winterfell."

"Would that I could join you. You could show me the way."

"The way?" Dunk frowned. "It's right up the kingsroad. If you stay to the road and keep going north, you can't miss it."

The Fiddler laughed. "I suppose not . . . though you might be surprised at what some men can miss." He went to the parapet and looked out across the castle. "They say those northmen are a savage folk, and their woods are full of wolves."

"M'lord? Why did you come up here?"

"Alyn was seeking for me, and I did not care to be found. He grows tiresome when he drinks, does Alyn. I saw you slip away from that bedchamber of horrors, and slipped out after you. I've had too much wine, I grant you, but not enough to face a naked Butterwell." He gave Dunk an enigmatic smile. "I dreamed of you, Ser Duncan. Before I even met you. When I saw you on the road, I knew your face at once. It was as if we were old friends."

Dunk had the strangest feeling then, as if he had lived this all before. *I dreamed of you, he said. My dreams are not like yours, Ser Duncan. Mine are true.* "You *dreamed* of me?" he said, in a voice made thick by wine. "What sort of dream?"

"Why," the Fiddler said, "I dreamed that you were all in white from head to heel, with a long pale cloak flowing from those broad shoulders. You were a White Sword, ser, a Sworn Brother of the Kingsguard, the greatest knight in all the Seven Kingdoms, and you lived for no other purpose but to guard and serve and please your king." He put a hand on Dunk's shoulder. "You have dreamed the same dream, I know you have."

He had, it was true. *The first time the old man let me hold his sword.* "Every boy dreams of serving in the Kingsguard."

"Only seven boys grow up to wear the white cloak, though. Would it please you to be one of them?"

"Me?" Dunk shrugged away the lordling's hand, which had begun to knead his shoulder. "It might. Or not." The knights of the Kingsguard served for life, and swore to take no wife and hold no lands. *I might find Tanselle again someday. Why shouldn't I have a wife, and sons?* "It makes no matter what I dream. Only a king can make a Kingsguard knight."

"I suppose that means I'll have to take the throne, then. I would much rather be teaching you to fiddle."

"You're drunk." *And the crow once called the raven black.*

"Wonderfully drunk. Wine makes all things possible, Ser Duncan. You'd look a god in white, I think, but if the color does not suit you, perhaps you would prefer to be a lord?"

Dunk laughed in his face. "No, I'd sooner sprout big blue wings and fly. One's as likely as t'other."

"Now you mock me. A true knight would never mock his king." The Fiddler sounded hurt. "I hope you will put more faith in what I tell you when you see the dragon hatch."

"A dragon will hatch? A *living* dragon? What, here?"

"I dreamed it. This pale white castle, you, a dragon bursting from an egg, I dreamed it all, just as I once dreamed of my brothers lying dead. They were twelve and I was only seven, so they laughed at me, and died. I am two-and-twenty now, and I trust my dreams."

Dunk was remembering another tourney,

remembering how he had walked through the soft spring rains with another princeling. *I dreamed of you and a dead dragon*, Egg's brother Daeron said to him. *A great beast, huge, with wings so large, they could cover this meadow. It had fallen on top of you, but you were alive and the dragon was dead*. And so he was, poor Baelor. Dreams were a treacherous ground on which to build. "As you say, m'lord," he told the Fiddler. "Pray excuse me."

"Where *are* you going, ser?"

"To my bed, to sleep. I'm drunk as a dog."

"Be my dog, ser. The night's alive with promise. We can howl together, and wake the very gods."

"What do you want of me?"

"Your sword. I would make you mine own man, and raise you high. My dreams do not lie, Ser Duncan. You will have that white cloak, and I must have the dragon's egg. I *must*, my dreams have made that plain. Perhaps the egg will hatch, or else—"

Behind them, the door banged open violently. *"There he is, my lord."* A pair of men-at-arms stepped onto the roof. Lord Gormon Peake was just behind them.

"Gormy," the Fiddler drawled. "Why, what are you doing in my bedchamber, my lord?"

"It is a roof, ser, and you have had too much wine." Lord Gormon made a sharp gesture, and the guards moved forward. "Allow us to help you to that bed. You are jousting on the morrow, pray recall. Kirby Pimm can prove a dangerous foe."

"I had hoped to joust with good Ser Duncan here."

Peake gave Dunk an unsympathetic look. "Later, perhaps. For your first tilt, you have drawn Ser Kirby Pimm."

"Then Pimm must fall! So must they all! The mystery knight prevails against all challengers, and wonder dances in his wake." A guardsman took the Fiddler by the arm. "Ser Duncan, it seems that we must part," he called as they helped him down the steps.

Only Lord Gormon remained upon the roof with Dunk. "Hedge knight," he growled, "did your mother never teach you not to reach your hand into the dragon's mouth?"

"I never knew my mother, m'lord."

"That would explain it. What did he promise you?"

"A lordship. A white cloak. Big blue wings."

"Here's *my* promise: three feet of cold steel through your belly if you speak a word of what just happened."

Dunk shook his head to clear his wits. It did not seem to help. He bent double at the waist, and retched.

Some of the vomit spattered Peake's boots. The lord cursed. "Hedge knights," he exclaimed in disgust. "You have no place here. No true knight would be so discourteous as to turn up uninvited, but you creatures of the hedge—"

"We are wanted nowhere and turn up everywhere, m'lord." The wine had made Dunk bold, else he would have held his tongue. He wiped his mouth with the back of his hand.

"Try and remember what I told you, ser. It will go ill for you if you do not." Lord Peake shook the vomit off his boot. Then he was gone. Dunk leaned against the parapet again. He wondered who was madder, Lord Gormon or the Fiddler.

By the time he found his way back to the hall, only Maynard Plumm remained of his companions. "Was there any flour on her teats when you got the smallclothes off her?" he wanted to know.

Dunk shook his head, poured himself another cup of wine, tasted it, and decided that he had drunk enough.

Butterwell's stewards had found rooms in the keep for the lords and ladies, and beds in the barracks for their retinues. The rest of the guests had their choice between a straw pallet in the cellar, or a spot of ground beneath the western walls to raise their pavilions. The modest sailcloth tent Dunk had acquired in Stoney Sept was no pavilion, but it kept the rain and sun off. Some of his neighbors were still awake, the silken walls of their pavilions glowing like colored lanterns in the night. Laughter came from inside a blue pavilion covered with sunflowers, and the sounds of love from one striped in white and purple. Egg had set up their own tent a bit apart from the others. Maester and the two horses were hobbled nearby, and Dunk's arms and armor had been neatly stacked against the castle walls. When he crept into the tent, he found his squire sitting cross-legged by a candle, his head shining as he peered over a book.

"Reading books by candlelight will make you blind." Reading remained a mystery to Dunk, though the lad had tried to teach him.

"I need the candlelight to see the words, ser."

"Do you want a clout in the ear? What book is that?" Dunk saw bright colors on the page, little painted shields hiding in amongst the letters.

"A roll of arms, ser."

"Looking for the Fiddler? You won't find him. They don't put hedge knights in those rolls, just lords and champions."

"I wasn't looking for him. I saw some other sigils in the yard. . . . Lord Sunderland is here, ser. He bears the heads of three pale ladies, on undy green and blue."

"A Sisterman? Truly?" The Three Sisters were islands in the Bite. Dunk had heard septons say that the isles were sinks of sin and avarice. Sisterton was the most notorious smuggler's den in all of Westeros. "He's come a long way. He must be kin to Butterwell's new bride."

"He isn't, ser."

"Then he's here for the feast. They eat fish on the Three Sisters, don't they? A man gets sick of fish. Did you get enough to eat? I brought you half a capon and some cheese." Dunk rummaged in the pocket of his cloak.

"They fed us ribs, ser." Egg's nose was deep in

the book. "Lord Sunderland fought for the Black Dragon, ser."

"Like old Ser Eustace? He wasn't so bad, was he?"

"No, ser," Egg said, "but—"

"I saw the dragon's egg." Dunk squirreled the food away with their hardbread and salt beef. "It was red, mostly. Does Lord Bloodraven own a dragon's egg as well?"

Egg lowered his book. "Why would he? He's baseborn."

"Bastard born, not baseborn." Bloodraven had been born on the wrong side of the blanket, but he was noble on both sides. Dunk was about to tell Egg about the men he'd overhead when he noticed his face. "What happened to your lip?"

"A fight, ser."

"Let me see it."

"It only bled a little. I dabbed some wine on it."

"Who were you fighting?"

"Some other squires. They said—"

"Never mind what they said. What did I tell you?"

"To hold my tongue and make no trouble." The boy touched his broken lip. "They called my father a *kinslayer*, though."

He is, lad, though I do not think he meant it. Dunk had told Egg half a hundred times not to take such words to heart. *You know the truth. Let that be enough.* They had heard such talk before, in wine sinks and low taverns, and around campfires in the woods. The whole realm knew how Prince

Maekar's mace had felled his brother Baelor Breakspear at Ashford Meadow. Talk of plots was only to be expected. "If they knew Prince Maekar was your father, they would never have said such things." *Behind your back, yes, but never to your face.* "And what did *you* tell these other squires, instead of holding your tongue?"

Egg looked abashed. "That Prince Baelor's death was just a mishap. Only when I said Prince Maekar loved his brother Baelor, Ser Addam's squire said he loved him to death, and Ser Mallor's squire said he meant to love his brother Aerys the same way. That was when I hit him. I hit him good."

"I ought to hit you good. A fat ear to go with that fat lip. Your father would do the same if he were here. Do you think Prince Maekar needs a little boy to defend him? What did he tell you when he sent you off with me?"

"To serve you faithfully as your squire, and not flinch from any task or hardship."

"And what else?"

"To obey the king's laws, the rules of chivalry, and you."

"And what else?"

"To keep my hair shaved or dyed," the boy said with obvious reluctance, "and tell no man my true name."

Dunk nodded. "How much wine had this boy drunk?"

"He was drinking barley beer."

"You see? The barley beer was talking. Words are wind, Egg. Just let them blow on past you."

"*Some* words are wind." The boy was nothing if not stubborn. "Some words are treason. This is a traitor's tourney, ser."

"What, all of them?" Dunk shook his head. "If it was true, that was a long time ago. The Black Dragon's dead, and those who fought with him are fled or pardoned. And it's not true. Lord Butterwell's sons fought on both sides."

"That makes him *half* a traitor, ser."

"Sixteen years ago." Dunk's mellow winey haze was gone. He felt angry, and near sober. "Lord Butterwell's steward is the master of the games, a man named Cosgrove. Find him and enter my name for the lists. No, wait . . . hold back my name." With so many lords on hand, one of them might recall Ser Duncan the Tall from Ashford Meadow. "Enter me as the Gallows Knight." The smallfolk loved it when a Mystery Knight appeared at a tourney.

Egg fingered his fat lip. "The Gallows Knight, ser?"

"For the shield."

"Yes, but—"

"Go do as I said. You have read enough for one night." Dunk pinched the candle out between his thumb and forefinger.

The sun rose hot and hard, implacable.

Waves of heat rose shimmering off the white stones of the castle. The air smelled of baked earth and torn grass, and no breath of wind stirred the banners that drooped atop the keep and gate-house, green and white and yellow.

Thunder was restless, in a way that Dunk had seldom seen before. The stallion tossed his head from side to side as Egg was tightening his saddle cinch. He even bared his big square teeth at the boy. *It is so hot,* Dunk thought, *too hot for man or mount.* A warhorse does not have a placid disposition even at the best of times. *The Mother herself would be foul-tempered in this heat.*

In the center of the yard, the jousters began another run. Ser Harbert rode a golden courser barded in black and decorated with the red and white serpents of House Paege, Ser Franklyn a sorrel whose gray silk trapper bore the twin towers of Frey. When they came together, the red and white lance cracked clean in two and the blue one exploded into splinters, but neither man lost his seat. A cheer went up from the viewing stand and the guardsmen on the castle walls, but it was short and thin and hollow.

It is too hot for cheering. Dunk mopped sweat from his brow. *It is too hot for jousting.* His head was beating like a drum. *Let me win this tilt and one more, and I will be content.*

The knights wheeled their horses about at the end of the lists and tossed down the jagged remains of their lances, the fourth pair they had broken. *Three too many.* Dunk had put off donning his armor as long as he dared, yet already he could feel his smallclothes sticking to his skin beneath his steel. *There are worse things than being soaked with sweat,* he told himself, remembering the fight on the *White Lady,* when the ironmen had come swarming over her side. He had been soaked in blood by the time that day was done.

Fresh lances in hand, Paege and Frey put their spurs into their mounts once again. Clods of cracked dry earth sprayed back from beneath their horses' hooves with every stride. The crack of the lances breaking made Dunk wince. *Too much wine last night, and too much food.* He had some vague memory of carrying the bride up the steps, and meeting John the Fiddler and Lord Peake upon a roof. *What was I doing on a roof?* There had been talk of dragons, he recalled, or dragon's eggs, or something, but—

A noise broke his reverie, part roar and part moan. Dunk saw the golden horse trotting riderless to the end of the lists, as Ser Harbert Paege rolled feebly on the ground. *Two more before my turn.* The sooner he unhorsed Ser Uthor, the sooner he could take his armor off, have a cool drink, and rest. He should have at least an hour before they called him forth again.

Lord Butterwell's portly herald climbed to the top of the viewing stand to summon the next pair of jousters. *"Ser Argrave the Defiant,"* he called, *"a knight of Nunny, in service to Lord Butterwell of Whitewalls. Ser Glendon Flowers, the Knight of the Pussywillows. Come forth and prove your valor."* A gale of laughter rippled through the viewing stands.

Ser Argrave was a spare, leathery man, a seasoned household knight in dinted gray armor riding an unbarded horse. Dunk had known his sort before; such men were tough as old roots, and knew their business. His foe was young Ser Glendon, mounted on his wretched stot and armored in a heavy mail hauberk and open-faced iron half-helm. On his arm his shield displayed his father's fiery sigil. *He needs a breastplate and a proper helm*, Dunk thought. *A blow to the head or chest could kill him, clad like that.*

Ser Glendon was plainly furious at his introduction. He wheeled his mount in an angry circle and shouted, "I am Glendon *Ball*, not Glendon Flowers. Mock me at your peril, herald. I warn you, I have hero's blood." The herald did not deign to reply, but more laughter greeted the young knight's protest. "Why are they laughing at him?" Dunk wondered aloud. "Is he a bastard, then?" *Flowers* was the surname given to bastards born of noble parents in the Reach. "And what was all that about pussywillows?"

"I could find out, ser," said Egg.

"No. It is none of our concern. Do you have my helm?" Ser Argrave and Ser Glendon dipped their lances before Lord and Lady Butterwell. Dunk saw Butterwell lean over and whisper something in his bride's ear. The girl began to giggle.

"Yes, ser." Egg had donned his floppy hat, to shade his eyes and keep the sun off his shaved head. Dunk liked to tease the boy about that hat, but just now he wished he had one like it. Better a straw hat than an iron one, beneath this sun. He pushed his hair out of his eyes, eased the greathelm down into place with two hands, and fastened it to his gorget. The lining stank of old sweat, and he could feel the weight of all that iron on his neck and shoulders. His head throbbed from last night's wine.

"Ser," Egg said, "it is not too late to withdraw. If you lose Thunder and your armor . . ."

I would be done as a knight. "Why should I lose?" Dunk demanded. Ser Argrave and Ser Glendon had ridden to opposite ends of the lists. "It is not as if I faced the Laughing Storm. Is there some knight here like to give me trouble?"

"Almost all of them, ser."

"I owe you a clout in the ear for that. Ser Uthor is ten years my senior and half my size." Ser Argrave lowered his visor. Ser Glendon did not have a visor to lower.

"You have not ridden in a tilt since Ashford Meadow, ser."

Insolent boy. "I've trained." Not so faithfully as he might have, to be sure. When he could, he took his turn riding at quintains or rings, where such were available. And sometimes he would command Egg to climb a tree and hang a shield or barrel stave beneath a well-placed limb for them to tilt at.

"You're better with a sword than with a lance," Egg said. "With an axe or a mace, there's few to match your strength."

There was enough truth in that to annoy Dunk all the more. "There is no contest for swords or maces," he pointed out, as Fireball's son and Ser Argrave the Defiant began their charge. "Go get my shield."

Egg made a face, then went to fetch the shield.

Across the yard, Ser Argrave's lance struck Ser Glendon's shield and glanced off, leaving a gouge across the comet. But Ball's coronal found the center of his foe's breastplate with such force that it burst his saddle cinch. Knight and saddle both went tumbling to the dust. Dunk was impressed despite himself. *The boy jousts almost as well as he talks.* He wondered if that would stop them laughing at him.

A trumpet rang, loud enough to make Dunk wince. Once more the herald climbed his stand. *"Ser Joffrey of House Caswell, Lord of Bitterbridge and Defender of the Fords. Ser Kyle, the Cat of Misty Moor. Come forth and prove your valor."*

Ser Kyle's armor was of good quality, but old and worn, with many dints and scratches. "The Mother has been merciful to me, Ser Duncan," he told Dunk and Egg, on his way to the lists. "I am sent against Lord Caswell, the very man I came to see."

If any man upon the field felt worse than Dunk this morning, it had to be Lord Caswell, who had drunk himself insensible at the feast. "It's a wonder he can sit a horse, after last night," said Dunk. "The victory is yours, ser."

"Oh, no." Ser Kyle smiled a silken smile. "The cat who wants his bowl of cream must know when to purr and when to show his claws, Ser Duncan. If His Lordship's lance so much as scrapes against my shield, I shall go tumbling to the earth. Afterwards, when I bring my horse and armor to him, I will compliment His Lordship on how much his prowess has grown since I made him his first sword. That will recall me to him, and before the day is out, I shall be a Caswell man again, a knight of Bitterbridge."

There is no honor in that, Dunk almost said, but he bit his tongue instead. Ser Kyle would not be the first hedge knight to trade his honor for a warm place by the fire. "As you say," he muttered. "Good fortune to you. Or bad, if you prefer."

Lord Joffrey Caswell was a weedy youth of twenty, though admittedly he looked rather more impressive in his armor than he had last night when he'd been face down in a puddle of wine. A yellow centaur was painted on his shield, pulling on a longbow. The same centaur adorned the white silk trappings of his horse, and gleamed atop his helm in yellow gold. *A man who has a centaur for his sigil should ride better than that.* Dunk did not know how well Ser Kyle wielded a lance, but from the way Lord Caswell sat his horse, it looked as though a loud cough might unseat him. *All the Cat need do is ride past him very fast.*

Egg held Thunder's bridle as Dunk swung himself ponderously up into the high, stiff saddle. As he sat there waiting, he could feel the eyes upon him. *They are wondering if the big hedge knight is any good.* Dunk wondered that himself. He would find out soon enough.

The Cat of Misty Moor was true to his word.

Lord Caswell's lance was wobbling all the way across the field, and Ser Kyle's was ill-aimed. Neither man got his horse up past a trot. All the same, the Cat went tumbling when Lord Joffrey's coronal chanced to whack his shoulder. *I thought all cats landed gracefully upon their feet*, Dunk thought as the hedge knight rolled in the dust. Lord Caswell's lance remained unbroken. As he brought his horse around, he thrust it high into the air repeatedly, as if he'd just unseated Leo Longthorn or the Laughing Storm. The Cat pulled off his helm and went chasing down his horse.

"My shield," Dunk said to Egg. The boy handed it up. He slipped his left arm through the strap and closed his hand around the grip. The weight of the kite shield was reassuring, though its length made it awkward to handle, and seeing the hanged man once again gave him an uneasy feeling. *Those are ill-omened arms*. He resolved to get the shield repainted as soon as he could. *May the Warrior grant me a smooth course and a quick victory*, he prayed as Butterwell's herald was clambering up the steps once more. *"Ser Uthor Underleaf,"* his voice rang out. *"The Gallows Knight. Come forth and prove your valor."*

"Be careful, ser," Egg warned as he handed Dunk a tourney lance, a tapered wooden shaft twelve feet long ending in a rounded iron coronal in the shape of a closed fist. "The other squires say Ser Uthor has a good seat. And he's quick."

"Quick?" Dunk snorted. "He has a snail on his shield. How quick can he be?" He put his heels into Thunder's flanks and walked the horse slowly forward, his lance upright. *One victory, and I am no worse than before. Two will leave us well ahead. Two is not too much to hope for, in this company.* He had been fortunate in the lots, at least. He could as easily have drawn the Old Ox or Ser Kirby Pimm or some other local hero. Dunk wondered if the master of games was deliberately matching the hedge knights against each other, so no lordling need suffer the ignominy of losing to one in the first round. *It does not matter. One foe at a time, that was what the old man always said. Ser Uthor is all that should concern me now.*

They met beneath the viewing stand where Lord and Lady Butterwell sat on their cushions in the shade of the castle walls. Lord Frey was beside them, dandling his snot-nosed son on one knee. A row of serving girls was fanning them, yet Lord Butterwell's damask tunic was stained beneath the arms, and his lady's hair was limp from perspiration. She looked hot, bored, and uncomfortable, but when she saw Dunk, she pushed out her chest in a way that turned him red beneath his helm. He dipped his lance to her and her lord husband. Ser Uthor did the same. Butterwell wished them both a good tilt. His wife stuck out her tongue.

It was time. Dunk trotted back to the south end of the lists. Eighty feet away, his opponent was taking up his position as well. His grey stallion was smaller than Thunder, but younger and more spirited. Ser Uthor wore green enamel plate and silvery chain mail. Streamers of green and grey silk flowed from his rounded bascinet, and his green shield bore a silver snail. *Good armor and a good horse means a good ransom, if I unseat him.*

A trumpet sounded.

Thunder started forward at a slow trot. Dunk swung his lance to the left and brought it down, so it angled across the horse's head and the wooden barrier between him and his foe. His shield protected the left side of his body. He crouched forward, legs tightening as Thunder drove down the lists. *We are one. Man, horse, lance, we are one beast of blood and wood and iron.*

Ser Uthor was charging hard, clouds of dust kicking up from the hooves of his grey. With forty yards between them, Dunk spurred Thunder to a gallop and aimed the point of his lance squarely at the silver snail. The sullen sun, the dust, the heat, the castle, Lord Butterwell and his bride, the Fiddler and Ser Maynard, knights, squires, grooms, smallfolk, all vanished. Only the foe remained. The spurs again. Thunder broke into a run. The snail was rushing toward them, growing with every stride of the grey's long legs . . . but ahead came Ser Uthor's lance with its iron fist. *My shield is strong; my shield will take the blow. Only the snail matters. Strike the snail, and the tilt is mine.*

When ten yards remained between them, Ser Uthor shifted the point of his lance upward.

A *crack* rang in Dunk's ears as his lance hit. He felt the impact in his arm and shoulder, but never saw the blow strike home. Uthor's iron fist took him square between his eyes, with all the force of man and horse behind it.

Dunk woke upon his back, staring up at the arches of a barrel-vaulted ceiling. For a moment he did not know where he was, or how he had arrived there. Voices echoed in his head, and faces drifted past him—old Ser Arlan, Tanselle Too-Tall, Bennis of the Brown Shield, the Red Widow, Baelor Breakspear, Aerion the Bright Prince, mad sad Lady Vaith. Then all at once, the joust came back to him: the heat, the snail, the iron fist coming at his face. He groaned, and rolled onto one elbow. The movement set his skull to pounding like some monstrous war drum.

Both his eyes seemed to be working, at least. Nor could he feel a hole in his head, which was all to the good. He was in some cellar, he saw, with casks of wine and ale on every side. *At least it is cool here*, he thought, *and drink is close at hand*. The taste of blood was in his mouth. Dunk felt a stab of fear. If he had bitten off his tongue, he would be dumb as well as thick. "Good morrow," he croaked, just to hear his voice. The words echoed off the ceiling. Dunk tried to push himself onto his feet, but the effort set the cellar spinning.

"Slowly, slowly," said a quavery voice, close at hand. A stooped old man appeared beside the bed, clad in robes as grey as his long hair. About his neck was a maester's chain of many metals. His face was aged and lined, with deep creases on either side of a great beak of a nose. "Be still, and let me see your eyes." He peered in Dunk's left eye, and then the right, holding them open between his thumb and forefinger.

"My head hurts."

The maester snorted. "Be grateful it still rests upon your shoulders, ser. Here, this may help somewhat. Drink."

Dunk made himself swallow every drop of the foul potion, and managed not to spit it out. "The tourney," he said, wiping his mouth with the back of his hand. "Tell me. What's happened?"

"The same foolishness that always happens in these affrays. Men have been knocking each other off horses with sticks. Lord Smallwood's nephew broke his wrist and Ser Eden Risley's leg was crushed beneath his horse, but no one has been killed thus far. Though I had my fears for you, ser."

"Was I unhorsed?" His head still felt as though it were stuffed full of wool, else he would never have asked such a stupid question. Dunk regretted it the instant the words were out.

"With a crash that shook the highest ramparts. Those who had wagered good coin on you were most distraught, and your squire was beside himself. He would be sitting with you still if I had not chased him off. I need no children underfoot. I reminded him of his duty."

Dunk found that he needed reminding himself. "What duty?"

"Your mount, ser. Your arms and armor."

"Yes," Dunk said, remembering. The boy was a good squire; he knew what was required of him. *I have lost the old man's sword and the armor that Steely Pate forged for me.*

"Your fiddling friend was also asking after you. He told me you were to have the best of care. I threw him out as well."

"How long have you been tending me?" Dunk flexed the fingers of his sword hand. All of them still seemed to work. *Only my head's hurt, and Ser Arlan used to say I never used that anyway.*

"Four hours, by the sundial."

Four hours was not so bad. He had once heard tale of a knight struck so hard that he slept for forty years, and woke to find himself old and withered. "Do you know if Ser Uthor won his second tilt?" Maybe the Snail would win the tourney. It would take some sting from the defeat if Dunk could tell himself that he had lost to the best knight in the field.

"That one? Indeed he did. Against Ser Addam Frey, a cousin to the bride, and a promising young lance. Her Ladyship fainted when Ser Addam fell. She had to be helped back to her chambers."

Dunk forced himself to his feet, reeling as he rose, but the maester helped to steady him. "Where are my clothes? I must go. I have to . . . I must . . ."

"If you cannot recall, it cannot be so very urgent." The maester made an irritated motion. "I would suggest that you avoid rich foods, strong drink, and further blows between your eyes . . .

but I learned long ago that knights are deaf to sense. Go, go. I have other fools to tend."

Outside, Dunk glimpsed a hawk soaring in wide circles through the bright blue sky. He envied him. A few clouds were gathering to the east, dark as Dunk's mood. As he found his way back to the tilting ground, the sun beat down on his head like a hammer on an anvil. The earth seemed to move beneath his feet . . . or it might just be that he was swaying. He had almost fallen twice climbing the cellar steps. *I should have heeded Egg.*

He made his slow way across the outer ward, around the fringes of the crowd. Out on the field, plump Lord Alyn Cockshaw was limping off between two squires, the latest conquest of young Glendon Ball. A third squire held his helm, its three proud feathers broken. "*Ser John the Fiddler,*" the herald cried. "*Ser Franklyn of House Frey, a knight of the Twins, sworn to the Lord of the Crossing. Come forth and prove your valor.*"

Dunk could only stand and watch as the Fiddler's big black trotted onto the field in a swirl of blue silk and golden swords and fiddles. His breastplate was enameled blue as well, as were his poleyns, couter, greaves, and gorget. The ringmail underneath was gilded. Ser Franklyn rode a dapple grey with a flowing silver mane, to match the grey of his silks and the silver of his armor. On shield and surcoat and horse trappings he bore the twin towers of Frey. They charged and charged again. Dunk stood watching, but saw none of it. *Dunk the lunk, thick as a castle wall,* he chided himself. *He had a snail upon his shield. How could you lose to a man with a snail upon his shield?*

There was cheering all around him. When Dunk looked up, he saw that Franklyn Frey was down. The Fiddler had dismounted, to help his fallen foe back to his feet. *He is one step closer to his dragon's egg,* Dunk thought, *and where am I?*

As he approached the postern gate, Dunk came upon the company of dwarfs from last night's feast preparing to take their leave. They were hitching ponies to their wheeled wooden pig, and a second wayn of more conventional design. There were six of them, he saw, each smaller and more malformed than the last. A few might have been children, but they were all so short that it was hard to tell. In daylight, dressed in horsehide breeches and rough-spun hooded cloaks, they seemed less jolly than they had in motley. "Good morrow to you," Dunk said, to be courteous. "Are you for the road? There's clouds to the east, could mean rain."

The only answer that he got was a glare from the ugliest dwarf. *Was he the one I pulled off Lady Butterwell last night?* Up close, the little man smelled like a privy. One whiff was enough to make Dunk hasten his steps.

The walk across the Milkhouse seemed to take Dunk as long as it had once taken him and Egg to cross the sands of Dorne. He kept a wall beside him, and from time to time he leaned on it. Every time he turned his head, the world would swim. *A drink*, he thought. *I need a drink of water, or else I'm like to fall.*

A passing groom told him where to find the nearest well. It was there that he discovered Kyle the Cat, talking quietly with Maynard Plumm. Ser Kyle's shoulders were slumped in dejection, but he looked up at Dunk's approach. "Ser Duncan? We had heard that you were dead, or dying."

Dunk rubbed his temples. "I only wish I were."

"I know that feeling well." Ser Kyle sighed. "Lord Caswell did not know me. When I told him how I carved his first sword, he stared at me as if I'd lost my wits. He said there was no place at Bitterbridge for knights as feeble as I had shown myself to be." The Cat gave a bitter laugh. "He took my arms and armor, though. My mount as well. What will I do?"

Dunk had no answer for him. Even a freerider required a horse to ride; sellswords must have swords to sell. "You will find another horse," Dunk said, as he drew the bucket up. "The Seven Kingdoms are full of horses. You will find some other lord to arm you." He cupped his hands, filled them with water, drank.

"Some other lord. Aye. Do you know of one? I am not so young and strong as you. Nor so big. Big men are always in demand. Lord Butterwell likes his knights large, for one. Look at that Tom Heddle. Have you seen him joust? He has overthrown every man he's faced. Fireball's lad has done the same, though. The Fiddler as well. Would that he had been the one to unhorse me. He refuses to take ransoms. He wants no more than the dragon's egg, he says . . . that, and the friendship of his fallen foes. The flower of chivalry, that one."

Maynard Plumm gave a laugh. "The fiddle of chivalry, you mean. That boy is fiddling up a storm, and all of us would do well to be gone from here before it breaks."

"He takes no ransoms?" said Dunk. "A gallant gesture."

"Gallant gestures come easy when your purse is fat with gold," said Ser Maynard. "There is a lesson here, if you have the sense to take it, Ser Duncan. It is not too late for you to go."

"Go? Go where?"

Ser Maynard shrugged. "Anywhere. Winterfell, Summerhall, Asshai by the Shadow. It makes no matter, so long as it's not here. Take your horse and armor and slip out the postern gate. You won't be missed. The Snail's got his next tilt to think about, and the rest have eyes only for the jousting."

For half a heartbeat, Dunk was tempted. So long as he was armed and horsed, he would remain a knight of sorts. Without them, he was no more than a beggar. *A big beggar, but a beggar all the same.* But his arms and armor belonged to Ser Uthor now. So did Thunder. *Better a beggar than a thief.* He had been both in Flea Bottom, when he ran with Ferret, Rafe, and Pudding, but the old man had saved him from that life. He knew what Ser Arlan of Pennytree would have said to Plumm's suggestions. Ser Arlan being dead, Dunk said it for him. "Even a hedge knight has his honor."

"Would you rather die with honor intact, or live with it besmirched? No, spare me, I know what you will say. Take your boy and flee, gallows knight. Before your arms become your destiny."

Dunk bristled. "How would you know my destiny? Did you have a dream, like John the Fiddler? What do you know of Egg?"

"I know that eggs do well to stay out of frying pans," said Plumm. "Whitewalls is not a healthy place for the boy."

"How did you fare in your own tilt, ser?" Dunk asked him.

"Oh, I did not chance the lists. The omens had gone sour. Who do you imagine is going to claim the dragon's egg, pray?"

Not me, Dunk thought. "The Seven know. I don't."

"Venture a guess, ser. You have two eyes."

He thought a moment. "The Fiddler?"

"Very good. Would you care to explain your reasoning?"

"I just . . . I have a feeling."

"So do I," said Maynard Plumm. "A bad feeling, for any man or boy unwise enough to stand in our Fiddler's way."

Egg was brushing Thunder's coat outside their tent, but his eyes were far away. *The boy has taken my fall hard.* "Enough," Dunk called. "Any more and Thunder will be as bald as you."

"Ser?" Egg dropped the brush. "I *knew* no stupid snail could kill you, ser." He threw his arms around him.

Dunk swiped the boy's floppy straw hat and put it on his own head. "The maester said you made off with my armor."

Egg snatched back his hat indignantly. "I've scoured your mail and polished your greaves, gorget, and breastplate, ser, but your helm is cracked and dinted where Ser Uthor's coronal struck. You'll need to have it hammered out by an armorer."

"Let Ser Uthor have it hammered out. It's his now." *No horse, no sword, no armor. Perhaps those dwarfs would let me join their troupe. That would be a funny sight, six dwarfs pummeling a giant with pig bladders.* "Thunder is his too. Come. We'll take them to him and wish him well in the rest of his tilts."

"Now, ser? Aren't you going to ransom Thunder?"

"With what, lad? Pebbles and sheep pellets?"

"I thought about that, ser. If you could borrow—"

Dunk cut him off. "No one will lend me that much coin, Egg. Why should they? What am I, but some great oaf who called himself a knight until some snail with a stick near stove his head in?"

"Well," said Egg, "you could have Rain, ser. I'll go back to riding Maester. We'll go to Summerhall. You can take service in my father's household.

His stables are full of horses. You could have a destrier and a palfrey too."

Egg meant well, but Dunk could not go cringing back to Summerhall. Not that way, penniless and beaten, seeking service without so much as a sword to offer. "Lad," he said, "that's good of you, but I want no crumbs from your lord father's table, or from his stables neither. Might be it's time we parted ways." Dunk could always slink off to join the City Watch in Lannisport or Oldtown; they liked big men for that. *I've bumped my bean on every beam in every inn from Lannisport to King's Landing, might be it's time my size earned me a bit of coin instead of just a lumpy head.* But watchmen did not have squires. "I've taught you what I could, and that was little enough. You'll do better with a proper master-at-arms to see to your training, some fierce old knight who knows which end of the lance to hold."

"I don't want a proper master-at-arms," Egg said. "I want you. What if I used my—?"

"No. None of that. I will not hear it. Go gather up my arms. We will present them to Ser Uthor with my compliments. Hard things only grow harder if you put them off."

Egg kicked the ground, his face as droopy as his big straw hat. "Aye, ser. As you say."

From the outside, Ser Uthor's tent was very plain: a large square box of dun-colored sailcloth staked to the ground with hempen ropes. A silver snail adorned the center pole above a long gray pennon, but that was the only decoration.

"Wait here," Dunk told Egg. The boy had hold of Thunder's lead. The big brown destrier was laden with Dunk's arms and armor, even to his new old shield. *The Gallows Knight. What a dismal mystery knight I proved to be.* "I won't be long." He ducked his head and stooped to shoulder through the flap.

The tent's exterior left him ill prepared for the comforts he found within. The ground beneath his feet was carpeted in woven Myrish rugs, rich with color. An ornate trestle table stood surrounded by camp chairs. The feather bed was covered with soft cushions, and an iron brazier burned perfumed incense.

Ser Uthor sat at the table, a pile of gold and silver before him and a flagon of wine at his elbow, counting coins with his squire, a gawky fellow close in age to Dunk. From time to time the Snail would bite a coin, or set one aside. "I see I still have much to teach you, Will," Dunk heard him say. "This coin has been clipped, t'other shaved. And this one?" A gold piece danced across his fingers. "*Look* at the coins before taking them. Here, tell me what you see." The dragon spun through the air. Will tried to catch it, but it bounced off his fingers and fell to the ground. He had to get down on his knees to find it. When he did, he turned it over twice before saying, "This one's good, m'lord. There's a dragon on the one side and a king on t'other. . . ."

Underleaf glanced toward Dunk. "The Hanged Man. It is good to see you moving about, ser. I feared I'd killed you. Will you do me a kindness and instruct my squire as to the nature of dragons? Will, give Ser Duncan the coin."

Dunk had no choice but to take it. *He unhorsed me, must he make me caper for him too?* Frowning, he hefted the coin in his palm, examined both sides, tasted it. "Gold, not shaved or clipped. The weight feels right. I'd have taken it too, m'lord. What's wrong with it?"

"The king."

Dunk took a closer look. The face on the coin was young, clean-shaved, handsome. King Aerys was bearded on his coins, the same as old King Aegon. King Daeron, who'd come between them, had been clean-shaved, but this wasn't him. The coin did not appear worn enough to be from before Aegon the Unworthy. Dunk scowled at the word beneath the head. *Six letters.* They looked the same as he had seen on other dragons. DAERON, the letters read, but Dunk knew the face of Daeron the Good, and this wasn't him. When he looked again, he saw that something odd about the shape of the fourth letter, it wasn't . . . "*Daemon*," he blurted out. "It says *Daemon*. There never was any King Daemon, though, only—"

"—the Pretender. Daemon Blackfyre struck his own coinage during his rebellion."

"It's gold, though," Will argued. "If it's gold, it should be just as good as them other dragons, m'lord."

The Snail clouted him along the side of the head. "Cretin. Aye, it's gold. Rebel's gold. Traitor's gold. It's treasonous to own such a coin, and twice as treasonous to pass it. I'll need to have this melted down." He hit the man again. "Get out of my sight. This good knight and I have matters to discuss."

Will wasted no time in scrambling from the tent. "Have a seat," Ser Uthor said politely. "Will you take wine?" Here in his own tent, Underleaf seemed a different man than at the feast.

A snail hides in his shell, Dunk remembered. "Thank you, no." He flicked the gold coin back to Ser Uthor. *Traitor's gold. Blackfyre gold. Egg said this was a traitor's tourney, but I would not listen.* He owed the boy an apology.

"Half a cup," Underleaf insisted. "You sound in need of it." He filled two cups with wine and handed one to Dunk. Out of his armor, he looked more a merchant than a knight. "You've come about the forfeit, I assume."

"Aye." Dunk took the wine. Maybe it would help to stop his head from pounding. "I brought my horse, and my arms and armor. Take them, with my compliments."

Ser Uthor smiled. "And this is where I tell you that you rode a gallant course."

Dunk wondered if *gallant* was a chivalrous way of saying "clumsy." "That is good of you to say, but—"

"I think you misheard me, ser. Would it be too bold of me to ask how you came to knighthood, ser?"

"Ser Arlan of Pennytree found me in Flea Bottom, chasing pigs. His old squire had been slain on the Redgrass Field, so he needed someone to tend his mount and clean his mail. He promised he would teach me sword and lance and how to ride a horse if I would come and serve him, so I did."

"A charming tale . . . though if I were you, I would leave out the part about the pigs. Pray, where is your Ser Arlan now?"

"He died. I buried him."

"I see. Did you take him home to Pennytree?"

"I didn't know where it was." Dunk had never seen the old man's Pennytree. Ser Arlan seldom spoke of it, no more than Dunk was wont to speak of Flea Bottom. "I buried him on a hillside facing west, so he could see the sun go down." The camp chair creaked alarmingly beneath his weight.

Ser Uthor resumed his seat. "I have my own armor, and a better horse than yours. What do I want with some old done nag and a sack of dinted plate and rusty mail?"

"Steely Pate made that armor," Dunk said, with a touch of anger. "Egg has taken good care of it. There's not a spot of rust on my mail, and the steel is good and strong."

"Strong and heavy," Ser Uthor complained, "and too big for any man of normal size. You are uncommon large, Duncan the Tall. As for your horse, he is too old to ride and too stringy to eat."

"Thunder is not so young as he used to be," Dunk admitted, "and my armor is large, as you say. You could sell it, though. In Lannisport and King's

Landing, there are plenty of smiths who will take it off your hands."

"For a tenth of what it's worth, perhaps," said Ser Uthor, "and only to melt down for the metal. No. It's sweet silver I require, not old iron. The coin of the realm. Now, do you wish to ransom back your arms, or no?"

Dunk turned the wine cup in his hands, frowning. It was solid silver, with a line of golden snails inlaid around the lip. The wine was gold as well, and heady on the tongue. "If wishes were fishes, aye, I'd pay. Gladly. Only—"

"—you don't have two stags to lock horns."

"If you would . . . would lend my horse and armor back to me, I could pay the ransom later. Once I found the coin."

The Snail looked amused. "Where would you find it, pray?"

"I could take service with some lord, or . . ." It was hard to get the words out. They made him feel a beggar. "It might take a few years, but I would pay you. I swear it."

"On your honor as a knight?"

Dunk flushed. "I could make my mark upon a parchment."

"A hedge knight's scratch upon a scrap of paper?" Ser Uthor rolled his eyes. "Good to wipe my arse. No more."

"You are a hedge knight too."

"Now you insult me. I ride where I will and serve no man but myself, true . . . but it has been many a year since I last slept beneath a hedge. I find that inns are far more comfortable. I am a *tourney* knight, the best that you are ever like to meet."

"The best?" His arrogance made Dunk angry. "The Laughing Storm might not agree, ser. Nor Leo Longthorn, nor the Brute of Bracken. At Ashford Meadow, no one spoke of snails. Why is that, if you're such a famous tourney champion?"

"Have you heard me name myself a champion? That way lies renown. I would sooner have the pox. Thank you, but no. I shall win my next joust, aye, but in the final I shall fall. Butterwell has thirty dragons for the knight who comes second, that will suffice for me . . . along with some goodly ransoms and the proceeds of my wagers." He gestured at the piles of silver stags and golden dragons on the table. "You seem a healthy fellow, and very large. Size will always impress the fools, though it means little and less in jousting. Will was able to get odds of three to one against me. Lord Shawney gave five to one, the fool." He picked up a silver stag and set it to spinning with a flick of his long fingers. "The Old Ox will be the next to tumble. Then the Knight of the Pussywillows, if he survives that long. Sentiment being what it is, I should get fine odds against them both. The commons love their village heroes."

"Ser Glendon has hero's blood," Dunk blurted out.

"Oh, I do hope so. Hero's blood should be good for two to one. Whore's blood draws poorer odds. Ser Glendon speaks about his purported sire at every opportunity, but have you noticed that he never makes mention of his mother? For good reason. He was born of a camp follower. Jenny, her name was. Penny Jenny, they called her, until the Redgrass Field. The night before the battle, she fucked so many men that thereafter she was known as Redgrass Jenny. Fireball had her before that, I don't doubt, but so did a hundred other men. Our friend Glendon presumes quite a lot, it seems to me. He does not even have red hair."

Hero's blood, thought Dunk. "He says he is a knight."

"Oh, that much is true. The boy and his sister grew up in a brothel, called the Pussywillows. After Penny Jenny died, the other whores took care of them and fed the lad the tale his mother had concocted, about him being Fireball's seed. An old squire who lived nearby gave the boy his training, such that it was, in trade for ale and cunt, but being but a squire he could not knight the little bastard. Half a year ago, however, a party of knights chanced upon the brothel and a certain Ser Morgan Dunstable took a drunken fancy to Ser Glendon's sister. As it happens, the sister was still a virgin and Dunstable did not have the price of her maidenhead. So a bargain was struck. Ser Morgan dubbed her brother a knight, right there in the Pussywillows in front of twenty witnesses, and afterwards little sister took him upstairs and let him pluck her flower. And there you are."

Any knight could make a knight. When he was squiring for Ser Arlan, Dunk had heard tales of other men who'd bought their knighthood with a kindness or a threat or a bag of silver coins, but never with a sister's maidenhead. "That's just a tale," he heard himself say. "That can't be true."

"I had it from Kirby Pimm, who claims that he was there, a witness to the knighting." Ser Uthor shrugged. "Hero's son, whore's son, or both, when he faces me, the boy will fall."

"The lots may give you some other foe."

Ser Uthor arched an eyebrow. "Cosgrove is as fond of silver as the next man. I promise you, I shall draw the Old Ox next, then the boy. Would you care to wager on it?"

"I have nothing left to wager." Dunk did not know what distressed him more: learning that the Snail was bribing the master of the games to get the pairings he desired, or realizing the man had desired *him*. He stood. "I have said what I came to say. My horse and sword are yours, and all my armor."

The Snail steepled his fingers. "Perhaps there is another way. You are not entirely without your talents. You fall most splendidly." Ser Uthor's lips glistened when he smiled. "I will lend you back your steed and armor . . . if you enter my service."

"Service?" Dunk did not understand. "What sort of service? You have a squire. Do you need to garrison some castle?"

"I might, if I had a castle. If truth be told, I prefer a good inn. Castles cost too much to maintain. No, the service I would require of you is that you face me in a few more tourneys. Twenty should suffice. You can do that, surely? You shall have a tenth part of my winnings, and in future I promise to strike that broad chest of yours and not your head."

"You'd have me travel about with you to be unhorsed?"

Ser Uthor chuckled pleasantly. "You are such a strapping specimen, no one will ever believe that some round-shouldered old man with a snail on his shield could put you down." He rubbed his chin. "You need a new device yourself, by the way. That hanged man is grim enough, I grant you, but . . . well, he's *hanging*, isn't he? Dead and defeated. Something fiercer is required. A bear's head, mayhaps. A skull. Or three skulls, better still. A babe impaled upon a spear. And you should let your hair grow long and cultivate a beard, the wilder and more unkempt the better. There are more of these little tourneys than you know. With the odds I'd get, we'd win enough to buy a dragon's egg before—"

"—it got about that I was hopeless? I lost my armor, not my honor. You'll have Thunder and my arms, no more."

"Pride ill becomes a beggar, ser. You could do much worse than ride with me. At the least I could teach you a thing or two of jousting, about which you are pig ignorant at present."

"You'd make a fool of me."

"I did that earlier. And even fools must eat."

Dunk wanted to smash that smile off his face. "I see why you have a snail on your shield. You are no true knight."

"Spoken like a true oaf. Are you so blind you cannot see your danger?" Ser Uthor put his cup aside. "Do you know why I struck you where I did, ser?" He got to his feet and touched Dunk lightly in the center of his chest. "A coronal placed here would have put you on the ground just as quickly. The head is a smaller target, the blow is more difficult to land . . . though more likely to be mortal. I was paid to strike you there."

"Paid?" Dunk backed away from him. "What do you mean?"

"Six dragons tendered in advance, four more promised when you died. A paltry sum for a knight's life. Be thankful for that. Had more been offered, I might have put the point of my lance through your eye slit."

Dunk felt dizzy again. *Why would someone pay to have me killed? I've done no harm to any man at Whitewalls.* Surely no one hated him that much but Egg's brother Aerion, and the Bright Prince was in exile across the narrow sea. "Who paid you?"

"A serving man brought the gold at sunrise, not long after the master of the games nailed up the pairings. His face was hooded, and he did not speak his master's name."

"But why?" said Dunk.

"I did not ask." Ser Uthor filled his cup again. "I think you have more enemies than you know, Ser Duncan. How not? There are some who would say you were the cause of all our woes."

Dunk felt a cold hand on his heart. "Say what you mean."

The Snail shrugged. "I may not have been at Ashford Meadow, but jousting is my bread and salt. I follow tourneys from afar as faithfully as the maesters follow stars. I know how a certain hedge knight became the cause of a Trial of Seven at Ashford Meadow, resulting in the death of Baelor Breakspear at his brother Maekar's hand." Ser Uthor seated himself and stretched his legs out. "Prince Baelor was well loved. The Bright Prince had friends as well, friends who will not have forgotten the cause of his exile. Think on my offer, ser. The snail may leave a trail of slime behind him, but a little slime will do a man no harm . . . whilst if you dance with dragons, you must expect to burn."

The day seemed darker when Dunk stepped from the Snail's tent. The clouds in the east had grown bigger and blacker, and the sun was sinking to the west, casting long shadows across the yard. Dunk found the squire Will inspecting Thunder's feet.

"Where's Egg?" he asked of him.

"The bald boy? How would I know? Run off somewhere."

He could not bear to say farewell to Thunder, Dunk decided. *He'll be back at the tent with his books.*

He wasn't, though. The books were there, bundled neatly in a stack beside Egg's bedroll, but of the boy there was no sign. Something was wrong here. Dunk could feel it. It was not like Egg to wander off without his leave.

A pair of grizzled men-at-arms were drinking barley beer outside a striped pavilion a few feet away. ". . . well, bugger that, once was enough for me," one muttered. "The grass was green when the sun come up, aye . . ." He broke off when other man gave him a nudge, and only then took note of Dunk. "Ser?"

"Have you seen my squire? Egg, he's called."

The man scratched at the grey stubble underneath one ear. "I remember him. Less hair than me, and a mouth three times his size. Some o' the other lads shoved him about a bit, but that was last night. I've not seen him since, ser."

"Scared him off," said his companion.

Dunk gave that one a hard look. "If he comes back, tell him to wait for me here."

"Aye, ser. That we will."

Might be he just went to watch the jousts. Dunk headed back toward the tilting grounds. As he passed the stables, he came on Ser Glendon Ball, brushing down a pretty sorrel charger. "Have you seen Egg?" he asked him.

"He ran past a few moments ago." Ser Glendon pulled a carrot from his pocket and fed it to the sorrel. "Do you like my new horse? Lord Costayne sent his squire to ransom her, but I told him to save his gold. I mean to keep her for my own."

"His Lordship will not like that."

"His Lordship said that I had no right to put a fireball upon my shield. He told me my device should be a clump of pussywillows. His Lordship can go bugger himself."

Dunk could not help but smile. He had supped at that same table himself, choking down the same bitter dishes as served up by the likes of the Bright Prince and Ser Steffon Fossoway. He felt a certain kinship with the prickly young knight. *For all I know, my mother was a whore as well.* "How many horses have you won?"

Ser Glendon shrugged. "I lost count. Mortimer Boggs still owes me one. He said he'd rather eat his horse than have some whore's bastard riding her. And he took a hammer to his armor before sending it to me. It's full of holes. I suppose I can still get something for the metal." He sounded more sad than angry. "There was a stable by the . . . the inn where I was raised. I worked there when I was a boy, and when I could I'd sneak the horses off while their owners were busy. I was always good with horses. Stots, rounseys, palfreys, drays, plowhorses, warhorses—I rode them all. Even a Dornish sand steed. This old man I knew taught me how to make my own lances. I thought if I showed them all how good I was, they'd have no choice but to admit I was my father's son. But they won't. Even now. They just won't."

"Some never will," Dunk told him. "It doesn't matter what you do. Others, though . . . they're not all the same. I've met some good ones." He thought a moment. "When the tourney's done, Egg and I mean to go north. Take service at Winterfell, and fight for the Starks against the ironmen. You could come with us." The north was a world all its own, Ser Arlan always said. No one up there was like to know the tale of Penny Jenny and the Knight of the Pussywillows. *No one will laugh at you up there. They will know you only by your blade, and judge you by your worth.*

Ser Glendon gave him a suspicious look. "Why would I want to do that? Are you telling me I need to run away and hide?"

"No. I just thought . . . two swords instead of one. The roads are not so safe as they once were."

"That's true enough," the boy said grudgingly, "but my father was once promised a place amongst the Kingsguard. I mean to claim the white cloak that he never got to wear."

You have as much chance of wearing a white cloak as I do, Dunk almost said. *You were born of a camp follower, and I crawled out of the gutters of Flea Bottom. Kings do not heap honor on the likes of you and me.* The lad would not have taken kindly to that truth, however. Instead he said, "Strength to your arm, then."

He had not gone more than a few feet when Ser Glendon called after him. "Ser Duncan, wait. I . . . I should not have been so sharp. A knight must needs be courteous, my mother used to say." The boy seemed to be struggling for words. "Lord Peake came to see me, after my last joust. He offered me a place at Starpike. He said there was a storm coming the likes of which Westeros had not seen for a generation, that he would need swords and men to wield them. Loyal men, who knew how to obey."

Dunk could hardly believe it. Gormon Peake had made his scorn for hedge knights plain, both on the road and on the roof, but the offer was a generous one. "Peake is a great lord," he said, wary, "but . . . but not a man that I would trust, I think."

"No." The boy flushed. "There was a price. He'd take me into his service, he said . . . but first I would have to prove my loyalty. He would see that I was paired against his friend the Fiddler next, and he wanted me to swear that I would lose."

Dunk believed him. He should have been shocked, he knew, and yet somehow he wasn't. "What did you say?"

"I said I might not be able to lose to the Fiddler even if I were trying, that I had already unhorsed much better men than him, that the dragon's egg would be mine before the day was done." Ball smiled feebly. "It was not the answer that he wanted. He called me a fool, then, and told me that I had best watch my back. The Fiddler had many friends, he said, and I had none."

Dunk put a hand upon his shoulder and squeezed. "You have one, ser. Two, once I find Egg."

The boy looked him in the eye and nodded. "It is good to know there are some true knights still."

Dunk got his first good look at Ser Tommard Heddle whilst searching for Egg amongst the crowds about the lists. Heavyset and broad, with a chest like a barrel, Lord Butterwell's good-son wore black plate over boiled leather, and an ornate helm fashioned in the likeness of some demon, scaled and slavering. His horse was three hands taller than Thunder and two stone heavier, a monster of a beast armored in a coat of ringmail. The weight of all that iron made him slow, so Heddle never got up past a canter when the course was run; but that did not prevent him making short work of Ser Clarence Charlton. As Charlton was borne from the field upon a litter, Heddle removed his demonic helm. His head was broad and bald, his beard black and square. Angry red boils festered on his cheek and neck.

Dunk knew that face. Heddle was the knight who'd growled at him in the bedchamber when he touched the dragon's egg, the man with the deep voice that he'd heard talking with Lord Peake.

A jumble of words came rushing back to him: *beggar's feast you've laid before us . . . is the boy his father's son . . . Bittersteel . . . need the sword . . . Old Milkblood expects . . . is the boy his father's son . . . I promise you, Bloodraven is not off dreaming . . . is the boy his father's son?*

He stared at the viewing stand, wondering if somehow Egg had contrived to take his rightful place amongst the notables. There was no sign of the boy, however. Butterwell and Frey were missing too, though Butterwell's wife was still in her seat, looking bored and restive. *That's queer,* Dunk reflected. This was Butterwell's castle, his wedding, and Frey was father to his bride. These jousts were in their honor. Where would they have gone?

"*Ser Uthor Underleaf,*" the herald boomed. A shadow crept across Dunk's face as the sun was swallowed by a cloud. *"Ser Theomore of House Bulwer, the Old Ox, a knight of Blackcrown. Come forth and prove your valor."*

The Old Ox made a fearsome sight in his blood red armor, with black bull's horns rising from his helm. He needed the help of a brawny squire to get onto his horse, though, and the way his head was always turning as he rode suggested that Ser Maynard had been right about his eye. Still, the man received a lusty cheer as he took the field.

Not so the Snail, no doubt just as he preferred. On the first pass, both knights struck glancing blows. On the second, the Old Ox snapped his lance on the Ser Uthor's shield, while the Snail's blow missed entirely. The same thing happened on the third pass, and this time Ser Uthor swayed as if about to fall. *He is feigning,* Dunk realized. *He is drawing the contest out to fatten the odds for next time.* He had only to glance around to see Will at work, making wagers for his master. Only then did it occur to him that he might have fattened his own purse with a coin or two upon the Snail. *Dunk the lunk, thick as a castle wall.*

The Old Ox fell on fifth pass, knocked sideways by a coronal that slipped deftly off his shield to take him in the chest. His foot tangled in his stirrup as he fell, and he was dragged forty yards across the field before his men could get his horse under control. Again the litter came out, to bear him to the maester. A few drops of rain began to fall as Bulwer was carried away and darkened his surcoat where they fell. Dunk watched without expression. He was thinking about Egg. *What if this secret enemy of mine has got his hands on him?* It made as much sense as anything else. *The boy is blameless. If someone has a quarrel with me, it should not be him who answers for it.*

Ser John the Fiddler was being armed for his next tilt when Dunk found him. No fewer than three squires were attending him, buckling on his armor and seeing to the trappings of his horse, whilst Lord Alyn Cockshaw sat nearby drinking watered wine and looking bruised and peevish. When he caught sight of Dunk, Lord Alyn sputtered, dribbling wine upon on his chest. "How is it that you're still walking about? The Snail stove your face in."

"Steely Pate made me a good strong helm, m'lord. And my head is hard as stone, Ser Arlan used to say."

The Fiddler laughed. "Pay no mind to Alyn. Fireball's bastard knocked him off his horse onto that plump little rump of his, so now he has decided that he hates all hedge knights."

"That wretched pimpled creature is no son of Quentyn Ball," insisted Alyn Cockshaw. "He should never have been allowed to compete. If this were my wedding, I should have had him whipped for his presumption."

"What maid would marry you?" Ser John said.

"And Ball's presumption is a deal less grating than your pouting. Ser Duncan, are you perchance a friend of Galtry the Green? I must shortly part him from his horse."

Dunk did not doubt it. "I do not know the man, m'lord."

"Will you take a cup of wine? Some bread and olives?"

"Only a word, m'lord."

"You may have all the words you wish. Let us adjourn to my pavilion." The Fiddler held the flap for him. "Not you, Alyn. You could do with a few less olives, if truth be told."

Inside, the Fiddler turned back to Dunk. "I knew Ser Uthor had not killed you. My dreams are never wrong. And the Snail must face me soon enough. Once I've unhorsed him, I shall demand your arms and armor back. Your destrier as well, though you deserve a better mount. Will you take one as my gift?"

"I . . . no . . . I couldn't do that." The thought made Dunk uncomfortable. "I do not mean to be ungrateful, but . . ."

"If it is the debt that troubles you, put the thought from your mind. I do not need your silver, ser. Only your friendship. How can you be one of my knights without a horse?" Ser John drew on his gauntlets of lobstered steel and flexed his fingers.

"My squire is missing."

"Ran off with a girl, perhaps?"

"Egg's too young for girls, m'lord. He would

never leave me of his own will. Even if I were dying, he would stay until my corpse was cold. His horse is still here. So is our mule."

"If you like, I could ask my men to look for him."

My men. Dunk did not like the sound of that. *A tourney for traitors,* he thought. "You are no hedge knight."

"No." The Fiddler's smile was full of boyish charm. "But you knew that from the start. You have been calling me *m'lord* since we met upon the road, why is that?"

"The way you talk. The way you look. The way you act." *Dunk the lunk, thick as a castle wall.* "Up on the roof last night, you said some things. . . ."

"Wine makes me talk too much, but I meant every word. We belong together, you and I. My dreams do not lie."

"Your dreams don't lie," said Dunk, "but you do. John is not your true name, is it?"

"No." The Fiddler's eyes sparkled with mischief. *He has Egg's eyes.*

"His true name will be revealed soon enough, to those who need to know." Lord Gormon Peake had slipped into the pavilion, scowling. "Hedge knight, I warn you—"

"Oh, stop it, Gormy," said the Fiddler. "Ser Duncan is with us, or will be soon. I told you, I dreamed of him." Outside, a herald's trumpet blew. The Fiddler turned his head. "They are calling me to the lists. Pray excuse me, Ser Duncan.

We can resume our talk after I dispose of Ser Galtry the Green."

"Strength to your arm," Dunk said. It was only courteous.

Lord Gormon remained after Ser John had gone. "His dreams will be the death of all of us."

"What did it take to buy Ser Galtry?" Dunk heard himself say. "Was silver sufficient, or does he require gold?"

"Someone has been talking, I see." Peake seated himself in a camp chair. "I have a dozen men outside. I ought to call them in and have them slit your throat, ser."

"Why don't you?"

"His Grace would take it ill."

His Grace. Dunk felt as though someone had punched him in the belly. *Another black dragon,* he thought. *Another Blackfyre Rebellion. And soon another Redgrass Field. The grass was not red when the sun came up.* "Why this wedding?"

"Lord Butterwell wanted a new young wife to warm his bed, and Lord Frey had a somewhat soiled daughter. Their nuptials provided a plausible pretext for some like-minded lords to gather. Most of those invited here fought for the Black Dragon once. The rest have reason to resent Bloodraven's rule, or nurse grievances and ambitions of their own. Many of us had sons and daughters taken to King's Landing to vouchsafe our future loyalty, but most of the hostages perished in the Great Spring Sickness. Our hands are no longer tied. Our time is come. Aerys is weak. A bookish man, and no warrior. The commons hardly know him, and what they know they do not like. His lords love him even less. His father was weak as well, that is true, but when his throne was threatened he had sons to take the field for him. Baelor and Maekar, the hammer and the anvil . . . but Baelor Breakspear is no more, and Prince Maekar sulks at Summerhall, at odds with king and Hand."

Aye, thought Dunk, *and now some fool hedge knight has delivered his favorite son into the hands of his enemies. How better to ensure that the prince never stirs from Summerhall?* "There is Bloodraven," he said. "He is not weak."

"No," Lord Peake allowed, "but no man loves a sorcerer, and kinslayers are accursed in the sight of gods and men. At the first sign of weakness or defeat, Bloodraven's men will melt away like summer snows. And if the dream the prince has dreamed comes true, and a living dragon comes forth here at Whitewalls—"

Dunk finished for him. "—the throne is yours."

"His," said Lord Gormon Peake. "I am but a humble servant." He rose. "Do not attempt to leave the castle, ser. If you do, I will take it as a proof of treachery, and you will answer with your life. We have gone too far to turn back now."

The leaden sky was spitting down rain in earnest as John the Fiddler and Ser Galtry the Green took up fresh lances at opposite ends of the lists. Some of the wedding guests were streaming off toward the great hall, huddled under cloaks.

Ser Galtry rode a white stallion. A drooping green plume adorned his helm, a matching plume his horse's crinet. His cloak was a patchwork of many squares of fabric, each a different shade of green. Gold inlay made his greaves and gauntlet glitter, and his shield showed nine jade mullets upon a leek-green field. Even his beard was dyed green, in the fashion of the men of Tyrosh across the narrow sea.

Nine times he and the Fiddler charged with leveled lances, the green patchwork knight and the young lordling of the golden swords and fiddles, and nine times their lances shattered. By the eighth run, the ground had begun to soften, and the big destriers splashed through pools of rainwater. On the ninth, the Fiddler almost lost his seat, but recovered before he fell. "Well struck," he called out, laughing. "You almost had me down, ser."

"Soon enough," the green knight shouted through the rain.

"No, I think not." The Fiddler tossed his splintered lance away, and a squire handed him a fresh one.

The next run was their last. Ser Galtry's lance scraped ineffectually off the Fiddler's shield, whilst Ser John's took the green knight squarely in the center of his chest and knocked him from his saddle, to land with a great brown splash. In the east, Dunk saw the flash of distant lightning.

The viewing stands were emptying out quickly, as smallfolk and lordlings alike scrambled to get out of the wet. "See how they run," murmured Alyn Cockshaw, as he slid up beside Dunk. "A few drops of rain, and all the bold lords go squealing for shelter. What will they do when the real storm breaks, I wonder?"

The real storm. Dunk knew Lord Alyn was not talking about the weather. *What does this one want? Has he suddenly decided to befriend me?*

The herald mounted his platform once again. *"Ser Tommard Heddle, a knight of Whitewalls, in service to Lord Butterwell!"* he shouted as thunder rumbled in the distance. *"Ser Uthor Underleaf. Come forth and prove your valor."*

Dunk glanced over at Ser Uthor in time to see the Snail's smile go sour. *This is not the match he paid for.* The master of the games had crossed him up, but why? *Someone else has taken a hand, someone Cosgrove esteems more than Uthor Underleaf.* Dunk chewed on that for a moment. *They do not know that Uthor does not mean to win,* he realized all at once. *They see him as a threat, so they mean for Black Tom to remove him from the Fiddler's path.* Heddle himself was part of Peake's conspiracy; he could be relied on to lose when the need arose. Which left no one but . . .

And suddenly Lord Peake himself was storming across the muddy field to climb the steps to the herald's platform, his cloak flapping behind him.

"*We are betrayed!*" he cried. "Bloodraven has a spy amongst us. The dragon's egg is stolen!"

Ser John the Fiddler wheeled his mount around. "My egg? How is that possible? Lord Butterwell keeps guards outside his bedchamber night and day."

"Slain," Lord Peake declared, "but one man named his killer before he died."

Does he mean to accuse me? Dunk wondered. A dozen men had seem him touch the dragon's egg last night, when he'd carried Lady Butterwell to her lord husband's bed.

Lord Gormon's finger stabbed down in accusation. "There he stands. The whore's son. Seize him."

At the far end of the lists, Ser Glendon Ball looked up in confusion. For a moment he did not appear to comprehend what was happening, until he saw men rushing at him from all directions. Then the boy moved more quickly than Dunk could have believed. He had his sword half out of its sheath when the first man threw an arm around his throat. Ball wrenched free of his grip, but by then two more of them were on him. They slammed into him and dragged him down into the mud. Other men swarmed over them, shouting and kicking. *That could be me,* Dunk realized. He felt as helpless as he had at Ashford, the day they'd told him he must lose a hand and a foot.

Alyn Cockshaw pulled him back. "Stay out of this, if you want to find that squire of yours."

Dunk turned on him. "What do you mean?"

"I may know where to find the boy."

"Where?" Dunk was in no mood for games.

At the far end of the field, Ser Glendon was yanked roughly back onto his feet, pinioned between two men-at-arms in mail and halfhelms. He was brown with mud from waist to ankle, and blood and rain washed down his cheeks. *Hero's blood*, thought Dunk, as Black Tom dismounted before the captive. "Where is the egg?"

Blood dribbled from Ball's mouth. "Why would I steal the egg? I was about to win it."

Aye, thought Dunk, *and that they could not allow*.

Black Tom slashed Ball across the face with a mailed fist. "Search his saddlebags," Lord Peake commanded. "We'll find the dragon's egg wrapped up and hidden, I'll wager."

Lord Alyn lowered his voice. "And so they will. Come with me if you want to find your squire. There's no better time than now, whilst they're all occupied." He did not wait for a reply.

Dunk had to follow. Three long strides brought him abreast of the lordling. "If you have done Egg any harm—"

"Boys are not to my taste. This way. Step lively now."

Through an archway, down a set of muddy steps, around a corner, Dunk stalked after him, splashing through puddles as the rain fell around them. They stayed close to the walls, cloaked in shadows, finally stopping in a closed courtyard where the paving stones were smooth and slick. Buildings pressed close on every side. Above were windows, closed and shuttered. In the center of the courtyard was a well, ringed with a low stone wall.

A lonely place, Dunk thought. He did not like the feel of it. Old instinct made him reach for his sword hilt, before he remembered that the Snail had won his sword. As he fumbled at his hip where his scabbard should have hung, he felt the point of a knife poke his lower back. "Turn on me, and I'll cut your kidney out and give it to Butterwell's cooks to fry up for the feast." The knife pushed in through the back of Dunk's jerkin, insistent. "Over to the well. No sudden moves, ser."

If he has thrown Egg down that well, he will need more than some little toy knife to save him. Dunk walked forward slowly. He could feel the anger growing in his belly.

The blade at his back vanished. "You may turn and face me now, hedge knight."

Dunk turned. "M'lord. Is this about the dragon's egg?"

"No. This is about the dragon. Did you think I would stand by and let you steal him?" Ser Alyn grimaced. "I should have known better than to trust that wretched Snail to kill you. I'll have my gold back, every coin."

Him? Dunk thought. *This plump, pasty-faced, perfumed lordling is my secret enemy?* He did not know whether to laugh or weep. "Ser Uthor earned his gold. I have a hard head, is all."

"So it seems. Back away."

Dunk took a step backwards.

"Again. Again. Once more."

Another step, and he was flush against the well. Its stones pressed against his lower back.

"Sit down on the rim. Not afraid of a little bath, are you? You cannot get much wetter than you are right now."

"I cannot swim." Dunk rested a hand on the well. The stones were wet. One moved beneath the pressure of his palm.

"What a shame. Will you jump, or must I prick you?"

Dunk glanced down. He could see the raindrops dimpling the water, a good twenty feet below. The walls were covered with a slime of algae. "I never did you any harm."

"And never will. Daemon's mine. I will command his Kingsguard. You are not worthy of a white cloak."

"I never claimed I was." *Daemon.* The name rang in Dunk's head. *Not John. Daemon, after his father. Dunk the lunk, thick as a castle wall.* "Daemon Blackfyre sired seven sons. Two died upon the Redgrass Field, twins—"

"Aegon and Aemon. Wretched witless bullies, just like you. When we were little, they took pleasure in tormenting me and Daemon both. I wept when Bittersteel carried him off to exile, and again when Lord Peake told me he was coming home. But then he saw *you* upon the road, and forgot that I existed." Cockshaw waved his dagger threateningly. "You can go into the water as you are, or you can go in bleeding. Which will it be?"

Dunk closed his hand around the loose stone. It proved to be less loose than he had hoped. Before he could wrench it free, Ser Alyn lunged. Dunk twisted sideways, so the point of the blade sliced through the meat of his shield arm. And then the stone popped free. Dunk fed it to His Lordship and felt his teeth crack beneath the blow. "The well, is it?" He hit the lordling in the mouth again, then dropped the stone, seized Cockshaw by the wrist, and twisted until a bone snapped and the dagger clattered to the stones. "After you, m'lord." Sidestepping, Dunk yanked at the lordling's arm and planted a kick in the small of his back. Lord Alyn toppled headlong into the well. There was a splash.

"Well done, ser."

Dunk whirled. Through the rain, all he could make out was a hooded shape and a single pale white eye. It was only when the man came forward that the shadowed face beneath the cowl took on the familiar features of Ser Maynard Plumm, the pale eye no more than the moonstone brooch that pinned his cloak at the shoulder.

Down in the well, Lord Alyn was thrashing and splashing and calling for help. "*Murder!* Someone help me."

"He tried to kill me," Dunk said.

"That would explain all the blood."

"Blood?" He looked down. His left arm was

red from shoulder to elbow, his tunic clinging to his skin. "Oh."

Dunk did not remember falling, but suddenly he was on the ground, with raindrops running down his face. He could hear Lord Alyn whimpering from the well, but his splashing had grown feebler. "We need to have that arm bound up." Ser Maynard slipped his own arm under Dunk. "Up now. I cannot lift you by myself. Use your legs."

Dunk used his legs. "Lord Alyn. He's going to drown."

"He shan't be missed. Least of all by the Fiddler."

"He's not," Dunk gasped, pale with pain, "a fiddler."

"No. He is Daemon of House Blackfyre, the Second of His Name. Or so he would style himself, if ever he achieves the Iron Throne. You would be surprised to know how many lords prefer their kings brave and stupid. Daemon is young and dashing, and looks good on a horse."

The sounds from the well were almost too faint to hear. "Shouldn't we throw His Lordship down a rope?"

"Save him now to execute him later? I think not. Let him eat the meal that he meant to serve to you. Come, lean on me." Plumm guided him across the yard. This close, there was something queer about the cast of Ser Maynard's features. The longer Dunk looked, the less he seemed to see. "I did urge you to flee, you will recall, but you esteemed your honor more than your life. An honorable death is well and good, but if the life at stake is not your own, what then? Would your answer be the same, ser?"

"Whose life?" From the well came one last splash. "Egg? Do you mean Egg?" Dunk clutched at Plumm's arm. *"Where is he?"*

"With the gods. And you will know why, I think."

The pain that twisted inside Dunk just then made him forget his arm. He groaned. "He tried to use the boot."

"So I surmise. He showed the ring to Maester Lothar, who delivered him to Butterwell, who no doubt pissed his breeches at the sight of it and started wondering if he had chosen the wrong side and how much Bloodraven knows of this conspiracy. The answer to that last is *'quite a lot.'"* Plumm chuckled.

"Who are you?"

"A friend," said Maynard Plumm. "One who has been watching you, and wondering at your presence in this nest of adders. Now be quiet, until we get you mended."

Staying in the shadows, the two of them made their way back to Dunk's small tent. Once inside, Ser Maynard lit a fire, filled a bowl with wine, and set it on the flames to boil. "A clean cut, and at least it is not your sword arm," he said, slicing through the sleeve of Dunk's bloodstained tunic. "The thrust appears to have missed the bone. Still, we will need to wash it out, or you could lose the arm."

"It doesn't matter." Dunk's belly was roiling, and he felt as if he might retch at any moment. "If Egg is dead—"

"—you bear the blame. You should have kept him well away from here. I never said the boy was dead, though. I said that he was with the gods. Do you have clean linen? Silk?"

"My tunic. The good one I got in Dorne. What do you mean, he's with the gods?"

"In good time. Your arm first."

The wine soon began to steam. Ser Maynard found Dunk's good silk tunic, sniffed at it suspiciously, then slid out a dagger and began to cut it up. Dunk swallowed his protest.

"Ambrose Butterwell has never been what you might call *decisive*," Ser Maynard said as he wadded up three strips of silk and dropped them in the wine. "He had doubts about this plot from the beginning, doubts that were inflamed when he learned that the boy did not bear the sword. And this morning, his dragon's egg vanished, and with it the last dregs of his courage."

"Ser Glendon did not steal the egg," Dunk said. "He was in the yard all day, tilting or watching others tilt."

"Peake will find the egg in his saddlebags all the same." The wine was boiling. Plumm drew on a leather glove and said, "Try not to scream." Then he pulled a strip of silk out of the boiling wine and began to wash the cut.

Dunk did not scream. He gnashed his teeth and

bit his tongue and smashed his fist against his thigh hard enough to leave bruises, but he did not scream. Ser Maynard used the rest of his good tunic to make a bandage and tied it tight around his arm. "How does that feel?" he asked when he was done.

"Bloody awful." Dunk shivered. "*Where's Egg?*"

"With the gods. I told you."

Dunk reached up and wrapped his good hand around Plumm's neck. "Speak plain. I am sick of hints and winks. Tell me where to find the boy, or I will snap your bloody neck, friend or no."

"The sept. You would do well to go armed." Ser Maynard smiled. "Is that plain enough for you, Dunk?"

His first stop was Ser Uthor Underleaf's pavilion.

When Dunk slipped inside, he found only the squire Will bent over a washtub, scrubbing out his master's smallclothes. "You again? Ser Uthor is at the feast. What do you want?"

"My sword and shield."

"Have you brought the ransom?"

"No."

"Then why would I let you take your arms?"

"I have need of them."

"That's no good reason."

"How about, try to stop me and I'll kill you."

Will gaped. "They're over there."

Dunk paused outside the castle sept. *Gods grant I am not too late.* His swordbelt was back in its accustomed place, cinched tight about his waist. He had strapped the gallows shield to his wounded arm, and the weight of it was sending throbs of pain through him with every step. If anyone brushed up against him, he feared that he might scream. He pushed the doors open with his good hand.

Within, the sept was dim and hushed, lit only by the candles that twinkled on the altars of the Seven. The Warrior had the most candles burning, as might be expected during a tourney; many a knight would have come here to pray for strength and courage before they chanced the lists. The Stranger's altar was shrouded in shadow, with but a single candle burning. The Mother and the Father each had dozens, the Smith and Maiden somewhat fewer. And beneath the shining lantern of the Crone knelt Lord Ambrose Butterwell, head bowed, praying silently for wisdom.

He was not alone. No sooner had Dunk started for him than two men-at-arms moved to cut him off, faces stern beneath their halfhelms. Both wore mail beneath surcoats striped in the green, white, and yellow undy of House Butterwell. "Hold, ser," one said. "You have no business here."

"Yes, he does. I *warned* you he would find me."

The voice was Egg's.

When Egg stepped out from the shadows beneath the Father, his shaven head shining in the candlelight, Dunk almost rushed to the boy, to pluck him up with a glad cry and crush him in his arms. Something in Egg's tone made him hesitate. *He sounds more angry than afraid, and I have never seen him look so stern. And Butterwell on his knees. Something is queer here.*

Lord Butterwell pushed himself back to his feet. Even in the dim light of the candles, his flesh looked pale and clammy. "Let him pass," he told his guardsmen. When they stepped back, he beckoned Dunk closer. "I have done the boy no harm. I knew his father well, when I was the King's Hand. Prince Maekar needs to know, none of this was my idea."

"He will," Dunk promised. *What is happening here?*

"Peake. This was all his doing, I swear it by the Seven." Lord Butterwell put one hand on the altar. "May the gods strike me down if I am false. He told me whom I must invite and who must be excluded, and he brought this boy pretender here. I never wanted to be part of any treason, you must believe me. Tom Heddle now, he urged me on, I will not deny it. My good-son, married to my eldest daughter, but I will not lie, he was part of this."

"He is your champion," said Egg. "If he was in this, so were you."

Be quiet, Dunk wanted to roar. *That loose tongue of yours will get us killed.* Yet Butterwell seemed to quail. "My lord, you do not understand. Heddle commands my garrison."

"You must have *some* loyal guardsmen," said Egg.

"These men here," said Lord Butterwell. "A few

more. I've been too lax, I will allow, but I have never been a traitor. Frey and I harbored doubts about Lord Peake's pretender since the beginning. *He does not bear the sword!* If he were his father's son, Bittersteel would have armed him with Blackfyre. And all this talk about a dragon . . . madness, madness and folly." His Lordship dabbed the sweat from his face with his sleeve. "And now they have taken the egg, the dragon's egg my grandsire had from the king himself as a reward for leal service. It was there this morning when I woke, and my guards swear no one entered or left the bedchamber. It may be that Lord Peake bought them, I cannot say, but *the egg is gone.* They must have it, or else . . ."

Or else the dragon's hatched, thought Dunk. If a living dragon appeared again in Westeros, the lords and smallfolk alike would flock to whichever prince could lay claim to it. "My lord," he said, "a word with my . . . my squire, if you would be so good."

"As you wish, ser." Lord Butterwell knelt to pray again.

Dunk drew Egg aside and went down upon one knee to speak with him face-to-face. "I am going to clout you in the ear so hard your head will turn around backwards, and you'll spend the rest of your life looking at where you've been."

"You should, ser." Egg had the grace to look abashed. "I'm sorry. I just meant to send a raven to my father."

So I could stay a knight. The boy meant well.

Dunk glanced over to where Butterwell was praying. "What did you do to him?"

"Scared him, ser."

"Aye, I can see that. He'll have scabs on his knees before the night is done."

"I didn't know what else to do, ser. The maester brought me to them, once he saw my father's ring."

"Them?"

"Lord Butterwell and Lord Frey, ser. Some guards were there as well. Everyone was upset. Someone stole the dragon's egg."

"Not you, I hope?"

Egg shook his head. "No, ser. I knew I was in trouble when the maester showed Lord Butterwell my ring. I thought about saying that I'd stolen it, but I didn't think he would believe me. Then I remembered this one time I heard my father talking about something Lord Bloodraven said, about how it was better to be frightening than frightened, so I told them that my father had sent us here to spy for him, that he was on his way here with an army, that His Lordship had best release me and give up this treason, or it would mean his head." He smiled a shy smile. "It worked better than I thought it would, ser."

Dunk wanted to take the boy by the shoulders and shake him until his teeth rattled. *This is no game,* he might have roared. *This is life and death.* "Did Lord Frey hear all this as well?"

"Yes. He wished Lord Butterwell happiness in his marriage and announced that he was returning to the Twins forthwith. That was when His Lordship brought us here to pray."

Frey could flee, Dunk thought, *but Butterwell does not have that option, and soon or late he will begin to wonder why Prince Maekar and his army have not turned up.* "If Lord Peake should learn that you are in the castle—"

The sept's outer doors opened with a crash. Dunk turned to see Black Tom Heddle glowering in mail and plate, with rainwater dripping off his sodden cloak to puddle by his feet. A dozen men-at-arms stood with him, armed with spears and axes. Lightning flashed blue and white across the sky behind them, etching sudden shadows across the pale stone floor. A gust of wet wind set all the candles in the sept to dancing.

Oh, seven bloody hells was all that Dunk had time enough to think before Heddle said, "There's the boy. Take him."

Lord Butterwell had risen to his feet. "No. Halt. The boy's not to be molested. Tommard, what is the meaning of this?"

Heddle's face twisted in contempt. "Not all of us have milk running in our veins, Your Lordship. I'll have the boy."

"You do not understand." Butterwell's voice had turned into a high thin quaver. "We are undone. Lord Frey is gone, and others will follow. Prince Maekar is coming with an army."

"All the more reason to take the boy as hostage."

"No, no," said Butterwell, "I want no more part of Lord Peake or his pretender. I will not fight."

Black Tom looked coldly at his lord. "Craven." He spat. "Say what you will. You'll fight or die, my lord." He pointed at Egg. "A stag to the first man to draw blood."

"No, no." Butterwell turned to his own guards. "Stop them, do you hear me? I command you. Stop them." But all the guards had halted in confusion, at a loss as to whom they should obey.

"Must I do it myself, then?" Black Tom drew his longsword.

Dunk did the same. "Behind me, Egg."

"Put up your steel, the both of you!" Butterwell screeched. "I'll have no bloodshed in the sept! Ser Tommard, this man is the prince's sworn shield. He'll kill you!"

"Only if he falls on me." Black Tom showed his teeth in a hard grin. "I saw him try to joust."

"I am better with a sword," Dunk warned him.

Heddle answered with a snort, and charged.

Dunk shoved Egg roughly backwards and turned to meet his blade. He blocked the first cut well enough, but the jolt of Black Tom's sword biting into his shield and the bandaged cut behind it sent a jolt of pain crackling up his arm. He tried a slash at Heddle's head in answer, but Black Tom slid away from it and hacked at him again. Dunk barely got his shield around in time. Pine chips flew and Heddle laughed, pressing his attack, low and high and low again. Dunk took each cut with his shield, but every blow was agony, and he found himself giving ground.

"Get him, ser," he heard Egg call. "Get him, get him, he's *right there*." The taste of blood was in Dunk's mouth, and worse, his wound had opened once again. A wave of dizziness washed over him. Black Tom's blade was turning the long kite shield to splinters. *Oak and iron guard me well, or else I'm dead and doomed to hell,* Dunk thought, before he remembered that this shield was made of pine. When his back came up hard against an altar, he stumbled to one knee and realized he had no more ground left to give.

"You are no knight," said Black Tom. "Are those tears in your eyes, oaf?"

Tears of pain. Dunk pushed up off his knee and slammed shield-first into his foe.

Black Tom stumbled backwards, yet somehow kept his balance. Dunk bulled right after him, smashing him with the shield again and again, using his size and strength to knock Heddle halfway across the sept. Then he swung the shield aside and slashed out with his longsword, and Heddle screamed as the steel bit through wool and muscle deep into his thigh. His own sword swung wildly, but the blow was desperate and clumsy. Dunk let his shield take it one more time and put all his weight into his answer.

Black Tom reeled back a step and stared down in horror at his forearm flopping on the floor beneath the Stranger's altar. "You," he gasped, "you, you . . ."

"I told you." Dunk stabbed him through the throat. "I'm better with a sword."

Two of the men-at-arms fled back into the rain as a pool of blood spread out from Black Tom's body. The others clutched their spears and hesitated, casting wary glances toward Dunk as they waited for their lord to speak.

"This . . . this was ill done," Butterwell finally managed. He turned to Dunk and Egg. "We must be gone from Whitewalls before those two bring word of this to Gormon Peake. He has more friends amongst the guests than I do. The postern gate in the north wall, we'll slip out there . . . come, we must make haste."

Dunk slammed his sword into its scabbard. "Egg, go with Lord Butterwell." He put an arm around the boy and lowered his voice. "Don't stay with him any longer than you need to. Give Rain his head and get away before His Lordship changes sides again. Make for Maidenpool, it's closer than King's Landing."

"What about you, ser?"

"Never mind about me."

"I'm your squire."

"Aye," said Dunk, "and you'll do as I tell you, or you'll get a good clout in the ear."

A group of men were leaving the great hall, pausing long enough to pull up their hoods before venturing out into the rain. The Old Ox was amongst them, and weedy Lord Caswell, once more in his cups. Both gave Dunk a wide berth. Ser Mortimer Boggs favored him with a curious stare, but thought better of speaking to him. Uthor Underleaf was not so shy. "You come late to the feast, ser," he said as he was pulling on his gloves. "And I see you wear a sword again."

"You'll have your ransom for it, if that's all that concerns you." Dunk had left his battered shield behind and draped his cloak across his wounded arm to hide the blood. "Unless I die. Then you have my leave to loot my corpse."

Ser Uthor laughed. "Is that gallantry I smell, or just stupidity? The two scents are much alike, as I recall. It is not too late to accept my offer, ser."

"It is later than you think," Dunk warned him. He did not wait for Underleaf to answer, but pushed past him, through the double doors. The great hall smelled of ale and smoke and wet wool. In the gallery above, a few musicians played softly. Laughter echoed from the high tables, where Ser Kirby Pimm and Ser Lucas Nayland were playing a drinking game. Up on the dais, Lord Peake was speaking earnestly with Lord Costayne, while Ambrose Butterwell's new bride sat abandoned in her high seat.

Down below the salt, Dunk found Ser Kyle drowning his woes in Lord Butterwell's ale. His trencher was filled with a thick stew made with food left over from the night before. "A bowl o' brown," they called such fare in the pot shops of King's Landing. Ser Kyle had plainly had no stomach for it. Untouched, the stew had grown cold, and a film of grease glistened atop the brown.

Dunk slipped onto the bench beside him. "Ser Kyle."

The Cat nodded. "Ser Duncan. Will you have some ale?"

"No." Ale was the last thing that he needed.

"Are you unwell, ser? Forgive me, but you look—"

—*better than I feel.* "What was done with Glendon Ball?"

"They took him to the dungeons." Ser Kyle shook his head. "Whore's get or no, the boy never struck me as a thief."

"He isn't."

Ser Kyle squinted at him. "Your arm . . . how did—?"

"A dagger." Dunk turned to face the dais, frowning. He had escaped death twice today. That would suffice for most men, he knew. *Dunk the lunk, thick as a castle wall.* He pushed to his feet. "Your Grace," he called.

A few men on nearby benches put down their spoons, broke off their conversations, and turned to look at him.

"*Your Grace,*" Dunk said again, more loudly. He strode up the Myrish carpet toward the dais. "*Daemon.*"

Now half the hall grew quiet. At the high table,

the man who'd called himself the Fiddler turned to smile at him. He had donned a purple tunic for the feast, Dunk saw. *Purple, to bring out the color of his eyes.* "Ser Duncan. I am pleased that you are with us. What would you have of me?"

"Justice," said Dunk, "for Glendon Ball."

The name echoed off the walls, and for half a heartbeat it was if every man, woman, and boy in the hall had turned to stone. Then Lord Costayne slammed a fist upon a table and shouted, "It's death that one deserves, not justice!" A dozen other voices echoed his, and Ser Harbert Paege declared, "He's bastard born. All bastards are thieves, or worse. Blood will tell."

For a moment Dunk despaired. *I am alone here.* But then Ser Kyle the Cat pushed himself to his feet, swaying only slightly. "The boy may be a bastard, my lords, but he's *Fireball's* bastard. It's like Ser Harbert said. Blood will tell."

Daemon frowned. "No one honors Fireball more than I do," he said. "I will not believe this false knight is his seed. He stole the dragon's egg, and slew three good men in the doing."

"He stole nothing and killed no one," Dunk insisted. "If three men were slain, look elsewhere for their killer. Your Grace knows as well as I that Ser Glendon was in the yard all day, riding one tilt after t'other."

"Aye," Daemon admitted. "I wondered at that myself. But the dragon's egg was found amongst his things."

"Was it? Where is it now?

Lord Gormon Peake rose cold-eyed and imperious. "Safe, and well guarded. And why is that any concern of yours, ser?"

"Bring it forth," said Dunk. "I'd like another look at it, m'lord. T'other night, I saw it only for a moment."

Peake's eyes narrowed. "Your Grace," he said to Daemon, "it comes to me that this hedge knight arrived at Whitewalls with Ser Glendon, uninvited. He may well be part of this."

Dunk ignored that. "Your Grace, the dragon's egg that Lord Peake found amongst Ser Glendon's things was the one he placed there. Let him bring it forth, if he can. Examine it yourself. I'll wager you it's no more than a painted stone."

The hall erupted into chaos. A hundred voices began to speak at once, and a dozen knights leapt to their feet. Daemon looked near as young and lost as Ser Glendon had when he had been accused. "Are you drunk, my friend?"

Would that I were. "I've lost some blood," Dunk allowed, "but not my wits. Ser Glendon has been wrongfully accused."

"Why?" Daemon demanded, baffled. "If Ball did no wrong, as you insist, why would His Lordship say he did and try to prove it with some painted rock?"

"To remove him from your path. His Lordship bought your other foes with gold and promises, but Ball was not for sale."

The Fiddler flushed. "That is not true."

"It is true. Send for Ser Glendon, and ask him yourself."

"I will do just that. Lord Peake, have the bastard fetched up at once. And bring the dragon's egg as well. I wish to have a closer look at it."

Gormon Peake gave Dunk a look of loathing. "Your Grace, the bastard boy is being questioned. A few more hours, and we will have a confession for you, I do not doubt."

"By *questioned,* m'lord means tortured," said Dunk. "A few more hours, and Ser Glendon will confess to having killed Your Grace's father, and both your brothers too."

"Enough!" Lord Peake's face was almost purple. "One more word, and I will rip your tongue out by the roots."

"You lie," said Dunk. "That's two words."

"And you will rue the both of them," Peake promised. "Take this man and chain him in the dungeons."

"No." Daemon's voice was dangerously quiet. "I want the truth of this. Sunderland, Vyrwel, Smallwood, take your men and go find Ser Glendon in the dungeons. Bring him up forthwith, and see that no harm comes to him. If any man should try to hinder you, tell him you are about the king's business."

"As you command," Lord Vyrwel answered.

"I will settle this as my father would," the Fiddler said. "Ser Glendon stands accused of grievous crimes. As a knight, he has a right to defend himself by strength of arms. I shall meet him in the lists, and let the gods determine guilt and innocence."

Hero's blood or whore's blood, Dunk thought when two of Lord Vrywel's men dumped Ser Glendon naked at his feet, *he has a deal less of it than he did before.*

The boy had been savagely beaten. His face was bruised and swollen, several of his teeth were cracked or missing, his right eye was weeping blood, and up and down his chest his flesh was red and cracking where they'd burned him with hot irons.

"You're safe now," murmured Ser Kyle. "There's no one here but hedge knights, and the gods know that we're a harmless lot." Daemon had given them the maester's chambers, and commanded them to dress any hurts Ser Glendon might have suffered and see that he was ready for the lists.

Three fingernails had been pulled from Ball's left hand, Dunk saw as he washed the blood from the boy's face and hands. That worried him more than all the rest. "Can you hold a lance?"

"A lance?" Blood and spit dribbled from Ser Glendon's mouth when he tried to speak. "Do I have all my fingers?"

"Ten," said Dunk, "but only seven fingernails."

Ball nodded. "Black Tom was going to cut my fingers off, but he was called away. Is it him that I'm to fight?"

"No. I killed him."

That made him smile. "Someone had to."

"You're to tilt against the Fiddler, but his real name—"

"—is Daemon, aye. They told me. The Black Dragon." Ser Glendon laughed. "My father died for him. I would have been his man, and gladly. I would have fought for him, killed for him, died for him, but I could not lose for him." He turned his head and spat out a broken tooth. "Could I have a cup of wine?"

"Ser Kyle, get the wineskin."

The boy drank long and deep, then wiped his mouth. "Look at me. I'm shaking like a girl."

Dunk frowned. "Can you still sit a horse?"

"Help me wash, and bring me my shield and lance and saddle," Ser Glendon said, "and you will see what I can do."

It was almost dawn before the rain let up enough for the combat to take place. The castle yard was a morass of soft mud glistening wetly by the light of a hundred torches. Beyond the field, a gray mist was rising, sending ghostly fingers up the pale stone walls to grasp the castle battlements. Many of the wedding guests had vanished during the intervening hours, but those who remained climbed the viewing stand again and settled themselves on planks of rain-soaked pine. Amongst them stood Ser Gormon Peake, surrounded by a knot of lesser lords and household knights.

It had been only a few years since Dunk had

squired for old Ser Arlan. He had not forgotten how. He cinched the buckles on Ser Glendon's ill-fitting armor, fastened his helm to his gorget, helped him mount, and handed him his shield. Earlier contests had left deep gouges in the wood, but the blazing fireball could still be seen. *He looks as young as Egg*, Dunk thought. *A frightened boy, and grim.* His sorrel mare was unbarded, and skittish as well. *He should have stayed with his own mount. The sorrel may be better bred and swifter, but a rider rides best on a horse that he knows well, and this one is a stranger to him.*

"I'll need a lance," Ser Glendon said. "A war lance."

Dunk went to the racks. War lances were shorter and heavier than the tourney lances that had been used in all the earlier tilts; eight feet of solid ash ending in an iron point. Dunk chose one and pulled it out, running his hand along its lenth to make sure it had no cracks.

At the far end of the lists, one of Daemon's squires was offering him a matching lance. He was a fiddler no more. In place of swords and fiddles, the trapping of his warhorse now displayed the three-headed dragon of House Blackfyre, black on a field of red. The prince had washed the black dye from his hair as well, so it flowed down to his collar in a cascade of silver and gold that glimmered like beaten metal in the torchlight. *Egg would have hair like that if he ever let it grow,* Dunk realized. He found it hard to picture him that way, but one day he knew he must, if the two of them should live so long.

The herald climbed his platform once again. *"Ser Glendon the Bastard stands accused of theft and murder,"* he proclaimed, *"and now comes forth to prove his innocence at the hazard of his body. Daemon of House Blackfyre, the Second of His Name, rightborn King of the Andals and the Rhoynar and the First Men, Lord of the Seven Kingdoms and Protector of the Realm, comes forth to prove the truth of the accusations against the bastard Glendon."*

And all at once the years fell away, and Dunk was back was at Ashford Meadow once again, listening to Baelor Breakspear just before they went forth to battle for his life. He slipped the war lance back in place, plucked a tourney lance from the next rack; twelve feet long, slender, elegant. "Use this," he told Ser Glendon. "It's what we used at Ashford, at the Trial of Seven."

"The Fiddler chose a war lance. He means to kill me."

"First he has to strike you. If your aim is true, his point will never touch you."

"I don't know."

"I do."

Ser Glendon snatched the lance from him, wheeled about, and trotted toward the lists. "Seven save us both, then."

Somewhere in the east, lightning cracked across a pale pink sky. Daemon raked his stallion's side with golden spurs, and leapt forward like a thunderclap, lowering his war lance with its deadly iron point. Ser Glendon raised his shield and raced to meet him, swinging his own longer lance across his mare's head to bear upon the young pretender's chest. Mud sprayed back from their horses' hooves, and the torches seemed to burn the brighter as the two knights went pounding past.

Dunk closed his eyes. He heard a *crack*, a shout, a thump.

"No," he heard Lord Peake cry out in anguish. *"Noooooo."* For half a heartbeat, Dunk almost felt sorry for him. He opened his eyes again. Riderless, the big black stallion was slowing to a trot. Dunk jumped out and grabbed him by the reins. At the far end of the lists, Ser Glendon Ball wheeled his mare and raised his splintered lance. Men rushed onto the field to where the Fiddler lay unmoving, facedown in a puddle. When they helped him to his feet, he was mud from head to heel.

"The Brown Dragon!" someone shouted. Laughter rippled through the yard as the dawn washed over Whitewalls.

It was only a few heartbeats later, as Dunk and Ser Kyle were helping Glendon Ball off his horse, that the first trumpet blew, and the sentries on the walls raised the alarum. An army had appeared outside the castle, rising from the morning mists. "Egg wasn't lying after all," Dunk told Ser Kyle, astonished.

———

From Maidenpool had come Lord Mooton, from Raventree Lord Blackwood, from Duskendale Lord Darklyn. The royal demenses about King's Landing sent forth Hayfords, Rosbys, Stokeworths, Masseys, and the king's own sworn swords, led by three knights of the Kingsguard and stiffened by three hundred Raven's Teeth with tall white weirwood bows. Mad Danelle Lothston herself rode forth in strength from her haunted towers at Harrenhal, clad in black armor that fit her like an iron glove, her long red hair streaming.

The light of the rising sun glittered off the points of five hundred lances and ten times as many spears. The night's grey banners were reborn in half a hundred gaudy colors. And above them all flew two regal dragons on night-black fields: the great three-headed beast of King Aerys I Targaryen, red as fire, and a white winged fury breathing scarlet flame.

Not Maekar after all, Dunk knew, when he saw those banners. The banners of the Prince of Summerhall showed four three-headed dragons, two and two, the arms of the fourth-born son of the late King Daeron II Targaryen. A single white dragon announced the presence of the King's Hand, Lord Brynden Rivers.

Bloodraven himself had come to Whitewalls.

The First Blackfyre Rebellion had perished on the Redgrass Field in blood and glory. The Second Blackfyre Rebellion ended with a whimper. "They cannot cow us," Young Daemon proclaimed from the castle battlements after he had seen the ring of iron that encircled them, "for our cause is just. We'll slash through them and ride hell-bent for King's Landing! Sound the trumpets!"

Instead, knights and lords and men-at-arms muttered quietly to one another, and a few began to slink away, making for the stables or a postern gate or some hidey-hole they hoped might keep them safe. And when Daemon drew his sword and raised it above his head, every man of them could see it was not Blackfyre. "We'll make another Redgrass Field today," the pretender promised.

"Piss on that, fiddle boy," a grizzled squire shouted back at him. "I'd sooner live."

In the end, the second Daemon Blackfyre rode forth alone, reined up before the royal host, and challenged Lord Bloodraven to single combat. "I will fight you, or the coward Aerys, or any champion you care to name." Instead, Lord Bloodraven's men surrounded him, pulled him off his horse, and clasped him into golden fetters. The banner he had carried was planted in the muddy ground and set afire. It burned for a long time, sending up a twisted plume of smoke that could be seen for leagues around.

The only blood that was shed that day came when a man in service to Lord Vrywel began to boast that he had been one of Bloodraven's eyes and would soon be well rewarded. "By the time the moon turns, I'll be fucking whores and drinking Dornish red," he was purported to have said, just before one of Lord Costayne's knights slit his throat. "Drink that," he said as Vrywel's man drowned in his own blood. "It's not Dornish, but it's red."

Elsewise it was a sullen, silent column that trudged through the gates of Whitewalls to toss their weapons into a glittering pile before being bound and led away to await Lord Bloodraven's judgment. Dunk emerged with the rest of them, together with Ser Kyle the Cat and Glendon Ball. They had looked for Ser Maynard to join them, but Plumm had melted away sometime during the night.

It was late that afternoon before Ser Roland Crakehall of the Kingsguard found Dunk among the other prisoners. "Ser Duncan. Where in seven hells have you been hiding? Lord Rivers has been asking for you for hours. Come with me, if you please."

Dunk fell in beside him. Crakehall's long cloak flapped behind him with every gust of wind, as white as moonlight on snow. The sight of it made him think back on the words the Fiddler had spoken, up on the roof. *I dreamed that you were all in white from head to heel, with a long pale cloak flowing from those broad shoulders.* Dunk snorted. *Aye, and you dreamed of dragons hatching from stone eggs. One is likely as t'other.*

The Hand's pavilion was half a mile from the castle, in the shade of a spreading elm tree. A dozen cows were cropping at the grass nearby. *Kings rise and fall,* Dunk thought, *and cows and smallfolk go about their business.* It was something the old man used to say. "What will become of all of them?" he asked Ser Roland as they passed a group of captives sitting on the grass.

"They'll be marched back to King's Landing for trial. The knights and men-at-arms should get off light enough. They were only following their liege lords."

"And the lords?"

"Some will be pardoned, so long as they tell the truth of what they know and give up a son or daughter to vouchsafe their future loyalty. It will go harder for those who took pardons after the Redgrass Field. They'll be imprisoned or attainted. The worst will lose their heads."

Bloodraven had made a start on that already, Dunk saw when they came up on his pavilion. Flanking the entrance, the severed heads of Gormon Peake and Black Tom Heddle had been impaled on spears, with their shields displayed beneath them. *Three castles, black on orange. The man who slew Roger of Pennytree.*

Even in death, Lord Gormon's eyes were hard and flinty. Dunk closed them with his fingers. "What did you do that for?" asked one of the guardsmen. "The crows'll have them soon enough."

"I owed him that much." If Roger had not died that day, the old man would never have looked twice at Dunk when he saw him chasing that pig through the alleys of King's Landing. *Some old dead king gave a sword to one son instead of an-*

*other, that was the start of it. And now I'm stand-
ing here, and poor Roger's in his grave.*

"The Hand awaits," commanded Roland
Crakehall.

Dunk stepped past him, into the presence of
Lord Brynden Rivers, bastard, sorcerer, and Hand
of the King.

Egg stood before him, freshly bathed and
garbed in princely raiment, as would befit a
nephew of the king. Nearby, Lord Frey was seated
in a camp chair with a cup of wine to hand and
his hideous little heir squirming in his lap. Lord
Butterwell was there as well . . . on his knees,
pale-faced and shaking.

"Treason is no less vile because the traitor
proves a craven," Lord Rivers was saying. "I have
heard your bleatings, Lord Ambrose, and I believe
one word in ten. On that account I will allow you
to retain a tenth part of your fortune. You may
keep your wife as well. I wish you joy of her."

"And Whitewalls?" asked Butterwell with qua-
vering voice.

"Forfeit to the Iron Throne. I mean to pull it
down stone by stone and sow the ground that it
stands upon with salt. In twenty years, no one will
remember it existed. Old fools and young malcon-
tents still make pilgrimages to the Redgrass Field
to plant flowers on the spot where Daemon Blackfyre fell. I will not suffer Whitewalls to become
another monument to the Black Dragon." He
waved a pale hand. "Now scurry away, roach."

"The Hand is kind." Butterwell stumbled off, so blind with grief that he did not even seem to recognize Dunk as he passed.

"You have my leave to go as well, Lord Frey," Rivers commanded. "We will speak again later."

"As my lord commands." Frey led his son from the pavilion.

Only then did the King's Hand turn to Dunk.

He was older than Dunk remembered him, with a lined hard face, but his skin was still as pale as bone, and his cheek and neck still bore the ugly winestain birthmark that some people thought looked like a raven. His boots were black, his tunic scarlet. Over it he wore a cloak the color of smoke, fastened with a brooch in the shape of an iron hand. His hair fell to his shoulders, long and white and straight, brushed forward so as to conceal his missing eye, the one that Bittersteel had plucked from him on the Redgrass Field. The eye that remained was very red. *How many eyes has Bloodraven? A thousand eyes, and one.*

"No doubt Prince Maekar had some good reason for allowing his son to squire for a hedge knight," he said, "though I cannot imagine it included delivering him to a castle full of traitors plotting rebellion. How is that I come to find my cousin in this nest of adders, ser? Lord Butterbutt would have me believe that Prince Maekar sent you here, to sniff out this rebellion in the guise of a mystery knight. Is that the truth of it?"

Dunk went to one knee. "No, m'lord. I mean,

yes, m'lord. That's what Egg told him. Aegon, I mean. Prince Aegon. So that part's true. It isn't what you'd call the true truth, though."

"I see. So the two of you learned of this conspiracy against the crown and decided you would thwart it by yourselves, is that the way of it?"

"That's not it either. We just sort of . . . blundered into it, I suppose you'd say."

Egg crossed his arms. "And Ser Duncan and I had matters well in hand before you turned up with your army."

"We had some help, m'lord," Dunk added.

"Hedge knights."

"Aye, m'lord. Ser Kyle the Cat, and Maynard Plumm. And Ser Glendon Ball. It was him unhorsed the Fidd . . . the pretender."

"Yes, I've heard that tale from half a hundred lips already. The Bastard of the Pussywillows. Born of a whore and a traitor."

"Born of *heroes,*" Egg insisted. "If he's amongst the captives, I want him found and released. And rewarded."

"And who are you to tell the King's Hand what to do?"

Egg did not flinch. "You know who I am, cousin."

"Your squire is insolent, ser," Lord Rivers said to Dunk. "You ought to beat that out of him."

"I've tried, m'lord. He's a prince, though."

"What he is," said Bloodraven, "is a *dragon.* Rise, ser."

Dunk rose.

"There have always been Targaryens who dreamed of things to come, since long before the Conquest," Bloodraven said, "so we should not be surprised if from time to time a Blackfyre displays the gift as well. Daemon dreamed that a dragon would be born at Whitewalls, and it was. The fool just got the color wrong."

Dunk looked at Egg. *The ring,* he saw. *His father's ring. It's on his finger, not stuffed up inside his boot.*

"I have half a mind to take you back to King's Landing with us," Lord Rivers said to Egg, "and keep you at court as my . . . guest."

"My father would not take kindly to that."

"I suppose not. Prince Maekar has a . . . prickly . . . nature. Perhaps I should send you back to Summerhall."

"My place is with Ser Duncan. I'm his squire."

"Seven save you both. As you wish. You're free to go."

"We will," said Egg, "but first we need some gold. Ser Duncan needs to pay the Snail his ransom."

Bloodraven laughed. "What happened to the modest boy I once met at King's Landing? As you say, my prince. I will instruct my paymaster to give you as much gold as you wish. Within reason."

"Only as a loan," insisted Dunk. "I'll pay it back."

"When you learn to joust, no doubt." Lord

Rivers flicked them away with his fingers, unrolled a parchment, and began to tick off names with a quill.

He is marking down the men to die, Dunk realized. "My lord," he said, "we saw the heads outside. Is that . . . will the Fiddler . . . Daemon . . . will you have his head as well?"

Lord Bloodraven looked up from his parchment. "That is for King Aerys to decide . . . but Daemon has four younger brothers, and sisters as well. Should I be so foolish as to remove his pretty head, his mother will mourn, his friends will curse me for a kinslayer, and Bittersteel will crown his brother Haegon. Dead, young Daemon is a hero. Alive, he is an obstacle in my half brother's path. He can hardly make a third Blackfyre king whilst the second remains so inconveniently alive. Besides, such a noble captive will be an ornament to our court, and a living testament to the mercy and benevolence of His Grace King Aerys."

"I have a question too," said Egg.

"I begin to understand why your father was so willing to be rid of you. What more would you have of me, cousin?"

"Who took the dragon's egg? There were guards at the door, and more guards on the steps, no way anyone could have gotten into Lord Butterwell's bedchamber unobserved."

Lord Rivers smiled. "Were I to guess, I'd say someone climbed up inside the privy shaft."

"The privy shaft was too small to climb."

"For a man. A child could do it."

"Or a dwarf," Dunk blurted. *A thousand eyes, and one. Why shouldn't some of them belong to a troupe of comic dwarfs?*

From master writers and editors

GEORGE R. R. MARTIN
&
GARDNER DOZOIS

come three stunning compilations featuring a diverse cast of
warriors, from the fireball-hurling to the starship-commanding

WARRIORS

★ **"An eclectic mix ... Highly recommended."**
—*Library Journal* (starred review)

**"An unpredictable assortment, where SF and
fantasy rub elbows with mystery, historical, and
military fiction, and even a Western .... The editors
succeed admirably in their mission to break down
genre barriers and focus on pure entertainment."**
—*Publishers Weekly*

WARRIORS 1
Paperback:
978-0-7653-6026-7
eBook: 978-1-4299-5442-6

WARRIORS 3
Paperback:
978-0-7653-6028-1
eBook: 978-1-4299-7020-4

WARRIORS 2
Paperback:
978-0-7653-6027-4
eBook: 978-1-4299-6946-8

TOR®
fantasy

tor-forge.com